FRIENDSHIP

DAVID DeGEORGE

WHISKEY CREEK PRESS
www.whiskeycreekpress.com

Published by
WHISKEY CREEK PRESS
Whiskey Creek Press
PO Box 51052
Casper, WY 82605-1052
www.whiskeycreekpress.com

eISBN: 978-1-63355-635-5
Print ISBN: 978-1-63355-752-9

Cover Artist: Molly Courtright
Editor: Dave Field
Printed in the United States of America

Dedication

To my nieces, Gabriella, Jamie, Joan, Libby, and Toni. And Grace, whom we unfortunately never got to know.

And to my nephews, Christopher and Zach.

Thanks so much for not caring whether I succeeded or failed. Your unconditional love and acceptance is what keeps me going, knowing you'll always be a friend to me.

Love you forever,

Dave

Chapter 1

Sophia Imeldo asked if tomorrow was the night, the two of them. Her boyfriend Arturo Dominguez assured it was, after the party. Their first time. The most intimate they'd gotten so far was French kissing, he having placed his hands on her chest. With an exhale, she pictured herself in his long arms and feeling his thin black hair through her fingers. He said he'd see her in second hour trig, told her he loved her. She said the same and placed her phone on the nightstand, then nestled under her powder blue comforter. Semester's end was imminent, their last at Stillwater High School, all seven of them. Would they stay in touch? They were all enrolled across town at Oklahoma State University, had planned to rent apartments though they hadn't so much as looked at one. Sophia promised herself to look at some next week, vowed she and the other six would remain friends until there was but one survivor.

Friendship

* * * *

The crew gathered at Stillwater Pizza for lunch the next day. A golden chandelier glowed in the center of the place, above the glass-covered buffet. In a booth, the seven discussed that night's party to be held at the vacant, one-room studio Sophia's mom owned. It had been the first place the woman and her former husband had bought, she hoping they'd reunite despite him moving out west. With another woman. Still, Sophia's mom left that morning for another visit with her ex.

By nine p.m. the one-room house thumped with music, bass tones the building's heartbeat.

"Where's Millicent?" Arturo asked.

Sophia brushed her short brown hair away from her eyes, then raised and lowered her shoulders. "Who knows?" she yelled over the din, saw their blue-eyed friend Andrea Todd already with an arm around a stranger on the ragged blue sofa.

Ted, Sophia told herself, his name the only thing she knew about him. She explained to Arturo perhaps Millicent was being fashionable then thought back to lunch and remembered the small, black-haired girl with even darker eyes had seemed someplace else mentally. Besides, Millicent Petrovich was absent at most nocturnal celebrations.

"Want some?" Renaldo Loveless pointed to his cup. Sophia peered over the rim, contents an odd yellow sprinkled with brown specks.

"Eggnog," the thin, well-chiseled, brown-haired, brown-eyed friend informed. "With a little…" He chuckled. "More than a little Crown Royal. Why wait till Christmas?" He repeated his offer.

The girl shook her head left to right, surmised this wasn't Renaldo's first drink, and went outside where dozens of kids chatted and danced, each with a drink in hand. She scrutinized the area then sighed at the fact the nearest neighbor was over a block away.

More cars pulled up.

Sophia returned indoors where Renaldo continued to drink and carouse. The girl spotted short, thin, red-haired Conrad Nessleton cramped in a corner by himself, beer bottle at his lips. Near Conrad, Wyatt Everson pushed a blue plastic cup past his long nose to dark lips that seemed darker due to his pale skin. Sophia doubted the cup contained alcohol, Wyatt having lectured others about their lack of discipline and self-restraint.

She went back outside, bumped into Arturo, viewed the crowd, and cringed. He inquired if she was okay.

"Things're getting a little out of hand."

Arturo chuckled. "It's a party, what'd you expect?"

She mentioned how everyone was drinking. Arturo held up empty hands, denied he was. When she countered he had been, he laughed, said to let her hair down. She grinned and replied hers was too short.

Arturo took her arm in his, led her back inside, and offered a dance as Maroon 5's "Sunday Morning" played. A couple more slow dances and Sophia's lips were in upward posture, her having consumed a cup of rum and Coke® from Arturo helping to improve her mood.

A girl asked Arturo to dance. Sophia stumbled aside.

"What's with her?" the girl asked, her eyes the color of daytime skies, golden locks spiraling past her shoulders, the contrasting dark bandana tied into her hair easily visible.

Arturo lifted a shoulder and snickered, dismissed Sophia as a previous steady, unable to let go.

The female shook her head. "High school girls. So immature." She introduced herself as Phoebe Martinson, a college freshman, and they danced a few numbers until a tall college guy cut in.

"Arturo, let's dance." A voice from behind the boy had him glancing over his shoulder.

"Oh," he said upon recognizing the person, his mouth long.

Sophia frowned. "Don't act so disappointed." She put her arms around him, no longer felt like she was on a Tilt-A-Whirl ride. He winked. At someone else. Sophia pushed her eyebrows together and tapped him.

"Huh?" He faced her then cast his glance to the ground and suggested they go inside for more drinks which they did, Sophia again with a buzz though her vision remained even.

For ninety minutes, she watched Arturo crane his neck at intervals though he remained by her side.

As the crowd size increased so did the noise, Sophia observing the large gathering, all either drinking or drunk. She advised they end the party.

Arturo checked his watch. "C'mon. Clock hasn't even struck twelve, party's just started."

The girl gave a sweeping gesture, asked him to look at everyone.

"Yeah. They're having fun."

She pointed to Renaldo, he in a discussion with a guy she'd never seen. The two young men raised their voices. The other guy pushed Renaldo.

Arturo stepped between them, retrieved his Polaroid, and asked to take pictures, photography a passing interest, his digital camera broken.

Sophia joined up with him and when things calmed, led him to the love seat, they trading kisses. Done, she opened her eyes then pulled away. He stared beyond her. She glanced over her shoulder, unable to guess whom he viewed. Conrad stood in the same corner, still with a bottle though he remained his usual, quiet self. Andrea laughed loudly at Ted's commentary on why people get drunk if the hangover's so bad, inched closer to him while he snaked his arm around her.

Arturo's rising distracted Sophia. She followed him. Profanity was uttered outside. Sophia ordered her boyfriend out there. He didn't move. She pushed him away and ran out. He caught up with her out of doors and they stopped in front of the action.

"Don't cut in on me when I'm with a woman," the guy— the same one who'd argued with Renaldo—said, clenched his hands and shifted to a fighter's stance then swayed and pushed Arturo, challenging him. Arturo extended an arm around the guy, suggested they talk as the girl the guy was with dissolved into the crowd, Arturo offering to drive this guy home. The stranger balked.

Sophia rushed in, ran her fingers through her hair, and smiled at the stranger. "Let me take him." She surveyed the boy, his sturdy build and brown hair. Her smile enlarged. "You live far?"

He denied he did, stumbled to Sophia's car, straightened up, said he was but a few blocks from campus, and winked.

"Good. It'll make a quick trip." Sophia put a hand on him, led him into the passenger seat, and jingled her keys at Arturo, said she'd be back shortly.

"Not too long," Arturo said. "Can't be without you."

She sighed then watched him head to the girl with long blonde hair. Sophia flattened her lips and glanced at the stranger in her car. The lips returned to their previous form. "C'mon." She peered at Arturo and slammed her door. Wheels stirred up noise as did the engine. The car sped down the road, Sophia murmuring profane sentences. She turned to the guy. Her heart raced. All her female confidants would envy this opportunity.

"Name's James," he said and smiled so bright Sophia felt she needn't have the headlights on. He sounded much more sober.

She searched for his hand, unable to think. "Oh." Uneven laughter. "You're a poet and don't even know it." She wanted to slap herself, gave the same, uneasy chuckle, and shook his hand.

The guy told Sophia where to turn and gave that smile. She offered her best welcoming grin. "Name's Sophia."

"You go to OSU?" Hopefulness was in his voice.

"No," she said then added, "but I will this fall."

He pointed at his place. Sophia pulled into the driveway, rocks and dirt crackling and popping. Two other cars were parked out here, house a dilapidated flat with cracked windows and siding that looked like it would fall off in a wind gust. Lights were on. Several figures moved past windows.

"Roommates," James explained, leaned to her, and grinned like he'd been told the winning lottery numbers. She did the same. They embraced, her tongue in his mouth. He groaned passionately, muttered she'd saved him from a fight, possibly an arrest, kissed her numerous times then led her to a supine position.

Sophia didn't resist, observed him undo his shirt, and thought of Arturo. Tonight was their night. Supposed to be. Yet she felt as ardent about this stranger as she had with Arturo.

They continued necking. A door slammed. The two froze. Shoes on wood. James sat up, looked through the windshield.

"Jesus, what's he doing?" James buttoned his shirt, straightened his hair. Sophia also rose and cleaned herself up. James rolled the passenger window down.

"Hey, man, it's you. Didn't know you were out here, thought someone had broken down and needed help."

James turned away from his friend and waved a hand. "Denny, you smell like a brewery."

"What about yourself?" The roommate eyed Sophia. "Hey, that's not Judy. Where is she?"

Sophia watched James give a harsh stare. "We're through, remember? She dumped me."

"Huh? Oh yeah. Sorry, forgot. That's too bad." Denny patted his friend's arm. "I see it didn't take long to…uh…get over her." Forced laughter.

James demanded his friend go back inside. The guy obeyed and James gave Sophia a long face, apologized, opened the door, and thanked her.

She clutched his forearm. "Wait. We were—"

"I'm sorry." James got out. "Maybe another day." He motioned to the house. "You know where I live. Stop by anytime." He picked up her hand, kissed it. "Sometimes things aren't meant to be. Later."

Sophia scowled—his last word was said like she was a buddy, she waiting for him to add, "Dude." He entered the house, the clamor of voices and laughter inside audible. She gritted her teeth, backed out, and sped down the street, rest of the drive an opaque memory.

A block and a half from the house, an odd glow caught her sight. On the same side of the street as the house. An orangish hue. She increased her speed, her stomach churning as if she watched a suspenseful movie. She parked several hundred feet away, small flames up ahead. Where the party had been. The fire, however, was contained. Sophia was relieved it had rained earlier in the week, the wooded area behind the backyard a threat for a brush fire during arid stretches.

Approaching the building, she debated notifying the fire department, house but a smoky pile of wood and bricks. A beam fell with a creak.

She moved to the house as if able to rescue anything though she could think of nothing worth saving. Two voices sounded in the near distance, east of the house. Sophia squinted in the semi-darkness, watched the two hurry away. One of them laughed. The pattern sounded familiar. Sophia's hair quilled like a porcupine's skin upon attack. She pressed her eyes shut as if doing so would change this person's tone. A second laugh. Feminine.

Laughter and conversation faded, Sophia alone with the night. Water emerged from her eye ducts. The girl drew in a long stream of oxygen and released it. She had misheard. Hopefully.

The house was nothing but a funeral pyre, orange specks glowing in spots. The teen thought about her mother's reaction then decided she wouldn't mention it and when the older woman saw the house, daughter would pass the incident off as anonymous negligence. Tomorrow she'd clean up as much as possible to soften the blow though why her mom would be upset about losing a quasi-condemned building, she couldn't fathom. She returned to the two who'd left. Had she guessed correctly on the male's laughter?

Nah, she told herself. *Just sounded like his.*

Once home, she called. The other line rang. And rang. And rang. She rationalized he'd turned his phone off. Finally, a click.

"Hello?"

The voice didn't sound familiar. Sophia's internal organs seemed to shut down. She pulled the phone away from her ear.

"Hello?" the voice spoke louder.

Chapter 2

"Arturo? You there?"

He responded he was. She inquired as to what happened, he explaining a flame lit up one side of the house in a sudden burst. "We got outta there quick."

Sophia frowned. "We?"

"Yeah. Everybody." Arturo offered condolences and when Sophia replied the place deserved to be demolished, Arturo concurred—too fast for the girl's comfort. She reprimanded herself she had no proof he was the one she'd seen. He inquired as to the damage and if she knew how it happened. Suspicions revisited Sophia but she answered in the negative, would check tomorrow.

When he offered no assistance, her breath hitched so she asked. He was silent a beat then said he'd forgotten to study a chapter for the chemistry final.

"Okay," Sophia said but believed his reply as much as if he said he had a fairy godmother. She mentally replayed the laughter she'd heard, listened to every laugh or chuckle he uttered now. None of it sounded as hearty as what she heard post-fire. Thirty minutes later, Arturo bade good night, professed his love, and invited her over after she cleaned up at the old place. Sophia told him she didn't know if she'd have time.

* * * *

In daylight, Sophia observed debris, burnt beams, and charred brick. Beer bottles and broken glass had their places. She saw a few crumpled, square plastic shapes, collected them. Polaroids. She continued probing.

Feeling the inspection complete, she stepped out of the rubble and, about to fold the photos into her pocket, temptation overcame her. She laughed at the first, Renaldo with raised cup, half of it spilling onto him. The second one had her chuckling as well. Until she brushed aside the embers stuck to it. Her grin did a complete shift. The snapshot flapped in her shaky hand. She tried to blink it away. No good. Her mouth trembled, eyes no longer dry. She told herself she was assuming bogus conclusions. When did they do it? Who took the picture? She noticed the photographer's arm extended in front of them, camera in hand. He had taken it because they were alone, his face—and hers—clearly seen, the two on the sofa, he with no shirt, she with just her bra, its contents ready to fall out.

Sophia crumpled the photo, cursed between sobs and denials, and looked at it again. Unchanged. She stuck it in her pocket, continued to tear up and sniff as she drove home, where she was a corpse, did not watch TV nor read, didn't even eat. Her phone rang several times though she didn't so much as flinch, let alone answer the call. When the doorbell ding-donged that afternoon, Sophia rolled over, buried her head in a pillow.

Late in the day, a voice mail: "Sophia, it's Arturo. Called but you didn't answer. Came to the house but no reply. You okay? Seemed testy last night. Call me as soon as you get this. Thanks. Bye." A click.

Sophia was hyperconscious about how he hadn't said "*Love you*," retrieved the photo from the oakwood coffee table, and stared at the images. Tears returned. It was over. James entered her thoughts. How had she forgotten him, his allure? They'd gone almost as far as Arturo and this girl.

Phoebe, Sophia thought she'd heard someone call the girl last night, asked herself why be mad at Arturo, she'd nearly done the same. Yet she hadn't then admitted she had no proof *he* had either. Her stomach roiled at that rationale. No doubt they had. She went in turns, denounced Arturo then condemned herself, fell asleep on the sofa, woke a few times before limping to bed, and experienced nightmares.

* * * *

Sunday was a blur, no calls or visitors, Sophia in bed till evening. Had her mom not been returning Monday, Sophia would have called school the next day claiming to be her mom to say the daughter was sick. Instead she rolled herself out of bed, surprised she didn't wreck the car on the drive to school.

At her locker, Andrea greeted Sophia with a wide grin and boisterous "Hello," then proceeded to fawn over Ted, how they'd hit it off, he *the* one, they to last forever. Sophia merely nodded, muddled to first hour, Andrea in tow.

"Are you listening?" the friend finally said.

"Huh?"

Andrea stood in front of Sophia's first hour classroom. "What's wrong, you ill?"

"Tired after that wild party."

"Still? Ted and I, we had the best time, really…"

"The house burnt down." Sophia tried to cut her off. Andrea did not hesitate until what her friend said registered.

"Your house?"

Sophia explained the old home, omitted the part about the photos. Andrea apologized, asked for details. Sophia's eyes glistened. "Don't want to talk about it." She brushed past her friend, sat down, only looked up when she was positive Andrea had left. A two-hour countdown to impact. What would happen? What to say? How to react?

Minutes lapsed like hours. In her second class, the teacher had to inform her that the end bell had clanged. Sophia meandered to third hour though not before stopping in the girls' room to release the contents of her innards.

As she neared the classroom, the vital organ in her chest pounded. She placed a foot across the doorway, saw the seat next to hers was empty, exhaled, and moved to her desk. The teacher stood, went to the front as the tardy bell rang, about to close the door. An arm prevented him.

Sophia's head seemed like a balloon that had no more room for expansion. She experienced double vision. The figure came into her sight. Carbon dioxide exited her mouth. The student, a boy the girl knew as Mark, hurried to his seat.

The teacher lectured though Sophia heard little, couldn't cease questioning where her boyfriend—soon to be ex boyfriend?—was.

After class, she met up with Renaldo, his breath giving an odor reminiscent of the party, he stating Arturo was sick. Sophia sighed. Then a thought: Was he doing his Ferris Bueller? With someone else? She displayed a straight face to Renaldo, who asked her to lunch and along the way, Conrad and Andrea joined them, it a quiet meal, Sophia consuming only a few bites. Andrea asked about Arturo, Sophia mumbling incoherently, others not pressing for clarification. Before lunch hour was halfway done, the group dispersed.

The rest of the day passed and Sophia's mood improved. Nightfall arrived as did her mother from work, daughter making no mention of the house. A second restless night.

* * * *

Third hour arrived faster the next day and, as yesterday, the girl experienced the bodily reactions at classroom's entrance as she peeked inside, his seat vacant. She walked to hers, about to spin around and face front. A voice stopped her.

"How are you?"

To Sophia, it seemed someone had turned on the air conditioning. Deliberately she shifted, whispered possible sentences. Her glance met his. She watched his expression, his lips at an upward bend. Hers moved the opposite way. Why was he so happy? From what he'd done after the party? Words moved to her lips. Sophia recalled James and her face flushed.

"You okay?" Arturo's smile receded.

Sophia asked how he was, where he'd been the previous day, Arturo joking about his mom's lack of cooking ability then started a confessive, "Ya know, I..." when the tardy bell rang and the teacher lectured.

The female teen contemplated what Arturo was going to say, hour's instructions passing through her like beer. When the bell rang, she gave a mouse-like squeak then collected her books. His unfinished sentence came to her. She rose and asked him.

"Oh. Was saying I..." He moved a hand in circles.

"You what?" She wondered if he knew she already knew. Maybe he'd discovered he'd left the snapshot behind. How would he know she'd found it? She chose not to rescue him.

Arturo ah-hemmed. "Ya know..."

"No, I don't. How would I if you haven't told me?"

"The fire." Arturo wiped his mouth with the back of a hand. "I know it upset you. And I'm sure your mom'll kill you." He stared at the floor. "Shoulda offered to help clean up."

Sophia noticed his eyes had some moisture. Was he addled because he hadn't helped? Or due to what he'd done with the other girl?

He whispered "Sorry," cleared his throat a second time, eyelashes in rapid movement. He shut his eyes, held the pose a second then looked at Sophia.

She felt as bad as he looked, thought of being in the car with James. Her eyes moistened. She sniffled and took Arturo's hand, led him out. "It's okay." She tried to chuckle. "Place was unlivable."

He re-requested forgiveness. She studied the soft eyes, sad smile, that smooth skin, put an arm around him, told him it'd be all right though she said this for herself. She walked him to class, her rational mind cursing her for being so forgiving, her emotional side assuring this would make the healing process easier. Didn't she want him anyway? She eyed the boy, his features, told him it was okay, the place was a dump, no one could live there. "Not even..."

"Roaches?"

Sophia laughed. "Took the word right out of my mouth."

The two grinned as they proceeded down the hall.

* * * *

Millicent watched Bobby Stephens saunter toward her, combed her long black hair, wished she could pull out her pocket mirror and check the eye-liner and shadow around her eyes. The guy was tall, a little gangly, brown hair and eyes, had a thin but glowing smile and muscles that rippled under a tight, blue shirt.

He walked past her without a glance. Millicent felt like she'd been sentenced to death row, went to class with her head down, only replied to friends in guttural tones. What was the point of going on? If only she was home now, could end it all there. No guy'd pay her any heed. Never had, never would.

Friday's lunch with the gang came to her. At least she was part of a group, wished she'd gone to the party but had felt too blah. In class Emily, the girl next to her, struck up a discussion, Millicent amnestic about her former mood.

* * * *

Sophia decided to tell her mom that night, the elder female in good spirits. As they watched the news, Sophia asked what was on.

"The news. Duh." The mother studied her offspring with squinted eyes. "Aren't you learning anything? You'll be in college this fall. Do you have a hint what you'll select?"

Sophia said she had time, freshman and sophomore years a homogenous schedule for students. The mother scowled and uttered a prayer that her daughter wouldn't be like those who went to college to party, their goal to be a full-time career student. She mentioned a thirty-year-old still in school, milking the experience as long as he was able.

Sophia insisted she wasn't one of those students.

"If you say so. I don't want you like celebrities, messed up before twenty-one."

"Will never happen."

"If you say so."

Sophia decided it best to get this over with before her mom drove past and saw the damaged structure or heard about it from someone else. She asked about her dad and the chances romance was brewing.

The older female sat up, leaned forward, eyes wider, and spoke in conspiratorial tones at a fast pace, said he was to visit a few weeks later on business.

Sophia leaned back. "Oh." When her mom criticized the detached response, daughter pointed out her dad was to be here on business. The woman admonished she'd arrange a romantic dinner with him at their old house then sat upright and declared she had to go and tidy the place. Sophia quickly dismissed the scheme, asked how her mom could take him there—"That old dump," she mocked—and questioned how he'd be impressed by it. Her mother explained the old memories would conjure up old passions. When Sophia suggested the fancy campus hotel, her mother declared the house the only possible place, it with positive memories for both, their first home.

Ms. Imeldo stood. "Need to check it out, get a jump on things."

"Mom." Sophia stepped in front of her. "Why the rush? You said it's not for several weeks."

"Because if I don't start soon, I'll procrastinate, he'll be here, there'll be no place to be together romantically, and he's gone, back to one of his sluts. I mean girlfriends."

Sophia half smiled, put a hand on her mother's shoulder. "Mom..." She blinked a few times then closed her eyes.

"Yes?"

Sophia opened her eyes and put her arm around her mother's neck. "You can't do it."

"Why not? Worth a try."

"I mean the house. You can't go there."

Ms. Imeldo's eyes became as small as Morse code dashes. "Why not?"

"It's..." Sophia gulped. "Not there anymore."

As quick as sashes thrown open, the older woman's eyes expanded. "What do you mean?"

"There was...a fire." Water collected in Sophia's eyes though not because of the event.

"A fire?" the mother said as if in a library. "What fire? How? When? Why?"

Sophia disclosed the facts. Realization swept over her mother's face like sunlight washing across land. She nodded then asked how she was going to reconcile with her ex. Her fingers curled. Her jaw spasmed. She took a heavy step toward her daughter.

More water from Sophia's eyes. She backpedaled, crumpled into a high-backed chair, nearly tipped it over.

"Answer me!" Ms. Imeldo shouted. "What did you do? How did it happen?"

Sophia protested she had no clue, admitted to her herself that was true, hollered she wasn't even there when it happened. Mother stepped to daughter, showed clenched fists.

"You'd better pray that's the truth because if I find out otherwise…" She turned her head up. "He'd never forgive me for what I'd do."

Sophia couldn't control her shaking, uttered, "Yes, Ma'am," and fled to her room, closed the door. Tears flowed although, again, because of the photo. The more she re-examined her recall, the more assured she was of her observations and conclusions. Her hands dug between the mattress and box springs, touched the slick, wrinkled rectangle. She viewed the photo. It hadn't changed, faces smiling at her, one familiar, the other not. She jammed it back under the mattress, crawled onto her bed, tossed her face into the pillow, and cried herself into unconsciousness.

Was the relationship changed irrevocably? Arturo had apologized, albeit not for what she knew he'd done. Not directly. Would he go to this Phoebe if she called? Was he with her now? Had he been with her since that night? Had the girl dumped him and he was now using Sophia to ease the blow? Or was he truly genuine?

The questions went unanswered, Sophia's alarm clock waking her the next morning. After their class, Arturo carried her books, paid for her lunch, helped with schoolwork. Though he'd said the words, Sophia waited to hear them again. For the reason she wanted. He didn't say them.

* * * *

Like on most nights, Renaldo sat alone, watched the tube, and guessed where his parents were: drinking at a friend's house, a bar, or some loud honky tonk. He looked at the bottles his parents kept in a seven-foot-high mahogany armoire behind an ebony bar they'd had installed. The contents tempted him. He wandered over, read the labels. Jack Daniels whiskey had always been a good friend but he craved something sweet. The Bacardi rum on the shelf above tasted bitter. He thought of what went well with it, licked his lips, and checked the refrigerator. Red cans aplenty. He grabbed two, pulled them open with a *ksssh*, poured the Coca Cola into a wide tumbler, and unscrewed the cap on the rum, poured shots into the cup. Several sips had him adding a liberal quantity from the bottle that'd been in the cabinet. He chugged the drink, made a second, drank it—then a third. A fourth. All became a blur. He rested on the sofa, skin at the top of his eyes as if weighted. His world was like an unlit room, door closed, his last thought to condemn his parents' negligence and addiction, the latter causing the former, outcome a pathetic, indulgent life.

* * * *

Conrad lay on his unmade bed, algebra book open though he wasn't reading it, instead surveying the room. A big, multi-paned window centered on the wall to his left allowed plenty of evening sun. He folded his arms over his chest, took in the peace and quiet. It didn't last long, his sister turning on her stereo at wall-thumping decibels. Their mother yelled to turn it down. The girl did although not enough for Conrad, final exams having him feeling as though his stomach muscles had sprung.

He focused on Friday's lunch at the pizza place. They'd plan weekend activities though he doubted he'd join them then, the noon rendezvous ample excitement for him, his mom sometimes ribbing him with the question of being a minister, it befitting his quiet personality though she mistook this demeanor for contemplation. Never religious, he believed in God, just not a controlling, planning one. Most of the time.

"Friday lunch," he said to bring his thoughts back to the pleasing. Yet he worried one of them would comment on his saying little at the party, particularly to girls, and make false assumptions about him. Had they already joked about it amongst themselves? He told himself he didn't care, knew it wasn't true, was patient, wanted the right girl, imagined introducing the gang to a new "friend," their facial appearances. Yet they'd have only a few more lunchtimes together.

Maybe in college, he thought and smiled. He'd have his girl then. All would be well.

The upcoming get-together spurred him. He returned to his studies.

* * * *

Andrea entered the house after her date, her mom asking how it went. The girl mumbled "Fine" and headed to her room.

"You get any?" younger brother Steve teased.

Andrea didn't smile. "Funny."

"I'll take that as a no. Good thing. That Ted dweeb is...well, a dweeb."

"Steven, be nice to your sister."

"Yes, Mother."

Andrea turned on the squawk box as a distraction, she and Ted having eaten a quick meal then watched an Oklahoma State theater play, something about two gay guys, she bored with it before the first scene concluded, Ted making jokes about the way one guy didn't lisp or how the other liked art and fashion. Andrea had frowned, informed Ted about his outdated, narrow-minded stereotypes, which led to a brief argument. Had they not been in public, Andrea was sure it would have escalated. Instead they were taciturn the second half of the show, Ted taking her straight home despite his earlier suggestion for ice cream.

TV noise was an insignificant distraction to Andrea. Though it was but their second time out, he didn't seem right. Like all the others, first contact perfect, each was Mr. Right. By the second, sometimes first *official*, date, he was Mr. Wrong.

She explained it away: lots of time to find the right one. But Friday was nigh. What would she tell Sophia? Mr. Right was the third Anti-Christ? She tried to imagine the fun things that'd come up. School would finally be over, they to join the adult world with real, mature males, college juniors and seniors. Men. Grown males who wanted to get out there and make big bucks.

She sighed, blocked out her brother's oral jab about Ted—"Dead," the boy ridiculed, the guy quiet when she'd introduced him—and awaited the time till Friday's gathering.

* * * *

Wyatt didn't fall asleep right away, same as every night since warning others about letting things get out of hand at the party. He'd done them a favor, there might've been serious injuries or death which would have brought numberless lawsuits against Sophia's mom, a rap sheet for some once the underage alcohol consumption became known. Yet the more he thought, the more uncertainty crept in. Friday he'd ask. But what if they turned against him, blamed him for the fire? Should he even broach the subject?

An hour later his mind shut down, consciousness replaced by dreamland, void of solution.

* * * *

Arturo's taste buds got little exercise at dinner, as they hadn't recently. When his mom questioned his lack of consumption, he claimed to be getting in shape. However, when she offered healthy foods and the son declined, she repeated her question. None of the parents had heard about the fire, as far as he knew. What if he told her? He knew she kept secrets as well as a rooster avoided announcing the new day. He muttered something about if he'd graduate, to which she gave a "Ha!" Arturo making honor roll every semester.

He added he had concerns about upcoming finals. And college. What if he didn't like his chosen major, housing management, he wanting to buy and sell homes, heard a fast living could be made doing such. Enrolling in a technical school for a realtor's license was not a choice, his parents demanding he be the first in their family to get a college degree.

And what about Sophia? She'd wavered on him, forgave him then criticized him. Did she know? How? Flames had consumed everything, he driving past it the next day. Nothing but bricks and burnt remnants. And they'd promised to do it that night, first time for either. That was now impossible for him thanks to Phoebe, whose pledge to call went unfulfilled. She hadn't revealed her number to him. Should he tell Sophia? She'd seen him flirting with the girl but had no inkling how far it'd gone. Might his apology for not assisting Sophia be sensed as confession for something else? Did it explain her ambivalence?

Long after the western skyline had lost its golden glow, the questions echoed in him with no answer reverberating back.

* * * *

Friday took its time arriving. Lunchtime had school halls filling, students like worker ants recognizing a cookout, parking lot a sea of moving metal and rubber.

Wyatt staked first claim to the booth, Sophia and Arturo pushing through the doors a minute later, then the rest of the gang en masse. They gathered at the food bar and chose their lunch. At the booth, dialogue sprang up while they ate,

Conrad saying they should've chosen a steakhouse, Arturo countering it was too expensive.

"Would cost ya what? Two cases of beer?"

The gang laughed, Renaldo responding with "Speaking of beer..." and asked others what they thought of last week's party and the fire, its cause, and who caused it. Voices rose.

"Arturo's saying you warning us about the dangers made us self-conscious, nervous," Renaldo argued with Wyatt.

"That didn't cause the fire."

"Sort of," Renaldo said.

"Whadya mean, sort of? Either it did or it didn't."

"It did." Renaldo sat back, crisscrossed arms over his chest.

"If you believe that, you're a dumbass."

Renaldo reached across the table, Wyatt ready to stand, Arturo in like posture. A voice broke their concentration.

"Guys, shut the hell up! Stop it!" Millicent shoved her chair back, it squeaking across tile. She pulled Arturo away, led him to his seat.

"He's the dumb fuck!" Arturo pointed at Wyatt. "I'll kick your ass, you—"

Millicent blocked Arturo, commanded him to tranquility then, with visual cues, forced Wyatt and Renaldo to calm. "Look at you, friends for so long. Are you going to ruin it due to one stupid party?"

"Stupid?" Arturo gave a uni-brow stare. "How would you know?"

Millicent withdrew, Sophia and Andrea patting the girl, Sophia scolding Arturo, repeated Millicent's comments regarding the boys ruining their friendship, asked them to think about that.

The boys exchanged looks. Sophia told them to speak.

No one did. She gave the order a second time, louder.

Wyatt extended a hand. "Sorry. Only warned you because things were way the fuck out of hand."

"Why do you have to be such an unfun tightass?" Renaldo asked.

Wyatt pushed fingers of the outstretched hand into his palm, arm going back.

A chuckle from Renaldo. Arturo and Conrad laughed. Wyatt opened his hand, lowered it, and offered it to Renaldo, who apologized, clasped Wyatt's hand in his, and shook. All four boys eased back.

"Better," Sophia said. "Thanks to Millicent. Saved you all from hurting each other. More important, from destroying a friendship. You need to thank her."

The boys did and Millicent smiled awkwardly, thanked them, and went quiet again. The group finished their meal and went for the exit. All except Millicent, who hastened to the restroom, looked in the mirror, wished she'd gone to the party, cursed, and bowed her head.

The door opened, Sophia asking how Millicent was, said she saw her rush in here, informed her the group was leaving. Millicent told her not to wait. Sophia exited.

Millicent gazed at her reflection. Her life was going no where, no boy would ever ask her out. She decided to do it tomorrow, a guarantee as good as Maytag's quality assurance. Or a Hawaiian weatherman's forecast for temperature in the eighties.

She walked out, chin up, body at a ninety degree angle to the floor. She beamed. No one noticed. Her body slackened.

* * * *

The following morning, Millicent tossed covers aside like it was Christmas morning and she was six years old again. She hurried to the kitchen—both parents asleep, she assumed, her brother's door also closed though she heard the *tap-tap-tap* of his laptop—and opened the same drawer her mother would have if it was time to carve the Thanksgiving turkey. She found one the right size. Everything was in order, note explaining all, this decision hers alone. Now was the time. Voices behind one door. Millicent startled. The object in her hand fell, landed with several metallic pings. She reacted as if seeing Medusa.

The mother's calling her name was like someone touching Millicent in a game of freeze tag. She retrieved the knife, seemed to reach the bedroom in one full bound, and shut the door.

A knob twisted. "Phil? That you?"

The mother's question was answered by silence. Millicent inhaled, she as unmoving as a sculptor's work. No sounds from the other room.

The teen exhaled. And put the knife to her wrist. The metal was cold but bearable. She paused. Should she be standing? Sitting? Did it matter? Her eyes watered. She shut them. This would make the event less painful, she not seeing the crimson seep out of her and wouldn't be tempted to puke. She pressed the knife harder. A pinch on skin. She winced, pushed deeper. A knock on the door.

Chapter 3

Prom night was clear, air warm and moist from a late afternoon shower, roads glistening in streetlights' wattage.

Arturo and Sophia sparkled in their outfits, unaware of anyone else, their final dance under a veranda beneath glowing stars. Afterward, they rode to Lake McMurtry and parked in the section known as Makeout Point that overlooked the waters. Done there, they repaired to their hotel room.

"C'mon." Arturo unbuttoned his shirt.

"What's the hurry? We got all night."

"Out there." He motioned to the sliding glass door that led to the hotel pool. When Sophia protested they hadn't brought swimsuits, Arturo grinned and dropped his pants.

Despite her face becoming hot, Sophia giggled. Arturo grabbed her, helped her undress then led her out, she with a hand over her face, said she hoped no one would see them.

Arturo slid into waters. "Just right. C'mon in."

Still warm-faced and giggling, arms tight over her chest, Sophia lurched in. He grabbed her and they swam quietly, observed the stars, and made out.

Back at their room, Sophia wrapped herself in the white terrycloth hotel bathrobe. Arturo asked what she was doing, retrieved the square foil package from his pants pocket draped over the padded chair, and flipped it between fingers. Sophia looked at it then him, then observed the king-sized bed with periwinkle spread. The name Phoebe formed mentally as did the image of the fire, two figures not far from it. She stuck her hands in the robe's pockets.

"Well?" Arturo hopped on the bed, pulled the covers on her side down. For a brief hiatus, Sophia wished her mother was more conservative, traditional, and strict.

"C'mon." Arturo patted the mattress. "It'll be great."

The event played larger in the girl's mind, strobed in her thoughts, closer, bigger, he with that bitch. She scowled. "How do you know?"

Arturo didn't flinch nor did his face lose color. He calmly extended a hand, drew her in, and held her. "I don't. Only basing it on what I heard."

"You had to hear it from someone before you believed it?"

The two laughed. Arturo kissed her, his hazel eyes seeming to stare into her deepest depths. He praised her beauty then reached for the belt on her robe, untied it. His grin expanded as he pushed one side of the robe away. "You'd look so much better with this off."

Though she blushed, Sophia wrapped herself around him, slid her other arm out of the garment. It fell in a hush on the brown carpet. Arturo undid the package, put its contents on though not without effort, his twitchy fingers unable to firmly grip the object.

"C'mon," she teased, on the bed. "Before I lose interest."

"Ready," he said after a lapse of silence and rolled on top of her.

To Sophia, she felt more ecstatic than she believed any drug high could have given her, other girl's name and images from that night dissolving the way burnt paper consumes itself, thought only of herself with him. Until time ceased.

They rolled away from each other. Arturo asked how it was, Sophia commenting it ended quicker than anticipated, Arturo agreeing though the possible meaning of his comment did not so much as register a tick on Sophia's dial of suspicion, her grin unwilling to recede. They held each other before falling asleep. Sophia's smile didn't fade.

The couple watched the sunrise, lovelier than the most exquisite painting. The journey home was a magic carpet ride to Sophia, everything in greater relief, brighter color, finer detail. They kissed goodbye at Sophia's house, each praising the other for a great smooch. And night. For Sophia it felt as if she moved to the door while in a child's moonwalk, blew a kiss to Arturo as he left. The past was just that. Forever.

* * * *

At graduation, the friends congratulated each other on the university grounds of Theta pond, the weather allowing the outdoor celebration, breeze blowing clouds across the sky at a steady pace, birds chirping above. A few owls hooted. Conrad joked about the fuss, asked who had died. Andrea shushed him, said it was the fact this moment was never coming back. When Conrad said it would a few months later, here on the college campus, Andrea scolded him, said that was different, they'd be on their own.

"How is that bad?" the boy said in full grin. "Now I can lay any chic I want, parents not around."

Andrea reacted like he'd said he didn't want the school year to end and when Conrad inquired as to why the girl's expression, she replied he didn't sound like himself. He asked what that meant, cupped hands on the brown belt that held up ironed black pants.

Wyatt, eavesdropping, tapped his friend. "She thinks you're gay."

Conrad pounded his foot. "Am not. Why would you say that?"

Wyatt poked his friend. "To get a rise out of you."

"I hope that's all." Conrad observed the skies. "You guys." He mingled with parents and relatives.

Renaldo came up to Wyatt, asked where the alcohol was.

"That all you think about?"

"Gotta celebrate. I've started already." He opened the front pocket of his black suit, showed the top of a Jack Daniels bottle. Wyatt asked what he was doing, gave a quick visual sweep. No adults saw them.

"What's a little drinkie poo?"

"If you're underage, it's a big deal," Andrea said.

Renaldo rubbed his shoulder on hers, said she disappointed him, had seemed the partying type. He laughed at how Andrea, at Sophia's party, was anything but sober, to which Andrea now warned he not breathe near any adults.

Renaldo mocked her, thumbed at Wyatt, and moaned he'd ruined the party.

"Let that shit go," Wyatt said, his tone louder. He looked around. No one stared his way. He lowered his timbre, lectured to abstain until after ceremonies. Renaldo sneered why, dared his friend to call authorities.

Wyatt's face pinched. He stiffened his shoulders, snapped at his friend. "Just take a break from the moonshine, huh?" He led Andrea away, amidst Renaldo's hissing "party pooper." Still, no adults noticed.

Arturo and Sophia stayed close to each other, a carryover from Prom night, classmates jesting as to their wedding date. The two enjoyed the teasing, sifted through the crowd, conversed with students they didn't even know. At one point, Sophia saw a figure in jeans and t-shirt, with blonde hair and blue eyes. The event swam in her mind, a flashback.

This person sauntered away, Sophia realizing it only looked like her. She eyed Arturo. He bantered with students and parents, oblivious to her suspicions. His gaze and hers merged. He smiled, led her to him, hugged her and told her the last few weeks had been his best then bragged it would only get better.

She sighed, broke out a grin, and hugged Arturo like he was her favorite stuffed animal. Things were going to get better.

* * * *

Millicent stood on the fringes of the gatherings, observed Arturo and Sophia clutching each other. Though she smiled at them, she felt she was Robinson Crusoe with no Friday. She withdrew further, surveyed the throngs, watched friends and classmates hug and kiss, exchange pats on the backs and handshakes. She sighed. Then hiccupped. A figure nearby. Bobby Stephens, moving in her direction. Her eyes were huge, her mind with numerous sentences and phrases, she unable to comprehend them all, let alone one. Bobby approached, Millicent with a logjam of words in her larynx. She opened her mouth. He smiled, Millicent positive he smirked at her mouth remaining open, as if to puke. Her face felt hot enough she feared it looked so red to him he'd think she belonged to a new race. She moved to him. And fell. The sidewalk seemed to welcome her with a grin. She shut her eyes, tensed, and expected the harsh contact of concrete on skin. Instead she landed softly, suspended inches above pavement. She opened her eyes. The distance between her and the path grew. She was upright. A hand held her.

"You okay?" Bobby asked.

Millicent could only gape at the boy's face, his high cheekbones like porcelain, his nose slightly upturned, lips small but the perfect shade of red. His brown hair was parted seamlessly in the middle. She seemed to look for miles into those brown eyes.

"Huh? Wha' happen?" Her tongue was a water balloon. She watched Bobby cringe, stuttered apologies, and thanked him, unable to cure her stammering. Bobby's mangled expression did not change.

"Sorry," she said, brushed herself off. "Kinda fell."

"Almost."

"Clumsy me." Millicent attempted a laugh but snorted.

"It's okay," Bobby said and searched the area, as if desperate to excuse himself. "I was…"

"Thank you," the girl said quickly to keep him from thinking up a reason to leave. She took in a long draw of air and gave a smile no model could have improved upon. Words formed in her brain. "I hope I—"

"Millicent!" An adult voice from behind. The girl shuddered.

A clap of hands. "C'mere, Grandma wants a picture with you."

Millicent's mom rushed up, turned the girl away, and chided the teen about wandering off, daughter feeling like her stomach had become a pile of large, sharp rocks. She checked over a shoulder. Bobby had moved away, nowhere to be found, as if a phantasm. She tried to look the other way but her mother's body was an obstacle, woman blathering about how she'd told her daughter since childhood to avoid anyone she didn't know. She placed Millicent beside the teen's grandmother and snapped pictures.

"Millicent, smile," the mother said. "And stop looking away, like you're trying to find something. Say cheese." She laughed. "Always worked when you were little. Now…"

She had them pose for several shots. Millicent surrendered her search, the boy long gone.

Of course, she thought. *I'm so boring, geeky, and clumsy. Next time I see a boy I like, I'm running the other way.*

She grumbled about her misfortune, forced smiles and a happy tone, wished to be in prison, that less agonizing. If only her mom hadn't intervened in the bedroom that morning.

* * * *

At a classmate's house, the graduation party lasted into the next day, soirée with no intoxicating beverages—until the parents escaped to their bedroom, whereby rum was added to Cokes, strawberry soft drinks metamorphosing into daiquiris.

Renaldo pulled out his stash, became the most easily-heard over the clamor, only quieted when a female classmate with curves, red hair, and dark eyes made darker by overdone black eyeliner sat next to him, and introduced herself as Katy, stated she'd watched him all year. She enfolded her hand in his, kissed him.

Renaldo fidgeted at the thought of commitment, reached for his concoction of rum, tequila, and gin, and downed a few shots. He stood, attempted to dance though no music played, and nearly crashed into a china cabinet, knocking over a few friends in the process.

Wyatt shushed him, asked Katy for help, she offering to drive Renaldo home, demanded the boy's keys, asked if he drove a gray Ford F-150 with black racing stripe. Renaldo slurred "Yes" and Wyatt inquired how she was to get home. Katy grinned, said she'd ridden here with a friend and lived in Renaldo's neighborhood. Wyatt instructed she call if Renaldo got out of control, gave her his cell number which she entered in her phone, thanked him then led Renaldo to his truck, told Wyatt it was but a ten minute jaunt.

She started the car. At the first traffic light she cursed upon seeing the light on the dashboard and informed Renaldo she'd make a quick stop for gas before dropping him off, at which point he could thank her. She smiled. "Right in this car."

Renaldo smirked and rubbed a shoulder on her, caressed her neck. She moaned pleasurably.

When she entered the vehicle after filling up, he requested the keys, said he'd sobered, promised to drop her off at her house. She yawned and floated her hand over his, dropped the keys in them with a *click*. Renaldo fisted them, kissed her, and commented she could thank him at her place then led her to the passenger side where they locked arms around each other's necks, their lips inseparable. He finally meandered to the driver's side and faced her. "On to bigger and better things."

He left the area doing sixty then ran a red light. Katy cautioned him to slow. He did. To fifty five. Katy mumbled for him to pay attention, pressed lips on his cheek. He insisted he was paying attention, looked at her, and said she was the finest female he'd seen.

"Watch the road," Katy said, though in a tone one uses during foreplay. She managed a peek ahead. And pulled away from him. "Stop!" She pointed. He did not do as told. "Renaldo! Look!"

The boy turned to the windshield and sat up, stared at the sight ahead. The license plate numbers and letters seemed as big as a billboard's at arm's length. He stabbed for the other pedal, only hit carpeted floor.

"Renaldo!" Katy pointed to the area below the dash. His foot found the pedal. The distance between him and the other car still shrank. The girl yelped. He hunted for the correct pedal. Metal squealed. The space between the vehicles grew. Renaldo released his breath, checked mirrors. No other cars near him. The car ahead receded from view.

"Too damn close," Renaldo said, added it was her fault. The girl sat up, wanted to know how. The side of his mouth closer to her inched up. "How can I resist looking at such a gorgeous babe?"

Katy laughed but warned him to watch out. He countered they were almost there, increased his speed, and passed another car despite her lecturing, turned on a side street then faced the girl. "God, you look great. Can I tear your clothes off now?" He stretched an arm to her side. She kissed his forearm then elbow, all the way up to his shoulder. The boy's face radiated as he watched her.

A rending crack like a huge branch breaking split their eardrums. They turned to the windshield. And shrieked.

Chapter 4

The car smashed the guardrail, bucked down the small ditch to a gurgling creek. The two exchanged wide-eyed looks.

"What the hell were you doing?" Katy said.

"You pulled me in your direction."

"I said keep an eye on the fucking road!"

"How can I when you're reeling me to you?"

She argued she'd had but a finger on him.

"Then that finger must be pretty damn strong."

"Never shoulda let you drive. Your parents aren't going to be happy when you get home."

Renaldo chuckled. She demanded to know why. He told her how his parents spent most nights. Katy gazed at him, blew air out of a corner of her mouth.

"Yeah, right."

Renaldo swore it was fact, said she could check for herself. She asked if this was his way of getting her into bed. He smiled, questioned if that wasn't what she wanted. The two laughed.

"C'mon." Renaldo opened his door, helped her out. She looked back at the mess, wanted to know how he'd rescue the car. He said he'd have it towed out after sunrise then grinned.

"Do I win the bet?"

Katy put hands on hips. "Haven't proven me wrong."

"Yet." Renaldo welcomed her up the road. They strode to the house, driveway unoccupied, door to the two car garage closed. At the tall, high-ceilinged brick porch, Renaldo opened the storm door then unlocked the French door and pushed it across tan carpet before reaching inside the door frame. A *click*. Lights hummed from recessed ceiling fixtures.

Katy viewed the vaulted living room ceiling and chandelier above a dining room table, glanced to the upstairs bedrooms, doors open, rooms unlit. No sounds came from them. "It is quiet. And dark."

"Told ya they wouldn't be upset," Renaldo said. "They're not here."

When Katy queried as to their whereabouts, Renaldo raised his shoulders, muttered, "Who knows?" and lowered his chin.

"It's okay." Katy rubbed him, kissed his neck.

Renaldo stiffened. "Who said I felt hurt?" He smiled. "How can I when I'm with you?"

Katy welcomed him to her chest, their noses touching, he pressing his lips on hers. They moved to the red sofa, continued their activities. He took off his shirt, assisted Katy then came into her.

"Too damn fast," Katy breathed.

"It'll slow down."

Katy separated from him. "This isn't your first?"

"No."

The girl opened her mouth. Mist formed in her eyes. She wiped them and sniffed, turned away.

"What gives?" He admitted he'd only done it twice.

"I thought it was *our* first."

He pushed her hair back. "It is. For us."

"I mean both of us."

"What difference does it make?" He tried to kiss her. Katy sat up, described how she'd dreamt she'd be his first, what it'd be like, how they'd do it.

"Well, this time was best." He pulled her back down and held her. "With someone I love. And who's beautiful."

Katy beamed, fondled his hair then pinched his butt. He yelped, asked why she did that. She giggled, said she wanted to since she first spotted his cute, little behind. He raised an eyebrow, said how girls always commented on a guy's great eyes or smile. Or his money.

"You have none of those," she teased. When he opened his mouth, she placed fingers over it, told him to relax. They held each other and fell asleep.

* * * *

Katy woke first, announced it was a few minutes past curfew, said she had to go, called her parents to inform them she was on her way.

"Call me," she said to Renaldo, who nodded, waved as she went down the street, then had pleasant, romantic dreams.

The next morning with rum and Coke in hand, he stared at the clear sky. High school was over, college fast approaching. At least he'd have classes that interested him.

And be with someone he could love. Truly love. And be committed to.

* * * *

A week after grades came out, the friends gathered at the pizzeria, spoke of college expectations then talked of where to live though no specifics were reached, Sophia stating she had a few leads, would keep them abreast of things.

"You keeping us abreast?" Renaldo tittered. "I like that."

"Grow up," Wyatt said. "Not in high school anymore. College is life. Your future. What you do there determines your future. Take care of yourself today and that'll take care of you tomorrow. And beyond."

"Yes, sir." Renaldo saluted Wyatt. "Benedict."

More chuckles. Wyatt glared at Renaldo who returned the look. The taller boy asked Wyatt if he wanted to go outside.

"Calm down," Andrea said, then chuckled. "You two need a woman."

"Already got one," Renaldo said.

All heads turned to him, a few requesting details. Renaldo orated about the graduation night party, neatly left out the car wreck, told how he and Katy had gone out since then, after he finished his shift at the university science lab where he prepared researchers' reports, a part-time job.

"Hopefully I can work this job and go to school."

The group congratulated him on his plans and his girl, Sophia inviting Renaldo to bring Katy. He cautioned it was too early.

Wyatt snorted. "Probably making it up."

Renaldo looked ready to spit. "You got a problem with me?"

"Was kidding. Like you." Wyatt clapped his friend's back. "Need to loosen up, don't be so uptight." He grinned. "Looks like you could use a nip."

The group collectively exhaled, Renaldo wishing for a belt. Wyatt pointed to his waist, offered his leather strap. Everyone moaned.

"Thought he'd like the offer," Wyatt went on. "Maybe he's gone to the dark side." He nodded toward another of the group. "Like ol' Conrad."

Chuckles from the group except Conrad. Wyatt offered his hand and apologized. They shook and Wyatt did the same to Renaldo, who sank two of his upper teeth on his lower lip.

Andrea and Sophia chatted up the topic of where to live though the group departed without reaching a conclusion.

On the way to Arturo's car, Sophia questioned him on his reticence. He responded he was thinking other things.

"Other women?" Sophia had an expression like a parent observing a teen's troubling behavior.

The boyfriend halted, she bumping into him. "What's that supposed to mean?"

She responded she was only asking, men thought only one thing. Arturo rubbed his temples and groaned, Sophia insistent it was fact. She called to Andrea before the girl closed her car door, asked for an opinion. The friend nodded, said that since guys did it, why shouldn't women? A tall, black-haired male in a small navy blue tank top that showed muscles as chiseled as a statue headed for the restaurant.

"With a guy like him." Andrea motioned her hand as if she'd touched a lit burner then whistled. "What a stud. May be my one. Let me find out." She started back to the entrance.

Sophia met her, grabbed her, and asked what the friend was doing. Andrea motioned to the tall guy.

"Remember? The stud?" She put both hands on Sophia. "You need help if you can't recall things that happened seconds ago. Senility isn't to hit until you're retired."

Sophia laughed then pushed her friend away and pointed a finger. "He's a lot older."

Andrea countered that was perfect, meant he was already making money.

Sophia sighed, wished the girl luck but with a frown, added, "Doubt it'll work." Andrea hastened back inside while Sophia watched the stranger and her friend strike up a dialogue, Sophia unable to decipher how things progressed. Arturo beckoned her to the car.

* * * *

Conrad stopped at a gas station before going home, sunlight glinting so sharp off the yellow and white roof covering the store the boy squinted despite sunglasses. He entered the store to pay, scanned the newspaper stack with six-inch headline screaming about a murder-suicide, smaller headline at the fold mentioning higher tuition costs. He snapped the paper open and read the lower article.

"You gonna buy that or spend all day here reading it?" the girl behind the counter finally asked.

Conrad didn't look up, said he'd buy it along with five lottery numbers and ten dollars worth of gasoline. The gray metal cash register dinged and the drawer slid open, the girl stating his cost. The boy felt for his wallet, continued to read, moved to the counter, and hit it at the waist. He grunted, extended a hand holding a twenty dollar bill, and looked up.

"Thank you." The sandy haired, green eyed girl in black and orange t-shirt took his bill.

Conrad didn't blink. "No, thank me. I mean, thank you."

The girl chuckled. Conrad continued to gape as if she was Aphrodite. She handed him his change and lottery ticket then asked if he was old enough to play.

Conrad stated he'd been eighteen for nine months, and accessed his driver's license. The girl viewed it then read the paper's title about tuition, asked if Conrad was at OSU. He told her in the fall and she inquired if the lottery was his way to earn a scholarship.

Conrad laughed awkwardly. His palms were cool while his body felt sunburned. One leg gave way and he fell toward the counter, elbow hitting it. She helped him back up and smiled. Conrad's throat went dry and he went to thank her but his tongue wouldn't shrink, lips feeling like inflated tires. He uttered *Aggh*, shuffled his feet, and displayed an uneven smile.

The girl repeated the question regarding tuition and the lottery. Conrad said his parents paid for most of it, the rest scholarship or grant money. The girl moaned she had to work part-time, grades not good enough for a scholarship.

"Well, we can't all be geniuses. Who'd do the grunt work for us brains?" Conrad smiled and she did the same then described her trouble with college algebra. Conrad promptly offered assistance then asked himself what he was saying, knew she'd reject the suggestion.

The cashier gave a small grin, twirled a lock of hair, and asked how well he knew algebra.

Conrad channeled thoughts. His mouth seemed to move on its own as he confessed he really didn't know it, had taken but one class.

"Thought you said you were eighteen."

Conrad gave an *Mmm-hmm*, wondered where she was leading. The girl explained Oklahoma high school students took two algebra classes, minimum before graduating.

"I was an exception." He tried to laugh, nearly choked then coughed, his head feeling like a drill was working both sides of it. "Clepped out of it."

The girl laughed. "CLEP is for college courses."

With his body feeling as if he'd descended into Lucifer's world, Conrad told the girl to keep the change—though he'd already taken it—and stumbled to the door, ran to his car like an outlaw pursued then halted, gathered his breath, fumbled for the fuel nozzle, stuck it in the car's tank, and squeezed. No gas came out. He pressed again. Nothing. His forehead gathered moisture, sun's rays not helping.

"You forgot something," a voice from behind said.

Conrad jumped as if he'd been caught cheating on a test.

Laughter. A hand on his back. He turned. And faced the girl.

"You forgot to choose the grade of gas. I assume being a college student with four years of bills ahead, you'd choose the regular unleaded, it's the cheapest." She touched the button and gripped the handle. Gas poured into the car's tank.

He thanked her though his voice quivered. She placed her hand on his, wanted to know why he bolted. The boy looked at her, the sensations returning: body warmth, slick hands. He grunted, "I dunno know," it coming out as, "I oh."

The girl's face brightened. "You seem a nice guy who could help with algebra. Would you mind? We can study at the library."

The suggestion of a public place had Conrad sighing. He moved his lips to form a *u* and inclined his head toward his chest. "Maybe we could do that."

She mentioned she was taking college algebra for summer school, had completed her freshman year.

Conrad imagined his friends' reactions. He with an older woman. He nodded. "Sure. Might be able to help though I only made Bs."

"That's good enough for me. I'm Dawn. Timberwolf."

"Dawn?" The distance between Conrad's eyebrows and hairline shrunk. "I hope that's with a W."

The girl chuckled. "I'm all woman."

"So I see." Conrad drank in her figure with his eyes. "I mean, it figures. I mean, forgive me, I…"

"It's okay." She promised it'd remain simple, they at the college library, second floor study room. They set a date and time, she writing them down along with her name and number for him. Her lips briefly met his face. She stepped away, waved, and returned to the store.

The nozzle clunked, Conrad spasming. He lifted the handle, a few drops dripping on his shoes. He reset the handle and gave a long look through the glass door. The girl chatted up a customer, turned as the older man exited, saw Conrad through the half open door, puckered her lips, and blew before the door closed. Through the glass, he volleyed the same. She took on another customer. Conrad entered his car and left, stuffed the white paper she'd given him into the glove compartment. Oh, would he have a story for the group.

* * * *

When she'd pulled out of the pizza place, Millicent's facial muscles sank, stomach as tight as the rubber band surrounding the core of a golf ball. It was back home to the jungle after visiting the oasis of the gang's gathering. She uttered oaths at her mom for knocking on her door the morning she'd wanted to end things. A long summer approached, she a waitress at a greasy spoon off Highway Fifty-one on the east side, its patrons with long hair, scruffy beards, missing teeth, and caps bearing logos of trucking companies. She thought of the catcalls and whistles, pinches on the rear, the comments:

"Hey, baby, you look tired. Wanna go to bed?"

"Got a band-aid? I scraped my knee falling for ya."

If only she hadn't obeyed her parents' order to apply. Her friends and the promise of being on her own helped make the future less daunting. And there was Bobby though she didn't know where he'd enrolled.

Back home, she sequestered in her bedroom, retrieved a calendar, counted the days until college, and let out a slow, heavy breath. A long summer indeed.

After dinner, she put on the restaurant uniform, trudged to her car, and left for a four-hour stint at the place. As she slogged to the door, hand on the thick, rectangular metal handle, she glanced back at *The Wharf*, an upscale seafood establishment, and imagined the salmon scent, her favorite spread, wafting through the dining area, low chandeliers dimmed, a bouquet of roses—pink, red, white—on the red, cloth-covered table. She would be in her best, a blue gown, candlelight between her and Bobby, he in tux with bow tie, hair slicked back, he having splashed on some male scent. Afterwards, they'd observe the stars. Maybe more.

"Honey, how's about taking my order?" a fiftyish man with brown beard and pony-tailed hair said, squeezed two fingers on Millicent's backside and grinned, gap-toothed.

Millicent frowned, hurried past the counter to the back, clocked in then peeked at the dining area. A group of older women seemed normal so she strode to them and took their order.

The evening passed faster than expected, only one other customer harassing her. She exited, planned her evenings: Out with friends tomorrow, next night spent considering college courses, next for relaxing, watching TV, and thinking of Bobby. She raised her head to the building across the street, watched customers enter and exit, pictured Bobby opening that tall, thick, wood door and holding it open for her.

"Let's go," she heard him say. And smiled.

"C'mon." The voice spoke louder. "It's late, ain't got much time. Gotta have ya back in fifteen minutes or your mom'll kill me, us, if I don't."

Millicent smiled. Until she discovered the voice wasn't part of her fantasy.

"Coming," a girl said, shoes clicking on pavement.

Millicent watched them. Her smile washed away, face as pasty and sick as the woman in the bathtub in *The Shining* after Jack Nicholson kissed her. Millicent rubbed her forehead, chanted for what she'd seen to disappear. His voice rumbled across the street.

"You look great. Did I tell you that?"

Feminine laughter.

Millicent watched. He kissed the girl, a quiet yet attractive red-head, Millicent not knowing her name. The two wrapped arms at the waist, he then opening the car door for her, she commenting how romantic he was, from the candlelight dinner to the rose he'd given, to always opening doors for her. He said he was glad he'd finally asked her out. They traded a quick kiss. He shut her door, walked to the other side, and passed a glance across the two-lane highway.

The girl in front of the diner hid her face behind a shoulder. Bobby opened his door, shut it, started the engine, and left.

Fighting back a crying jag, her legs like she'd caught a debilitating flu bug, Millicent staggered to her car, glad the cruiser that patrolled the area on occasion wasn't around. They'd have interrogated her then requested she put a finger on her nose, one leg up. She doubted she'd have passed.

In the car, her chest swelled and shrank and her throat hitched. She turned the engine over and headed home, her depression chilling her like wintertime. Her eyes blurred and she blinked away tears. Her throat seemed as if attacked by streptococcus.

The car sliced through blackness. Despite eyes like broken waterworks, Millicent made it home, collected herself, and ran past the living room where her mother sat in the white recliner, eyes shut, a book face down in her lap, the once-lit glass lamp off thanks to the plug-in timer beneath the brown mahogany table.

The teen paused, taken by the humorous, slack-jawed pose. She called to her mom who stirred, blinked, rubbed her eyes, and sat up. "Oh. How was work?"

Millicent's face was like a horse'd just shat in the room. "Hate the goddamn fucking place. Not to mention the job." She kicked off work shoes as if punting a football, first one landing harmlessly on carpet. The second one went high. A clang as it hit the black metal floor lamp. "It sucks!" She went to the kitchen, tears flowing again.

"Millicent?" Mrs. Petrovich, now fully conscious, stood. "What's wrong? Something happen?"

The daughter knew no way she'd tell the truth. Not the whole truth anyway. She railed about the job, the harassment while the scene of the boy and girl at his car flipped over and over in her mind, a constant loop.

"Why didn't you say so? Had no idea," the mom said.

"Because you never pay attention, don't give a damn about me, only that bitchy, bratty brother, that spoiled *brat*."

An upstairs door creaked, father in blue pajamas and white t-shirt wanting to know why the ruckus.

Mother wrapped arms around daughter, told Millicent to tell him. The girl described as she had to her mom, had no trouble showing hurt, even if misplaced.

The parents stood over Millicent—she now collapsed in a kitchen seat—and took turns massaging the girl's back. After all was said, the father considered legal action but following Millicent's protests and careful thought, decided they had little evidence.

"I just want another job. Or a break from things. Please?"

"Let's wait till sunrise." Mrs. Petrovich patted Millicent, hugged her, the father agreeing, said they cared for their daughter, wanted her to succeed better than they had.

Millicent stared at her dad, events of yore coming to her: the days he helped her catch butterflies or fireflies in a jar after dark. Taught her hopscotch. Things her girlfriends' fathers had wanted nothing to do with. She smiled, wiped an eye, and agreed to a next-day discussion. The trio moved in unison to their rooms, gave the usual nighttime wishes.

Millicent closed her door, didn't turn on the light, shuffled to the bed, lay on it, and stared into blackness. Was it worth continuing? The only boy she'd felt attraction to loved someone else. She would live and die alone, no family, nothing. If only her mother hadn't intervened.

She listed possibilities: Gun. Drugs. Alcohol. Rope.

The last sounded tempting, others not easily accessible, she not knowing the first thing about firearms, her parents owning none, alcohol and drugs too risky, she fearful she'd only pass out, wake up with a hangover or a high and be punished or taken to a psych ward. How to get some rope? She had many belts, none strong enough to hold her. She felt her eyes wanting to close as replays of childhood summers, outdoors with her dad, drifted in her mind. Tears found their way out.

The emotions swayed back and forth in her. Give up or experience another day? Even if it seemed tomorrow held no signs of improvement? Assume things would get better? Or get it over with now?

These flooded her mind, filled the void in her brain. Her eyelids became heavy and soon her eyes moved rapidly back and forth.

Chapter 5

The haze of first light forced Millicent to open her eyes. Last night's events came to her. She pulled the bed sheet to her face.

A hand rapped the door. The knob turned, space opening between door and frame.

"Millicent?"

The girl looked at her mother then rolled away, maternal figurehead gently stating she understood, asked for forgiveness.

Millicent turned over. "I hate that place." She scowled at what happened there along with the incident across the street, and forced phlegm down her throat.

"We understand now. Your father and I discussed this. Are there any jobs you like? Weren't you thinking about teaching?"

The girl contemplated the words. Tell her parents? The father wanted her to follow his trail, obtain a business degree, and take over his office supply store. What would he say when she told him otherwise?

"Millicent?"

The teen blinked, looked at her mother who repeated the questions. Millicent pondered teaching. It seemed uplifting, helping others learn things. So how to let her father down easy?

"Possibly," she said. "I'm not sure what I want to do. However, yes, I've thought about it."

"There's an opportunity."

Millicent sat up. "Huh?"

"A summer job teaching."

The younger Petrovich shook her head, informed her mother of the requirements for teaching. The mother chided to be realistic, Millicent wasn't going to be hired now as a teacher. She rubbed the sheet blanketing her daughter's legs, suggested a day care job as an assistant doing grunt work or cleaning up after kids, this allowing the girl to see if she liked it. The woman mentioned local daycares, admitted they weren't structured schools but it was a start.

The girl smiled. "Sounds okay."

"Good. C'mon." Mrs. Petrovich claimed she knew someone who worked part time at such a place.

Not since her initial yearning for Bobby did a day seem to offer more to Millicent than just moving through it. They visited the place, it actually a person's home with wide living room and French patio doors and smaller family room with hearth, mantle, and fireplace and several bedrooms transformed into classrooms. Toys, games, and coloring books were scattered about, cries and yells creating a din like Bedlam. A boy and girl fought over a puzzle. A baby was changed by a worker. Several other children were read to. A few in the large-windowed, bright kitchen ate pancakes, oatmeal, and cold cereal.

Millicent observed the chaos then listened to her mother with her friend and the daycare owner and asked herself if she could handle what she'd seen. Watching the kids being read to and seeing their wide eyes as they asked—or were asked—about the story made her insides warm.

Her mom waved her to the door. In the car, she told the girl the daycare wasn't hiring but mentioned larger places that might need part timers.

The teen filled out applications, got to speak with one lady but was not hired. Her mom encouraged her, said if all else failed she might try Wal-Mart.

Millicent frowned. Not exactly a dream job, standing all day, dealing with angry, impatient customers. But her mom had her apply there as well as a few university jobs. By the time they got home, the younger female wanted sleep, glad the waitressing nightmare was over. Her brother told her Sophia had called.

"What for?" Millicent asked.

Her brother grinned. "I know a great way to find out."

"Ha-ha-ha." Millicent stuck out her tongue and called her friend, wished her mom would give her a cell phone, Dad suggesting it but Mother saying it was unnecessary.

"Good news," the friend said, declared she'd found a rental, wanted everyone to meet the next day for pizza. Millicent immediately agreed.

Sophia chuckled. "Heard there were new employees at the pizza place. Real studs."

Millicent snickered but uneasily. No boy would take interest in her, just old men with beards, body odor, and missing teeth. The two bade goodbye. Millicent slept well that night.

* * * *

Arturo picked up Sophia the following day when the sun reached its highest point. She asked what took so long as her mind pictured the night of the fire despite the fact it'd happened weeks ago and he hadn't so much as uttered a name beginning with the letter P since apologizing the day after the house had burnt. He smiled, backed out of the driveway, and put a hand on her thigh. At a stoplight he kissed her until the car behind them honked, light having changed to green. Sophia couldn't avoid smiling.

* * * *

Conrad traveled to the restaurant in record time, pictured the bug eyes, dropped jaws, the unblinking stares. He constructed verbal jabs for Wyatt's gay comments, parked in the lot, hopped out, rushed in, and scanned the room, it absent his friends. Sophia'd said noon. He checked his watch. The minute hand scraped past the smaller one at the top of the circle.

Then again, he thought, *have any of them been prompt?*

He found the corner booth, his body and mind as if juiced.

* * * *

Renaldo wished the time before their get-together would speed up. Though Katy wasn't going, she working at a clothing store, he had pictures to show. Since meeting her, his urge to be inebriated had decreased though Friday and Saturday nights were tempting. His job deterred him as well—it enjoyable though it was simple data collection and errand running for research involved in testing gasoline additives and their environmental effects. Renaldo asked about the research but the scientific jargon had him thinking his supervisors suffered amnesia regarding the English language. His desire to learn the results, however, had him pondering a science major. Right now, he opted for the more important, urgent situation. His chest swelled as he visualized everyone's reactions.

* * * *

Andrea was the lone occupant in her car, would make no mention of the guy she'd pursued the last time the group had converged. Sophia had been a prophetess, the guy much older. And not as handsome as Andrea had presumed, chest and arms more flab than muscle. Plus, he claimed he was taken. The girl cringed at his explanation. Mr. Right finding Mr. Right. No way indeed she'd bring it up.

* * * *

Wyatt arrived next, commented no one had ever made it here before he did.

"First time for everything, huh?" Conrad laughed. Within ten minutes, the booth was full and they ate, Sophia describing what she'd seen, handed out brochures of a new complex with all the amenities.

"Now the important question," Wyatt said. "How much?"

Conrad insisted that wasn't the important question. When Renaldo and Wyatt asked simultaneously, Conrad folded his arms. "Duh?" He motioned his head at the girls.

Wyatt frowned, demanded to know when Conrad became such a ladies' man.

Renaldo cackled. "Never."

All the boys not named Conrad laughed. Conrad moved his head from one side of his body to the other, clicked his tongue off the top of his mouth. "If only you boys knew."

With grin seeming to extend beyond the ends of his face, Wyatt jabbed Renaldo. "Listen to him. Real expert on women."

The two guffawed.

Conrad smirked, chin out. "Am now."

Wyatt laughed louder. "What the hell're you talking about?"

Conrad sat back. "Got me a girl." He awaited gasps, then praise. A hush at the table instead, all reacting like Conrad spoke gibberish.

"Didja hear? Have a girlfriend."

"Uh, buddy." Wyatt placed an arm on Conrad. "When we say girlfriend, we mean actual, human flesh female. Not those plastic things you blow air into."

Laughter from all except Conrad. Renaldo congratulated Wyatt, asked when he was to debut on *The Tonight Show*, Wyatt bragging he had his own show. The two poked each other's side. Sophia chided them, encouraged Conrad to speak.

The boy said nothing, cinched arms over his chest, and swallowed. Sophia said he must have had good news, begged him to tell.

"I met a girl," Conrad said slowly and passed a glance at each. "The other day while getting gasoline." He glared when he got to Wyatt. "A real one. And older."

Wyatt *who-hooed*, laughed again. "He's lost his mind."

"You have to have something before you can lose it," Renaldo responded.

"You're the first guest for my talk show," Wyatt said, the two roaring.

Sophia cursed at them to shut up, spoke to Conrad. "You met a girl? Older?"

"Mmm-hmm."

"How much older?"

"He means he helped an old lady across the street," Arturo chimed in, high-fived with the other boys, then asked when his own TV debut would be.

"Guys, shut up!" Sophia yelled. Other patrons looked over. Sophia slid down in her seat, told the others to keep quiet, again allowed Conrad his chance.

"Was filling up with gas and this girl…"

He told what happened. Wyatt smiled smugly, ribbed Renaldo, and said the girl must be a real heifer. Conrad glared. Wyatt said he was joking then put a hand on Conrad.

"Watch him," Wyatt said of Renaldo. "Might hit on your girl. Remember, he's usually drunk, thinks the Man Upstairs created him as a present for the females."

Renaldo's smile went missing. He protested he wasn't always drunk.

"I said usually."

Conrad seized the opportunity and laughed, razzed Renaldo.

"Guys, haven't had a drink in..."

Wyatt checked his watch. "One hour. Let's call Guinness Book of World Records."

More group laughter. Renaldo was mute then bent his lips in an upward arc, told how since meeting Katy, he'd gone a spell without drinking seriously.

Wyatt asked what that meant. When Renaldo said he'd had but one drink a day the past two weeks, Wyatt sarcastically gave an *ooh* and shook his hand as if he'd touched fire. Renaldo countered it was the first step.

"He's right," Millicent said.

Whatever others were doing they stopped in mid-motion.

"Give him a chance," Millicent continued. "Not everyone goes cold turkey. Most go in gradations."

Arturo whistled. "Gradations. When did you become an English major?"

Laughter.

"It's true, damnit."

The group had expressions like the girl had pulled out a semi-automatic rifle. Millicent bowed her head and gave a hushed apology. Sophia reassured her as Andrea touched Millicent's hand, told her to show no restraint.

Millicent propped elbows on the table. "Just be careful what you say," she lectured then shut her eyes. "Words hurt."

Wyatt scoffed. "What happened to sticks and stones?" He sermonized political correctness made everyone weaker, all needed to take their lumps early so they'd be steeled for future criticisms.

"Not true." Millicent quoted research that showed those harassed at an early age were more likely to become delinquent.

Wyatt flicked his hands. "So we just shelter and protect everyone, never expose them to failure?"

"Not at all." Millicent agreed life had disappointments, one just needn't be bombarded with them, added how sensitive children were and too many harsh comments damaged their psyche. "Besides, do you think if African Americans heard the word nigger everyday, it'd make them stronger?"

Wyatt squirmed, felt the others' stares. "I'm only saying we can't be soft. That's what makes people snap, they're treated with kid gloves then are hit with reality. Life's no amusement park." He sat up. "Anyways, if one is confident, ridicule doesn't hurt. If someone called me fatso, it wouldn't hurt. Why? I know it's not true. Only when it's true does it hurt. People can't accept their weaknesses."

"I see your point," Renaldo said and smiled. "Benedict."

Six others chortled. Wyatt told Renaldo if he repeated that name, he'd get the beating of his life.

Renaldo snarled he wasn't afraid then eased back, agreed words hurt when the person believed they were true or worried others believed them to be true. He argued if someone called an anorexic fat, it would hurt since the insultee thought it true, not because it was.

Solemn glances met, slow nods were traded.

"Anyways," Arturo said, "why the hell did we come here in the first place?"

Skittish laughter. Sophia picked up on her earlier announcement of the apartment and the costs then requested feedback.

Arturo bragged how organized his girl was, said it was the right place. Renaldo and Wyatt gave positive reviews, Conrad saying the price was right, Andrea agreeing. Sophia turned to Millicent, mentioned she was the only one who hadn't responded.

The girl said a few words, her lips barely parting. Wyatt encouraged her to speak up.

"Okay," Millicent nearly shouted. "I like it, it's fine." She sank down, asked if that was loud enough. Sophia reached over, touched Millicent, said to have courage to state her mind, alluded to how impressed she was of her friend's monologue and knowledge of child psychology. She chuckled. "You've probably said more today than you did during all other luncheons."

Millicent gave a tender smile. "Guess when I know something, I speak up."

"Because you're confident about it," Wyatt said and paraphrased his previous statement. Millicent nodded.

"Back to our point." Sophia wanted to know if they all liked the apartment, Millicent replying they should see it first. Sophia suggested they check now and ordered the group to their cars, she and Arturo to lead the way. As they slid out of the booth, Sophia extended a finger, spoke to Millicent. "That waiter's cute. Whadya think?"

The boy glanced in their direction. Millicent faced the floor. Sophia nudged her toward him.

"Doesn't want me." Millicent hastened to the door. Sophia, in tow, tried to bring her friend back in. Too late.

"Why'd ya do that?"

Millicent mumbled he wasn't her type. "Anyways," she said sarcastically, "if you love someone, let them go. If they love you, they'll come back to you."

"Whatever."

"We'll be back soon, he'll still be here, and I can tell him then I have the hots for him, want to have his children."

Sophia laughed, slapped her friend's side. "What's gotten into you today, girl?"

Millicent smirked, said there were many sides to her.

The group's apartment tour went well, no dissenting voice though all, other than Renaldo, agreed they'd have to talk it up with their parents.

* * * *

The next day the place was theirs, the seven congratulating each other, debated who was sharing what apartment with whom. After some dickering, the girls agreed to live in a three-room bungalow, Arturo and Renaldo in a two bedroom place, Wyatt and Conrad in another. A quick stop at the pizzeria was unavoidable.

"So when will we meet whatshername?" Wyatt said to Conrad who quickly retorted his date was tonight. Wyatt and Arturo *oohed*, demanded to know her name. When Conrad said "Dawn," Wyatt smiled.

"That spelled dee-oh-enn?"

Conrad frowned, answered the question, and promised they'd meet her soon. His lips quickly did a flip on his face. "You guys'll be so jealous."

Wyatt tapped Arturo. "Probably a transvestite."

"Transsexual."

Hysterics from the two.

Conrad sank in the booth. "What's your guys' fucking problem?"

Arturo and Wyatt paused, stared at their friend with half grins, and joked as to when Conrad had last cursed. With his own smile, Wyatt stated swearing wasn't good for the monastery.

Conrad hit a fist on the table. "Motherfuckers, stop it! I'm serious!"

Arturo and Wyatt halted. The girls stared at Conrad, who retreated, said how yesterday's talk was right, words did offend. He promised to bring Dawn the next time they congregated here. "Will show you damn fuckers."

Loud guffaws from the other guys, Renaldo wanting to know why Conrad was suddenly potty-mouthed, asked if they needed to wash his mouth out with soap. They laughed harder.

"Fuck you, bastards."

The trio continued their laugh fest, Conrad finally smiling, joked sometimes one profanity did more for a person than hours of prayer.

All of them laughed, Arturo saying he'd have to use that one. Conrad reminded them of his promise though they did not set a date to reunite.

Telling his parents he was going to tour the campus with a neighbor friend—*Which*, he told himself, *was true*. At least, halfway—that evening, Conrad gave adios to his parents then left to join his neighbor friend Steve.

At the huge, constantly running fountain in front of the university library, the two went separate ways. Conrad viewed the towering four-story building, a long brick promenade between fountain and marble steps leading to a series of tall, wooden doors with glass running top to bottom. He pulled at one of the twelve behemoths, barely able to open it, had to catch it with a palm before it closed, then entered the tiled, high-ceilinged foyer and observed the ivory steps to the right and left that led to a second floor of shelves seeming to push through the roof. Ahead, a hall led to a back room of more shelves and books, check-out section to the left with a long, granite counter.

He found the elevator, entered, pressed the button numbered "2," and sighed at the ease with which he'd gotten here.

The doors dinged shut. Elevator hummed, red digital number above changing from 1 to 2. Another ding. Doors vibrated, opened. Conrad stepped out hastily, almost bumped into a student, turned, and stumbled into a desk. A couple of students tittered. Conrad gathered himself and paced down the hall, eyed the ever closer end leading to the second floor study room. He turned the knob and opened the door, his face like a five year old who'd ran downstairs on Christmas morning to discover no presents under the tree.

Chapter 6

Where was she? He checked his watch. Still a few minutes. Or had he remembered the correct time and date? He groped his pockets, paper not there. He checked his backpack but didn't find the sheet. Now he couldn't call her. Where was she? He sighed—he was early, sat at the round wood table, opened his backpack, and let books slide out, found the needed one and reviewed notes.

Five minutes, no Dawn. The present became the past, the future turning into the present. Ten minutes. Fifteen. He remained the room's lone occupant, checked his cell phone. No calls. Why hadn't he realized at the gas station this was a joke, she'd never choose him to date, let alone study with?

He shoved stuff into the backpack, his eyes hot. He sank teeth on his tongue and opened the door. The guys were right, he'd never have a woman, monastery sounding more promising.

He trudged toward the elevator. The door donged, slid opened. Someone exited. Conrad lowered his head, slipped between doors, they about to shut. A hand stabbed between the two.

"Where're ya going? We had a date, didn't we?"

Conrad jerked his head up. His backpack slid off his shoulder as he gaped. Dawn. In tight, red halter top and cutoff denims so short he thought he saw some bush by the upper right thigh. He pushed his shoulders back, folded his lips tight, and ordered his eyes back into their sockets. "Oh, right. Sorry. Thought I was on the wrong floor." He forced laughter.

Dawn closed then quickly opened an eye then apologized, asked if he was waiting long. He claimed he'd just arrived. She led him back to the room, sat at the table, rescued her books and a laptop from her OSU backpack, and spread the books, one a thick, blue text with *College Algebra* in white calligraphy. Conrad sat opposite her.

The girl displayed a long face. "Not there. Here." She patted the chair to her right. "For when we take a break. Am right-handed."

Conrad wiped at the sweaty skin between lip and nose, scratched the back of his neck, sat in the chair, and seized the algebra book, flipped it open. Dawn giggled he had no idea what chapter she needed.

"Just thought I'd get started." He reached for his knapsack. It slipped. He went to retrieve it. It dropped a second time.

"Butterfingers." Dawn laughed and leaned in Conrad's direction. His hand touched hers, it as soft as a pillow. They exchanged glances, hers a magazine cover smile. She squeezed fingers around his hand. He felt his lips curve up though shakily, yet drifted toward her. She shut her eyes, planted lips on his lower left cheek. Silence for a stretch, followed by smacking moisture. They separated.

"How was it?" she said, words lush.

"Fine," Conrad said then condemned himself for being so plain, tried to conjure romantic language. His mind was as blank as a re-formatted computer.

"Fine? That's it?" Dawn inched closer. "Let me improve my grade, Teach."

She was millimeters from his face. Sweat from his forehead dribbled into his eye. He rubbed it, pushed his chair away for elbow room. Its legs squeaked like a foghorn. He apologized, wiped his nose, sniffled then wiped the eye.

"It's okay." Dawn kissed him, long. He groaned she deserved an A. They moved apart and she swiveled to her laptop. Conrad reclaimed the algebra book, asked what chapter they needed, kept alternating glances from the book to her. She reached across, opened to the correct page, fingered the problems, he able to help yet wondered if she feigned ignorance.

Twenty minutes later, Dawn announced they needed a break and slid an arm behind his neck. He forced saliva down his throat as she pursed her lips. He wiped his forehead, kept asking himself why the hesitation, leaned in then asked internally what he was doing, she moving way too fast. He withdrew then came closer, a pendulum on the upswing. His mouth hit hers, hard. He tried to mutter a reaction but his lips were on the girl's. He cloaked her in his arms, their faces together.

"Awesome," she whispered.

Conrad exhaled. "Definitely."

She kissed him again.

"Uh...shouldn't we..." Conrad spoke between breaks. "Get back to studying?"

"Soon enough."

They finally went back—with snatches of passion, Dawn undoing the buttons on his shirt, he too busy kissing to protest.

Ninety minutes later, Dawn gathered her items.

Conrad's face was blank. "Done?"

"Yeah, we've done all I needed." She smiled. "Thanks." She rubbed a hand on his chin. "You've helped so much, almost made algebra interesting. Though I still don't see how I'll use this in the real world."

"Makes you think in a different way."

"Or gives math teachers a job, keeps unemployment down."

Conrad laughed, looked at her long, smooth, wavy hair, the green eyes melting him. He laughed at her joke some more, said he had to remember that one.

Dawn's mouth curved. "Lemme give you something you'll always remember."

Conrad thought about her implication, recalled where they were, and pushed his chair away, stood, and fumbled to collect his possessions. "I...I...don't think we should go for that. Not here." He shoved things into his backpack, attempted to zip it. The zipper stuck. Books fell. He ha-ha'ed. "Clumsy me." He squatted, gathered notebook, old high school algebra book, and pencils, then stood, his glance straight with hers.

"Of course not here." Dawn let out a hot breath. "My place."

To Conrad, it seemed winter had arrived. She surrounded him in her arms, so gently he was unaware until her chest touched his. They exited and she went to the elevator, its doors squeaking toward one another. She sprinted, Conrad trailing. Dawn jumped, arm extended, and touched the doors. They slid apart. She crashed into a corner, he landing on her. The doors made contact with each other.

A possible scenario stopped any blood flow in the area beneath Conrad's waist: Her house, apartment, wherever, he in bed, on his back, wrists behind him, metal rubbing against them, she with the key to the cuffs, on top of him, he between her legs.

The carriage doors opened and she led him out. He tried to break free. She pulled him back to her. He pried some more, she trying to open the huge, front glass door, asked why he resisted.

An idea. He mentioned he had no protection. She dismissed that with a wave, said she was on the pill. He didn't budge. She looked ready to strike him. He mentally examined why he questioned this moment. Every guy wanted it. And he was but eighteen. How many older guys would pay mucho dinero for this opportunity? He recalled wisecracks at the pizza place regarding his sexual preference. When they found out, he'd be a god in their eyes, Wyatt and Renaldo asking *him* for advice. Sweet revenge. Jealousy was great.

He looked at her the way a car buff eyes a '57 Chevy. Blood flow near his groin returned. "Let's go."

"All right." She applauded, led him to her place a few blocks away.

Minutes later, they were in her bedroom, she making a contest out of it, see who could get undressed first. They tied. She jumped on the bed, led him over while giving instructions. The further they progressed, the more instinct took over for him.

Dawn chuckled. "For someone so uncertain, you seem to know what you're doing."

To Conrad, it felt like a July Fourth fireworks that featured only firecrackers, guessed it was because he'd always imagined the initial time would be with *the* one, on the biggest day of his life. The thought of telling his friends reinvigorated him. He went over his speech so many times his mind felt it was now made of the same compounds as planet Venus. Conrad convinced himself it was going to be a celebration, envisaged their reactions.

A tap on his shoulder.

"Huh?"

"Was talking to you. You've suddenly become distant."

"I'm listening."

She crawled onto him, fondled his chest, teased he had more hair than her last partner, a college senior.

The words had Conrad mummified. Her last partner? How many other guys were there? Was she really interested in him? He could hear the guys' response if he turned those thoughts into words. This made him gag.

She asked if he was okay. He debated if he should inquire about her other guys, decided to stay quiet, and checked the time. His eyes seem to want to jump from their sockets. He pushed her aside, sprang up. When she wanted to know what he was doing, he babbled he had to get home or his dad would kill him if he was even a minute late. He viewed her clock. It would be close. He told her soon enough he'd be on campus and they'd get together then. He smiled. "A lot."

She ran a hand up his chest, said waiting that long would seem like waiting for Last Judgment. He offered to go out Friday, explained curfew that day was two a.m.

"Wow," she droned. "Two in the morning. What a grown man you are."

"C'mon." Conrad eyed the time as he kissed her. Nearly too late. She clutched his chest again. He pried her hands off, hurried to the door, saw her look at him as if he'd said he'd never return. He delivered a kiss, promised he'd call once home, and waved. She did the same, her wave like a child turning the hand as if opening a door. Conrad halted. The words—threats—of his father had him moving again.

As soon as his feet met the ground, he sprinted, aware his car was at the library, then drove home as if qualifying for an open wheel race, surmised a few blocks from the house he had time to spare. He combed his hair with a hand, smoothed out his clothes, and lectured himself not to say too much or act fidgety.

The figure in the red recliner appeared to have been sitting there all night, counting down the minutes, he the first thing Conrad saw after pushing the door open.

"There you are." The father moved his wrist toward his nose. "Right on time," he growled as if disappointed.

"Like I promised." For Conrad, trying to keep his tone even was as hard as pushing a truck uphill. He slithered in the direction of his bedroom.

"That's it?" the father bellowed.

"What?"

"You're not going to tell me how the tour went?"

Conrad lifted then dropped his shoulders, let his thoughts simmer before speaking. "Was good, saw where classes will be then caught a late movie at the OSU theater, grabbed a bite afterwards, and I returned home." Another step toward his room.

A cackle. "That's it? You expect me to believe that?" The man viewed his watch. "Out this late and no encounters?"

"Excuse me?"

"C'mon." The older male cackled. "I was young, haven't forgotten those days." He grinned. "Had some good nights. Slept well, if ya know what I mean."

Conrad squinted. Had another person possessed his father's body? He denied anything happened.

The father smiled, waved his son over, slung his arm around Conrad, and squeezed gently. "C'mon. Nothing happened? No woman?"

"Well..." Conrad smiled, released a breath. "Maybe one girl..." He pressed the words in his throat back down and turned so his dad could only see him in profile. Spilling a half truth might work. He smiled coyly, lifted a shoulder. "She's cute."

The father sat up. "That's more like it. Anything happen?"

Conrad rubbed lips together. "Umm… We did...kiss." His eyes felt like they'd never blink.

The father sat unspeaking, ran a finger back and forth under his chin. He asked how it was.

"Good," Conrad admitted.

The man nodded, smiled, and sighed, said he'd feared his son hadn't any attraction to women. Conrad assured his father he did, took the opportunity to say good night then hurried to his room and went to bed, drifted in and out of sleep with his lips up. He planned what he'd say to friends. It was going to be a great college debut.

* * * *

Two weeks of filling out applications and Millicent remained unemployed, managed but one interview at a daycare and felt she'd underwhelmed her possible employer, though afterwards, a four year old girl asked Millicent when she would be working there. Millicent sank to one knee, introduced herself, and said she'd only had an interview. When the girl asked what that was, Millicent said it was like trying to make a new friend. The girl shook her head in agreement, asked to play a game, and Millicent did, though after a few minutes another girl asked the four year old to play and the two ran off.

Millicent stood, watched the two throw a small plastic ball, smiled, and left, thought how she might've liked this job.

Two days later, the girl's mother handed her the phone. It was the woman who'd interviewed Millicent. She offered a part-time job.

"Really?" Millicent couldn't hold back the smile, commented on the disappointing meeting, woman concurring, said it was watching the girl with the four year olds that told her Millicent might be a good hire, how she seemed a natural. She instructed Millicent to come that Monday. The girl thought of the day her mom had knocked on the bedroom door. Or how she'd seen Bobby with another female. It was as if those events had happened to another Millicent.

The weekend couldn't be completed fast enough.

* * * *

The seven were unable to meet again until the first week of August. In their booth, they updated one another, Millicent congratulated on her job though she admitted it was part time.

"But now I know what my major will be."

Arturo and Sophia planned what they'd do that fall, she saying how college appeared easier, class time half that of the high school routine.

"The rest is party time!" Arturo hit palms with Renaldo, then Wyatt before kissing Sophia. He promised lots of memories—"Road trip!" he yelled as Sophia smiled—and time spent together. When the girl cautioned free time was for studying, Arturo hissed, said that was what all-nighters were for. Besides, he was going into real estate; no one had to be on the Dean's list to get a job in that field, it was all about selling.

Sophia argued he'd have to study to pass the realtor's exam.

More air passed through Arturo's pressed lips. He promised he'd ace the test then hit palms with Renaldo. "For now, it's party time!"

Sophia half smiled.

"What about you?" Wyatt said to Conrad. "Ya know, you've only got four years to get laid."

"How do you figure four?"

"That's all you'll get on your own." Wyatt displayed teeth and arched lips. "Then it's back to living in Mommy and Daddy's house until they retire or kick the bucket. By then, you'll be too old, no woman—or animal—will want you." He snapped fingers. "Time's a wasting."

Conrad laughed. The others observed him. He laughed louder.

"What?" Sophia said at last.

"What?" Conrad's grin expanded.

"You want to say something. Out with it."

The boy viewed each person.

"C'mon," Andrea begged.

Conrad pleaded one of the guys to ask, said it was a man thing, and predicted the girls would scoff or grumble, perhaps utter profanities. When Sophia repeated her question, Conrad sat up, spoke slowly.

"The one thing every male says he has to do before twenty-one or he's a pussy, will never get any the rest of his life."

Renaldo chortled. "You're lying."

Conrad denied it. Renaldo asked for details. The other boy described what had transpired and how he felt, then exchanged glances with Arturo, Renaldo, and Wyatt. They were as if the weather was being forecast. Conrad leaned in, spread his arms. "Didja hear me?" He repeated what he'd said but in *Reader's Digest* format.

The other boys' postures stayed stiff.

"Guys? You there?" Conrad waved a hand in front of Arturo, snapped fingers in front of Wyatt, and poked Renaldo. "Hey."

Wyatt folded his arms.

Conrad slid toward the friend. "You okay? You look ill."

"You? With another woman? A real woman? Hah! The San Andreas Fault will break away before any woman—or man—spends time in bed with you."

Renaldo chuckled.

Conrad looked to Arturo who turned to his own girl. She told him to look elsewhere, she wasn't dating Conrad.

The other girls laughed.

"Who cares anyway?" Millicent said.

"Who cares?" Conrad stood. "Who cares? It's the most important thing a guy can do, a rite of passage, from boy to man! Any guy who doesn't think it's a big deal is either gay or has no libido." He sat, seat cushion groaning under him.

Wyatt's face was a map of wrinkles. "You mean it's true? You really…"

"Hell yeah. Can't you tell? Look at me. Do I look like I'm describing how I made perfect cookies?"

Andrea and Sophia laughed. Wyatt sat up, leaned to Conrad. "You really did it?"

"No shit, Sherlock. Wouldn't say it if it wasn't true."

"Well, then you've committed sin," Wyatt said.

Conrad's eyes went high in their sockets. He chided Wyatt that was a concern between himself and the Higher Power and he'd worry about it when Judgment Day arrived. He smirked, accused Wyatt of jealousy, how he always attempted to spoil a good time.

Wyatt bolted upright, denied this.

"You sure do." Conrad beamed. "Benedict."

The others grinned and gave hushed *oohs*. Wyatt pounded the table, said he was only trying to let them know right and wrong, had to save them since they weren't doing it themselves.

Conrad held his hands in mock prayer. "Pray for him. Has multiple personalities. First, he's a normal teen then believes he's Benedict Arnold. Now a new persona, Jesus Christ." He raised then lowered his arms in front of Wyatt, chanted hosannas.

Wyatt locked fingers around Conrad's wrists, warned him not to go too far.

"Me? You're the one condemning others."

Wyatt uttered words through teeth. "Not everyone. Just you. Watch it." He released his grip.

Conrad re-settled himself. "Was kidding, lighten up."

Sophia petitioned for calm. Conrad reiterated he was teasing then extended a hand to Wyatt. "Water under the bridge?"

The left side of the other boy's mouth curled down. His friend jeered, encouraged him. Wyatt's lips went up at last to friends' applause. He shook Conrad's hand. The group collectively eased back.

"I'd still like to meet her," Wyatt said.

"Who are you pretending to be now? My parents?"

Wyatt shrugged. "Just want to meet the girl who did the impossible, bonked Conrad." He gave a sly but friendly uptick of the lips.

Conrad shook his head, snickered, and promised he'd bring Dawn—"That's Dee-aye-dubbayou-enn," he stated— next time they got together.

Sophia commented sarcastically how interesting this conversation was, had so long desired to hear a man's first time, added she had to visit the ladies' room as a result.

Conrad defended himself, blamed the others' denial. Sophia headed to the back of the restaurant, boyfriend in tow. The others huddled by the front door, discussed their moving date and getting utilities turned on at their new places as well as enrollment. The discussion soon shifted out of doors, Arturo and Sophia joining them.

A man approached, his tight fuchsia shirt rippling over well-toned body fibers, his matted, moussed black hair reflecting the sun's glow. Sophia tapped Millicent, wiggled a finger, and asked her friend's opinion.

"Uh-huh." But Millicent didn't move. Sophia goaded her to speak to him. The other girl ducked behind her friend, said no way he'd want an ugly duckling. Sophia admonished the girl's hypersensitive self-criticism, to which Millicent noted her friend hadn't disagreed with her statement.

The man approached. Sophia slipped away from Millicent, the quiet girl an island.

The man passed. Millicent *ugghed* then gave an exclamation like someone had pinched her behind. The guy looked at her as if she was some kind of oddity then entered the restaurant.

Sophia hit Millicent's wrist. "Why didn't you say something? He looked at you."

"He wondered why a freak like me would be seen in public."

Sophia repeated Millicent was too self-critical, requested Andrea's support.

"Huh?" Andrea said, busy in dialogue with the other guys. Sophia pointed to the man, he now in the buffet line.

"Oh, he's hot. Why didn't you point him out to me?" Andrea looked through the door.

"Him?" Arturo said. "The one in pink? You're kidding." He gained Renaldo's attention, told him to look. "That pink th'irt i'th th'o pretty on him, ithn't it? Bet it goes with his pink pump'ths."

The boys guffawed, girls rebuking them for stereotyping. Andrea praised the guys' dark hair.

"That mound of grease?" Wyatt said. "You could drown in it."

The boys laughed some more. Andrea shushed them as she swept to the entrance, said it was time to find her man. The boys hooted, pretended to place bets. Sophia put a thumb to her ear and extended her pinky finger to her lips, said she needed her bookie.

Millicent, however, lowered her head and turned her back, stated she was leaving. Sophia answered an affirmation but continued to monitor her other friend. Millicent rushed to her car, slammed the door, and sped away. Arturo wanted to know what that was about but Sophia dismissed it as nothing, she still focused on Andrea.

Arturo told Sophia they were to leave. She held up a finger, kept watch. He grasped her elbow, pulled her to him. When she resisted, he pulled harder then slowly led her away. The others followed, Arturo soliciting a date to move into their places. They all agreed, Sophia promising to notify Millicent and Andrea. She watched Andrea and her new acquaintance chat then added unless Andrea had found her Mr. Right. The others sniggered.

* * * *

Moving day. Sophia took charge, helped others unpack. Conrad arrived with a stranger next to him, introduced Dawn. The way Arturo and Wyatt held their glances on the girl had Conrad moving his mouth down then up. Arturo, he told himself, was taken, no surveiling of him required, that was Sophia's chore. Wyatt, though honest and trustworthy in other matters, was a concern so Conrad stood right next to Dawn when she shook hands with Wyatt, Conrad attempting to block his friend's view of the female. Nothing sinister happened. The group unpacked.

"Done at last," Sophia said after parents had given final hugs and advice. She announced they were on their own, no one to tell them what to do or when to study or to go to class.

Arturo jigged. "Party time!"

"Who's up for pizza?" Sophia said.

Arturo halted. "Pizza? That's no celebration." He grabbed her, spun her in his arms, and kissed her. "I'm talking about a *real* fun time. Out there." He pointed in the direction of the strip, Washington Boulevard, the main party drag, every building on the block a bar or club.

"Too tired." Sophia yawned. "They're not open now anyway. And you can't get in, aren't twenty-one."

Arturo informed there were ways around that then hit his wallet with a palm, bragged he and Wyatt looked older, no one would suspect them. And if they were let in, they had to let the rest of the friends in, it was just good business.

Sophia reminded him no bars were open now.

"Fine, we can eat," Arturo conceded. "Who's up for a supreme?"

Others rolled tongues over lips or rubbed stomachs. Dawn asked where they were going. Everyone faced her as if she'd claimed to be a transsexual, Conrad wanting to know what rock she had been under. Dawn pinched him, lectured she wasn't from here, had only lived in Stillwater a year. He reminded her they'd come in his car, led her to it as everyone went to their vehicles.

* * * *

At the restaurant, Dawn's eyes were shut as she chewed. She moaned as if massaged.

"Told ya it was good. Try some more." Conrad gave her a slice. She ate it faster than the first, said she wished she'd known about the place last year. "Is delicious," Conrad agreed and wrapped an arm around her. They met at the lips. Wyatt stuck a finger in his mouth and gave barnyard-like noises. Arturo droned he was eating.

"Really?" Conrad faced his friends. "Well, then, why don't I—we—keep at it? If it spoils y'alls appetites, more for us two."

"Cocky, aren't we?" Sophia said. "When did you become big man on campus?"

"When I met her." Conrad plunged lips on Dawn's cheek. "Best thing for me."

The girls gave *awws*. Sophia turned to Andrea, requested where the latest Mr. Right was. Andrea said not to worry, they had a date that night at *The Wharf*.

"Wow. Big spender, isn't he?" Sophia said.

Andrea held out her hand, wiggled the third finger, it with a large, blue sapphire ring. Sophia breathed through pursed lips, gained Millicent's attention then lifted Andrea's hand.

"Look at it."

"Material things don't interest me. I'm not a gold digger." Millicent harrumphed.

Andrea withdrew the hand, flipped the ring on her finger with a thumb. "What's that supposed to mean?"

Millicent countered Andrea knew exactly what it meant.

Andrea smiled, accused her friend of the j word.

"Jealous of a jackass?"

Andrea's lips did a one eighty and she stiffened. Sophia stretched a hand to Andrea, put a finger of her other hand over her lips as she looked at Millicent, advised they take a long breath. Andrea accused Millicent of being the instigator, the latter retorting it was the other's fault. Sophia said it didn't matter, then laughed, asked Millicent if she was taking bets on how long this guy would last. Millicent deliberated then smiled, even apologized to Andrea, who accepted. Sophia brought them back into the conversation, looked at Conrad and Dawn as they hugged and kissed at intervals and teased each other. She took Arturo's hand and pressed his flesh. He gave a quick smile but continued to speak with Renaldo. Sophia dipped her head, unaware of Dawn's behavior as the newbie listened to Arturo but focused visually on Wyatt. When Wyatt's glance met hers, she smiled. Under the table, she stretched a leg to his and waved at him, her hand hidden below table's edge.

* * * *

"Did you see those two at lunch?" Sophia asked Arturo that night at her place, Millicent saying she'd forgotten stuff at home and would spend the night there, Andrea on her date.

Arturo asked which two.

"Who do ya think?"

The boy munched tortilla chips, grunted he didn't know. Sophia muttered if boys paid attention to anything that didn't have to do with them having sex.

"Guess not." Arturo laughed. "Because I don't know what you're talking about."

Sophia told him how Conrad and Dawn were unselfconscious in displaying their affections, seemed like they were meant to be.

"Yeah." Arturo chewed more chips as Sophia romanticized how lovely it was when two people felt so comfortable around each other they could express themselves in public.

"Yeah." He finished off his chips. "Sure is." He didn't look at Sophia. The girl spun, took a heavy breath, saw a pan on the stove, and slammed it on a burner.

Arturo leapt as if watching a scary movie, asked profanely what she was doing.

"Nothing," she stated though her voice broke with the answer. She took a cup out of a cupboard and slammed it on Formica.

He wanted to know if he'd said something wrong.

She faced him. "Why can't *we* be like that?"

"What?"

She huffed. "More romantic. Like them."

"We are."

"How?"

"Like this." Arturo stood, smiled, and picked up Sophia, bounced her in his arms, carried her to the bedroom, mattress still void of sheets. He set her gently on the springs then rested atop of her. "Ya know," he began, his lips contacting hers, "I prefer bunk beds."

Sophia pulled her lips off his. "What?"

"Yeah…" Arturo kissed her. "I love being on top."

The two chuckled, undid their pants. Finished, Sophia grinned as wide as her face would allow then made a quick meal which they shared.

* * * *

The first week of school had the seven seeing little of each other as they acclimated themselves to the campus and its buildings, their schedules, and location of classrooms. Not until the following Wednesday did they reconvene though Conrad and Dawn managed a movie, Andrea and her guy using the campus athletic facilities—he obsessed with his health—to play racquetball and swim in the Olympic-sized pool.

"What a week," Conrad said. "Seems only a day has passed."

Dawn informed it'd slow, college much less busy than high school, lots more down time. "Or, as parents say, study time."

Arturo raised a glass. "Or, as we say, party time." He and Dawn clinked glasses, he then kissing Sophia. Andrea, her boyfriend Chuck now with them, did to him what Arturo had done with Sophia.

"I'm impressed," Sophia said. "You've been an item how long?"

Andrea granted it hadn't been long. Her friend edged toward the new guy, laid a hand on his side. "I think you must know this is a record for her with one guy."

Andrea retorted Sophia was just wishing she had such a macho man as her suitor.

Sophia placed hands on Arturo's chest. "Have one."

Andrea heckled Arturo couldn't lift an empty grocery bag. Sophia sat up, watched her friend and boyfriend make contact at the mouth.

"He can lift me," Sophia said, nuzzled with Arturo. The other female pumped her hand on Chuck's arm, stated his bench press maximum. Sophia said there was more to a man than how many metal plates he could push away from his chest. Andrea said Chuck was all that and more.

Sophia crisscrossed her arms. "Well I don't care. This isn't a competition, there's no prize for having the better guy."

"That's because I have him." Andrea nudged against her boyfriend.

Sophia muttered the word describing a female dog. Millicent tapped her, assured it was just who Andrea was and tittered, wagered the relationship would extend but a fortnight. The two of them reflected smiles.

Movement across the table. Conrad and Dawn traded bites of Italian bread. Sophia tried to gain Arturo's perspective but he was too preoccupied in a debate about the upcoming football schedule with Renaldo and Wyatt.

Dawn pushed herself away from Conrad and viewed Wyatt. The right side of her mouth perked up.

Wyatt retreated as far back against the booth as possible then rubbed hands on his leg. She stayed her expression. He finally looked aside.

Renaldo stood, excused himself, and when Arturo inquired as to his friend's intentions, Renaldo hesitated then said he needed some change from his car to play one of the restaurant's video games. Arturo teased they were so old and boring, no one would want to play them. Renaldo only said he'd be back, Arturo questioning why his friend took his cup with him.

Renaldo stared at the plastic. "Didn't realize it. May as well hold onto it now that I have it." He exited before hearing Arturo's reply.

* * * *

In his car, Renaldo searched for the real reason he'd come out here. Though still interested in Katy, the novelty of love collected dust spots on his heart and he yearned for what he loved long before she entered his world. He convinced himself Katy hadn't meant what she'd said during sex, it was simply uttered in a moment of passion. No way she'd date a sot.

I'm not a sot, he argued to himself. *Just have a nip once in a while.* He opened the glove compartment. There it was, clear glass with white label, words *Bacardi Gold* in black. He untensed.

The bottle rolled off the owner's manual, its destination the floorboards. He imagined it smashing, dark liquid diffusing on the car's floor like some kind of virus spreading across one's innards. He slapped fingers on the glove compartment lid. The bottle glided to his digits. He wrapped them around the container, opened it, and drew it to his lips as if he'd just crossed the Sahara. Liquid down his throat. He smiled and his joints eased. He poured a liberal quantity into the cup, exited the car, and rejoined the group.

"What happened to you?" Arturo said.

Renaldo did not blink. "Huh?" He was glad his skin tone was olive, knew it hid the redness he felt come over his face.

"You act like you just lost your virginity."

"Maybe he has," Wyatt said.

"Funny," Renaldo grumbled, went to the soft drink machine, added Coca-Cola to his cup then returned to the gang, requested access to the booth, and said little, didn't need them smelling his breath. Suspicions were not raised.

* * * *

That night on the worn, brown cloth sofa Arturo's parents had given him for the apartment, Renaldo reunited with his friend Bacardi, Arturo with Sophia, Katy having been asked at the last minute to work late. After all the rum found its way into the boy's stomach, Renaldo went to his bedroom and retrieved another bottle from the closet shelf, drank some straight then mixed the rest with Coke.

"Ahh, best I've felt since the night I met her." He held up the empty bottle, read the words Jim Beam then muttered, "Reunions are nice," and tossed the bottle in the trash.

By the time a knock on the door stirred him out of a respite from consciousness, Renaldo had regained sobriety. He opened the door, saw the figure, and ran a shirt sleeve over his mouth, bit down on the cotton material.

"Hi, honey." Katy went to kiss him. He shifted his head at the last instant, her lips wetting his jaw. He excused himself, went to the kitchen, and drank a long swallow of Coke. Upon his return, she gathered him to her bosom, cooed she'd missed him, smothered her mouth on his.

Renaldo's eyes were wide. He watched her, she with eyes shut, noises from her sounding like she'd reached orgasm. His attempts to extricate himself failed. She finally separated, eyes remaining shut.

"Beautiful," she groaned. "You're the best kisser."

Renaldo thanked her and, seeing her eyes stay shut, did a hurried reconnaissance, glad it was the one time he'd been tidy.

She ushered him to the sofa where they lounged in front of the ebony entertainment center and watched TV. Renaldo sensed the craving but restrained himself, made periodic glances to his bedroom closet. When Katy questioned his actions, Renaldo explained he was checking the time. Katy laughed and pointed to the clock on the DVD player above the TV. Renaldo gave a slow pass of his hand over his face, slid down on the sofa, closer to Katy, asked her to forgive his stupidity. When she acquiesced with a kiss, he exhaled, wondered if he'd qualify for a part in a university drama.

Her softness allowed him to forego his desire, although not totally.

Chapter 7

The door to the girls' apartment clanged open a few afternoons later.

"Hey," Andrea said to Millicent, who sat at the circular pine table, English composition book and laptop open. Andrea led Chuck in, strode past her friend. The other girl looked up, half aware of the two.

"See?" Andrea smirked. "She's a real study geek, guys are the last thing on her mind."

The young man laughed, noise making Millicent think she was at the zoo with animals that did tricks with beach balls. He joked Andrea was going to be the next Jay Letterman.

Millicent pursed her face, though the guy's physique was good enough to qualify for Mr. Universe.

Andrea held his arm. "Look at him. So muscular. Perfect bod. On a scale of one to ten, I score him a twelve."

"How can you rate me a twelve on a scale where ten is max?"

After a quick silence, Andrea laughed. "Such a kidder. What a guy. A regular Mensa."

Chuck's face dimmed. "Why'd ya call me that? I'm no perv."

Millicent couldn't suppress laughter though she covered her mouth with both hands. Andrea shushed her, disappeared into her room, reappeared in shorts and t-shirt then gushed how much Chuck had taught her about racquetball.

Millicent snorted.

"Bless you," Chuck said.

Millicent couldn't reply, her hand covering all but the upper corners of her smile.

Andrea hit Millicent. "He said bless you."

The other girl said thanks, Andrea quickly rambling about Chuck's knowledge. Millicent snickered, said he'd taught her a lot already.

Chuck scratched his head, wanted to know how he'd taught Millicent anything as they'd just met. She turned in her chair, faced him. "I learned from osmosis."

"Who was he?" Chuck said.

Millicent pinched the inside of her mouth to keep it from expanding.

"Well, gotta go." Andrea smiled at her roommate. "Some of us have a life, a real love, don't need to be bookworms."

Millicent's lips sagged. When Chuck questioned who'd want to be a worm, Andrea rushed him out, told her friend not to stay up, winked, and said not everyone was meant to have somebody, let alone a gorgeous stud. She shut the door before her friend could reply.

"Bitch," Millicent said and tried to return to her studies but couldn't, rubbed teeth tighter the more she thought about her friend's snarkiness. The reminder of that night had her flinging her books across the room. She stared at the wall, thought of her job, kids wanting to play hide and seek, draw, paint, or just sit with her, the way they put on no airs, had no expectations of others. She smiled and collected her books, resumed her studies.

When Sophia came home, Millicent griped about Andrea's treatment, Sophia attributing it to Andrea's first true love.

"Yeah, she been with him for so long," Millicent scoffed.

"For her, it's a lifetime," Sophia said. "For me, I'm patient, willing to wait it out."

"Easy for you. You already have someone."

Sophia pointed out Millicent only focused on the positives of a relationship, said there were lots of struggles and arguments, give and take.

The other girl accepted that as truth and focused on her next work day.

* * * *

Wednesday night at Arturo's apartment, Sophia kissed him, he announcing it was one day to party time. Sophia created creases on her face as she mentioned it was two more days until Friday. The boy patted her like a child who wanted to know how Santa Clause made it around the world overnight, reminded her Thursday was dollar cover at the bars, drinks a buck for eight ounce draws, two for longnecks. Everyone would be there, all the women.

"All of 'em?" Sophia gave a scornful laugh. "Why would I care? I'm no lesbo."

The boys chuckled. Renaldo extended an arm around her. "One important thing he left out. All the men will be there too. The big, muscular studs, the smart guys, the deep, philosophical ones. Even the geeks. It's party night in Stillwater!"

He and Arturo smacked hips, snapped fingers. Sophia blocked her vision with a hand, questioned the two regarding their manhood, asked Wyatt, who laughed.

"They're not my type."

"That's right." Renaldo stopped dancing, stood by Wyatt. "You like the geeky, bookish guys."

Arturo and Renaldo chortled, Renaldo pointing to Wyatt's open American History book, joked the boy liked studies more than sex. Arturo laughed, contributed how there was one positive: with a book, Wyatt wouldn't have to hear *Not tonight, honey, got a headache.*

"Which is all he'll ever hear from females!" Renaldo yelped.

Wyatt slammed his book shut, stated he craved sex as much as the others. "I just don't brag about it like women are some kind of trophy."

Arturo said they were, traded playful jabs with Renaldo. Wyatt retorted they'd be jealous when he graduated cum laude.

"What'd he say about come?" Renaldo said.

"Said he comes loudly."

Both boys roared. Sophia ordered restraint, Conrad opening his bedroom door and asking about the commotion.

Renaldo and Arturo teased they had another study geek, Renaldo theorizing Dawn was a transvestite, Arturo saying she had big shoulders, a deeper than usual voice.

Conrad protested she was all woman.

"How would you know?" Renaldo said. "You've never done it with her."

Conrad's facial tone darkened as he glared. "We sure did."

"Yeah, right." Wyatt moved to the other guys, put an elbow on Arturo's shoulder. "Anyone can say they did it. Him? Please. Mr. Rogers had a better chance of performing sex on his show."

The other boys howled, shook Wyatt's hand. Conrad maintained it had happened, his voice squeaking. When asked for details, he demurred, turned to Sophia. The three males verbally assaulted him like politicians in a debate. Sophia spoke above them to cease, asked why they needed to know.

Arturo smiled. "See? Even you know he didn't do it. That's a girl's way of saying a guy didn't."

Sophia put her arm around Conrad, said she thought highly of a guy who didn't think only of how many girls he could bed before graduation. Conrad mumbled appreciation but escaped to the bathroom. The other boys, tired from their antics, sat on the sofa.

Sophia took advantage of the sudden, test-like quiet to demand how they were going to enter a bar under aged. Arturo waved her away, said he knew a guy who worked at a club. When she asked what if this guy refused entry, Arturo reached for his wallet, said a few extra Lincolns would open the doors for them.

"And how are you gonna get alcohol if a bartender cards you?"

Arturo petted the girl's head. "Why would he? They'd have already let me in, checked then."

"S'pose he gets suspicious?"

"That's easy. Anybody above twenty-one would buy it for us for a minimal fee."

"This is costing a small fortune. Is it really worth it?"

Arturo asked the guys if it was. Renaldo nodded emphatically. Wyatt did the same. Conrad exited the bathroom and Wyatt asked him. Conrad nodded so fast it looked like his head would disengage from his spine.

"See?" Arturo pressed the side of his face against Sophia's, led her in a dance move. "It'll be fun. How 'bout it?"

"Get me the hell out of your possession and I'll think about it."

Arturo released her, Sophia looking at each of the boys.

"All right," she relented and Arturo promised a great time.

"Sure you're not going off with some other babe?" she asked slyly.

Arturo flashed teeth. "You're the best babe I know."

Sophia grinned, placed her head on his shoulder, checked the clock with Roman numerals above the wood mantle of the brick fireplace, said she had to study. Arturo offered his room. She declined and when he requested going to her place, she said tonight was not the night. He opened his mouth but she put her hand over it, said the following day looked better, believed the partying would put her in the mood. She stepped away, waved as she exited, and blew a final kiss.

Arturo pledged a great night, lots of music and partying, drinks flowing as freely as water melting from polar ice caps placed in the Gulf of Mexico. And many women. When Conrad said he had a girl as did Arturo, the latter hesitated, face in freeze frame. After a few seconds, he smiled.

"I meant for Wyatt. And Renaldo."

Conrad stated Renaldo had a girl too.

"Then, Wyatt, damnit. We just want to have a good time." He stared down Conrad. "Do you?"

"He's afraid of sex," Wyatt ridiculed.

"Told you, already did it."

"Allegedly," Wyatt said in low tone, lips barely moving.

Conrad reaffirmed it was fact. When the others didn't ease up on the taunts, Conrad thumped to his room and slammed the door. Wyatt joked the boy was doing the sound of one hand clapping.

A gaggle of laughter from the trio ensued.

* * * *

Andrea pranced in front of Millicent the succeeding evening, wanted an opinion of her tight-fitting blue top with hip-hugging jeans.

Millicent, though no longer envious of Andrea for having taken Chuck, mumbled it wasn't something she would wear and when Andrea requested she speak up, Millicent answered slowly and loudly. Andrea huffed the girl was jealous, warned it was one of the deadly sins. Millicent, tired, retreated to her room.

Sophia entered the apartment whereupon Andrea requested she critique the outfit. After a pause, Sophia nodded, said it looked nice, and added quietly, "For you." When Andrea told her to clarify, her friend didn't stammer, said the color wouldn't look good on herself but it reflected Andrea's eyes nicely. The girl in the blue top smiled though it was a jagged line.

Sophia entered Millicent's room, asked if she was ready.

"Don't feel like going." Millicent, on her bed, rolled away. Sophia sat by the girl, quizzed the roomie about her health. The other female did a one-eighty, poked a finger at the door, lipped *Bitch*, and pretended to throw up. Sophia suppressed laughter, whispered they'd stay as far away from Andrea as possible, not only to avoid her but her genius boyfriend.

Millicent smiled and rose. Sophia helped her pick out attire, soon had Millicent in a ribbed yellow shirt with khaki shorts, Sophia choosing a pink and black ensemble from her own room, then led the other two out.

"You sure seem excited," Millicent said.

Sophia told of her and Arturo having just dined at an Italian restaurant and now had a night of dancing and more ahead, explained the freedom from a long week—two assignments plus an upcoming test—had her feeling like the rodeo bull right before the gate opened.

They met the guys in the apartment parking lot, Conrad informing them he and Dawn might join them later. The boys ridiculed he was in fact too scared to really party. Sophia admonished that some took longer to warm up and get crazy.

"He's a guy, not a car," Arturo said. "Every guy wants beer, sex, and women. Since the last two go together, every guy wants beer and sex."

"Well, normal guys," Renaldo said as Wyatt and Arturo moved their craniums up and down.

Sophia led them to their cars, Arturo telling all to meet at The Depot, the most popular bar on the strip. When Sophia warned they'd better have no obstacles gaining admittance, Arturo said it'd be easier if she gave a little feminine attention to the guys at the door, promised to take care of the rest, hit his wallet.

"Hope so," the girl said.

It was easier than expected, Andrea and Chuck waved in, no questions. Arturo had intentionally omitted shaving the past two days. His college-aged friend smiled and let him enter. Renaldo had no problems once he saw Katy inside, bouncers letting him through as the girl sidled next to employees. Wyatt slid in behind, undetected.

"Maybe it's good Conrad stayed away," Arturo said. "He's too jumpy, those guys'd spot him easily and we'd all be denied entrance."

"He's such a dweeb anyway. A good time could explode on him like a Molotov cocktail and he'd miss it," Wyatt said.

Sophia repeated her chastisements as they sat down, Arturo requesting her presence on the dance floor. A few tunes later, he had Chuck get the group drinks. When Sophia declined a banana daiquiri, her boyfriend chided her to loosen up. She demanded what was that earlier on the dance floor. He coaxed her to have a few sips. Then half the cup. Before long, she'd drank the whole concoction and was speaking freer, louder. Several more drinks and she offered to dance with Renaldo, then Wyatt, Millicent.

"You okay?" Millicent grinned. "Never seen ya this loose."

"Just having fun. Can't a girl let her hair down?"

"As long as it doesn't fall out."

Sophia cackled and led Millicent onto the floor. A few girls strolled past Arturo, one sneaking a look, he returning the expression. The girl led her friends back to the guys and chatted up Arturo who never clued her in on Sophia though he made several glances to his girl. When Renaldo leaned over Arturo's shoulder and said they shouldn't be doing this, Arturo brushed him aside, said they were having fun and talked up Renaldo like he was a new car on sale. Renaldo was mute, cup of beer near his lips, Katy at the table behind him with Everclear, she observing Millicent and Sophia.

When Arturo pushed Renaldo toward the new girls, Renaldo motioned to Wyatt, said to try him. He leaned into a black haired girl, she with a long neck and large gold earrings, told her Wyatt was pre-med from a rich family. The girl rushed the table, took Wyatt onto the floor though after three songs he was back with friends. When the girl grunted he fit the arrogant doctor type, Wyatt laughed, said what she didn't know was good for her, and threatened Renaldo with groin surgery though he grinned while saying it. Renaldo yawned, said he'd tried to help. They watched Arturo and Sophia glide to and fro while Train's *When I look to the sky* sang how one felt a loved one's presence when absent.

The couple rejoined the group, Sophia sobered up though Arturo continued his journey to meet the pink elephants. She watched him, pushed his cup down after a few more drinks, and mothered him to slow down.

"This is party time," Arturo slurred and assured her he was fine. She quizzed him as to the capital. He spread his arms.

"Washington, D.C."

She corrected him, said it was Oklahoma City.

"Not for the U.S."

"I didn't say U.S."

"You didn't say Oklahoma either." Arturo tapped Renaldo. "Did she?"

Renaldo gave a sad smile to Sophia, admitted Arturo was right.

"I'm so sober I can recite the alphabet backwards." Arturo glared at her. "The English alphabet."

She called him out.

"..zee, why, ex, dubbayou, vee, you, tee, ess..." He touched the back of Sophia below her belt line. "God knows I love that letter. We all want a good piece of it."

The girl poked him, told him to at least take a break for a minute.

"Will do." Arturo put his cup down, held out his wrist, and observed his watch, mentioned thirty seconds had expired then forty five then counted down with ten seconds left.

"Okay." He picked up his cup. "Waited a minute." He finished off the drink, smacked his lips, and stood.

Sophia probed as to his destination. He said nature called and did she want to go with him. The girl's face was a prune and she used a hand to ward Arturo away. "Though I'm watching you."

He traipsed to the restroom. Sophia conversed with others at the table then saw Arturo exit the men's room and bump into a girl who rolled her tongue at him then over her lips. He grinned. But glancing back at the table and seeing Sophia look his way, he resumed his forward progress.

"I'm back. You happy?" Arturo flipped his chair around, sat with chest pressing the chair's front, and set his cup down. Sophia peered over the lip. He picked it up, claimed it was the same one he had before getting up.

"You took it into the restroom?" She smiled.

Arturo laughed. "'Course not." He took her hand and the two danced a few numbers.

Back at the table, Arturo renewed his boozing, had trouble finishing sentences. Each time Sophia complained they should go home, Arturo took another swig, said this was his first night out as a college student and no one was going to ruin his freedom celebration.

"From what?" Sophia heckled.

"Parent's iron-fisted grip. Now I can do what I want, when I want." He stood, arms wide. "I'm a man now!"

"And you're sure acting like one." Sophia joined him. "An immature one."

"Fine." Arturo moved to the dance area, chatted with a curvy brunette. The two put hands on each other, oscillated with music.

Sophia turned away, harrumphed, and started to go for another drink but sat down, talked with Millicent yet kept looking to the spot where couples moved. Arturo remained with this girl a few songs. Next he was with a thin, brown-haired girl, finally stumbled into his seat, his speech worsening. Sophia stated if he drank any more, she was leaving. The last word hadn't so much as disintegrated in the air and he took a swallow of beer. Then another.

"I meant if you got another cupful. Will let you finish that one."

Two gulps later, Arturo smacked the cup on the table, gasped, *Ahhhh*, and said he was going back for more. Sophia insisted she wasn't bluffing. Arturo rose. Sophia reached into her purse. He stepped toward the bar. She retrieved her keys, jingled them. He viewed the objects then her, she with straight face, her eyes small. The young man motioned her to the door. The girl stomped a foot then swam through the crowd. A student passed Sophia as she exited. The door clanged and Sophia rushed out. The entrance wheezed shut.

Arturo fought through the throng, waited in line at the bar, requested a screwdriver, washed down one quarter of it heading back to his friends then crashed into someone. His cup conceded to gravity, a portion of its contents spilling on his wrist.

"Shit for brains. Watch where the fuck you're going," he said.

The other person, though with their back to him, spoke before turning. "No one tells me who the fuck I should look out for. You're the one who needs to watch their ass because I'll kick it, whether I'm a woman or not."

Arturo's voice calmed but he told the girl she needed to watch where she went. He raised his glance and took in the face. The cup fell out of his hand. He caught it with the other, spilled more of its contents. The two jumped back, alcohol splashing at them, rest of it staining the floor. They looked at each other.

"Phoebe," he said, more a question than statement as he viewed the figure.

The wavy marks on her forehead waned. Her mouth broke out in a semi-circle. "Arturo, how ya doing? Thought you'd forgotten me."

"I'm fine. And you?"

"Great. How's college life?"

"Excellent. We're having a great time partying."

"We? You mean you and whatshername?"

Despite the anger at Sophia smoldering in his belly like charcoal embers, Arturo clenched his cup upon Phoebe not remembering Sophia's name. The snapping of dented plastic had him loosen his grip. He gathered himself, replayed that night mentally. The feeling. For the first time. The way she'd taken control, shown him what to do. His shoulder sank. "Her name is Sophia," he said, the way a parent warns their child never to talk back.

"I knew that. Sorry." Phoebe put a hand over her brow and turned in various directions.

"Went home."

"Too bad. Sick?"

"No. Guess she was tired."

"Some just don't want to get out and enjoy life, huh?"

Sharp, crooked lines on Arturo's forehead. He narrowed his eyes, distanced himself from her. She asked where he was going, he telling her he was returning to friends. The girl raised a hand, moved a finger toward herself.

"I'd rather not," he said.

Her eyes became dark. "What's wrong?" Her hand sank to his wrist. "Wasn't it special?"

His face felt warm. He found his head slowly moving toward his chest. "Was decent enough."

"Decent?" Phoebe's turn to take a step in reverse. "That's it? The night you became a man thanks to me—*decent*?"

Arturo wrapped a hand around her arm, his cup still in the fingertips of the other hand. He pressed against her. "Meant a lot to me. Thank you very much. But that's over."

Phoebe pushed his hand away. He released his grip. She withdrew. "I don't want to bring it back, want to work on the future. I s'pose I'm too late."

"It's okay." He found her hand, put his fingers between hers. "You're really good. It's just not right. That night was special. Really. Thanks." His lips touched her knuckles gently.

She blushed, requested one dance, to which he obliged. When a slow dance followed, they did not part. Nor after a third tune. At the end of the fourth, he said he had to return to his friends. She followed. By the time he noticed her at the table, he'd already begun conversing with the gang. He nodded, continued speaking with friends.

Wyatt questioned if Conrad was going to make it, rose then sat back down. "Probably didn't have a date and doesn't have the guts to party, get drunk, or ask a girl to bed."

Millicent admonished him, Wyatt protesting that was what guys did, looked at Arturo and Renaldo who chuckled agreement. Millicent rebuked them again, Katy and Phoebe backing her up with a "Yeah."

"Oh really?" Arturo swung around to Phoebe, spoke in a low tone. "And what about at Sophia's graduation party?"

Phoebe glared, led him away, warned him to never speak of the event in front of others. When he accused her of being in a rush to do him so she could brag she'd gotten a younger man, Phoebe denied it. He glowered. She bowed her head.

"Somewhat." She raised her head and gave a firm glance. "But you wanted it too, bragged to all your buddies."

"Did not."

"Yeah, right." Phoebe moved in a circle. "Hey, everybody, listen. I have a first here." Her hand went above Arturo's head and she pointed an index finger down. "This guy claims he never bragged to anyone about his first. You believe that?"

A few jeers, guys telling Arturo if it was true, something was wrong with him. He faced the girl, his eyebrows in a v. "Well I didn't. I mean, I did."

She squinted. "You're not making sense."

His turn to pull her aside. "I didn't tell them"—he nodded toward his table—"Not about us. I bragged to them Sophia was my first, told them about her and me on Prom night."

"Oh." Her tone softened. "I see. Congratulations."

"I'm sorry. It's just not right." He leaned to her, touched his mouth lightly on hers. She pulled him to her, he unable to escape. Finally able to lift her arms off his back, he rushed to his table and sat down, friends gazing at him as if he'd fallen from above. Phoebe remained in the same spot, unblinking. Arturo rushed to the bar before she broke from her trance, pushed past others, grabbed a cup, not caring what was in it, and drank.

Phoebe came to him. His body pounded. He took a drink. She approached. He went to dodge her. She grabbed him.

"It's okay," she said. "I understand. Just wanted to have you one last time."

Arturo paused mid-drink, shook his head, and held up his other palm. She gripped it.

"Just a kiss. One final time." She lowered his cup, gave him a kiss though he kept his arms against his hips. Her mouth lifted and a gap opened between them. Phoebe waved, added, "If ever..." but turned before finishing, Arturo not wanting to hear the rest anyway and, back at his table, sank, nearly missed his seat. He finished the contents of his cup, crinkled the container in his hand, seized Wyatt's cup, and drank what was in it before the friend could protest, stood, and swayed though not just from the alcohol.

"Hold on." Wyatt held his friend.

Arturo affirmed his sobriety. And fell. Wyatt caught him, stated he had to take the boy home, cops on patrol sure to arrest Arturo should he try and weave his way back.

"I's fine. Can even add. See?" He held out both hands. "Six and six is twelve."

Wyatt assured it would be okay. Once home, he gave Arturo black coffee and led him to bed.

* * * *

As she moved to her bedroom, too exhausted to change into appropriate attire, Sophia felt the sting of salt in her eyes, rubbed it away, and flopped onto the bed. She drifted mentally, half in dreamland, half awake. A face she'd seen before leaving the bar came to her as did the name and where she'd seen this person originally. Too tired to go back and confront him, she convinced herself he'd already left the bar and taken this other person to some cheap motel. Sophia's eyes burned. She dug through her purse, touched the sharp, crumpled plastic, and pulled it out, stared at it, aware of what it was, even in the dark. A reunion for those two tonight, the name strong in her mind. She wished she'd forget it. With wet cheeks, she entered the sandman's territory.

Chapter 8

Wyatt returned to the bar, Arturo having fallen asleep as soon as he'd laid down. Wyatt watched Renaldo finish another drink, Renaldo moving as if to dodge the visual contact, wanted to know what was wrong.

"Nothing." Wyatt obtained another beer and sipped it, only his second cup that night.

Renaldo grabbed a full cup, drank. "C'mon."

"What? We going somewhere?"

"You want to say something. I can take it." Renaldo took a long gulp.

"It really was nothing. I forget."

"If you forget, how can you know it was nothing?"

Wyatt grasped his container, it making popping noises. He took a drink then exhaled. "I really don't remember. Honest."

Renaldo said he did. Wyatt leaned back, looked at his friend. "Was going to say take it easy with that."

"This?" Renaldo lifted the drink. "You're worried about me and some beer that's mostly water?" He laughed. "Do I act like I need to be taken home?"

Wyatt stated everyone acted differently.

"So you have no clue if I've reached my limit."

"I just..."

"I'm fine." Renaldo nudged Katy, she getting to know Millicent. He had her observe him, state her conclusions.

"You've done well in controlling your consumption since we met." She kissed him.

"See?" Renaldo said gruffly. "I'm fine."

"Just take it easy," Wyatt said.

"I will. But thanks for your concern." Renaldo curled fingers around his cup, brought it to his lips, swallowed several times, and took Katy's hand, offered a dance. Before proceeding out, Renaldo leaned in on Wyatt, said to watch for anything wrong. On the dance floor, he spun Katy, dipped her a few times then glared in Wyatt's direction. Wyatt began small talk with Millicent, checked on the couple occasionally. Each time, they were as smooth as professionals.

The song ended and the couple revisited their seats. Wyatt viewed Renaldo's new cup, the liquid in it up to the rim. Wyatt remained silent, avoided Renaldo, and asked Katy if they planned on auditioning for a dance contest. The girl chuckled, said she'd had difficulty keeping pace.

Seeing Renaldo's smirk, Wyatt shrugged. Renaldo tapped his cup against Katy's, drank, and put his arm around his girl, the two making contact at the mouth.

A couple of more trips to the bar soon had Renaldo speaking like he was at an assembly trying to quiet the crowd. Katy rose, mentioned an early class tomorrow.

Renaldo scoffed. "You don't have class till ten-thirty."

The girl said she needed beauty sleep.

"C'mon," Renaldo growled, seized her wrist, and led her in a few dance steps. Katy backed away, moaned they should leave, and offered to take him home.

"I drove here. Besides, *I* should take *you* home."

Katy reminded him she'd also driven here. He demanded he take her back. She protested and asked for Wyatt's assistance. Renaldo came to him as if a soldier, Wyatt an enemy combatant.

Wyatt held up his palm then moved his fingers. "Gimme the keys."

"I'm fine. Is a short drive anyways."

"Then let me drive," Wyatt said. "We'll be there before you can get even more drunk."

"I'm not drunk."

"Then before you get drunk. C'mon." Wyatt reached for his friend's arm. Renaldo stepped back. Katy moved beside her boyfriend, whispered promises if he let his friend take them back. Wyatt looked at her. She fingered an okay, said Renaldo would be out soon after they put him in bed. Wyatt gave no response. The girl reiterated her proposal to Renaldo, who opened his fingers, metal falling into Wyatt's hands with a *clink*.

"Thanks." Wyatt drove the three to the apartment, Katy's prediction nearly accurate, Renaldo going right to bed though he didn't fall asleep, mumbled for Katy to join him. The other two shut his door.

Wyatt offered to drive the girl to her car. She thanked him then smiled, asked why he was still single. Wyatt bent his wrist. "I prefer the dark th'ide."

They laughed and he led her out, returned her to her car. Katy thanked him again, ran her tongue from one side of her mouth to the other. The distance between them decreased.

Wyatt's legs weakened. He thought of Renaldo's reaction. The group's. Katy was cute but his heart did not warm up nor did its beats per minute increase. She leaned into him. He watched the lips purse, tried to lift his foot. Too late. Her mouth brushed next to his. And slipped past, to his cheek. She gave a quick kiss and backed away.

"Thanks for helping me. And Renaldo." She went to her car, started the engine, and waved before leaving. Wyatt felt like he was in water at the North Pole. The hum of the engine faded. He warmed up, slowly entered his car, and sat, stared dumbly into early morning blackness, finally stuck the key in the ignition, and twisted it clockwise. The car awoke and he drove away.

* * * *

Back at his place after two classes the next day, Conrad tried to work an assignment. His mind floated to the previous night. Why hadn't he done it then? Perfect opportunity, she in debt to him after he'd assisted her again with her work. The study mood had faded, replaced by a tryst on the sofa. At his place, no less. Dawn had started to disrobe. Conrad watched and the more he did, the more he felt like he was in a panic room that had become an oven. Salty water like tiny rivers dribbled down his forehead. He brushed it away. More formed. His mouth felt like lit gasoline. He slithered, sprung away, dashed to his room, and locked the door.

"Where're ya going? What's wrong?" Dawn rapped on the door.

The boy could not breathe, clawed through his dresser drawer then saw the trash can near it, scattered it contents on the floor, seized the bag, and held it over his mouth, breathed in and out. His heart rate and pulse decreased. He let go of the bag and collapsed on the bed.

Fingernails tapped the door, Dawn repeating her question. Conrad got up then paused. No way he could say it to her face, she'd slap him. Or force herself on him.

A fist on the door, more questioning.

"Sorry," Conrad said through the wood barrier. "Not feeling well. A headache." He cursed himself. "I mean, might be coming down with some kind of flu bug."

"Oh, great. Thanks." The hand slid away from the door. "Now you tell me."

He said it'd just started, suggested it could be allergies.

Dawn asked if she'd done something to upset him. He responded she hadn't and he'd call in the morning. She persisted, he giving the same response before going quiet. Calling his name three more times with no answer, Dawn sighed heavily and left. Conrad did not fall asleep until after two that morning and not before condemning himself to Lucifer's lair.

He now noticed his eyes watered. He wiped them, went outside, and heard Arturo retching from his apartment. Conrad shook his head and went back in, wished his problem was that simple, pain to be gone by day's end.

He took possession of his cell phone, checked for messages. None. He threw the object aside. After a few minutes of non-movement, he retrieved the phone and pressed the first three numbers. His thumb balked. He turned the phone off, sank on the bed, and decided to call that night, eat his humble pie then ask if they could go out.

He sat up. It might work. The gang's get together. He groaned. Today was Friday. They were meeting Saturday. He rationalized he wasn't in the mood now and an extra day to prepare could only help. He napped off and on for the next few hours, phone at his side, he cradling it, thumb climbing and sinking on five numbers before he quit.

Tomorrow, he promised himself. Today was left for preparing what to say.

* * * *

Despite an evening of minimal sleep, Sophia was up early yet she did not so much rise as sleepwalk, considered blowing off class. One thing propelled her: The cute guy in front of her in Psychology. He was tan and trim, said little to others, took copious notes.

Not a partier, she thought. *Nor a philanderer*.

She soon was dressed, her hair combed. Recollections of last night had her choke up but she regained calm. He would regret his choice.

The walk to campus was distracted by internal thoughts, Sophia preparing what to say then how she'd parade him in front of Arturo, brag how much smarter this guy was— "Obviously he is. Chose me and you didn't," she'd sneer— then kiss him and wave her ex goodbye.

As she neared class, the words and ideas melted. Her teeth clicked involuntarily. She had trouble holding her books when she spotted him in the second row. Her heart sang out a classical music concert until a reminder had her cursing: Their teacher assigned seating by last name. She sat and looked at him. His face betrayed no emotion.

"Hey, how's it going?" a female said. The male voice in the second row spoke:

"Great. How're you?"

To Sophia, it was like watching a sad-ending movie, the kind that won the Oscar. She listened to the girl say she had trouble with her car again, guy promising he'd look at it after class, motioned her to the empty seat on his left. She reminded him of the assigned seating and he assured her no one would recognize. The girl grinned, seemed to skip to the spot, hugged the guy, pecked his cheek as she sat, and put his hand on hers. The teacher came in and began her lecture.

Sophia was first out the door an hour later, books so tight against her skin they left a mark. At the apartment—glad to discover the place unoccupied—she opened some textbooks but gave up when nothing registered in her memory, the scene frozen in her brain, a snapshot like one of the frames of a plane crash. A buzz on her thigh. She fished out her cell phone, checked the I.D., and shoved the plastic and metal back in her pocket. "Hell if I'm gonna answer him."

The phone continued its plea. She pulled it out, tossed it in a nightstand drawer, slammed it shut, and promised herself no contact with him until they met up at the pizza parlor. She fell asleep, an uneven, nightmare-consumed nap, was no further refreshed upon awakening.

* * * *

Wyatt awoke and got out of bed an hour prior to his eight-thirty class although he'd experienced less than half a dozen hours of sleep. She'd only pecked his cheek, certainly hadn't been totally sober. But he had to tell Renaldo, it was the truth. But serious enough to tell? And was it a permanent truth or a passing one? Might this one lead to more?

Not reaching a decision before class time, Wyatt collected his things, didn't so much as change out of yesterday's clothes, grabbed a cap, pressed it on his head, and went to class, recalled very little of it or the succeeding one, and sauntered home.

"Hey, Wyatt," Renaldo said from the sofa, had apparently invited himself in—they giving each other spare keys. "How's it going?"

Wyatt, glad the low-browed cap hid his face, stopped on the way to his room when he heard the cheeriness in his friend's tone. "Hmmm?"

"Last night was crazy, huh?"

"Sure was." Wyatt started toward his room.

"Hold on."

Wyatt stood in freeze frame.

"How'd it go?"

"How did what go?" Wyatt felt his backbone grow cold. None of his possible responses sounded good.

"Duh, last night." Renaldo lifted a cup to his lips, Wyatt observing the near empty contents of black coffee. Renaldo rubbed his head and groaned, said he was glad the after effects were almost gone.

"I don't know," Wyatt said of his friend's question, whereupon the friend laughed, said Wyatt seemed to have forgotten more of last night than he had. Wyatt inquired as to his pal's recollection.

Renaldo stretched out on the sofa, grabbed the cloth of half melted ice cubes next to him, pressed it over his eyes, and stated what he could of the evening. He stopped short of Wyatt taking Katy to her car.

"I'm impressed." Wyatt awaited more interrogation. With no further commentary from his friend, he had his answer.

Renaldo pushed the cloth deeper into his eyes, muttered he'd missed the best part of the evening. Wyatt guaranteed he hadn't, awaited a question about Katy. The still hung-over student rolled over and snored.

Wyatt shut his door, tried to convince himself he'd done the right thing. A difficult task. By nightfall, his mind's self-criticisms quieted enough that he fell asleep.

* * * *

For Conrad, Saturday passed faster than expected, Arturo and Renaldo inviting him to join in a basketball game at the university recreational center. Despite interest in the game, Conrad was slow and short, managed but one shot though the trio won. He then beat his friends in a game of HORSE on a trick, behind the back reverse lay up.

Not until he'd entered the apartment did Conrad remember Dawn. He checked the time. Two hours before the group met. He picked up the phone. His fingers seemed paralyzed. He mentally commanded them to press numbers but they did not obey. He set the phone down, would shower to make himself enticing. As if she could somehow smell him over the phone. He heard the bathroom door open then close. Water rushed out of the showerhead.

"Damnit." Conrad held the phone, fingers taking the same posture. He decided to get it over with, a normal person had no difficulty doing so, would even be excited. He imagined he was Wyatt, how the friend did what needed doing, painful or pleasurable.

With shoulders in, jaw out, Conrad rattled off a speech to himself, so engrossed his fingers hit the numbers without him realizing it. The ringing brought a resurgence of paralysis. A door seemed to slam inside his throat, his hand as if marble. The phone slipped. He moved his other hand beneath it, and pushed it back up to his ear.

Two more rings. A click. Then the recording.

Conrad sighed then grimaced, wanted this over with, gathered words, and debated the tone. Sad? Happy? Pretend nothing was wrong? Or just—

The beep stopped him in mid thought.

"Uh…Conrad? I mean...Dawn? It's Conrad. Don't delete this message, let me explain. I'm really sorry about the other night, forgive me." He chuckled though with little emotion. "I'm just a young virgin, ya know." The words made his face hot. "I mean, I'm not, I'm a man. Well, not quite a man, I..."

"Hello?" A live voice.

Conrad choked back words, coughed and hit his chest, reached for the cup of water he'd left on his dresser, took a gulp, and sibilated.

"Conrad?"

The boy's face became hotter. "Uh… Yeah. Hi. How are ya?"

"Fine..."

"I just...I'm sorry." Conrad fell on the bed, released all the air in his lungs, shut his eyes, and said how nervous he'd been despite it not being his first time, was afraid he wouldn't be as good the second time. "Musta had a panic attack," he explained. "Couldn't help it, I..."

"It's okay." Dawn laughed. "Heard the phone, checked the number but when I read whose it was, I..."

"Wanted to hang up."

"No. Calm down. It's okay, I just dropped the phone in surprise, couldn't answer until you were leaving your message." Another chuckle. "Had to laugh at what you said. No guy would admit he was a virgin unless he thought it'd impress a girl."

"Well, I'm not. Anymore."

"I know."

"In fact, I'm ready for another," he said. Fearing he came off too aggressive, he corrected himself that didn't mean he had to do it now.

Dawn giggled. "A noncommittal response. Thought about politics?"

"Naw, no way I could lie for a living."

Dawn laughed. Conrad apologized again. She replied she understood, there was nothing to forgive, feared she'd scared him off.

"You did. But don't worry, looks aren't the only reason I left."

"Watch it or you won't get a second chance," Dawn teased.

They laughed and she agreed to his offer to join the group for dinner.

"Perhaps more," she said. "If the mood's right."

"I dunno..." Conrad drawled. "I'm coming down with a headache." He tittered and she laughed, asked if tonight would work.

The boy gulped, discovered sweat on his chest though he'd cooled off since they'd played basketball. Thinking how he won HORSE relaxed him so he concentrated on that. "You want home court advantage?"

"Huh?"

"Sorry, that was sportspeak, meant where we'd go after dinner."

"Men. Always thinking sports."

"Not always."

"Sports and sex."

"There you go. So where do we..." He couldn't finish the sentence. She said they'd decide after eating and he agreed. "And Dawn..."

"Yes?"

"I'm really sorry and..."

"Shut up, already, it's forgiven."

"Thanks. Bye."

They hung up, Conrad punching the air just as the bathroom door opened. Wyatt asked if he was okay. The other boy collected himself, worked to hide his grin. Wyatt cringed, wanted to know if Conrad was high.

Yeah, the other boy thought. *On love.* He visualized Dawn. *And this time I won't let the opportunity pass.* He rubbed his palms.

"You're definitely not okay." Wyatt flung his towel across his shoulder, announced he was done, suggested Conrad needed a shower to cool off.

"Or have sex in," Conrad responded gleefully, pondered the possibility of he and Dawn in there, hot bath with body lotion, oils, bubbles, steam rising above them.

"You're off your rocker." Wyatt distanced himself from his roommate. Conrad skipped into the bathroom and shut the door, pictured he and Dawn together.

* * * *

Saturday dragged longer than Friday for Sophia, her classmates' words and actions repeating in her mind. She reminded herself it didn't matter, she had only wanted the student as a revenge pawn. But was the one she *really* wanted right for her? Or vice versa? Arturo had called numerous times Friday, left messages but hadn't stopped by. Today he'd made but one call, hours ago, hoped she'd be at the pizzeria.

Millicent knocked on Sophia's door, asked if she was going. When Sophia didn't respond, Andrea told Millicent to come along, Sophia unwilling to get over her men, too immature to forgive and forget.

Sophia flung the door open, told Andrea she could learn from her how to get real love and maintain it. "Watch."

"All right, girl. Get him," Andrea said.

Sophia halted at her friend's now encouraging words, requested her friend explain the change of attitude.

Andrea raised a shoulder. "Had to try anything to get you outta that room."

"Thanks," Sophia said although she maintained her expression and the trio went to the restaurant.

* * * *

The gang slid into their usual booth, this time Sophia and Arturo not together—her doing—his expression similar to someone who'd received an F in a class where they'd scored one hundred on all their work. She spoke with Millicent. Arturo began a discussion with Renaldo, Wyatt listening. Conrad and Dawn joined this group, Renaldo teasing the boy if his zipper had been opened yet, the man inside now free. Conrad frowned. Dawn put her arm in his. He smiled at Renaldo who showed no reaction. Conrad then kissed Dawn's cheek. She responded in kind and they laughed together.

Wyatt watched their giddiness, decided immediately to stay mum about the last time he and Dawn were here. It'd been a misunderstanding on his part—as was his take on Katy—confirmed by what he now saw.

A cell phone rang. Everyone looked down at or reached for theirs. Andrea held up a finger, stated she was the lucky one.

"Or perhaps unlucky," Wyatt snickered, others tittering.

Andrea held the phone to her ear. And smiled. "Hi, honey." She spoke to the group. "He's such a sweet guy, always calls to ask how I'm doing even if we just saw each other an hour ago."

Sophia faced Millicent, hid her expression from Andrea with a hand as she pretended to puke. The two giggled as their friend's speech, once animated and fast, slowed.

"Oh," Andrea said. "Too bad. Okay. See ya then. Love you." She held out the phone for all, turned up the volume so they could hear Chuck tell Andrea the same to her then put the phone away, said Chuck wouldn't be coming but he and her would meet later. "Said he wanted to talk," she concluded.

"Uh-oh," Arturo warned.

Andrea squinted. "What uh-oh?"

"You don't know? C'mon." Arturo waved his arm at the rest. "We all know what that means."

"Doesn't mean it's true in this case," Andrea said.

"Right," Wyatt said. "And guys don't want sex with girls they're attracted to." He shot a glance at Conrad, grinned slyly. "Or, at least, ninety nine point nine percent of them."

Arturo and Renaldo yukked, also flashed glances at Conrad, who fiddled with the salt, pepper, and napkin holder, wiped his mouth with a napkin then turned to his girl who smiled and leaned on him. Conrad let out a breath, commented coolly some guys had more patience than others, knew how to treat women.

"Yeah, right," Renaldo said. "They just say that because they know they aren't getting any."

Arturo and Wyatt laughed.

"You guys are so damn immature." Dawn moved further into Conrad's side. "Women want a man who's mature, much deeper than just wanting sex."

"Then she's gonna have a long wait." Arturo exploded in laughter.

"A lifetime." Renaldo high-fived Arturo then Wyatt.

"Whatever." Dawn pulled her arm free of Conrad, crossed hers over her chest, and sank in her seat.

Sophia advised they be certain they were with the right person. "Most guys…" She stared at Arturo. "Get a girl once then move on." She swallowed. "Unlike women."

Andrea concurred, men more about accomplishment, females concerned with others, were better listeners, which was why they gave birth.

Millicent jerked her head back, gazed at her friend, wanted to know who'd just possessed her mind. Andrea furrowed, requested a translation.

"Tell her, Sophia."

Andrea switched to her other roommate, said the words to her. Sophia spoke to Millicent, said she didn't have telepathy. Millicent glared while Andrea volleyed her look back.

"Since you forced me." Millicent's back formed a right angle with her thighs. "You're not exactly deep."

Andrea's jaw drooped. She pressed for more information.

"Look at you. Bragging and showing off about your boyfriend, how in love you are, how great you are for him."

Andrea smiled. "It ain't bragging if it's true."

"It sure is." Millicent's voice rose as she extended a forefinger. "If you talk but it's true, that's bragging. If you talk and it's not true, *that's* lying." She sank, viewable from just the shoulders up. "Don't mean harm, I'm just saying." A heavy exhale. "Tired of hearing how great you have it."

"You're just—"

"Right, I'm jealous." Millicent cut her off, pushed herself up. "Part of me is." She held thumb and finger close together. "That much. Rest of me is annoyed. Confidence requires no approval from others, narcissism does."

The group nodded. Sophia complimented the girl. Andrea, her lower lip between teeth, spoke.

"You're saying I'm a narcissist?"

"You are a little insecure," Millicent said, Sophia chuckling. "A little?" to which Millicent said she'd seen worse. Andrea inquired what to do, the girls saying to tone it down, said they'd give her credit if she deserved it.

Andrea thanked them, said she still believed men cared only about achievement while women cared about others.

"Yes." Sophia fixed her gaze on her boyfriend. "Why is that, Arturo?"

The boy laughed quick yuks, wanted to know why they continued on this subject.

Sophia rose. "Because we want to talk about more than getting someone into bed. Or how, because your girlfriend wants to go home and you don't, you tell her to go to hell and reach for a slut." Tears like raindrops from Sophia's eyes. "And it's the same one he tried to hit on months ago when they..." She choked. "They..." She cried. "You see him with her again and know they did each other later that night."

Arturo's face was like he now grasped a scientific theory. He joined her in upright position, they inches from each other. "I danced with a bunch of girls, yes. But had sex with them? Hell no!" His words and tone raised a few eyebrows, one mother covering her young daughter's ears.

"Not all of them," Sophia said. "Just one. The same one you hit on at our party."

"We didn't even go home together. We talked, danced, went our separate ways, nothing more."

"And the others?"

"You just said I only did it with one." Arturo laughed humorlessly. "Never made it to first base with that one, let alone any others." He curled a lip up, nodded then sat back down. "That's why you didn't return my calls, came here alone, and didn't sit next to me." He put the palm of each arm on the opposite biceps, asked how long they'd been going out but did not allow her to respond, asked his friends if anything happened that night, said they were all there then looked at Conrad with thin eyes. "That is, those of us who know how to party."

Conrad put a fist in the palm of his other hand. Dawn pushed his hands down, extended an arm behind his back.

"You were all there," Arturo went on." Did I leave with anyone? I may have been plastered but I sure as hell know I didn't leave with anyone. Wyatt? Tell the truth."

Wyatt's trachea swelled and shrank. He sipped water, looked at Arturo, who nodded, then viewed Sophia. "It's true. He left with no one."

Arturo thanked his friend, who mumbled he was just telling the truth. Arturo requested Sophia sit back. The girl did and he professed he loved her, said he was sorry he hurt her, hadn't thought rationally, argued it was the past.

Sophia stared at Wyatt then moved to Arturo, put a hand on his shoulder, he doing the same to her. They leaned into each other and kissed. The gang applauded. Arturo drug a finger past Sophia's eye and wiped away the wetness.

"Now," Arturo said. "We finally ready for dinner?"

They all agreed, helped themselves to the buffet, and ate until satiated, all reclining in their seats. Sophia sighed, asked if others believed in the afterlife and if they confessed their sins on their deathbed and were truly repentant, would God forgive them and allow immediate entrance into heaven?

Arturo's forehead creased. "Where did that come from?"

"Theology class. You could use some religion, ya know. But what do you all think?"

No one said anything, looked at their plate or glass.

"I think God won't grant us immediate entry if we're sorry, just give us a more lenient sentence," Wyatt finally said.

"Can we change subjects?" Arturo asked.

Conrad squirmed, looked at his watch, and announced he had to study. Dawn turned to him like he said they were breaking up. He nodded. "Studying. You and I. Algebra."

"Huh?… Oh, I guess we do."

The pair stood, others allowed them out, and the two said they'd see everyone later.

Wyatt moved as if receiving an electric shock. Arturo inquired about his condition.

"I'm fine." Wyatt maintained a downward glance.

"Don't look it."

"Have a headache, I guess."

Arturo pulled at his friend's hand. Wyatt's arm stayed stiff.

"Whatsa matter, wanna take my temperature, too?" Wyatt glared. "Mommy?"

The other boy lifted his hand in surrender. Wyatt looked out the window. Dawn glanced to the restaurant then spun around, strode to her blue Ford Focus. With body half-turned, she looked back again. Wyatt faced the group, his chest as if he was running a race.

"You sure you're all right?"

"Fine. Leave me alone."

Arturo again requested they change the subject.

"To what?" Sophia said then added in a sharp tone, "Like does a guy want a girl for anything other than a companion in bed?"

"Seems to me," Wyatt said, "women want men for it too."

Sophia chortled, sprayed spittle across the table, choked and coughed, consumed a few gulps of her drink. She cleared her throat, laughed some more. "Girls wanting a guy just for that? Get over it."

"It can happen." Wyatt twisted in the booth, wanted to tell them though no one would believe him. And he had no proof. Had to tell Conrad first anyway. To his face. It'd be the second thing he'd do, first one being he had to make sure he wasn't fantasizing something into existence.

Sophia asked Wyatt for an example. He cleared his throat, ran his hand across his mouth, and sat up, the girl sing-songing, "We're waiting."

Wyatt's mind worked like a super-microprocessor yet it could not meet the girl's demand. He hemmed and hawed, frittered with his cup then lifted a finger. "Britney Spears." He went on how she was all over Justin Timberlake and Kevin Federline.

Sophia smiled sadly, gave a *tssk, tssk*, and told Wyatt if that was all he could produce, he'd lost the argument. When he asked her to expound, she said Britney's name as a question and ran circles around her ear with a finger. The other females laughed, slapped palms.

"It's true," Wyatt said.

"How do you know?" Andrea asked.

"I just do."

The girl snorted. "Must think it happened to him."

Millicent and Sophia chuckled with Andrea. Wyatt's teeth merged but before his mind alerted him to possible harm, his mouth let the words out. "It has."

The girls froze. Then redoubled their laughter.

"Like when?" Sophia said. "And with who? Where?"

Wyatt processed what he'd said, wondered if his face showed discoloration. "Take my word for it. It happened."

"When?" Sophia repeated.

Wyatt scratched his head, whispered, "Long time ago," and when Sophia wanted to know how long ago and said it must have been in kindergarten because girls weren't as smart then, Wyatt rose.

Sophia teased he couldn't bear the pressure of a woman's questioning, claimed he'd lied just to win a battle of the sexes argument.

"It happened, damnit, I swear," Wyatt growled.

Everyone looked at him as if he'd pointed an Uzi. He apologized but continued to slide out of the booth. "Later," he said though in a tone as if meaning to say *Never again*, and shuffled out.

"What's up with him?" Arturo said, others moving to the window as if witnessing an accident.

Andrea gave a "Who knows?" said she was off, and exited, the rest advancing to the door as if on cue.

"Wait," Arturo said to Sophia who asked why. He took her hand, offered to drive her to Boomer Lake and watch the sun vanish into the horizon.

"I dunno," the girl said stiffly. "Don't you want another woman?" She dramatically put a finger to her temple. "Whatshername?"

Arturo stuck hands in his pockets. "Let it go. Nothing happened."

Sophia asked Renaldo, who reiterated his friend's words, and moved to her. "Remember, Wyatt said so."

The girl inhaled, held the pose for a spell, found Arturo's hand, stuck her fingers between his, gazed at him then released her breath. "Let's go." She chuckled. "Anyways, Andrea was my ride. Guess I have no choice."

Arturo frowned until Sophia added she was joking and the two went hand in hand to his car.

"Well, it's just us," Renaldo said to Millicent. "By ourselves."

"Uh…" Millicent put her hands behind her, took a step back.

Renaldo laughed. "I mean, we're done here. Let's return to our apartments." He led her to his truck.

* * * *

"I know," Sophia said to Millicent later that night. "But she's our friend, hasn't always been like this, only since she's been dating these guys this year. Ted and whatshisname."

"Airhead?"

The two giggled, Sophia confessing they weren't exactly the ones to know true love, assumed the guy must have good traits, ones Andrea liked enough to forgive his flaws. Millicent questioned how Andrea could ignore them, Sophia chuckling she thought the same. They gossiped a few minutes when the door swung open. Andrea stood in its frame, remained there, as if a force field prevented her entry. Her eyes were reminiscent of one who'd witnessed a car crash.

"Andrea?" Sophia welcomed her in. The friend did not reply. Millicent approached, waved a hand in front of her fellow tenant. The girl was unresponsive.

"Andrea?" Sophia gently touched her, helped her cross the threshold then led her to the blue lounge chair. The recliner leg popped up, almost tossed Andrea off, she still in catatonic state.

Millicent and Sophia called Andrea's name, Sophia squeezing the girl's hand, Millicent continuing to move hers in front of Andrea then snapped fingers. The female did not react.

"C'mon, girl, break out of it." Sophia mimicked Millicent's behavior. "What happened? Tell us?"

Andrea's lips opened. The other two awaited words. None came out. They prodded her. The lips moved, about to form words. The girls leaned in, an intake of oxygen suspended in each one's lungs.

Chapter 9

"He…" Andrea fought to bring the words out. "We... Us..."

"Yes?" Sophia motioned her hand. "He? We? What?"

Andrea turned as if in slow motion. "Can't believe it."

"What?" Millicent said. "Are you okay?"

The girl in the chair barely shifted her head. "He said we should…" Andrea's mouth twitched. "Said we should see other people, it was his fault, and..."

"You could still be friends," Millicent said.

Andrea faced her. "Right."

"Oh boy." Sophia sat on the sofa cushion's edge.

Millicent squatted in front of Andrea, asked if she was sure that's what he said. Andrea gave a head bob.

"Happens to all of us," Sophia said.

"Yeah," Millicent replied, sat on the arm of the chair, and patted Andrea, stated Chuck wasn't that good, plenty of other men were available.

Sophia lifted a finger. "I know. Let's have a girls' night out. We'll get drunk, have a great time."

Andrea wiped her eyes. "If you think it'll work." She stirred to an upright position.

Sophia asserted it would and all this would be forgotten. She tee-heed. "Besides, how many times have you dated a guy and broken up with him before the next weather pattern came in?"

Andrea chuckled, sat up further but wanted confirmation the idea was a cure. Sophia giggled, estimated how many guys they'd see, Millicent contributing her guess. Andrea gave hers, Sophia saying it was a bet.

"A gentleman's bet," she added then corrected herself. "A lady's bet." She put her hand on Andrea's, Millicent doing the same. They all smiled and Andrea thanked the two, said she was sorry for being so egotistical and show-offish, said she'd thought Chuck was right for her, had felt so elated she had to tell everyone.

"It's okay." Sophia hugged her. "As long as you know you did wrong and are sorry."

"And won't do it again," Millicent said.

"I won't," Andrea promised. "And please hit me if I do."

"We will," Millicent said as Sophia's forehead broke out in lines. Millicent lifted her shoulders. "What?"

Sophia held her stare until Andrea thanked them a second time. The three exchanged a hug, Sophia vowing a wild night.

* * * *

Conrad hopped out of his car, rushed to Dawn's side, opened the door, and waved her out then questioned if this was the right place, offered the scenario of his friends returning before the two were done. She told him the first few times always went fast.

"You know this?" Conrad's voice squeaked.

She shrugged, admitted she'd hooked up a few times.

"A girl?"

Dawn punched him, wanted to know why men fooled around and were praised while girls were scorned. Conrad did not open his mouth, fished his keys out of one pocket, other one containing the tiny, foil package.

At the apartment door, Conrad's key did not fit. He took a second stab. Same result. His hand beaded sweat. He lost possession of the keys, uttered a meek apology, picked up the chain, and tried the lock. Dawn offered assistance, Conrad telling her he'd do it. Another failure. Dawn chuckled, took the key, and held it up.

"Your car key." She jingled it, grinned then held up another key. "Your apartment key. Watch." She gave a teasing, how-to speech until she twisted her wrist and the key did not turn. She pushed at it, grunted, and kicked it.

"Hold on." Conrad ran the key out, held it as she had to him. "This for the door lock." He gripped a key of similar color and shape. "This is for the deadbolt. See?" He stuck it in, flipped his wrist. The bolt clacked. Conrad took the other key, undid the door lock, turned it, and pushed. The door opened. He smiled. "That's how you unlock a door."

"You were the one who tried your car key," Dawn retorted and snickered. "I at least had the apartment one."

"But I was the one who got us in." Conrad's insides hummed. Blood raced through him at record speed. He had trouble moving his Adam's apple up and down, caught sight of his open bedroom door, glanced at her, and tried to think of an excuse. "Uh…" Blood flow sounded in his ears. His head throbbed. He spotted the TV. Maybe a movie, a romantic comedy. Too long, he decided, wished he had a clever line. Only one idea reached his lips. Once he said it, he wished there was a string tied to the end of his words so he could reel them back.

"Uh...how about some foreplay?" His face became hot, his knees unsteady.

Dawn's face was as red as *his* felt. "Excuse me?"

"I...I mean...I..."

Dawn laughed, laid a gentle, soft hand on him, said to relax, and offered a massage. Conrad accepted—until she suggested he step into his room.

"Why not out here?" he said and once more wished he'd kept his mouth shut.

"Calm down." Dawn's laughter increased. "You *are* nervous. C'mon, I'll lead. Like before. First, the massage."

"Wait." Conrad dipped under her arms. She lowered them, caught him. He complimented her on her quickness, to which she replied she had experience. She soothed him, rubbed the area between neck and shoulders.

"Ahh." The boy shut his eyes.

"There." Dawn led him to his bed, set him on his front, and gave a full massage.

"Now," she said when complete, undid the button on his jeans, and slid his pants off. Conrad's head pounded like a drum at a rock concert. He wet his lips.

"Here." She held up the package, handed it to him. He gripped it with thumb and finger of both hands. The package did not tear. A second attempt netted the same. A third time, nothing. After a fourth try, Dawn seized the object.

"Watch." She stuck it between her teeth and pulled at it then handed it to him.

"Thanks." The foil slipped from his trembling hands to the mattress. He picked it up, pulled out the condom, and wished, like last time, he could do it without one, asked her if she wasn't on the pill. She said she'd ran out and wasn't taking any chances. He looked at the condom, it much smaller than he'd anticipated. How would he fit that thing on? And by the time he did, the urge in him might be gone. He looked at it again then her. His mind flashed pulsating signs: Quit. Take control. Do nothing. Fake it. Did guys do that? Never. This was the only thing males wanted from the time they reached puberty to the day dirt was shoveled on them.

But he already had his first time, reached his goal of manhood. Would this time be better? Should he tell her to forget it? Or just relax? He breathed.

She lay on him, went back and forth, up and down, groaned. He mimicked her behavior. Feelings overtook him. Again, it happened too fast. They remained in this pose, twin bed barely wide enough for them. She asked how it felt.

"Great. Like last time. Thought it was supposed to be longer this time."

She promised it would on the next. They kissed then held each other.

"Ya know—" Conrad began. A thump cut him off. He sprang up, nearly knocked Dawn to the floor. They were back. What would they say? What would it be like to be seen naked with another woman?

He stopped himself. Why be ashamed? They'd praise him. He lay back down and prepared a victory speech.

No noise on the other side of the door. Conrad listened. All quiet, no voices, no door shutting. He scanned the room and with assistance from the complex's outside lights, noticed a book on his desk had fallen to the carpet.

"Damn," he said and when Dawn queried if something was wrong, Conrad hastily said the book falling had scared him. They both got into their clothes and went to the living room, Wyatt showing up minutes later.

Conrad's mouth spread across his face until Wyatt passed him, unaware.

Dawn laughed giddily, said it was time for her to go back. Conrad gave a similar laugh, said he'd gladly drive her back. At her place, she kissed him and they agreed to get together in a few days. He waved as he left then drove to the apartment as fast as the speed limit would allow, thought of what he'd say to Wyatt. He entered the place, his smile still intact.

Wyatt, on the sofa, looked up from the television. "You okay?"

"Better'n okay. Awesome."

"You look ready to burst." Wyatt acted like someone at the rear of a truck, telling the driver to back up. "Out with it."

Conrad said Wyatt wouldn't believe, like last time.

"C'mon, tell me." He led Conrad to the couch, huddled next to him. "Out with it."

Conrad's chest seemed as big as Schwarzenegger's. "We did it! A second time!"

"Did what? Who's we?"

"We!" Conrad hopped up and down, laughed, and tossed his head back. "Us. Her. And I!" He jabbed to the sleeping area. "In there. Together."

"Kissed?"

Conrad nearly toppled over backwards. "No, dipshit. I mean the whole way! Around the bases. A home run! Again!"

A smiled forged its way onto Wyatt's face. He pressed his hands on the sofa. "You did?"

Conrad's eyes became huge. "Yes! Again!"

"Way to go." Wyatt slapped hands with his pal, Conrad turning a somersault on the floor, hit the scratched-up end table, and knocked over a cheap ceramic lamp with Dallas Cowboys logo though it didn't fall, simply rolled to and fro on the table. Conrad set it upright.

Wyatt clapped Conrad's back then asked if he was joking.

"If I'm lying may the University of Oklahoma beat OSU every year in baseball from now on."

Wyatt whistled—Conrad was a big OSU baseball fan. "You aren't kidding. Way to go!" He hit Conrad so hard the friend coughed.

Wyatt went to the refrigerator and tossed a beer, Conrad catching it inches off the carpet. Hissing like steam from an iron sounded from two cans. The two raised the aluminum, tapped them, and drank. Conrad choked, bubbles dripping out of his mouth.

"Take it easy. Slow."

Conrad sipped his beer, answered Wyatt's questions, and said he and Dawn were getting together in a few days to study. Wyatt kidded him, asked when he had overtaken Conrad's body, joked only he would concern himself with studies after losing his virginity.

The two drank another toast. Conrad chugged the rest of his beer, wiped his mouth, and belched.

Wyatt fisted a hand, thumb pointing to the ceiling. "Way to go."

Conrad smiled.

* * * *

Fall break came and went, everyone going home for the four-day weekend, a respite from one another. Thanksgiving also had everyone at his or her home. Finals week had them busy cramming for exams, they not congregating until halfway through the first week of Christmas vacation, Arturo and Sophia welcoming Katy and Renaldo as they arrived, Katy declaring her boyfriend's drinking was on the decline.

She hugged him. "He's really hanging in there. I know he'll improve." They smooched and Renaldo smiled though the mention of alcohol had his taste buds wishing the restaurant served drinks, needed a break from all the semester's thinking, his part-time job not helping. He pushed the desire away, placed his lips on Katy's. They smiled, sat down together.

Conrad, Dawn, and Wyatt arrived at the same time, Conrad and Dawn hand in hand. None of the guys teased him, had praised him since he'd proven the first time was no fluke.

Millicent came, Andrea a short time later. The group debated happenings for the break, Arturo asking Dawn why she was still here, she replying she was to leave for Tulsa the following day, parents out of town on business until yesterday. Conrad put his face on hers. "I'll miss her."

"I'm sure you will." Arturo punched his friend's arm then asked Wyatt if he was depressed.

"What for?"

Arturo ridiculed how Wyatt seemed more interested in studying than in going out or dating and now that school was out for a month, he must be down.

Wyatt fisted hands on the table. "I party. You've seen me."

"Not often. When you do, you just sit at a table sipping beer." Arturo laughed. "Real men don't sip."

Wyatt glared. "Or eat quiche, right?"

"Guess not."

"Since when did you become the arbiter of what defines a real man?"

Arturo whistled. "He's so busy learning new words and studying, he never has time for girls. Look at Conrad, even he's doing all right."

Conrad smiled then frowned, asked what Arturo meant by "Even he..." The other boy waved hand, said he meant nothing then questioned Wyatt further about dating. Wyatt thumped his fist, asked what it mattered.

"Guess you haven't made it yet," Arturo said, Renaldo and Conrad chuckling.

Dawn inspected Wyatt and smiled. "I think it's admirable he's in no rush. One athlete never had sex until almost forty."

When Arturo bellowed, "Who?" and Dawn said she couldn't remember, Arturo heckled she'd made it up.

With chin out, Dawn said she hadn't. Arturo wanted proof. Dawn reiterated she didn't know his name, only that he played basketball so Arturo asked for which team did the guy play.

"A good team back in the eighties. Won some championships, I think." She smiled at Wyatt.

"Well, a basketball player makes tons of money," Arturo said.

Wyatt crossed his arms. "So if I make a lot of money, not having had sex is no big deal?"

Arturo concurred. Wyatt wanted him to explain what that had to do with it.

"Because that's how we judge others," Sophia interjected. "The more you make, the better you are as a person."

Millicent moved her head. "How stupid. Some of the richest were real bastards. John Gotti. Al Capone. Bernie Madoff. Even those who weren't criminals aren't so friendly. Donald Trump can be a horse's ass, humble not a word in his vocabulary."

"But he's successful," Arturo said. "Today's psychoanalysts think if you're not making a lot of money, there's something wrong with you."

"Not everybody can become wealthy," Sophia said. "Some just have talent in a profession where they don't get paid a lot. Is that their fault? Like teachers, they don't get paid much."

"They don't work a full year," Arturo said. "A professor makes good money."

"I'm talking school teachers. Isn't that what you want to be, Millicent?"

The girl nodded. When Sophia asked why, Millicent shrugged, said she liked kids.

Arturo grinned. "She wants to molest them."

Millicent stared knives at the boy. He raised a hand then lowered it and Millicent reclined, said kids were fun, creative, easy to please and amuse. "Teaching them to do something is great satisfaction," she said. "You should see them, so excited when they get it right."

"See?" Sophia said. "It's what she likes. Why judge someone based on how much they make?"

"It's easy to do," Arturo said. "A lot easier than getting to know them."

Sophia hoped she'd judge based on who a person was, how much they helped others. Arturo argued others might want a profession that didn't necessarily help others so why should they be punished, accused Sophia of doing the thing she claimed to be against.

"We all do this," he said. "You complain when others protest yet are doing the same thing, only protesting them. Like political dissent. Both sides say they're for free speech—except when someone says something against that side's beliefs. What happened to free speech?"

The others moved their heads back and forth.

"Look at you." Sophia smiled. "You can play this game. It's intriguing, makes ya think, wonder about things. Life."

"Isn't that what college is for?" Wyatt said.

"And you're good at that. One of the few things you *are* good at." Arturo laughed then quickly held out his hand, said he was kidding. "Really, I wish I had your work ethic, able to do what needs to be done, a business before pleasure mindset. That's what gets you good grades, which leads to making good money." He chuckled how if Wyatt made enough, he could have any girl he wanted.

The females razzed Arturo. He argued it was true, quoted an old show where someone joked guys married girls for their looks, girls married guys for their job titles.

"What a myth," Sophia moaned, held Arturo's hand. "I love you, no matter how much you'll make."

"Oh, really? And what if the job I loved was a low-paying profession and I was poor?"

"I'd still love you." Sophia turned to Katy then switched back to her boyfriend. "Just how poor are we talking?"

"See?" Arturo said.

"Well, maybe."

"No maybe. Money is an important thing to a girl when she's dating a guy."

"And men?" Andrea asked.

"They want money," Arturo replied. "But have to earn it themselves."

"While the woman's barefoot and pregnant, right?"

Arturo protested he hadn't said that, said there are double standards everywhere. Girls couldn't sleep around, guys always had to be the breadwinner, had to make the first move and pay for dates, girls weren't supposed to take charge, couldn't get angry or were ridiculed for fighting.

"Cat fight." Renaldo grinned. Katy looked at him like someone who'd tasted something sour. He replied he was joking then saw a bus drive past, ad on its side displaying a drink. He excused himself, grabbed a cup by the soda fountain, filled it with a soft drink then peered at the group, they involved with their theories. He rushed to his car, found the bottle in the glove compartment, added some of its contents into the cup, drank a shot then jogged back inside and rejoined the group.

"I agree with some of what you said," Andrea commented. "There're just more limitations for women."

Arturo and Wyatt disagreed and Sophia intervened, said they were getting nowhere. "Besides." She ran her tongue over a lip. "I'm hungry."

"If that isn't a change," Arturo said. "You wanting to pig out, me wanting to debate."

"You're right." Sophia did a half turn, looked to the window. "Nope, it's okay. Sky's still up."

"Maybe it's the first horseman," Millicent kidded.

Sophia chuckled and asked what guy wouldn't find her entertaining. Millicent smiled then frowned, said Arturo's comment was factual, girls to be the quiet ones who shouldn't make the first move. Sophia said that had changed.

"I don't see it," Millicent droned.

"Well, we'll change it. Our generation."

Wyatt gave a bland "Huh," commented every generation said this, they the ones who'd change things, would take care of the environment, improve government, society.

Sophia answered every generation falls short of grand goals but every little change contributed to society's betterment, how if one took each group's contributions and combined them with the one before, they'd see results.

"True," Wyatt said. "But values, beliefs, and the like change slowly. If at all."

"So we do our part," Sophia said.

"Right." Arturo patted his stomach. "But we always do better on a full stomach. C'mon."

Sophia smiled. "My darling. Back to his old self. So disciplined."

Arturo countered she was the one who'd mentioned eating and pushed his way out of the booth to the buffet.

"Did I leave out romantic?" Sophia said to her boyfriend's chuckles.

"Way to a guy's heart is through his stomach," Andrea replied.

"I shouldn't talk, I'm starved too. C'mon."

They followed Sophia's lead, soon had empty plates.

Sophia began another commentary to which Arturo sat up and said it was time to go, yawned he was too tired for philosophy.

"What happened to my man of the world?"

"He's full." Arturo extended a hand, assisted Sophia. "C'mon. I'm going back to the apartment to sleep this off."

"My man of the world."

The gang smiled as the couple waved goodbye.

Andrea watched them and released a long, slow breath. "So unfair. They get it right the first time. Me? Every guy is Mr. Wrong. And when I find Mr. Right, he doesn't want me. So unfair."

Millicent shifted her head upward and exhaled. "Some don't realize how good they have it."

Andrea asked her to explain. Millicent spoke longer than she ever had with the group, told Andrea how she had guys wanting her every week while others merely asked for one opportunity and never got it; the ones who had everything complained they had nothing. Then when the single opportunity did come to those who'd wished for it, the ones who had everything came in and stole it.

Andrea lifted a shoulder, claimed taking chances was the only way and would allow one to avoid torturing themselves with *What ifs*. Each had to give their best shot and, worst result, they'd have peace of mind.

"I guess." Millicent sighed. "I'd rather wait for the right chance. Why try if it's going to fail?"

"Because the right chance may never come. And you can learn from failure."

"Doubt it." Millicent sank. "If so, why do we keep making the same mistakes?"

Andrea nodded, asked why the friend hadn't spoken up earlier but before Millicent responded, Renaldo and Katy said it was time to go and all agreed.

Dawn stood. "C'mon, Wyatt."

"Honey," Conrad said, "Wyatt can take care of himself." He pulled her to him. "My apartment?" He simpered. "Could use some more home field advantage."

"Sorry." Dawn forced a yawn. "Never shoulda ate so much. Bet I gained ten pounds."

Conrad told her she looked fine, could have had ten pizzas and wouldn't have gained an ounce. He attempted to lead her out. She freed herself, said she had to pack to go home the next day, apologized, and gave a quick sweep of her lips on the side of his face, rubbed a thumb over his mouth, promised she'd be back before he realized she was gone then went to her car. He waved as she drove off. Wyatt straggled out, he and Conrad with a quick conversation before Conrad left. Wyatt moved to his car.

* * * *

A block away, the blue Ford Focus did a one eighty, drove back to the eatery, girl susurrating a message to the heavens it wasn't too late. She knew his car, had memorized the license number. Another innocent one. Pure. What a challenge they were. And what a reward. She rehearsed a speech, pulled into the lot, and searched. The car wasn't there.

"Damnit." She checked where he'd parked. An empty space. "Shit. If only I'd come back earlier."

A white Chevy Impala from around the building's rear. She smiled, leapt out of her car, and allowed air to seep out of one of her tires, acted as if recalling a funny joke then rushed in front of the white car, crisscrossed arms above her head.

The other car stopped. He opened the door, stepped out, asked what she was still doing here, and if something was wrong.

No, she thought. *Everything's right. Perfect.* She portrayed an embarrassed smile.

Chapter 10

Dawn continued with the smile, chin tucked to her shoulder, moved a hand to her forehead, and heaved a breath. "Such a stumblebum." She praised herself for remembering at least one thing from Freshman Comp, told Wyatt she must have run over a sharp object, her tire flat, and she'd come back on the off chance one of them might have lingered. Her smile increased. "Looks like I got lucky."

Wyatt checked the tire. "Guess you did. Could call a tow truck."

"Uh-uh." Dawn explained she had no cash and her dad wouldn't let her have credit cards, even for an emergency. Her smile remained. "Can you help?"

"Let's see." Wyatt squatted, inspected the tire, asked if she had a car jack and when she replied in the negative, adding she didn't know what it was, Wyatt stared at her, she continuing to grin. He dug out his jack, raised the car, and put the spare on.

"There." He wiped his hands and instructed her to drive to the repair place a few miles away.

She smiled again, softly placed a hand on his arm. "Mind following me? You know how car repair guys are with women."

Wyatt agreed, said he had no plans, motioned her to her car, and led the way then offered a ride home when the mechanic said it'd be a few hours till they checked her car. Dawn wished she could have jumped into Wyatt's arms, instead sprinted to his vehicle, and slipped inside. Upon sliding into the driver's seat, Wyatt chuckled dryly, asked if police were chasing Dawn. She responded she was in a hurry to go home and relax.

Wyatt followed her directions, parked at her place. "There ya go."

She thanked him and offered a drink, told him she had long desired to show off her place.

He delayed.

"Just a quick look. And a drink."

Wyatt granted he could use some liquid refreshment.

Dawn grinned, opened the car door, and led him to the place, bragged she decorated it herself, no help from roommates—who, she mentioned softly, were gone. Inside, she led him to a sofa, mixed him a rum and Coke, and joined him, snuck an arm behind his back, her face next to his. "You really are a nice guy."

"Thanks."

"And so pure."

"What?" Wyatt lifted her hand off him.

She eased closer. He sat up, inched away from her.

"Don't be shy. You don't want those others teasing you forever about...well, ya know." She sank her lips on his.

Wyatt pulled away, said they couldn't do this, she dating his friend. She denied any commitment, placed lips on his again, forced her tongue past his teeth. Muted cries from the boy. They subsided within the minute. Soon they were on her bed. She undid his clothing, he returning the favor.

"How was it?" she said after they'd caught their breath.

"Better than anticipated," Wyatt said and chuckled.

"Figured you'd say that. Your friend said something similar."

"Conrad?"

"Who else?"

The boy sat up. Dawn asked if he was okay.

"Umm..." He tossed the covers aside, leapt out of bed. "Shouldn't have done this." He jumped into his pants, put on the shirt, gathered his shoes and socks. "So wrong."

She tugged at him, wanted to know how.

He froze, nearly dropped his possessions. "What?"

She asked again.

"Duh. You and Conrad? Dating?"

She had a blank face.

"You're dating him. And more."

She frowned. "He told you?"

"No shit. He's a guy."

She raised and lowered eyebrows. "Thought he wasn't the typical, braggart male. But don't worry. C'mere." She rolled across the bed to him.

He hurried toward the room's door. "Have to go. But you were great. Sorry." He sprinted to the front entrance, bumped into it before opening the door, rushed to his car, and sped away.

Dawn watched the car disappear.

Maybe he only needs a little more encouraging. Didn't expect him to be more afraid than Conrad. She smiled. *But that's what's fun, making the shy types men. Just have to do a little more work with him.*

Her smile grew.

* * * *

At the first traffic light, Wyatt shut his eyes, head on the wheel, caught his breath, and asked himself how he could have done that, why he'd done it, how to tell Conrad. If he should tell him at all.

He collected himself, concentrated but his mind couldn't formulate an answer.

Have to tell him, he finally decided.

No way he could lie. If so, he'd be like the others, couldn't be objective about himself, honest about his strengths, weaknesses, or past transgressions. So tell Conrad now? Or later, let him down easy?

He decided on the latter, figured he'd go home, cool off, and relax with family.

Yeah, he thought and sighed. *It's Christmas break, won't see Conrad for weeks. Things'll have calmed. Dawn said she was leaving tomorrow anyway. All will be forgotten next semester.*

He allowed a grin to creep up. He wouldn't see them until the New Year. Things would be fine. He drove slowly, arrived home, and behaved normal though a few times someone's conversation drifted away in his mind, the speaker having to check if Wyatt was listening, boy claiming to be drained from finals. After a few days, he was back to his original self.

* * * *

As Dawn loaded her car, a voice sounded from behind. "Hey."

She paused, about to smile then saw it was not the member of the group she'd last seen. She dropped a suitcase. "Oh."

Conrad laughed. "Don't sound so disappointed. Good morning." He kissed her. She kept her arms at her side. He took her bag and put it in the trunk. "Glad I saw you off." He placed other things in the car. They stood in front of the driver's door.

"See ya when you get back." He kissed her.

"Sounds good." Dawn shut her door.

"Life is great," Conrad said and grinned. "Couldn't be better, could it?"

She smiled and drove off but did not wave.

* * * *

On campus, Renaldo and Katy parted outside her apartment, she in her car, motor running, said she would call when she arrived at her grandparents' house in Enid, seventy miles northeast of Stillwater, she to spend Christmas with family. They wished each other a happy holiday, she hinting at returning for New Year's Eve.

Renaldo heated up. The one night to binge and not be criticized. He made her promise she'd celebrate with him. She only nodded while moving gearshift from park to drive and pulled away. He blew a kiss. She rolled down the window and returned the gesture, waved then drove away.

"Damn," he said, tried to defeat the craving but it was like Custer at Little Bighorn. He entered his car, went home to the dozens of bottles awaiting, hoped his parents would be there and his mom in one of her lecturing, albeit hypocritical, moods regarding alcohol and its dangers. His throat was like he'd finished a box of salted crackers though no other liquid would quench this desire.

The home was as quiet as an exam room. He rushed toward the bar. A figure walked into his path.

"Whoa!" His mom drew a hand to her chest, brushed strands of straight black hair into place, inquired as to her son's well-being. He admitted to a little sadness with Katy having left and his mom smiled, rubbed his back.

"Don't know where I'd be without your father." She laughed. "No one likes a good time as much as I do except him."

Without him, you'd probably be sober, Renaldo wanted to say but knew one couldn't argue with an alcoholic. "Gotta enjoy life," he replied instead.

"Is too short. Which reminds me." The mother called her husband to get up, smiled, and winked at her son. "There's more partying to do!" She clapped then did a bad rendition of one auditioning for a dance show.

Renaldo felt his facial temperature increase though his Mom blocking access to the room—as the urge crescendoed like a tsunami wave—made him smile.

"C'mon," the mother said to her husband, he in their bedroom, a distraction to Renaldo though only for a few minutes, his dad now ready. The couple ate breakfast despite the clock showing post meridian, and said goodbye to Renaldo as soon as the last morsel was consumed, woman snapping fingers in her husband's direction. The man growled he wasn't her pet, stood, and paused.

"Let's spend some time together, all of us, right here. We never do. Just a few hours."

Renaldo felt like the death row tenant who'd learned executive clemency had been issued. He gazed at his mom. The mother led her husband by the shoulder to the garage, mocked his statement then asked why didn't he have this attitude fifteen years ago when his son really needed it. She glanced over her shoulder, blew Renaldo a kiss, promised they'd be back before he could blink, opened the door, shoved the old man out, and closed the door without looking back.

"Shit!" Renaldo glanced to the barroom, the cabinet. His tongue did its usual movement outside his mouth. A few steps later, his hands caressed wood, the texture as sensual to him as Katy's breasts.

He swung the door wide, cradled a container to his chest, unscrewed the cap, and read the label.

"Everclear. Perfect." He took a half shot then poured some into a cup, added orange juice, and downed that faster than light traveled. He then mixed rum and Coke, sweetness contrasting with alcohol. He filled and emptied the cup three times, the ratio of rum to Coke increasing with each refill. He grabbed the Jack Daniels bottle, took a few gulps then squeezed his eyes shut. Done with that, he drank more rum and Coke, mixed his fourth glassful, staggered to the living room sofa, and collapsed onto it like he'd been shot.

An hour later, his cell phone rang. He didn't hear it. The caller left a voice mail.

Chapter 11

Millicent spent most of Christmas break at the daycare, worked an eight hour shift several times, liked reading stories and teaching kids the alphabet. Concerns about next semester's classes and her friends getting together were as distant in her mind as thirty years into the future.

* * * *

Christmas vacation couldn't end soon enough for Wyatt. His mom, aware of her son's unusually subdued demeanor, asked if the first semester had been rough.

Though fidgeting, he gave a denial, spent most of the time in his room, glad he hadn't given the girl his cell or home number though the latter could easily be found. He turned on his TV atop the about-to-collapse ebony stand, channel-surfed through every station three times before turning the television off. He looked out the window to kids throwing a football in pale sun, heard laughter and chuckles. He sighed. To be a kid again. Before girls mattered.

If I tell Conrad, he thought, *will Dawn continue to hit on me?*

Was it a heat of the moment encounter? Did girls have such occurrences? Should he tell his friend?

He rolled onto one side of the bed then the other, finally lay on his back, and decided to wait and see. He napped and awoke feeling better, his answer more concrete. It was the best choice.

* * * *

Sophia and Arturo spent their free time together, she continuing her philosophy questions, he inquiring why she kept at this, which spurred the memory to flash in Sophia's mind like lightning bursts on a rainy night. She pushed the image away, offered to cook Arturo dinner, her mom visiting her own parents, Sophia's grandfather having had simple surgery.

"Dinner. And a movie," she said playfully.

Arturo grinned. "How about X-rated? And live." He held her. "It'll be your all-time favorite movie."

"Already is." She giggled and the two embraced.

Dinner went well, Arturo saying it was the best meal he'd eaten then led her to her bedroom. Once more, the images clouded her mind as she groaned all kinds of hosannas and praises on Arturo as if he was the Second Coming. The thoughts and pictures waned.

Done, the two professed each other's dedication. For Sophia, this was the greatest Christmas she'd know. So far.

* * * *

Andrea shopped with her mother both before and after the holiday and went out with her older sister, a student on break from Baylor University. They went to several bars where Andrea's sister bribed the bouncers to allow the younger sibling in, Andrea accepting any offer to dance with a guy who fit her perfect-man image. None of them offered a second dance despite her asking. She met a guy at a retail store but after two dates, decided he wasn't right.

* * * *

Conrad's break was the best he'd experienced. Not only was it twice as long as high school's, he had a girlfriend, called everyday—several times on occasion—and felt like each afternoon was a perfect summer day. Yet when he asked if she couldn't wait to reunite and she said, "Of course not. Am counting the days," to him it sounded flat. Once, she laughed when he'd discussed an aunt's illness. Conrad asked what that was about. She paused, told him to repeat what he'd said then apologized she'd misheard. He found himself wishing he could jump ahead in time to the end of the break.

* * * *

New Year's Eve had the gang at *The Depot*, Andrea with her usual perspective.

"Hey," she yelled to Millicent. "Why haven't you been out on the floor?"

Millicent twitched, sipped a peach wine cooler, said she didn't like to dance, and conveniently omitted the fact no guy had asked her. Andrea encouraged her to go up to the next boy she found cute and lead him out, pointed to her own beer.

"This'll help ya get right out there." She belched then laughed. "See? I never do that sober."

Millicent's face was as wrinkled as a seventy-year-old. She persisted she didn't like dancing. When Andrea teased she would wind up a maid, Millicent clenched her teeth. Andrea bragged she'd found a guy, pointed to the boy next to her, and tagged him with a kiss.

"Yeah. Like last time was right." Millicent looked at the guy. "Why don't you tell him?"

Andrea didn't move. Millicent continued.

"Oops, sorry." She smiled. "Probably hurts too much so *I'll* tell him." She went up to the young man and explained Andrea's dilemma.

"All right, enough," Andrea chided. "He doesn't need to know everything." A ballad played. Andrea offered a dance. When the boy accepted, the girl stuck her tongue out at Millicent who said she was doing as Andrea requested, letting her know when her ego got out of control.

Andrea halted, cleared her throat, and thanked Millicent, asked forgiveness for nearly backsliding. The friend smiled, wished Andrea luck, and pushed them out on the floor then sank in her seat, her mouth a straight line. Though she hadn't liked dancing since her mom had forced lessons on her at five, Millicent wished she could be out there. With her Mr. Right. Instead, she drank her wine cooler. Almost done, a figure in her line of vision had her choking. The guy had a great, wide smile, small pink lips, his teeth white, hair perfect, wore an ironed, navy blue polo and jeans. She lipped a request to the Man Upstairs.

The boy moved closer. Millicent heard Andrea's words mentally, stiffened her legs, about to push off of her chair. Words like broken jigsaw puzzle pieces scattered through her mind.

The boy stepped forward, his glance in her direction. Millicent felt as if she'd been catching August rays for three hours. Her tongue was the world's largest caterpillar, she finding it impossible to close her mouth. She felt paraplegic.

The distance between he and her shrank. Andrea's words again. Millicent's body came loose. She stumbled, caught herself, and approached him.

A person blocked the area between Millicent and this guy. A female. She chatted with the boy. He nodded, took her hand, and led her out. The two danced, each step a poker in Millicent's gut. She sank down toward her chair. And hit the floor instead.

"Wow, you act about as drunk as I feel," Renaldo said from behind.

The girl crawled back onto her chair, yelled for Arturo to bring a beer then snatched it from him and drank as if it was her favorite. Arturo and Renaldo applauded, Arturo asking his roomie when Katy was to arrive. The other boy looked, didn't see her, went to the bar, and ordered a drink then another. On his fifth request, the bartender said that was enough. Renaldo grumbled but returned to his table.

* * * *

Wyatt spent the night with arms over his chest, did not have so much as a swallow of beer. Conrad sat next to him at one point, spoke quickly regarding Dawn's return. Wyatt excused himself to the men's room, splashed cold water on his face, and returned, quiet so long, Sophia and Andrea questioned his health, he explaining he felt tired, girls giving a *Hmmm* then left, Sophia to Arturo, Andrea to the dance floor. An hour later, Wyatt excused himself, girls wishing him well.

"Me too," he muttered and when they inquired what he meant, he shook his head. At home, he stayed up with family but maintained his quiet demeanor.

* * * *

Renaldo dialed her number. No answer so he left a message and tried again thirty minutes later. Still no answer. He hung up, mouthed an epithet, turned, and offered double what the person behind him had paid for their beer then downed it.

"I'm going to have a good time anyway," he said, got up, and danced, hooted, waved fisted hand, drew a girl's attention then another. Both bought him drinks.

"Looks like it's gonna be a great evening," he cackled and slammed each drink. When the girls left him, he returned to his friends, drank some of their alcohol, then, with a deep sigh, opted to leave.

* * * *

Andrea left the bar alone, the guy she'd been with having left an hour earlier. At Campus Corner, she rode toward the fire station with her foot on the pedal, even where the street curved, station blocking her view of oncoming traffic. She saw no headlights and withdrew a breath then sucked it in just as quick.

A truck from the opposite direction swerved across the double yellow line. She honked. The driver paid no heed. She repeated her action triple time. The other driver neared her then drifted back to the correct lane. Air seeped out of the girl's mouth. She pulled it back in, oncoming vehicle sliding back to the wrong side. Andrea hit the horn and swerved. The other car slipped back to their lane and went past her. Gray truck with black racing stripe.

"Jesus!" Andrea observed the other driver and gasped. Did she see correctly? She took a second look, over her shoulder. Wasn't he still at the club? She hadn't seen him leave. Then again, she'd been too busy with any available man to know.

Who else drove that model of truck in that color and racing stripe? And while drunk? No one. The driver looked like him. What to do? Confront him? He'd deny it. She had no proof she could later show him. Besides, they were friends.

An object in front of her disrupted her thinking. Her foot methodically slammed the brake. The car lurched, threw her toward the wheel. She braced herself, did not hit the wheel then was thrown back. The squirrel scampered away.

"Damnit, Renaldo, if I don't make it home alive or in one piece, I am coming after you." She allowed her nerves to calm, went home with no further incidents.

* * * *

"Damn, too close." Renaldo heaved as he rescued the truck from near disaster, his foot pressure on the pedal decreasing. He glimpsed the rear view mirror. No sirens in its panorama. Streetlights blazed a haloed path, moving objects seeming to go faster than usual. He maintained a speed pertinent to a school zone, checked mirrors, and sighed each time they remained as black as his surroundings.

With one final turn then a straight shot to his house, Renaldo put weight on the right side pedal. Speedometer needle razored higher. He thought of the mahogany cabinet and gunned the engine, went hand over hand on the wheel. The back end shifted further to the left than the front. He bucked in his seat. The right front side went up at an angle. A thump. A metallic crack then a crunch of metal. Renaldo went further ahead. His hands lost control of the wheel, his head destined to contact glass. He cringed and awaited the clink of glass shards. Silence. The distance between he and the shield protecting him from the elements went on the upswing. The sensation of leather on his back, though harsh, was a relief as was the rear of his cranium hitting the head rest. He slumped. The car settled at an incline.

Renaldo sat up, the bent metal stick with red octagon sign angled away from him. He clambered out and staggered to the front bumper. Only a couple of dents. He re-entered the vehicle, backed up, and slowly progressed home. Certain his mom and dad hadn't called it a night, he weaved his way to the front door, and after four tries, unlocked it.

He swayed to the cabinet, did a battle with its doors, opened them, clutched the closest bottle—Scotch—took a couple of shots, and gave an "Ahh!" then sauntered to his bed, and crashed. Unconsciousness followed.

* * * *

When clocks chimed twelve times and "Auld Lang Syne" played, Conrad called Dawn, said although the old *When Harry Met Sally* movie was her favorite and it was New Year's Eve, he wasn't proposing, wished she was with him, asked when she would be back. The surrealism of her low-keyed reply to the obvious partying going on behind her found Conrad lifting his eyebrows. He assumed it meant she wanted some quiet. A candlelight dinner with him. He hung up to her bland "Miss you," and rejoined his friends. It was to be a good year. A great one. The best. Until the next year. And the one after that.

* * * *

Arturo drove Sophia home but only after making a stop at their apartment. They joked about who'd get the advantage of familiar surroundings, settled on her place, and were done in minutes, after which he dropped her off at her mom's, they in a long embrace good night. Sophia waved from behind the glass front door as he left, seemed to float to her room, and slept peacefully.

* * * *

The New Year had Wyatt feeling better. A week remained to prepare should he have to change tack. He had to tell him, pleasurable or not. The more he thought about Dawn, however, the warmer his body became. He scolded himself then defended his actions, his mother, noticing the angst, questioning him. He brushed it off as concern for the upcoming semester, each one tougher.

His mother shook her head. "Always the perfectionist. You'll never be satisfied."

Wyatt shrugged. The phone rang and his mother answered then held it out and grinned. "A young lady. Sounds cute."

The boy hid his face, stammered it must be a sales call or something to do with enrollment, perhaps tuition. "Hello?" His trembling hand barely held the phone, he certain of her voice before she spoke.

Dawn told him she missed him and couldn't wait to return. They conversed though she did most of the talking, he responding with an occasional gruff, "Yeah,", "Sure," and "Uh-huh." When those went unheeded and after his mom exited the room, he told Dawn he wasn't interested. She said he'd change his mind next time she had him alone.

For Wyatt, repressing that moment was as easy as a rich, sex-starved man at a bachelorette auction trying to prevent himself from bidding. He forced a calm tone, Dawn ending the conversation with the promise she would change him. Wyatt had trouble putting the phone back in place, had even more difficulty explaining to his mom who the girl was, gave half truths. This had to cease.

* * * *

The New Year's Eve celebration was a blur to Millicent, she drunk for the first time though it did little to mask how she felt. Another blown opportunity. He was handsome, seemed a nice guy, good at dancing, might have gotten her onto the floor. But, of course, he chose someone else.

Millicent drank more, spoke louder with each swallow, Arturo and Renaldo saying how getting drunk loosened one up, allowed them to be themselves. The girl rubbed her jack-hammering head, replied if this was being herself, she didn't want it. Renaldo patted her, said she had to accept this mood, appreciate how it brought out a side of her guys loved.

Millicent stayed seated, fearful if she tried to stand, she'd soon become good friends with the porcelain bowl in one of the stalls behind the door labeled *Ladies*. By the time friends decided to leave, she felt aware enough to drive home, her trip with no problems. She slipped into her room and into bed but didn't meet with sleep. The more she queried why she always came so close with men only to fail, the more the water rose to her eyes. She condemned Andrea, how easy the girl had it while she, Millicent, needed help the way a debt-laden woman needed a high paying job offer yet received none, no matter how much she prayed.

Thinking of her next work day, it in less than thirty hours, had her smiling, if only briefly. Why couldn't boys restrain their urge? How was she to get a guy if none wanted her? Her mother had warned not to even hint interest or those boys would have her in bed faster than an F5 tornado could destroy a mobile home.

She flipped back and forth, no position comfortable then pretended she was with Candice, a five-year-old who always wanted to see how many numbers she knew before needing assistance. Soon enough, Millicent slept.

* * * *

Not until after the first two weeks of a new semester did the friends go to the pizza place.

"Never told me about your break." Arturo put an arm on Conrad, he with Dawn. About to tell Arturo, Conrad looked at Dawn, she glancing elsewhere. He asked if she was okay. She nodded.

Renaldo entered, said Katy was at the library and had called New Year's Day, contrite, said she'd been so busy with family she'd forgotten their bash and her cell had been off all day while being charged.

Andrea came alone, Sophia teasing her about not finding Mr. Right on New Year's Eve. "You'll find him tonight," Sophia reassured her. "And the next night. And the next."

They laughed as Millicent sauntered in, head down. Andrea asked if the girl was still upset over what she, Andrea, had said at the bar. Millicent shook her head, said the apology showed Andrea had matured.

"So why the somberness? Vacation's over but is it that bad?"

Millicent said she just didn't feel in a great mood, almost hadn't come then thought being with them might perk her up.

* * * *

At the apartment, Wyatt kept checking the clock. It was time. He'd told Arturo he'd be there, had to find out how Dawn would treat him. For fourteen days he'd awaited the right time yet avoided the apartment whenever Conrad had said she was coming. Now was it. If nothing else, to see how Dawn would behave. What if she hadn't changed? How to tell Conrad? He pictured the friend bawling as he fell into someone's arms. One good thing, Wyatt thought, was Conrad wouldn't challenge him to a fight. But how would this harm his friend? Their friendship? Might Dawn deny the fling, say Wyatt made it up? Would she tell Conrad yes, it was over, she'd moved on? Perhaps she'd blather how it wasn't his fault, nothing personal, and they could still be friends.

He opted to stay with his plan and headed to the place despite his stomach feeling no need for sustenance.

The drive seemed a cross country trip. Wyatt meandered to the door, the way his shoulders felt making him sympathetic to Atlas. He gripped the entrance's handle. His feet went forward.

"Over here, slowpoke," Arturo said.

"I'm being fashionable." Wyatt smiled as he scanned faces, met Conrad's, and promptly acted as though he was a floor inspector then hurried to an empty spot in the booth. He snuck a peek. She acted like they'd never met. He turned to Arturo but before escaping sight of her, watched her chest go out and her mouth curve, eyes gaining brightness. She wiggled fingers at him, Conrad on her other side.

Half of Wyatt's body landed on the cushion, other half on air. He rebalanced and pushed himself into position.

Arturo chuckled. "Got a hangover?"

Wyatt did not laugh, Arturo now with a blank stare. Wyatt gave an incoherent excuse but received no response and forced himself not to view her, this as easy as trying not to move while standing on hot coals. He wrung his hands under the table, shuffled feet, sat up, slouched, leaned then sat back up, none of these poses desirable.

The others talked though Wyatt comprehended little, kept internally repeating, *Don't look her way, focus on everyone else.* Four times he proposed they go to the buffet but was drowned out by someone's conversation. The urge became too strong. He slid a glance. She sat up, her face brighter, pressed an eye shut, quickly opened it then ran her tongue at a corner of her mouth. His sight went to Arturo, Sophia, Andrea, Millicent. "I think that's wrong," he said.

"What's wrong?" Sophia asked.

"What you were just saying."

"That we wanted pepperoni pizza?" Sophia chuckled. "Why? Is it poisoned?"

"He's the one who poisoned it." Andrea smiled. "Probably spit in it."

Arturo creased his face, let out exaggerated yelps, said they'd ruined his appetite. The others rolled their eyes. Renaldo threw a straw at Arturo, advised he not take drama. Arturo laughed, said late night talk show hosts didn't have to worry about Renaldo stealing their job. The two chortled some more, Arturo asking if they were ready to eat. All jumped up except Wyatt, Conrad bumping him, Wyatt as stiff as the Cardiff giant.

"Hey," Conrad pushed. "Time to eat."

Wyatt stepped away, Conrad flashing past. She was next, her figure visible out of his eye's corner.

When the booth became unoccupied, Wyatt slid to the opposite end, watched friends choose their food then prayed anyone but Dawn be first to return.

The girl stood at the buffet closest to the booth. Wyatt stuck a fingernail between teeth and gnawed. She swerved to the buffet's other side, Andrea taking Dawn's spot, then made a straight line to Wyatt. He beamed as she sat next to him.

"You okay? You're looking at me like I'm your girlfriend."

"You are."

Andrea's eyes became small.

"You're a girl," Wyatt said. "And a friend so you're a girlfriend." He could not even force himself to laugh.

She pushed herself a few inches away and checked the others, waved Millicent over, got up, and permitted the other girl to sit in the booth then gave a wrinkled-brow stare at Wyatt before sitting down.

Wyatt's joints eased. The others sat, Conrad and his girl last to arrive. Wyatt saw her look at him. He put a hand to his cheek and leaned on it, fingers against his eye creating a manual wall. Conrad sat. Dawn continued. To the booth's other side.

Wyatt jolted. What had he been thinking? Why hadn't he been thinking? She asked him to squeeze in. He said there was no room. She argued there was, requested everyone slide down. When all protested, Wyatt pointed to Conrad and the spot next to him. She frowned but did as told. Though he tried to avoid looking to her, Wyatt caught a few passes, turned away each time.

Sophia chewed then spoke. "You think God or whoever created us put us here for a specific purpose?"

"Who knows?" Arturo wiped his mouth. "Okay, why did I answer that?"

"Because I'm teaching you how to be intelligent and it's finally sinking in."

Huh-huhs from the rest.

"Seriously," Sophia continued. "Why are we here? Do we have a purpose? Do things happen as part of a greater plan?"

"Perhaps some is destiny," Wyatt said to distract himself from Dawn. "Like people who meet and are immediately attracted to each other." He looked Dawn's way then quickly back to Sophia. "Maybe it is to be. But when someone forces themselves on another..." He frowned at Dawn, who rose and sank discreetly in the booth. "...that's a choice. Free will."

"So He doesn't have a plan?" Arturo said.

"Attaboy, you're listening." Sophia patted her boyfriend.

"No, He doesn't." Wyatt leaned back. "What better way to explain why good happens to bad people and vice versa?"

The group moved heads up and down in unison.

"I mean, September eleventh," Wyatt said. "That was part of His plan?"

"Of course not," Sophia raised her voice. "It's—"

"But if *He* has a plan, wasn't that part of it? And what about the Holocaust? Did that..."

"Okay, okay." Sophia held up a hand. "You win."

"Not trying to win," Wyatt said. "Just asking questions. Like you." He shifted his vision on Dawn. "I don't know. Maybe there is a big programmer up there with a plan but we ignore it. Ya think?" He glared at Dawn though Sophia responded agreement, said she wasn't trying to win either, only wanted to know how others felt.

Wyatt narrowed his eyes. "What do you think, Dawn?"

The girl returned the expression, confessed she believed in a plan though only a vague one. Her eyes became smaller.

"There are some who deny their opportunities for a big moment, ya know?" Her stare darkened.

"Well, we've worn out this subject." Arturo put his arm around Sophia. "Why don't we have some free will of our own, if ya know what I mean."

"Sounds great." Renaldo pulled out his cell phone and texted Katy. A ding a minute later had him look down. "Gotta go. Said she'll be studying a while and needs help." He typed and spoke as he did. "See ya soon." He shoved the phone in his pocket, stretched, and requested the others move to let him out.

"Oh no, we're keeping ya in line." Sophia grinned. "*We* have a plan. Keep ya here as long as possible."

Renaldo pushed her playfully, others toppling from this action, Renaldo forcing his way out, hands raised. "I won! Was meant to be. See ya." He left amongst waves and catcalls.

"The problem," Wyatt went on, "is no one knows what's meant to be and what's our own choice."

"Thought we nixed that debate," Arturo said. "Let's get a pick up basketball game going."

"After eating all this?" Wyatt yawned. "Don't have the energy."

"Aw, c'mon. We can burn off what we ate. Conrad?"

"Sounds good. Wanna come?" he asked Dawn.

The girl turned away, said she had school work and later, a shift at the gas station.

"Okay. See ya before you go to work." Conrad kissed her, got up with Arturo, they again offering Wyatt to join them.

He passed a short look Dawn's way then spoke to the guys. "Sorry. Gotta complete some assignments."

Conrad mentioned how Wyatt had said he was tired. Wyatt nodded to which Conrad asked how he could do homework. Wyatt clenched his jaw, words exploding in his mind like fireworks. Should he say them? Now was not the time. But he had to tell him. When? His head felt like it was in a tourniquet. He sighed. "Maybe I'll take a nap first."

"Guess that means we have to ask the girls to play," Arturo said. "Sophia?"

She agreed and all except Dawn and Wyatt went to the door.

"Aren't you going with them?" Wyatt asked.

"Said I had school work. Then my job."

"First, we must talk."

Dawn slid closer. "I'm listening."

Wyatt waved to the rest as they stood at the door then watched Conrad, whose face looked like he'd been poked with a sharp object. Wyatt glanced down. The others exited.

"Now," Wyatt began. "Let's get this straight. That was a one-time thing, a fluke. I'm not interested. I betrayed my friend." He thought of the name the others tagged him with and forced air down his lungs. "There's no attraction, I'm sorry. You're a great-looking girl, don't get me wrong. Conrad's lucky to have you. And you should appreciate him, he's supremely loyal, like a dog."

Dawn touched Wyatt's hand. "I want a man, not a pet."

Wyatt pulled his hand away. "Sorry." He stood. "Just can't let this go on. It's wrong." He headed toward the door. She grabbed him, turned him around.

"How is it wrong?"

"Didn't ya hear me? He's my friend."

"So? It's not like he and I are married."

"But he and I are friends."

"Are you?"

A pause. "Yes."

"You hesitated." She smiled. "Who's more important? Him or me?"

The inside of Wyatt's pants grew hot. It was a no-brainer, emotionally. The memory of the moment, combined with the current one, had him sweating and fearing his zipper would break. His thoughts shifted to Conrad then how he would feel if he'd found out Conrad humped his girl. His body cooled. "You just don't understand our friendship. Bet you never had one. A real, true one where you know your friends have your back. I can't betray them. Doubt you'd understand that."

Dawn stuck out her lower lip. "And I doubt you know anything about having a good time. What do we have in life but memories? Good times, having fun. Are you ever going to have those?" She shrugged. "All this talk about loyalty, self-respect, honesty, they're overrated. Who cares about those if you can make a lot of money, be successful, and enjoy life? I know you enjoyed what we did. I did. I only hope someday you won't look back and say, 'Damn, wish I'd done it with her again. And again. Forever'." She moved to the door.

"Not to worry, I won't," Wyatt said yet his groin heated up. He winced and swung back into the booth to hide himself. The door opened. She looked at him. He gritted his teeth, waved her out. She sighed and left.

He watched the car leave, remained seated another ten minutes. Driving home, he nearly turned around several times, toward her house. On each occasion, he pictured Conrad cheating on him as well as how the others would ridicule him with their moniker.

He made it to the place, glad the overeating had drained him although he surmised his constant questioning also had something to do with how he felt. He fell asleep, still unsure.

Chapter 12

Upon waking, Wyatt figured the hard part would be telling Conrad. He opened his American history book, aware of the upcoming quiz. Forty-five minutes later, he'd memorized none of what he'd studied, words he'd say to Conrad the only thing he could remember: *She's not right for you. There are better women. This wasn't meant to be.*

By the time voices penetrated through the door, Wyatt had a decent speech prepared.

Arturo and Renaldo entered, Renaldo holding up a twelve-pack, favor from an older friend. Seeing no one behind them, Wyatt exhaled. Footsteps outside. Another knock. The door opened, Sophia peeked in, then entered, and shut the door.

Wyatt relaxed as before. A third noise, a clang of metal. Wyatt's face went long. Conrad entered, Wyatt certain now wasn't the time. His gut ached so he drank his green tea, no sugar, and tried to watch television, hoped to make his friends' discussion background noise. It worked the other way around, Conrad eventually announcing he was on his way to Dawn's before she left for work.

"Hey," Wyatt said as the boy turned the knob.

"Yes?"

Wyatt paused, his words not sounding so good after all. He stayed silent. Conrad repeated his question.

"Maybe we should go out sometime," was all Wyatt could think to say.

"You have a crush on him?" Arturo teased.

Wyatt gave a smile though it receded hastily. He rephrased the request, said he needed help with algebra. Conrad told him to name the day. Wyatt said he would and Conrad left. Wyatt sank on the sofa, Arturo, Sophia, and Renaldo joining him, Arturo offering a beer. The friend declined. For now, avoiding Dawn as much as possible was his only answer.

* * * *

Not until Tuesday did Wyatt ask Conrad for assistance, softened the blow with a little bribery via take-out he'd gotten at a steak and burger place.

"Thanks," Conrad said, though Wyatt instructed they study first. After a sixty-minute session, Wyatt offered a break.

Conrad pulled a dish to him, set the food on it. Wyatt asked how he was. Conrad told of being with Dawn the day before, said though they were in the initial stages, he hoped four or five months would make things clearer, after which they'd get serious, perhaps move in together for a few months. Following that, he said he'd take the final step, planned possible ways he'd ask her. At Christmas with a big box and the question inside in fancy calligraphy. With a teddy bear, the ring on its finger. Or on her birthday.

Wyatt whoa'ed, gave Conrad the cliché of taking things one day at a time. Conrad pointed out that was what got the ant in trouble. Wyatt furrowed his brow. Conrad referenced the Aesop's fable of how one insect prepared for winter as the other took it day to day.

"I'm just saying you've got your whole life," Wyatt said. "Relax, enjoy this time before you enter the real world."

"I am enjoying it, thanks to Dawn. She's great, has really shown me how a relationship works."

"Well, now that you have some experience, you might try for someone better."

"Better?" Conrad stopped chewing.

"Yeah. The first isn't always the best. Sometimes things seem right when they aren't."

"Sure." Conrad took a drink. "Whatever." He turned the algebra book to his side of the table. "Ready?"

Wyatt studied the other boy, he showing no recognition. "Okay."

The next chance came an hour later, Conrad saying how tough his English Literature assignment had been, Dawn nearly losing her temper with him. Wyatt sat up, grasped Conrad's wrist. "See? Women get moody, bitchy, Dawn included."

When Conrad disagreed, Wyatt pointed out they hadn't had a crisis.

Conrad pressed his back into the chair, facial features as if he'd caught Wyatt trying to steal something. "Whadya mean?"

"I mean you don't know people unless you hit a rough patch."

Conrad let go of his pencil, motioned with his fingers. "What?"

Wyatt's turn to sit up. "What?"

"You want to tell me something. What? Dawn say something?"

"Uh-uh. Just want to caution you about women. They—"

"I had this talk with my dad and in much more depth. You guys think I'm a geek but I'm more confident than you realize. Now tell me."

Wyatt knew he had no choice. He put his arm around his friend. "Have to tell you."

"What?"

Wyatt leaned in, inhaled, counted to five, and let the breath out. "Dawn and I, we...." He put a hand over his mouth and withdrew from Conrad. "Had a moment together. Her and I." He ah-hemmed. "In bed."

Conrad's eyes became bulbous. His Adam's apple bobbed. He folded his arm. "I don't believe it."

"It's true." Wyatt gave some details.

"You're making it up."

"Why?"

"Jealous? Wish you had somebody?"

"I'm telling the truth. I'll call her."

"No. I know you're lying but even if you're not, I want to talk to her face to face, see her reaction."

"I'm sorry." Wyatt sank a heavy hand on his friend's shoulder. "Had to tell the truth." He displayed hands in surrender mode. "Never happen again, I swear." He crossed the hands as if a referee signaling an incomplete pass. "Not that I don't find her attractive but she's yours, told her I wasn't interested." He hugged Conrad who did not return the favor. "I'm so sorry."

Conrad was immobile. Wyatt moved away, said if they needed to talk, he would. He watched Conrad's chin vibrate, his eyes blurry. Conrad raised a forearm to them.

"I understand." Wyatt went to pat his friend.

Conrad's arm changed direction. Toward Wyatt. It landed on the bridge of his nose with a harsh crack. Wyatt toppled.

"Bastard!" Conrad cried. "Fucking liar! I'll show you!" He pirouetted, wrapped fingers around the doorknob, sprinted out, and slammed the door. The building rattled. Feet on concrete like a soldier on march. They pattered off.

Wyatt wiped his nose, red droplets on a finger. He ran his shirt sleeve over the nose. More red dots. He grabbed a paper towel from the kitchen and rubbed it on his nose until no red appeared on the sheet.

"Damn," he whispered, limped to his room, shut the door, and fell on the bed. Nearly an hour passed before he drifted off.

* * * *

Conrad's tires lost some rubber on the way to Dawn's, he hardly able to see through visual wetness, nearly missed the police car, radar pointed at the street. He raised his foot off the pedal though only for half a block. Not until he reached her place did the foot come off again. He jumped out, slammed the door, stomped to the house, and hit the doorbell many times then wiped his eyes.

A chubby brown-haired girl opened the door. Conrad had met her twice, Dawn introducing her as Colleen. She asked what he wanted.

"Dawn. Need to talk to her. Now." He fisted hands. When Colleen didn't respond, he brushed her aside. "Dawn?"

"In here. I'm coming."

"No, I am!" Conrad rushed to her bedroom door. She moved the door from its frame just as he arrived. Both stepped back.

"Sorry," Dawn said.

"I'll bet," Conrad fumed.

She held up a hand. "What's wrong?" She stayed silent for a pause then nodded, stiffened. "Wyatt talk to you? What did he say?"

Conrad admitted such, told her.

The girl scoffed, accused Wyatt of lying, slid her hands around Conrad's midriff, lifted them up to his back then wiped away the leftover water in his eyes. "He's lying." She kissed him. "He came on to me. I warned I'd kick him between the legs if he didn't stop. When he didn't and I followed through, he was so humiliated he ran out and sped away."

Conrad nodded, about to sigh, then retreated a step as his brow sank. "Why didn't you tell me this when it happened?" He watched her face, frozen. She then smiled, sidled back up to him, arms quickly around his neck.

"Too upset. Then I figured what you didn't know wouldn't hurt you. Anyways..." She put her lips on him. "I felt embarrassed, feared you wouldn't believe me, accuse me of wanting to ruin your friendship." She smothered his face with her lips, pushed him into the room, and shut the door. They helped each other shed their clothes.

* * * *

The next day, Conrad returned to the apartment, Wyatt at his car. The two stood like old west gunmen.

"I appreciate you telling me what happened," Conrad called out sarcastically, stepped toward the other boy. "Though I got the real scoop from Dawn. Thanks anyways."

Wyatt rushed up and grabbed Conrad's shirt collar, demanded the friend tell him what Dawn claimed. When Conrad finished—omitting how it ended—Wyatt pushed him back.

"If you want to believe that lying bitch, nothing I can do. But when sex takes priority, nothing else matters. So live in your fantasy world. Just don't cry to me when she cheats again. Later."

Wyatt entered his car and left, Conrad remaining where he was long after the sound of the vehicle faded. Turning to the apartment, Conrad thought then shook his head. She was telling the truth, Wyatt too embarrassed. Perhaps she'd told Wyatt she was going to press charges.

Yeah, he thought, entered the building. *That's it. Wyatt wouldn't have waited a month if she'd come on to him, would have bragged to us.* Yet he wondered, *If she said they didn't have sex, why would Wyatt claim they did and say she came onto him? Because*, his mind said, *What guy doesn't want a woman coming on to him?* But Wyatt? When did he boast? Then again, no guy, even Wyatt, waited a month to tell someone.

Conrad pushed this out of his consciousness, watched TV, Arturo soon coming over. Conrad said nothing of Wyatt's claim or Dawn's reply.

* * * *

The following series of Saturdays had everyone doing their own thing, each saying they had other plans then, eventually, mid-terms.

An invite by Renaldo to the bar one Thursday brought them together, Wyatt continuing to avoid Conrad, didn't speak to him at their place. Once he knew Wyatt would be there, Conrad promptly declined and, when asked why, replied he was too tired.

Millicent also declined, claimed a next day exam although she did anything but study, her mood improving little since the incident—*Non-incident*, as she called it—with the guy on New Year's Eve. She visualized herself at eighty: Gray haired, wrinkled, stooped, cane in hand. Alone. No children, family, nor friends. Attempting to dismiss this as unnecessary pessimism didn't help, she unable to avoid shuddering.

Deciding the group had her self-conscious about being alone—even Conrad, the one who would've been voted most likely to wind up a virgin, had someone—she chose to avoid them a while—hearing of or seeing others succeed at what she wanted causing acute inferiority. Fortunately the job helped her mood, kids never asking what her grades were, what her major was, or if she had a boyfriend.

She sighed. In less than half a day she'd be at work, concerns forgotten, if only temporarily. It was enough to help. For now.

* * * *

Renaldo hadn't picked Thursday due to it being dollar cover night and two dollar draws for longnecks but because it'd been nearly two months since his last drinking event. Or, as he called it, his last *serious* drinking event, the previous nights and weekends nothing more than having a beer, not getting so much as a buzz. Mid-terms were over, he'd done well, and spring break was nigh, the whole gang to South Padre Island, Texas, *the* party spot for spring breakers in south central U.S.

When asked, Conrad hemmed about other plans.

"Other plans? Like what? Studying?" Renaldo boomed. When Conrad said he was tired, Renaldo stated break wasn't for a couple of weeks. Conrad said he couldn't afford it. Renaldo reminded him he'd already paid. Conrad said he'd think about it.

Wyatt had given a like response.

"What's wrong with you people?" Renaldo had said. "You act like you're over the hill. C'mon." He rallied the other five to get excited.

Katy pressed herself to him. "You'd better be careful down there." She made fingers in a V, pointed them at her eyes then his. He laughed, proclaimed he'd been dry since New Year's.

"Okay," she relented. "We'll see."

"I promise."

Thursday evening was like other nights at the bar: lots of dancing and drinking although Renaldo held his own. At the end of a slow dance with Katy, he rewarded his discipline with a long neck, chased that with a shot of Tequila then a second before he returned to the group, stayed quiet.

Evening passed into early morning. Renaldo drank a beer each time a friend danced with Katy then consumed more in a corner. At one point, he, with two cups in hand, brushed past Andrea.

"Isn't that a little much? Ya know, we shouldn't even be in here."

"Aw, they don't care, wouldn't have let us in if they did, bribery or otherwise. Have fun."

When Andrea commented she didn't need drinks to do that, Renaldo scorned she only said that because she had trouble holding her alcohol and couldn't admit it.

She put a hand on him. "You'd better stop or you might have a wreck if you decide to drive."

He asked what she meant then saw Katy look at his cups and glare. "First one," he told her, said he'd gotten the second one for her at which Andrea faced Katy and stated it wasn't true. Renaldo confessed it was his second. Andrea offered to bet he'd had more. The boy made faces at her then, with a straight look, demanded proof she knew of his exact consumption. She mentioned New Year's Eve, the serious harm he could have caused.

Katy joined the two. "New Year's Eve? What harm?"

"Nothing." Renaldo set one of his cups surreptitiously on a table behind him. "Nothing happened. We went out, had a great time."

"He nearly crashed into me while driving."

Renaldo accused her of being the drunk one that evening, claimed he'd gone home without so much as a cop suspecting him of wrongdoing.

"Probably don't remember," Andrea said.

"Neither do you!" he shot back. "Anyways, how did you know it was me? Coulda been anyone."

Andrea chuckled. "In a gray truck with black racing stripe?"

Renaldo watched Katy's eyes gain a steely edge. "I barely had anything," he pleaded.

"All it takes is one or two." Katy slapped the cup out of his hand, seized his arm, and ordered him to leave with her.

Renaldo pulled free. "I'm staying! Night's still young."

"Then I'm leaving. We're through!" Katy stomped away.

"Thanks a lot!" Renaldo shouted at Andrea who shrugged, said he should be thankful she hadn't done worse, could've had him arrested that night.

"Snitch," Renaldo snarled. "Bitch!"

Andrea slapped him then did the same as Katy. Renaldo returned to the bar.

* * * *

Wyatt sat alone at the group's table. A tap at his shoulder. He turned. And stopped halfway. "Oh no." He stood, watched Arturo spot this and motion to Sophia, Wyatt knowing Arturo would ask his girl what was happening.

Dawn's arm went around Wyatt. He pushed it down. She repeated the gesture, this time slapping the other arm on him. He tried to duck. She pulled him in, kissed him.

"Told you we're through." Wyatt squirmed free and started towards the door, now close enough to Sophia and Arturo he knew they'd hear him. "You screwed my friend. Then me. Literally and figuratively. You meet a guy, come on to him until you've got him in bed then move on to another and get him. And so on."

"Which is why you should be thanking me." She smiled. "Saved you from future mockery."

"So? You lied to Conrad, continue to lead him on, and now he and I are avoiding each other." He glanced at Arturo and Sophia, they as if hypnotized.

Dawn's arms on Wyatt distracted him.

"Forget about Conrad, he's a guy," the girl susurrated. "I'm much more enjoyable than he'd ever be."

"Sorry." Wyatt escaped her possession. "It's over. See ya." He started then looked back, Dawn unblinking. "I mean, I hope I never see ya." Out the door, into light-filtered darkness he went, drove away, and checked the time. Probably too early, Conrad still awake. He rode in his car until he surmised the roommate had gone to sleep.

* * * *

"What was that all about?" Arturo asked.

"Don't know," Sophia said. "Did he say they—"

"I believe so. Maybe we can find out." Arturo hurried to the lot and checked. Wyatt wasn't there nor was his car. "Should we ask Conrad?"

"No, it's their problem, don't need us meddling." Sophia pointed. "Don't go asking Conrad any personal questions or I'll slap you."

"I won't, promise."

"Good. They need to work this out." She started to say, "Like we did" but held back, would have choked up if she hadn't. "Let's go home."

"Why? We're having fun."

Sophia recalled the night of the fire and though they were on the path to recovery—had recovered—she used great effort to repress the tears, forced a yawn, and said she was tired. The photo flashed in her mind in sync with her heartbeat. But they'd reconciled. Why had she kept the picture? She had no answer.

"Let's go home," she said again and led Arturo to the car, he inquiring if she was all right. She put a hand on her forehead, claimed she'd had too much to drink.

Arturo laughed that she could only be punch drunk.

"No," she said and though it took great effort, smiled. "Didn't drink any punch."

Her boyfriend laughed some more then stopped, held her, and planted a kiss on her. "You are too funny." He looked at her. "Did I ever tell you I love you?"

"Not enough."

"Well, I love you, I love you, I love you." He kissed her forehead. "That'll make you feel better, the way a mom's kiss heals her kid."

"Thanks." Sophia laughed but in a broken way. He opened the car door for her. She looked at him like she was Linus, he the security blanket, thanked him, and entered.

He drove her back, she reminding him not to ask Conrad or Wyatt about Dawn. He promised, leaned in to kiss her. The picture again in her mind as well as that night at the club despite being told by all nothing had happened between him and that girl. Phoebe, she now recalled, wished she hadn't. A tear escaped her eye.

"You okay?" Arturo wiped it away.

The girl answered in the affirmative. He frowned, asked what it was. She said she was fine, had something in her eye, rubbed the spot, said it was now okay, and reiterated to herself she should move on. He'd asked—begged—forgiveness. And she'd given it. She smiled. "Thanks."

"Sure," Arturo replied.

She watched him inch closer, his eyes now shut, lips curved up. She did the same, thanked the Almighty they had made up, unlike Conrad and Dawn. Or Wyatt and Dawn, could only guess where that was headed. Her arms went around his body. He did the same. They fell in the front seat, undid their pants, and climaxed quickly. However, Sophia did not feel complete.

Chapter 13

At Conrad's apartment the next week, he and Arturo planned spring break. Wyatt entered and started toward his room. Arturo called him, led him to Conrad.

"Sophia told me to stay out but how is this good? Conrad told me his version. What's yours?"

Wyatt stared down Conrad. Arturo asked Conrad to leave the room then asked for the other boy's side. Done, Arturo called Conrad out, described what had been said. Conrad protested Wyatt had come on to Dawn. Wyatt swung an arm. Arturo intervened, said this wasn't helping.

"Conrad?" Arturo faced his friend, told him what he'd seen at the club with Dawn and Wyatt, said Sophia would back him, asked Conrad if he wanted a girl who cheated. The other boy fiddled with his hands in his lap, said he wanted evidence proving Dawn had done as Wyatt professed. Arturo repeated the night's events, how Sophia saw it too.

"Well…" Conrad sighed. "I love her. I really do. Thought she might be…ya know."

"There're lot more," Arturo said. "No guy wants to get married anyway. Why do you think man invented golf? To get away from the old hag."

The three chuckled.

"Now, Wyatt." Arturo looked at him. "You admit you shouldn't have done what you did?"

"I guess."

"You guess?" Conrad growled.

"Okay, I admit it. I'm sorry. But I came clean. We're friends. That means more to me than sex."

Arturo bug-eyed.

Wyatt laughed. "Maybe not sex." He offered a hand to Conrad. They shook. Arturo stood while the two clapped each other's back.

"Problem solved." Arturo's face shone. "Sophia'll be so proud."

The three shook hands, sat, and watched TV.

"Ya know," Arturo said to Conrad during a break, "Dawn's not your kind of girl."

"So who is?" Conrad's eyes pinched. "And where is she? Did I miss her, too involved with Dawn? How will I know?"

"Dude," Arturo admonished. "Calm down. Way down. You sound like a girl."

Conrad started to speak. The other two put hands at their ears, Arturo then pretending to be in front of a commode, bent over. Wyatt laughed, Conrad managed a smile, and they watched television.

* * * *

In his room that evening, Conrad listed questions mentally like flip cards. Did he really want it to be over? What if she was the one? But she'd cheated, no longer wanted him. Or so Wyatt said. Was he lying? The guy always told the truth. And had said he'd broken things off with her. Conrad felt there was one thing left to do. He went to the front door, told his friends he had an errand. When they asked, he said he'd tell them when he got back.

At Dawn's front porch, they talked, she not allowing him in, betrayed no emotion.

"So you're okay with it?" Conrad said.

"Why be loyal to guys when they never are?" She sneered. "All men are created equal. They all want to cheat."

Conrad frowned, said he wasn't that way but it didn't matter, it was over between them as far as he was concerned.

The drive back was difficult, his eyes manufacturing a few tears. Wasted time. Why had they met if it wasn't meant to be? Had he missed out on the right girl? His friends' mockery of such questioning had him cease the interrogating.

Back at the apartment, he informed his friends though the questions continued, a revolving door in his mind. The two praised him, promised a night on the town. Though he didn't say it, Conrad felt more like going to bed. For a few days. Instead, he followed them, had a couple of drinks at *The Depot* but spent his time at their table.

That night, he slept poorly. And the next. That week. On four occasions, he grabbed his phone and prepared a speech. Each time he hit the *off* button after pressing the first three numbers.

* * * *

The day following her argument at the club, Katy's phone vibrated in class. She checked the number. And tossed the receiver back into her purse. Only after classes and dinner and homework did she play back what he'd left her, numerous calls and texts. She wished she had the courage to hit *delete all*, instead read or listened to what he'd said. They were the same, he requesting forgiveness, promising he'd change, said he'd do whatever to get her back. Though he didn't seem the type to do anything drastic, Katy had trouble thinking anything else. She dialed his number. A click.

"Listen, Katy, honey, don't hang up. I'm sorry, won't do it again. Please."

No reply.

"I promise, I won't. I mean it. Katy?"

The girl remained unresponsive.

A heavy breath. "I won't drink anymore, I swear. Please, Katy..." Sniffles. "I love you."

"You swear you won't drink?" the girl said at last.

"I do, I swear. Never again."

"If I see any hint showing you broke your vow, I'm gone. This is it, no more. You promise?"

"I do."

"Good. I hope you're right." She let out a long, slow stream of air, said he was a nice guy, independent, and hard-working, went to college full time and worked, most guys having trouble just going to school. She suggested he harness his desire to play.

"Work hard, play hard, I say."

"No, you should slow down, enjoy things. This time won't ever come back, is the most exciting period for us. We're young, full of hope, our whole lives ahead. Before long, we'll be women and men, out in the real world with real concerns."

Renaldo sarcastically thanked her for the pep talk. She said she was only advising to enjoy things now, not ruin them. For her. For him. Them.

A short silence.

"So," Renaldo said. "When are we going to party?"

"That's it, I'm hanging up."

"Katy, I'm joking," Renaldo said quickly.

"You sure?"

"Positive. Just had to get it out of my system." His voice calmed and he invited her over, Arturo not back till later. He offered a candlelight dinner then confessed it'd be Chinese take out, said he'd still light some candles. She asked if he had any and he allowed he didn't, requested she bring some then laughed. "But I *will* light them."

She chuckled. He promised soft music—"I do have that," he teased—and no alcohol. Katy sighed, said she'd be over.

The night was quiet, the noisiest moment when Renaldo dropped beer bottles, a few still full, into the trash bag with a *clink* then tossed the bag in the outside dumpster. Not long after dinner, they were in bed, Arturo waking them later upon his arrival. Katy left the next morning but not before Renaldo made her agree to a following date. She departed with the feeling this was the beginning of something good. And long-lasting.

Renaldo stayed in bed, spring break almost upon them. He imagined he and her on the beach. Perfect situation to ask. But that was the future, he now entering a new phase of his life. A better one. A non-dependent one. He would avoid his parents' fate after all.

Chapter 14

South Padre was a great time despite more rainy days than sunny ones, Arturo and Sophia spending most of the break by themselves, he thinking next year he'd ask.

* * * *

Although he went in a downer mood, Conrad had fun, swam in the ocean, and saw some sites. One afternoon he and Millicent soaked up rays, chatted future plans, upcoming classes, and next semester's course load. Conrad spoke of other signature moments, gave details of his breakup, how he worried the right one had passed him by.

"Thought only women did that," Millicent said.

"A few guys, I guess." Conrad closed his eyes. "Though I'm the only guy I know. I just wonder."

Millicent assured him he'd be successful. He mumbled, "I dunno," got up, and took another swim.

A while later, Andrea ran past, a guy behind her, arousing Millicent who watched the two chase each other into the ocean. Millicent smirked. Would Andrea ever be patient? The couple splashed each other, soon with arms intertwined. The girl on the beach shook her head, offered a prayer for her own chance with the right person, would never let it go nor give up so fast.

A muscular, older guy stopped in Millicent's path of vision, ten feet from her. She estimated him to be mid-twenties. He didn't so much as turn her way. She pleaded mentally, contemplated why she wasn't like Andrea, her mother's reprimand about approaching men sounding in her internal speaker. Such actions were what got girls raped, assaulted, or killed. Give a guy an inch, the mother would say, and he'd take a life.

The guy walked on. Millicent's sadness resurfaced. Not even being on an idyllic beach with hundreds of available men improved her lot. She joined Conrad in the water.

* * * *

Renaldo kept his promise despite ubiquitous temptations, distracted himself during slow times by thinking what he'd do with her that night, how he'd use a different approach, she on top. Or a little foreplay. A candlelit room.

He and Katy jumped and splashed in the water, walked along the beach, he noticing alcohol wasn't needed for a good time. What might life be like without her? He shivered though the sun's rays saturated him. For an instant, he desired to seize her, set her down on the sand, envelope her with kisses, and ask. But it was too soon—*way too soon,* he reminded himself. Her response would send him right back to Jack Daniels and his other neighbors in that mahogany cabinet. He licked his lips. Her leading him back into the waves allowed the desire to pass unfulfilled. The time would come, he worried. Soon enough.

* * * *

The weeks after spring break were tumultuous, one test or term paper succeeding another, friends not at the pizza parlor until the week before finals.

"So, Conrad," Renaldo said after others praised him when he said he still hadn't touched alcohol since his vow to Katy, said his many tests, assignments, and part-time job had him away from taking a nip. He drank his Pepsi. "Gotten over Dawn?"

"Oh yeah," Conrad said though his jaw flinched and he frowned, dropped his pizza slice, and pushed the plate away.

"He never liked women," Wyatt said. "Why do ya think it was easy for him? He's not exactly, shall we say, a man's man."

The guys chuckled. Even Sophia and Millicent displayed dimples.

Conrad extended his tongue. "Yeah, well, y'all wish you'd had a relationship with someone that attractive."

Andrea smiled. "Not me."

"Me neither," Millicent said.

"I might," Sophia replied. "If the sex was good."

Everyone chortled. Arturo looked at Conrad, asked if it was good.

"How would he know?" Wyatt kidded.

The guys—except Conrad—laughed to where they held their stomachs. The girls, though smiling, hinted sympathetic facial views. Conrad shoved his dish against the salt/pepper/napkin holder at the table's center. Metal rang out. Arturo flinched and Renaldo grimaced, the girls covering their ears. All gazed at Conrad. He spoke as though upper and lower jaw were wired together.

"What the hell do any of you know about my relationships?"

Wyatt arched his lips. "Relationship."

"Whatever. But I did it before you did." Conrad's nostrils flared, mouth a wrinkled *I* on its side.

Wyatt scowled. "Only teasing."

"So was I. And I'm telling the truth about me and Dawn."

"I am too."

"How do we know?"

"Ask her."

"Probably bribed her to do it. Or say you did it."

The others roared, Arturo patting Conrad who smiled like he'd found the right girl.

"Fuck you," Wyatt seethed.

"Bet you wish that'd happened instead of with her."

No one other than Wyatt had a serious expression, Renaldo with tears, girls with face-splitting grins. Conrad's smile expanded and he sat back.

"Bastard." Wyatt stretched across the table. "I'll kick your ass."

Conrad opened his arms and muttered, "Was kidding. And like Mommy says, those who tease you care about you."

Grins widened. Arturo reassured Wyatt it was a joke.

"Yeah, well..." Wyatt looked at Conrad.

"Sorry." Conrad held a hand out. The other boy shook it then sat back.

They said little the rest of the time, Wyatt getting a few digs at Conrad, mimicked the friend's behavior and response of "Was kidding" when Conrad seethed amidst the chuckles. After the third incident, Conrad stood.

"Whatsa matter?" Arturo asked and his friend stated he had last minute cramming to do, mumbled "See ya," pushed himself out of the booth, and left.

* * * *

"Ridiculous," Conrad said at the apartment. "Always making fun of my relationships." Wyatt's comment sounded in his mind. "Relationship," he hissed. "Then they ridicule me like *I* should be ashamed. *He* betrayed *me*. Benedict." He slammed his door, flung himself on the bed, and pouted. He and Dawn were no longer. A small shower on his cheeks. He shoved his face into a pillow. Why had it happened this way? Tears flowed, he hopeful they'd wash away the pain. His heart still hurt as he fell asleep, choices scrolling through his mind. He'd do it. Or, rather, sleep on it then reconsider.

In morning light, he reached a decision. No grand announcement, no press conference amongst them, wouldn't so much as tell them unless they asked if he had plans for next semester. He could afford it, part of his education a scholarship. Slightly more expensive. But he'd have privacy. Peace and quiet. Most important, no more memory of what had been, could have been. Or, at least, it wouldn't be at the front of his mind, no objects nor people constantly evoking past events.

He turned the idea over in his thoughts, like a child examining a new toy. Same answer every time.

* * * *

Finals week atmosphere saturated the campus, each of the gang huddled in his or her bedroom.

The last day had the *r-r-r* of box tape being unrolled and pressed onto packages full of clothing, kitchen supplies, and stereo equipment; voices grunted as couches, chairs, and tables were carried out to pickup trucks and a moving van, parents and siblings offering assistance.

"That does it." Arturo wiped hands on his jeans as the others stood quiet and nodded, arms folded over chests. "Guess we'll meet up come August."

Most of us, Conrad thought, already mentally cataloguing possible places he'd check out. *A home,* he told himself. *With backyard where I can enjoy the peace, listen to the sounds of nature. Or go inside and fuck any girl with complete privacy. And no one to steal her away.*

The jibes from the last time they were at the pizzeria pierced him like a sword at his aorta. He asked himself if this was what he really wanted to do. Nearly four years of friendship destroyed as quick as a beach home in a hurricane.

Sophia said she'd miss everybody, even if they were just across town and for but a few months. Conrad felt a sting in his eyes, she putting into words his thoughts save for the part of a few months. Yet those comments, the approving laughs, the failure of his first, perhaps only, relationship stung more than the emptiness of knowing he wouldn't see them.

"Hope you're not getting all mushy," a voice jarred Conrad back to the present. He steeled his eyes, moisture on them evaporating like steam. He blinked, faced the speaker. "Sure thing, Benedict."

Wyatt said nothing, his smirk replaced by a reddened face. With parents surrounding them, he asked Arturo to help him shove things tighter into his car. The rest exchanged hugs and handshakes, promised to stay in touch.

"Let's meet in a few weeks," Sophia said.

They all showed approval though no date was set. In a short time, the parking lot in front of the three apartments was empty, sounds of engines fading into the distance like a shrinking storm.

Chapter 15

Not until a few days following the mid-summer celebration that ends with pyro-technics in the night sky did the friends satiate their appetites with an all-you-can-eat pizza buffet.

"Am starved," Renaldo said, blamed his full time job though he said he enjoyed the work. He and Katy became more intimate, he thankful for her presence, his parents continuing their habit, he seeing less of them than any time he could recall, spent most nights visiting Katy. As they curled up on a red love seat and watched *Casablanca* the night before the group met, he asked aloud about his parents' behavior, what made them do what they did.

"Why so introspective?" Katy said.

Renaldo credited Sophia's desire to be Aristotle. Katy kissed him, teased he should ask Sophia. They made out, his questions never answered.

* * * *

Millicent worked at the daycare, felt more alive than ever, seemed to learn more from the kids than they did from her, worries of having her man of the world no longer front page, bold headlines for her psyche. She contemplated such questions only when seeing Arturo and Sophia or Renaldo and Katy hugging and kissing, found herself gaining solace with the morbidly joyful realization Conrad's relationship had ended.

Upon entering the pizza place, she inquired as to Conrad, he the only one absent. Arturo separated from Sophia, checked the table then the restaurant.

"Didn't know he wasn't here." He looked at his watch. "Still early."

"Besides," Wyatt sniffed, "he's probably out screwing the first girl he sees, is the second coming of Hugh Hefner after all."

This time no one laughed. When the big hand on her watch passed several numbers, Sophia phoned Conrad, received voice mail, and reminded him of their luncheon. The group then ate their fill, sat around, and discussed fall enrollment. Sophia viewed her phone. No messages. She wondered aloud about Conrad, Wyatt again trying to slide sarcasm into the dialogue. Sophia frowned and the boy shrank while the rest fidgeted, offered meek responses before Sophia suggested they go by his house. No one offered to volunteer, Sophia included. The subject changed, Renaldo mentioning his earlier questions with Katy.

"The missus and I were on the sofa together and—"

"Missus?" Arturo said. "You guys elope?"

Renaldo's face went red. "I mean, Katy and I were on the sofa together—"

"Doing what?" Arturo grinned.

"Whadya think?"

The guys laughed, girls smirking, Katy's face the color of blood as she hit and mildly scolded her boyfriend.

"Seriously..." Renaldo brought up past discussions, posed the question of if things were meant to be.

Sophia looked to Arturo, he still busy eating. She knocked crumbs from his hand. He looked at her as if he'd been punished for getting all A's. She pinched his arm, said he should listen, might do him good.

Wyatt argued how events could be twisted, as with Nostradamus's predictions, how every time a tragic event unfolded, his followers would search his quatrains for one that fit the circumstance. "Kind of self-fulfilling, eh?"

"I have a thought," Renaldo said. The rest reacted as if in a hospital delivery room, nurse coming out to announce the news.

Renaldo raised his glass. "Let's par-tay!!" He chugged his soft drink and kissed Katy, who giggled.

Sophia and Millicent rolled their eyes, Arturo's thumb went up. Wyatt said nothing. Andrea whooped, gave Renaldo a slap of palms.

"Sounds great!" Andrea yelled. "Let's go!"

Sophia studied her. "You've been awful quiet. Everything good?"

"Slow summer," Andrea moaned. "Had but one summer school class, couldn't even find part time work although I wasn't going to take any job. No way I'm doing this." She made a fist, flipped the hand counterclockwise. "Burger flipper I ain't."

"That's why you're down?" Sophia replied.

"No. It's just been slow. And Mr. Right walked out on me again."

The gang chuckled, Wyatt and Arturo kneading their foreheads, Sophia wanting details. Andrea described her dad's company picnic where she met a guy, went out a few times before he abruptly ended it.

Sophia's lips sank. "Why?"

Andrea gave a *Huh*. "Said it was him, not me."

"Oh no." Sophia rubbed her eyes. "What'd ya do to him?"

Andrea placed a hand on her chest, said true friends never blamed one another, only supported them.

Sophia responded these were not true circumstances, made quotation marks when saying *true*. "We know ye, girl." Sophia touched Andrea gently. "Every guy is the one. You go too fast. Guys don't want fast women, want to control the pace." She passed a glance at each male. "Right?"

The guys nodded, Sophia responding, "See?"

Andrea agreed she rushed things but her guys wanted that. Sophia bequeathed her advice a second time. Andrea yawned she just wanted the break over, stood, and offered to meet at the bar, ten-ish.

Renaldo was up as if he'd been poked in the rear though his face was a smile. "Let's do it."

Katy pulled him down and before she got halfway through, "Now, Renaldo..." he swore he'd have one beer all night.

"Two, tops," he edited quickly.

"One," she said.

"Please?" he begged. "Only two. No more." His hand went up. "Promise."

"Only two." Katy displayed index and middle finger up. "I'm counting."

Renaldo smiled. "Didn't know you were that good at math."

She hit him but grinned. The group retreated, met at the door, and synchronized their agreement. That night they danced and partied, Renaldo keeping his word.

* * * *

Renaldo and Katy spent more time together, went on double dates with Sophia and Arturo, Sophia mentioning to the others they had to renew their leases. She sighed it was another year closer to graduation. And the real world. She instructed Arturo to research buying real estate, he replying he'd been checking local sales.

"Fortunately, you don't dally about that." Sophia put her hand on his. "My boyfriend, real estate tycoon."

The two smiled and kissed.

* * * *

The succeeding get together had all but Conrad present again, he claiming to be busy with schoolwork or family. On his own, however, he'd perused the classifieds, made a few calls, saw a house he liked, parents approving of it. Next week he'd sign the forms, tell friends about it sometime thereafter.

Friendship

* * * *

"Why isn't he here?" Sophia hit her hand on the restaurant table two weeks before fall semester, said she'd reminded him about the lease. Arturo squeezed her hand, asked her philosophical questions. She ignored them, said this had to be done, why were others so negligent, she having to rescue them?

"Thought you liked being there for others, feeling needed."

"Not with this." She picked up her phone, dialed, took the Lord's name in vain, and left a firm message, warned she wasn't going to do all the work if he wouldn't cooperate, concluded with "You'd better call" then pressed the *off* button so hard she shook her thumb, uttered more expletives.

"Mrs. Hitler, come to life," Renaldo said.

About to glare, Sophia saw him and the rest with upturned mouths. She respired and requested forgiveness. Her phone didn't ring and she checked the door every time it chimed. No Conrad. Her nails sank into her palms. She threatened bodily harm if he didn't show.

Ten minutes later, the number of friends at the table was the same. Sophia pounded a fist. Arturo petted her like a beloved dog. She shrugged him off, thrust out her cell phone, pounded the numbers, and announced each. The line rang. And rang. She cursed, awaited the recording, prepared what to say.

"Hello?" Conrad spoke as if they were best friends.

"H-hello?" she stammered, his live voice causing the prepared speech to drain from her mind, his tone causing her to speak calmly as she described the situation.

"Well, I have something to tell you regarding this."

Sophia lowered her eyebrows toward one another.

Chapter 16

"First, I'm right here in the parking lot," Conrad said.

Sophia gave thanks then snapped for him to get inside. The door opened and the girl turned off her cell phone and watched Conrad do the same, waved him to the table.

"Hey, guys." He straggled in as Sophia demanded to know where he'd been, why he hadn't called.

"Excuse me," Conrad spoke over her. "But I rented on campus to get *away* from my mother."

Sophia's eyes grew tinier. "Yes sir, Mr. Bigshot-I-am-a-man-because-I-was-in-bed-with-somebody."

Chuckles from the rest.

"And won't be doing it for a long time," Wyatt contributed.

More laughs.

Conrad flipped the bird. "Funny. However, you're to blame."

"For what?" Wyatt demanded.

"For what I'm about to say." Conrad sat, others with countenances like dogs who'd heard the bell.

"Well?" Arturo said.

"Tell us," Sophia added.

"C'mon," Millicent said.

"It's nothing personal. Just a choice I made."

The group's expressions changed, they now as if family members outside an intensive care unit. Conrad assured them he'd thought about it a long time, wanted to tell them when it felt right.

"Tell us what?" Andrea motioned her hand toward herself. "We're waiting."

"I..."

"Oh my God," Wyatt said and groaned. "Don't tell us."

Sophia cringed. "Tell us what?"

Wyatt stretched an arm, palm up. "He's coming outta the closet."

The gang gasped then moaned the way people do after seeing a fake scare in a movie.

"Shut up," Conrad snapped. "Now I know I made the correct decision."

"What are you talking about?" Andrea said.

"Yeah. My God, tell us," Millicent chimed in.

Sophia chuckled when Millicent used profanity, you knew you'd been waiting too long.

All eight laughed.

"Okay," Conrad said. "Promise you won't get mad?"

Sophia crumpled a napkin. "Enough already."

"Like I said, nothing personal. But..." Conrad released air from his lungs. "I'm moving out."

No one responded, their faces alike: Wrinkles below the hairline or at both ends of their eyes, noses curled.

"Moving out?" Arturo said. "Of where?"

"Okay, not moving out." Conrad forced a smile. "Moving on, somewhere else."

Gasps. Heads turned toward one another.

"Not out of town," Conrad said. "Just...somewhere else."

Arturo's mouth was limp, Millicent was matter of fact, Wyatt like he'd been told a show he never watched was canceled, Renaldo still interpreting the statement, Andrea's shoulder touching her ear, Katy's face indifferent. Only Sophia had a long face, her eyes as if he'd said he was leaving the country.

Conrad pointed out he'd be but a few minutes away, his chuckle sounding like a plate across a wood cabinet. "No big deal. Just want to try it out for a few months."

Sophia wanted to know why. Wyatt echoed her comments though his voice was like a cop questioning a suspect. Conrad did not respond for half a minute then looked down and shifted his head left to right. "Need a break," he mumbled.

"From what?" Andrea said.

"Us?" Sophia placed a hand on the boy.

Conrad answered, "No," then cracked a broken smile. "It's not you, it's me."

Renaldo, Arturo, and Wyatt all looked to the heavens, Wyatt muttering, "Gimme a break. We're friends, not lovers."

"Some of us are." Arturo reeled Sophia to him and smiled.

With slitted eyes, Wyatt requested more information from Conrad. The other boy did not answer. Wyatt motioned a hand as if calling his dog.

"What?" Conrad laughed. "Thought you didn't want to get this personal, intimate, we're friends not lovers. Don't worry, though, we'll still see each other. Might join ya here if ya let me know."

"Might?" Sophia said. "You will, won't you?"

Conrad looked at the floor, commented he'd never noticed how many cracks were in it.

Sophia asked again. Conrad's view didn't shift. She said it a third time. He gave a low-tone, "I guess."

"Don't sound so enthusiastic," Wyatt said.

"I just..." Conrad exhaled a thick breath. "Need a break from everything." He pushed arms closer to his chest.

"You said that." Wyatt wriggled fingers, raised his voice, said he wanted the truth.

"That *is* the truth." Conrad's tone was that of an innocent accused of a felony.

Wyatt reclined, replied his friend was hiding the real reason.

"I'm not gonna take this," Conrad groused.

Wyatt repeated his words.

Conrad slammed a hand on the table, stood, and said that was enough, he was never coming back. He stepped to the door.

"Look at chicken little," Wyatt teased. "Runs when he has to stand up for himself." He flapped arms. "Bok-bok-bok."

Conrad's glance met Wyatt's, the former's eyes as if afire while he thrust a finger. "You!" he bellowed. "You're the damn reason!"

Patrons stared. Sophia shushed Conrad.

"Fuck you." Conrad hit his chest. "Don't tell me to be quiet! I'm an adult, able to live on my own. And that's what I'm doing." He shoved his index finger toward Wyatt's face. "Because of you!"

"Me?" Wyatt gave a quick *yuk*. "What'd I do?"

Conrad laughed. "What'd you do? Not much. Merely ruined my relationship with a girl. First *true* love." His voice broke and he blinked rapidly, cleared his throat then thrust his face in front of Wyatt's. "It's your damn fault!" He withdrew. "Hope you can sleep at night. Asshole." He glanced at Sophia, his voice mimicking a five year old. "Sorry for swearing, Mommy. Do I have to go to my room now?" He shoved his backside at her. "Gonna give me a spanking, Mommy?"

"You little shit." Arturo shot up, tried to escape the booth but Sophia restrained him. He ordered her to let go. She told him to be quiet as an employee headed toward them—a muscular, mid-twenties guy with tattoos on both arms.

Sophia pushed Arturo down, led Conrad to the booth's edge, and had him sit. The employee asked if something was wrong then warned if they had any more disruptions, they'd be out the door and he'd call police if needed.

Sophia said it was okay. The man displayed fang-like teeth, said he would be watching, and went back to his duties. The girl requested Conrad state his side of the story.

"Said what I had to. He ruined my relationship." With a thick swallow and eyes down to pinpricks, Conrad stared at Wyatt and wiped at the moist corner of an eye. "Hurts too much being with you guys. Always mocking me, saying I'm gay."

"Not always." Arturo displayed a tiny smile. "Sometimes you seem depressed."

Sophia rapped knuckles on Arturo's arm. He cursed her.

"Hope you're happy…," Conrad said to Wyatt, mouth as if ready to spit. "…Benedict. Appropriate, huh?" He walked away, lifted an arm to the top half of his face, ran it across then reached for the door, and swung it wide. It clacked as it shot back, caught itself, and closed with a soft *click*.

The others slumped.

"Thanks a lot, Benedict," Renaldo whined.

Wyatt protested it wasn't his fault, Conrad chose to feel pain instead of moving on.

"How can you say that?" Sophia said.

Wyatt said he'd done so, said feelings were a matter of choice.

"So every emotion we feel is our own doing?" Sophia's eyes were as narrow as Conrad's had been.

"Sure. You choose to feel sad or happy."

"So all who lost loved ones on September eleventh *chose* to feel sad?"

Wyatt flicked a crumb at Sophia. "Sometimes you're so dense, so wrapped up in this philosophy bullshit, you don't hear the comment."

Sophia put fisted hand under her chin. "Go ahead. I'm listening."

"All I'm saying is he has to move on. Was six fucking months ago." Wyatt looked to the kitchen. The tattooed guy didn't come out. "In this case, yes, he must get over it. He's upset, I understand. I was."

"You?" Andrea said as if Wyatt had confessed he was gay.

"Yes, me. I have feelings." The boy's face was like he'd chewed something bitter. "But that's nobody's business. Move on, they'll go away. Unless you're a wuss."

"So it's not your fault the relationship ended?" Sophia asked.

Wyatt tapped Sophia's head. "Hello? Anything in there? Listen. Stop with the quasi-psychology lessons. Sure, I shouldn't have done it. But she became bored and wanted someone else." His tone eased. "Why he still wants her, who knows? I don't want somebody who sleeps around."

"Unlike yourself," Sophia replied.

"Why are you persecuting *me*? I apologized, broke off the relationship. Conrad's still thinking about it, blaming someone else."

"He's right," Arturo said. Wyatt extended a hand and heaped praise on his friend.

Sophia was open-mouthed. "How?"

"Conrad has to get over it."

"But Wyatt betrayed Conrad," Andrea added. "That's okay?"

Arturo waved his hand. "No, no, no. He screwed up, no pun intended. And yes, that's his fault." A corner of his mouth lifted as he turned to Wyatt. "Ever think of changing your name? Benedict fits, ya know."

Wyatt's jaw drooped, his face a lighter tone of peach. Arturo laughed, reassured his friend he was behaving properly, the affair happened, nothing could change it.

Sophia shook her head, wanted to know how these two held such cavalier attitudes.

"Me too," Andrea said.

"Renaldo?" Sophia said.

The boy started to speak then looked to Katy. "Depends."

"C'mon," Arturo said. "What do you *really* think?"

Renaldo viewed the girls then the guys, looked at Katy, and made her promise she'd keep her cool.

With downturned mouths, all the girls groaned. When Renaldo protested he hadn't said anything, Sophia said his non-reply spoke for him. The guys stared, mouths open, girls demanding to know what their problem was. Both sides argued, finally agreed to disagree, and went home.

"I still don't believe you guys," Sophia said to Arturo as he drove and when he said he didn't want to discuss it, Sophia said she did. They went back and forth. By the time he'd reached her house, they weren't speaking. She mumbled, "Thanks" and slammed the car door, sprinted to the house without looking back, opened and closed that door as if trying to shut out a cold night.

Her cell phone rang. She saw the number, pressed talk. "What?" she said firmly. He demanded to know why the fuss. She gave a hasty, "Good night" and hung up.

Arturo called Renaldo. "What the hell happened? Why is she so damn mad at me?" He then dialed Wyatt. Both agreed with Arturo, Wyatt inquiring what to do regarding a roommate. Arturo offered all three guys rent an apartment like the girls, called Renaldo, who approved the new agreement.

* * * *

Sophia did not fall asleep at her usual time, thought about each question: Did Arturo really think it wasn't a big deal, someone betraying a friend with their mate? Was he doing this? Why? With whom? She filed through her memory to moments where he hadn't been with her for stretches. Like now, they living at home, not near each other. But no way he'd bring a girl home, let alone sleep with her there. And during the semester? She had no memories of them not together. Or were those times he was gone a while innocently forgotten? That might explain his defense of Wyatt. If one thought themselves generous, they had to do generous things. And if someone cheated, they could never criticize another cheater even if no one knew the first individual had. One had to remain consistent to themselves mentally. She told herself she was working her mind—and heart—into a fevered paranoia. She shut her eyes, rehashed the question of if she was being hyper-paranoid until she fell asleep.

Chapter 17

At her parents' place on the sofa as that evening passed into early morning, her mom and dad long having retired for the night, their bedroom door closed, Katy asked Renaldo if he agreed with the other two guys. He looked at her, girl's stare making his innards a bed of nails. He considered answers, imagined her reaction to each and what it would be like without her, then ran his tongue outside his mouth. Bottles flashed in his mind like strobe-lighted signs. He wasn't going to be his parents, gathered her into his chest, tightened his grip, and said he never wanted her to leave, made her vow she wouldn't. She did. With unblinking expression, he stated he did not agree with the other guys' carefree attitude. "But," he continued, "Conrad shouldn't dwell on it. Yes, Wyatt is to blame, never should have betrayed a friend but Conrad must move on."

Her turn to hold him tighter. She asked if he felt bored with her. He denied he did.

She giggled. "I mean besides during sex."

Renaldo narrowed his eyes. "That's what you think? All I want from you is sex?"

"Well, you're a guy."

Renaldo let go, turned away.

"I'm sorry." Katy slid her arms around him, made him face her. "I just know what I hear."

He protested he loved her for more than that, stared at her, said he loved her more than she understood. She hugged him and led him down on the couch then said she wanted to stay with him forever.

"And me with you," Renaldo breathed.

They unclothed and quietly he came into her. They relaxed, fell asleep for a spell, he then leaving, his chest muscle pumping faster and stronger than ever. He strummed his fingers in tune with Los Lonely Boys' "How far is Heaven" on the radio, felt he was already there.

* * * *

The gang signed their leases and once unpacked, relaxed in the girls' apartment, Wyatt the last to finish.

"Over here, Benedict," Renaldo said.

Wyatt was like he'd tasted a lemon. "What was that for?"

"Only kidding," Renaldo tittered. Then, in an undertone, "Though the name fits."

Wyatt clutched the boy's shirt. Renaldo swung free, shirt giving a quiet *rip*. The teaser looked at it, fabric loosened though not torn. "What was that for?"

"You know exactly what it was for."

"I was kidding."

"See? You knew what it was about, trying to get a rise outta me."

Arturo and Sophia chuckled it had worked. Wyatt transferred his expression to them, breath now audible. Arturo put a hand out. Sophia told Wyatt to relax, make a fist, and think about his reaction.

"Now, open your hand," she said. "Let it go." She held her clenched hand up. "Open your hand, let it go." She motioned several times, Wyatt moaning to cease, gave quick thrusts of his throat.

"I shouldn't have done it, okay? There I said it." He licked his lips, massaged his temples.

"Thought you were over it," Sophia said.

"You keep revisiting it."

"Well," Sophia moved her head slightly forward, "People get what they deserve. You reap what you sow."

"What the hell does that mean?" Wyatt curled his fingers.

"What you get is based on what you give. You get what you deserve."

"So victims of rapists and serial killers bring it on themselves?"

Sophia motioned her head up and down, said those people put themselves in a vulnerable position.

Wyatt slapped a palm on his forehead, uttered a plea to the Deity to help his friend. "So those who died on September eleventh—"

"Stop that bullshit. I'm not talking about that."

"So everything doesn't always come back to you?"

"I don't know." Sophia sighed. "I mean, it does. I mean, most times. Generally speaking…" She watched Wyatt's grin expand the longer she talked. "... I mean, on the whole, the majority of the time."

Wyatt snickered her philosophy classes were a waste of money. Andrea tittered. Millicent gave a brief smile. Renaldo nodded, Katy mirroring him. Sophia shifted to Arturo, who scrunched shoulders inward, one end of his mouth up, other down.

"Well..."

"Dunno," Arturo muttered.

"But—" Sophia began.

"Let's forget this namby-pamby philosophy and get down to business," Wyatt cut in. "Like deposits due on the utilities we just set up."

They discussed finances, upcoming semester, class schedules, and what they'd do for fun. Arturo gloated he'd soon be of legal age, had started kindergarten a year late as a result of family circumstances, bragged he wouldn't have to sneak to buy a beer or get into a club. "Don't worry," he teased. "I'll buy ya alcohol. For a fee, of course."

Sophia did not smile, scolded Arturo for being too interested in having a good time.

"Isn't that what college is for? Why do ya think we have all this free time?"

"If your grades drop, you'll lose that scholarship. Then ya won't get a good job."

Arturo spread his arms, looked at her like she'd charged him with genocide. "I've barely partied." He elbowed Renaldo. "I have not yet begun to party."

The two chortled. Sophia cautioned Arturo, who placed his head on her shoulder, told her he had control of things. Hadn't he already checked homes and inquired about the process of buying and selling? She warned it took more than that; he had to graduate and pass the realtor's test.

"Let's take it one day at a time," he said. "Enjoy this while we've got it, won't be long before it's gone." He smiled at her.

"All right," she acquiesced.

Arturo hugged her, kissed her, swore he wouldn't falter.

* * * *

The first half of the semester faded into memory. At their favorite nightclub, Arturo reminded everyone how he'd soon be able to enter legally though none of the others were questioned, the guys he knew still working the front door. He promised everyone drinks on his birthday. "Will even buy Benedict's. Anything to loosen him up."

"Ya know," Wyatt grumbled, "Getting tired of that."

"Why?" Arturo took a drink, smacked lips, gave an "Ahh," and said the moniker fit.

Wyatt curled one lip over the other, stood, and stared at Arturo, promised he'd make sure no one would call him that anymore. When Arturo asked how, Wyatt grabbed his friend's shoulders and pushed him to one side. Arturo caught himself. Both glared.

Sophia and Millicent squeezed between the two, Sophia gently sitting her boyfriend down. Millicent attempted the same with Wyatt, he squirming until free. Millicent stumbled, landed on a chair unevenly.

"Listen," Wyatt said. "I screwed up but Conrad was the one who chose to leave. If you call anyone Benedict, let it be him. I'm gone!" He pushed those in his path aside and left.

"What's with him?" Arturo said. "I was joking. Why is everyone so hypersensitive?"

* * * *

On the dance floor, Renaldo observed his friends but stayed close to Katy, danced every slow song with her, unaware he hadn't had, let alone craved, a drink. He spent the night at her place, she making breakfast in bed. It was just a matter of time until he asked her *the* question, spring break but five months away. He'd make each day feel like the twelve days of Christmas.

A week later, Renaldo's phone sounded. He smiled and gave a cheery, "Hi, honey" when the tone from the other end had his jaw sinking. "Okay. Be right over."

"What's wrong?" Arturo asked, he and Wyatt now over their spat though the latter had skipped the next go around for pizza.

Renaldo rolled his tongue along his mouth. "She said we need to talk."

"Oh God." Arturo moved to his friend, put an arm around him. Renaldo swung free, denied problems, they more passionate than ever.

"So what could it be?"

"I'll find out." Renaldo gripped his keys and licked his lips a second time. Stopping home first to see what was in the cabinet became an option. He chose to hear her news first. This couldn't be the end. Could it?

He headed out.

Chapter 18

"Hi." Katy opened the door, her smile innocuous enough. Like she'd invited him to dinner. She led him in. Renaldo glanced around, nothing out of the ordinary. She offered a seat on the sofa. The TV was not on nor the stereo, the quiet hurting his ears. His tongue did its action, enough times he felt he'd become a lizard.

Katy sat with him, her white t-shirt wrinkled. Renaldo noticed a wet spot near the sleeve, assumed she'd stained it and wiped it clean. Yet no food was out and no smells wafted from the kitchen, it free of pots and pans, cups or dishes. He observed her, his mind churning out possibilities: Breakup. She wanted to see other people. Was seeing someone else. She was ill, dying. Having trouble in school.

He chased the thoughts away, only one solution to finding out. "So what do you want to tell me?"

"I know we're not ready for this." She clasped hands in her lap. "I'm not even sure it's right, just a symptom."

"Symptom?"

Katy seized his forearm with both hands, gripped, and repeated her statement, had him swear he'd tell the truth and not get mad.

He took his free hand, clasped it on hers. "What is it?"

She swiveled away, hand to her eyes, asked forgiveness, and condemned herself aloud for what might be a misdiagnosis.

"About what?"

"I'm not sure it's even right." Katy stood.

"You said that." Renaldo rose, spun her around. Her eyes were not dry. He felt his own burn and blinked rapidly. "What is it?" he rasped. "Tell me."

"I..." Katy examined the floor.

He took her hands. "What? You what?"

"I think I..."

"What?"

Katy sucked in oxygen, Renaldo nearly able to see words wanting to tumble out of her mouth. He encouraged her, professed his love, no matter the circumstances. Even if she was dying.

Katy laughed hollowly then turned away. Her shoulders trembled. She gave soft cries.

"Honey." Renaldo touched her as if she was china. "What's wrong?" He twisted her around. "Tell me." A tear dribbled out of one of her eyes. "You are okay, right? Not anything life threatening?"

"Nothing like that. I may be overreacting. It is but one clue. A misleading one, perhaps."

"What clue?"

She wiped her eyes. "I missed my period."

Renaldo repeated the words in question format, interpreted them, his insides as if he watched a magician unable to put the sawed-in-half woman back together. "Did you say…"

"Period." She retrieved a tissue from a box on a table, tapped it to one eye then the other, and gave a long sniff. "Thought I'd warn you because you're the only one I've been…" She forced a smile. "Screwing around with."

"You're sure? I mean about your period."

"Mmm-hmm. I think so."

"Honey, you must be sure. Maybe it's late."

"I doubt it." She sighed. "I guess I—we—will have to wait and see."

"Well…" Renaldo re-processed the information, exhaled. "Like you said, wait and see. And pray." He shoved fingers through his hair then covered his face with both palms. "How could this happen? Weren't you on the pill?"

She said she was then added it wasn't fool-proof.

He slithered his tongue in and out, wanted rum and Coke, followed by a shot of whiskey. A six pack. A case, wanted to slam each beer. His mind sketched how she'd looked in eight months. Stains appeared under the armpits of his shirt. He swiped the back of a hand across his hairline. Oh, how the cool touch of a glass bottle would feel on his lips.

He centered his thoughts on Katy, brought her to him so fast she gave an "Oww!", her eyes expanding. He clutched her. "Let's just think about each other," he whispered, ran his hands up and down her back. "Calm down, think logically."

Quiet ensued. He sighed. "Have to wait and see."

"You're right." Her lower lip turned blue, jaw as if a Pogo stick. Water droplets fell from her cheeks to the floor or on his shirt. "Wait and see. And pray."

The couple held each other, Katy's sniffles the only noise. Renaldo felt his shirt become moist. She turned on the television and the two watched a show about how the Roman Empire fell, one of the causes overpopulation, how after wars, many countries' birth rates rose.

Renaldo spent the night though they did not have intercourse. When brightness infiltrated their sleep, they considered the future, their choices if she was pregnant, the simplest, quickest, and best option also the toughest. He concluded with the same statement of waiting though with little conviction. Would they tell the others?

"No way," Katy said firmly. "Certainly not before we know for sure."

* * * *

The next day the group gathered at the restaurant, Wyatt there this time. Arturo thanked him for making it. Wyatt mumbled he had nothing better to do.

Sophia asked Renaldo and Katy what they'd been doing, Renaldo saying "Classwork," said this semester was more difficult.

"And it'll only get harder," Sophia intoned.

"Exactly." Renaldo looked at Arturo. "Have to take it easy on the partying, buckle down, and take care."

Arturo laughed. "Of what?"

Renaldo's finger went to his friend. "Yourself." He glanced at Katy then bowed his head, viewed the area between her chest and waist, turned back to Arturo, looked past him to Sophia, and moved his chin in her direction. "And her. Take care of her." He shuffled his feet. "Never know what curveball life will throw."

"True," Arturo said but with a raised shoulder.

"When did you become Mr. Straight and Narrow?" Sophia said.

Renaldo shifted his focus to his girlfriend. Her face seemed to have no pigmentation. Under the table, her hand restricted blood flow in his leg. He pulled it free though not without seeing her eyebrow-merging demeanor. He spoke to Sophia.

"A little maturity, perhaps the realization what I do now will impact the rest of my life, determine my salary. The better the lifestyle, the less problems one has."

"I doubt that," Sophia said.

"It's true." Renaldo felt Katy pat his leg, passed a short glance to her with approving smile. "I mean, ya never see a rich guy breaking into other people's home."

"Why would he?" Millicent asked.

"My point exactly. The more money you've got, the fewer problems you have. Fewer problems, the better life is."

Sophia argued happiness didn't come with money and if it did, there'd never be a celebrity at the Betty Ford or Mayo Clinic.

Renaldo countered he hadn't said happiness, claimed that was indefinable, as ephemeral as mercury. Sophia contended it was the struggles and tribulations that made one stronger, setbacks and failures learning experiences. Renaldo came back with the comment people didn't learn from mistakes because if they did, they wouldn't repeat them and society would be close to perfect, every generation committing fewer and fewer errors.

"Or," he asked, "is it God's will for us to screw up?"

Sophia stiffened.

"All I'm saying," Renaldo went on, "is failure teaches you how not to do something, doesn't tell you the right way unless there are a very limited number of obstacles or choices along with a guarantee you'll succeed." He observed everyone. "And we know the only two things guaranteed in life."

The others mumbled the archaic joke.

"Only success teaches you how to succeed," Renaldo finished. When Andrea asked how someone could succeed without failing first, Renaldo waved a hand at her, said to look to successful others and see how they did it.

"Life doesn't have an owner's manual," Wyatt said to uneasy laughter from the rest.

Renaldo stated it did: Learn from others' mistakes, don't make them yourself.

Heads went up and down. Sophia leaned past Arturo and stared at Renaldo like he'd just descended through the roof from a spacecraft. He half-smiled, repeated his comments about maturity, and looked at Katy. She patted his leg and he credited his maturity to her, kissed her to cheesy, "Awws" from the girls and mocking ones from the guys, Arturo and Wyatt pretending a stomach virus forced their inner contents out of their mouths.

"She is a godsend," Renaldo went on, Katy's hand now sliding up and down his thigh. "Don't know what I'd be without her."

"A virgin?" Wyatt joked.

Renaldo snapped his head around, face warm. "Watch it, Benedict."

Wyatt's countenance became the color of school bricks, he promising the next person to call him that would suffer.

Arturo and Renaldo wriggled their fingers, muttered, "Whooo," to which Wyatt sardonically added he was only following the plan, cast a thin-eyed expression at Sophia.

"What'd I do?" she said in a high tone.

Wyatt quoted her belief about a purpose, everything happening due to a creator's plan.

Renaldo asked himself—for the hundredth time since receiving the news—what the plan was for he and Katy. Like always, no answer came forth. "What about us?" he blurted to Wyatt.

Katy acted as if she'd been goosed, her nails digging into his skin. He cried out, others looking at him. Sophia asked if they were okay.

"Fine," Katy said before Sophia finished her question then fiddled with a napkin. "Everything's good. Couldn't be better." She gave a small grin.

Sophia told her not to be secretive. Katy turned to Renaldo. He only nodded. She then viewed the others and gave a dramatic breath. "If you insist. We're thinking about living together."

Renaldo wrinkled his brow and nose.

"Marriage?" Andrea and Millicent said.

Katy looked at Renaldo. "Oh sorry, hun." She chuckled. "Guess they'd find out soon enough. No wedding here, no engagement." She wiggled fingers. "No jewelry. We talked and chose to wait." She turned to her boyfriend. "Didn't we, hun?"

"Huh?" Her grip on his leg jolted him. "Yes, we did, decided to wait for now. We'll, umm, see how she feels in the future."

Katy's grip tightened though she smiled, bragged Renaldo always let her decide important issues.

Arturo requested a change of subjects, rubbed his stomach.

"Men," Sophia chided. "Always thinking the same things."

"I'm not a man," Arturo said. "Am still a boy. You're always saying I act like one."

Sophia frowned, rolled her eyes.

All except Katy shifted to the buffet. She grabbed Renaldo, gently pulled him down.

"What?"

"Watch what you say," she whispered.

Renaldo fussed he'd said nothing, Katy warning she didn't want to so much as hint what might have transpired. She loosened her grip. He got up slowly, gave his word, put a hand over closed mouth, and twisted fingers as if turning a combination lock. Katy stayed mute about the subject though the more he thought about a family, the more his opinion swayed in the opposite direction. He fantasized teaching his son to play sports. Or his daughter how to read, recalled picking up Millicent from the daycare, thought of the kids' openness, a four year old showing him her finger painting then requesting his help. For a few seconds, it felt like she was his daughter, he thinking she'd called him "Daddy," though when he looked at her, she was busy. Millicent said kids had bad moments but the good ones outnumbered them.

A wry smile on Renaldo now. Did he want it? He shivered.

* * * *

The succeeding morning, Katy bought a home pregnancy test, concerned about its accuracy despite the label claiming better than ninety percent. She could not stay seated or stand in place for more than thirty seconds. Enough time elapsed. She picked up the device, checked the color. And closed her eyes, allowed air to rush out of her mouth. She set the test down, leaned on the counter, and reminded herself it wasn't always accurate. She didn't care. It was a done deal. She found her phone, dialed him.

* * * *

To Renaldo, it seemed a grenade had landed in his gut. Though he sighed audibly, he pressed eyes shut and swallowed despite the pain from doing so. In a ragged tone, he thanked her although his mouth was a straight line. "Maybe next time," he droned.

"What's that?"

"Huh?" Renaldo recalled his words and snapped into a clear state. "I dunno. Just, I guess, you have to make sure. All the way sure."

"You sound disappointed. Kids are fun, make you forget your worries but God knows I'm not ready for that. *We* are not ready, are we?"

Renaldo did not answer, too busy imagining picking up his daughter from school, swinging her around. Or playing hide and seek with his son. Katy's voice rising as she repeated her question brought him back to the here and now. "Guess not."

"I'll have a family," Katy reassured. "Someday."

"Yeah. Someday." Renaldo's voice was like the teacher's in *Ferris Bueller's Day Off.*

Katy asked if something was wrong. Renaldo responded he was tired, contrived a yawn. She giggled it was only morning. He laughed and they talked of Thanksgiving, finals, Christmas break, and New Year's Eve. She praised him for his abstinence from alcohol, said perhaps they'd have a conversation a few years hence, only the test result would be positive. And they would want it to be.

"Maybe," Renaldo said flatly.

* * * *

A week and half after Thanksgiving break, Katy felt nauseous, thought how a classmate had the flu, Katy wishing she hadn't picked up the student's book after it'd fallen off the girl's desk. Upcoming finals distracted her and not until the Wednesday of finals week—her last exam that week—did she think about the symptoms. Arriving home with some free time and no anxieties about school, she became acutely aware of the pains: Achy back, nausea, fatigue, last of which she surmised being due to stress from finals. When the symptoms did not abate, the idea came to her.

"Oh, God, no," she whispered, dug through the belongings she'd taken home, found the test kit. Did she want to know? Hadn't it already told her? No way she'd go to a doctor while with her parents. Maybe after Christmas, her mom and dad to visit New Orleans, Mother wanting to celebrate the twenty fifth anniversary of when her husband had proposed to her on Bourbon Street on New Year's Eve, they not to return until after spring semester began.

She put the kit away. This was a festive time, free of worries. And bad news.

The day after Christmas she took the contraption out. And put it back. Too soon.

Early the following day, before too much time had passed, she took the test, checked the color. And fell to the bed, hand over her eyes. She got up, looked at it again. Same color. She tested a second time. Same results. Now she did feel sick though not due to what was inside her. She reached for her cell phone.

"Hello?" a groggy voice answered. It cleared when Katy asked how he was. They'd talked on Christmas and yesterday so he asked why the call.

"Oh that." Katy's voice trilled as she said she was checking how he was. He replied he'd told her less than twenty-four hours ago. She laughed dryly, joked she'd forgotten, was getting senile in her old age, and followed that with more bland laughter. When he asked if she was ill, she became mute. He said it again. She stammered. He addressed her by name, same question.

"I... I think we have to talk."

"We're doing that now."

"In person."

Renaldo's turn to not speak for an interlude. "Did you see a doctor?"

"No. Uh-uh. Definitely not."

"Did you test again?"

"I...ummm..."

"You did, didn't you?"

Katy sniffed. Her eyelashes batted at a rapid pace. She rubbed a finger over an eye, her breathing shallow. She confessed.

"And...."

"I think I'm pregnant."

Renaldo laughed. "You *think* you're pregnant?"

She told him the results. He reminded her they weren't one hundred percent. She promised to see a doctor after her parents left for New Orleans. Renaldo offered to take her, said it would be their secret. Katy mentioned the lightness of his mood and bit her lip, asked if he'd been drinking.

Renaldo laughed, said he hadn't so much as thought of alcohol once during the break, swore he wouldn't drink when they went out on New Year's Eve. She congratulated him.

* * * *

Two days later, the six remaining friends plus Katy lunched at the pizzeria. A debate evolved about how much they controlled their lives, how much was their own choice.

"Let's just say, hypothetically," Katy began, lowered her chin to view her stomach, "you were given a responsibility you didn't want, say a family member needed constant care, how would you deal with that?"

"I'd take care of 'em," Wyatt said quickly. "Someday I may need someone to care for me."

"What if it was so expensive you couldn't afford it?"

"I'd still do it. As best I could."

"But you couldn't," Katy said. "Was too much money, too much of your time. And you didn't know how to care for them or treat what they had."

"Hire someone," Sophia suggested.

Katy shook her head. "Too expensive. What would you do?"

Arturo scratched his forehead. "Raise money?"

"Suppose you couldn't."

All exchanged blank miens. Katy viewed Renaldo who flinched. She gripped a hand on his leg. "Should we care for someone even when we don't have the means to support them nor the emotional maturity to care for them?"

Wyatt creased his eyes. "What're ya supposed to do, euthanize them?"

"I'm just wondering, as we said, how much choice we have in life and how much is thrust upon us." Katy exhaled, slid lower in the booth, still focused on Renaldo, and chewed her tongue. The boyfriend only moved his cranium from one shoulder to the other.

Katy checked her stomach again. It seemed to have grown. Could she raise a child with no assistance from her parents, they having lectured no one should have premarital sex? Adoption was a possibility but she didn't want to be constantly concerned if the child's new parents were abusive or if her child would forgive her or hate her. There was but one choice.

The group had no further answers, ate their fill of pizza then returned to their homes.

* * * *

Next afternoon Renaldo sat on the sofa at his parent's house, hands between shaking legs. When would she call? He'd taken her to the free clinic this morning for the sonogram and urine test. She was supposed to call when she got the results this afternoon. Why hadn't she? He viewed the time. Almost thirty minutes past the time she was to have responded.

The phone had him jumping up. He checked the ID. Some California number. He cursed and let the call go to voice mail. No message was left.

The doorbell rang.

No doubt a salesman, Renaldo thought, sat back down. A second ring. A third, followed quickly by a fourth.

"Damnit." He opened the door. Katy came forward.

"Thought you were gonna call."

She shook her head, said it'd be best to tell him in person.

"Well?" he said though he knew the answer.

Katy whispered they should sit down. Renaldo hurried her to the couch. "Well?"

Katy looked out the window. Water formed in her eyes and her body convulsed. "They said I'm...pregnant." She fell to his chest and sobbed.

"Oh." Renaldo let out his breath, his lips an exact one eighty from hers. His heart beat faster, more pleasant than he'd ever known. The earlier images moved to the front of his mind: Teaching his daughter to read, playing ball with his son, the daycare experience. What would be his child's first word? When would they take their first steps? He listed things he'd have to buy.

Katy freed herself from him. "Ya know we have no choice."

"No choice?" His mind would not let go of the visuals.

"Of course." The girl sat up then shut her eyes. "I—we—can't afford this and adoption would be too difficult."

To Renaldo, it seemed the rhythmic motion in his chest had ceased. His mouth fell open, his body as if ice. "You mean you want..."

"An abortion. Yes." She cried, fell to him again, her arms on his shoulders, said the decision was hard but it had to be done.

Renaldo suggested both of them get full time jobs.

Katy withdrew, shook her head multiple times. "No way, uh-uh. It'd lead to a vicious cycle of poverty we'd never get out of nor would the child. My parents won't help. Your parents..." She scoffed. "Well, they can't take care of themselves, forget about you. Or a grandchild."

"What did you say?" Renaldo found his voice on the increase despite the disdain of nearly twenty years.

Katy said it a second time, how Renaldo hadn't shown much faith in them either.

Renaldo shot up. "But they're my parents!"

"So?" Katy rose. "Only you can criticize them?"

"Yes. They're my mom and dad, no one's lived their lives, experienced their hardships." He closed then opened his eyes, asked himself if he'd really said this.

"There's no way I'm having this child. We can't do it."

"Adoption," Renaldo said but regretted that, wanted to raise the child.

Katy stated her fear of constantly wanting to know about the child, which made her cry harder.

"What about me?"

"What about you?"

He explained he was half the reason this baby had come into existence, wanted to have some input.

"Okay. What do you want to do?"

Renaldo swallowed. "Keep it."

Katy scowled a laugh. "Last time you said you didn't want it."

"Changed my mind." He told her of the day care incident.

"We know nothing about child rearing," she said and sobbed.

"So we learn," he said, nearly shouting. "We'll go to Millicent's daycare, get some experience for a few months."

"I've thought about this, all the choices, costs versus benefits. We can't do it."

"But I want it."

"We can't do this just because we want to. What about the child? Can't subject him or her to a life of poverty, possibly divorce or—"

"You don't think we can last?" Renaldo's arm started to move up, his hand a fist.

She stated the majority of under twenty-one marriages wound up in divorce, asked how that would be fair for a child. Renaldo argued they'd find a way, re-quoted Sophia once having said one was only given as much as they could handle. Katy retorted with Wyatt's comeback then: If one was only given as much as they could handle, suicide would not be in our vocabulary. The dispute escalated until Katy looked out the window, Renaldo checking over her shoulder, saw two neighbors peering toward the house.

"I'm going home," Katy mumbled.

"Fine." Renaldo led her out, did not wave to her, went inside, and stared at the cabinet.

No, he told himself. *Will only make it worse.*

He picked up the phone, put it back, and lay on the sofa, dozed off and on, did not get up until the following afternoon, thought about their plans of welcoming a new three hundred and sixty-five day cycle. Should he ask? Would she agree? They'd had some time away from each other, might be able to talk calmly. He'd ask about tonight, promise not to discuss the matter, tonight the night everyone let loose more than any other evening.

He dialed her number. It rang. He whispered for her to answer. More ringing. Mentally preparing what to say, he heard the click.

"Hello?" she said. Renaldo questioned her mood, Katy saying she was better, had time to think. She inquired how he was. He told her, added quickly they weren't going to discuss the matter.

"Let's focus on today. It's New Year's Eve. We had plans."

"Yeah... and?"

The boy inhaled, counted to five then released the air. "Want to go out? Like I said, won't mention it, we'll focus on celebrating the New Year."

She did not answer then gave a heavy, drawn out breath. "Guess so. Could use a night to let go, forget this damn thing, if only for a few hours."

"Great. I'll be there around ten. See ya."

"Thanks," she said, words spoken as if she had laryngitis. "For being there for me. Most guys would have fled. Appreciate it. Love you."

He echoed her words, hung up, and sat down. Her poverty argument made sense. Her other concern had him shaking his head. A broken marriage? He pictured court proceedings, she gaining custody. His throat hurt. He stood, went to the location. Fingers caressed the handle. His tongue made a path across his mouth.

"Honey?" a voice from the bedroom. "You finally back? Honey?" The mother entered the foyer. "Oh." She mechanically said hi, asked how her son was.

Renaldo frowned. Christmas had been a downer, parents giving him but two presents, the couple also exchanging gifts: case of beer for him, wine coolers and hard fruit punch for her, husband making Margaritas. Couldn't she at least pretend to be glad to see him? He forced saliva up to his tongue.

"What do you think you're doing?" She grabbed Renaldo's hand that held the cabinet door handle.

The son's eyes narrowed. Saliva inched closer to the tip of his tongue.

"We've lectured you about this," the mother said then tried to laugh, red-faced. "Not that we set any kind of example." She laughed harder. "Other than do as we say, not as we do."

Renaldo puckered his lips, ready to release the liquid. His mother smiled and lowered her hand.

"You're old enough now, I'm sure you know what to do."

The boy gaped as his mom exited. He released his hand from the cabinet. The front door opened.

"Honey, c'mon," the father said.

"See ya later, son," Mother called out then admonished her husband, said the beer run could have waited, they going to a New Year's party followed by a trip to a bar. The father broke out a beer anyway, chugged it, and tossed it to Renaldo, told him to finish it off, which the boy did.

"And recycle the can," the woman said. "We're not totally wasted. I mean, wasters. We take care of the environment."

The husband belched. "Most of the time."

The couple chuckled and waved goodbye, the woman warning Renaldo about drinking and driving.

Seconds after he shut the front door, Renaldo opened another door, grabbed a few bottles, and poured a little from each into a glass. He tried to stop himself with the contemplation of raising offspring though Katy seemed determined to end the pregnancy. Wouldn't a child give him a concrete, permanent motivation to do away with the bottle?

"But *she* wants to end it," he muttered, took a swallow of the elixir, smiled, and took a second drink. Then another. Another. More. His confusion eased though he knew this was transient.

When he arrived at Katy's, he'd sobered up enough she wouldn't be suspicious. She said they were going to have a great time, wouldn't talk about it. Silence was the subject of conversation the rest of the way.

At the bar, they danced a few numbers, Renaldo even turning down a drink from Arturo whose birthday had been right after Christmas, he bragging about being of legal age, this his first chance to celebrate.

"Don't worry," Arturo told Renaldo. "Someday you'll be there."

Renaldo looked at Katy, smiled. "Not that I need to be. Get a natural high being with her."

Katy blushed, kissed him, and sat in his lap. An announcement it was thirty minutes to the end of the year blared over the speakers. The two remained quiet through a series of songs.

"So," Renaldo checked the girl's stomach, "thought about it?"

"Can we talk about that tomorrow?" she said though in an even tone. "Said we were going to have a good time."

"Just wondering."

She warned him not to brainwash her. In negotiator-like tone, he said he only was asking if she'd thought about it.

"I have. Now let me be."

A slow song. She asked him to dance. He declined.

"C'mon." She took his hand, led him out, and pointed to the clock, big hand squeezing closer to the little one. She insisted they had to be on the dance floor when they said goodbye to the old year, hello to the new one.

Renaldo pressed about a decision. Her teeth merged as she informed, pausing between each word, he would know the next day.

"Better think fast." Renaldo moved his hand toward the clock. "It's almost here."

"Very funny. Not," she snarled.

"Just give me a hint of where you're leaning."

The announcement of one minute to the New Year.

"Haven't made any decision. Will let you know in the morning."

Renaldo opened his mouth. She stuck a finger over it.

"I mean after sunrise," she said. "Maybe later. Noon-ish."

"Noon-ish?"

Thirty seconds, the voice boomed.

"What's the rush?" Katy said.

"I just feel we need to talk about this."

"Why now?"

"Why not now?"

Katy separated from him. "What's your problem?"

"What's yours?"

"Answer my question, damnit."

"You answer mine."

"Ten seconds," the voice yelped.

Bar-goers chanted with it. Nine.

"Why can't you fucking wait till tomorrow?" Katy said.

Renaldo stuck out his chest, batted his eyes, and spoke in a high, feminine-like tone. "Us guys just have to know how someone feels."

Three seconds.

"Feel this!"

Two seconds. Katy reared back.

One second.

Her fist contacted Renaldo's mid-section.

"Happy New Year!" everyone yelled. Glasses clinked, alcohol was chugged, kisses and hugs were traded, couples held each other. A chorus of "Auld Lang Syne" broke out.

"How does that feel, bastard?" Katy marched out and hailed a cab.

"Stupid bitch!" Renaldo yelled when he caught his breath. "Wouldn't know a good man if everyone told you. Most guys'd leave or force you to have the goddamn abortion. Not me! I'm facing my responsibilities. Gimme a son, daughter, I don't care. Bitch!"

Nearby, Arturo asked if his friend was drunk. Renaldo gave an exaggerated stumble, pretended to fall. Arturo reached out.

"I'm not as think as you drunk I am occifer," Renaldo said sarcastically, eyebrows low. "Do I look drunk?" He moved away from Arturo, muttered, "Fuck you."

Arturo caught up to his friend, asked what the boy had been talking about, and to whom, then scanned the interior. "Where's Katy?"

"Who cares?" Renaldo hastened to the bar, in a sprint by the time he reached it, ordered two double Scotches, drank the first before the second had been prepared.

Arturo seized his arm. Renaldo broke free. And smiled, turned slowly. "Am taking it slow, see?" He sipped his drink, ambled to the table, sat down, and left the drink untouched for five minutes then sipped it again.

Arturo stayed with him until the old song "Heaven" by Bryan Adams played. He went to Sophia, she with Andrea and Millicent. Renaldo mumbled "Thank God" when Arturo took Sophia in his arms, her eyes misty, this the first romantic song they'd ever danced to.

"Hell with them." Renaldo searched, found someone to get him beer, worried Arturo might try and stop him. When a few songs passed with no Sophia or Arturo in sight, Renaldo got the drinks himself, several with one bartender, several with another. "Hell with that bitch!" he said, went bottoms up, and pounded the table. "What about *my* choice? I helped create it! Bitch!"

He consumed more liquor, bummed off a guy behind him, got up, and weaved his way to the bar without raising suspicions. Back at the table, he downed his drink then checked his watch.

"Late enough," he muttered, stood, and meandered through the crowd toward the door. A familiar figure caught his sight, this person with a second figure—one he also knew, hadn't seen since Conrad bolted the group. The first was male, second female, she with sandy hair. No separation between them. They smiled at each other, exchanged words. Their lips met. For quite a stretch.

"Hmmm." Renaldo pushed the door open. "Thought that was over." He gave one final check. "Guess Benedict is alive and well tonight." Renaldo strode to his truck and drove away, vehicle sliding from one side of the double yellow line to the curb and back. A couple of times he crossed the yellow lines. The sight of the university black and white had him slowing down, speedometer needle fuzzy in his vision, it reading either fifteen or five miles. He slowed even more.

Rounding campus corner, he drifted to the other lane. And did not retreat. A horn from a car in the opposite direction. Renaldo went hand over hand on the wheel, away from this driver. They passed without incident. Only after a mile away from campus did Renaldo breathe. He increased his speed, city cops not as picky as campus fuzz though he knew there'd be plenty of police out on this night. He obeyed the speed limit, approached the turn to his parents' home.

Aware of what happened last year, he decreased his speed and avoided the sign—now upright, in place—the way a horse rears away from a spot where it'd had a previous fall.

"Made it." He checked mirrors. No autos with city seal followed him. His foot fell to the pedal on the right. Speedometer needle zinged clockwise though to Renaldo the numbers and needle were a blur, he guessing it displayed a speed somewhere between forty and fifty.

A *zttt* above. Outside. Where light once shone, the roadway went dark.

"Where am I?" Renaldo squinted, saw something. Or thought he did and swerved.

The truck bumped the curb, jostled Renaldo forward, and continued on though the tires made a much quieter conversation. Renaldo, however, bucked up and down, noticed the green color underneath wheels then looked back up. A thick, wide obstacle of nature greeted him, its roots planted years ago. It won the battle with the boy's car.

Renaldo tipped forward, head hitting the steering. Things went white, as if a lightning flash, then black. He collapsed into the seat, a red line above his left eye and on his forehead. He did not feel it, his eyes shut, body limp.

Chapter 19

Barking and whining. Renaldo's head pounded like a bullet train had ridden a path through it. He opened his eyes, swayed and gripped the wheel, twisted the truck key away from him. A *r-r-r* from the engine allowed his memory to come alive. He groped for the handle. The door popped open—and stopped halfway. Renaldo kicked it, squeezed through the opening, stumbled, re-righted himself, and surveyed the damage: Metal like pocked skin, front bumper on the ground.

"Shit." Renaldo sank to the hood, warm steel making him stand. He kicked the truck, nearly fell, straggled up the road, and repeated utterances to the Almighty that no one see him. Over his continuing, head-thumping buzz, he contemplated scenarios, first one most believable: A New Year's Eve drunk ran him off the road. Calling police was of no assistance. He'd sell the pickup for parts and scrap, use the money and his savings to buy something decent.

He made his way home, muscles un-tensing upon discovering the house vacant. He wandered to his bed, walls and doorways never having been such good friends. The moving hand of the clock hadn't made two circuits in advance of Renaldo slipping into the fairy tale land of night.

When he came to with enough strength to rise, the house was unresponsive to his query of others' presence. Reading the clock's digits, he deduced his parents had returned and gone out again, the hour for low-priced drinks upon them.

After nourishment of chips and crackers—washed down with a leftover can of beer—Renaldo ventured to his vehicle and retrieved his cell phone, dialed a towing company, and had them haul the pickup to a salvage yard, sale of parts more then he'd expected. A taxi ride to a dealer had him with a newer pickup.

At home, memories of last night had Renaldo preparing an oration. He dialed her, aware not to mention the *accident*. When she'd notice the new car, he'd bring out the "Driver hit me" spiel.

"Hello?" Katy said deliberately.

"It's me. Need to talk."

A thick exhale from the other end. "Already did. More than twelve hours ago."

"That wasn't talking," he snapped then spoke in a slower, lighter tone. "We have to hear each other out, can't make rash decisions we'll regret."

"I know what I must do."

"Can we talk about this? In person?"

Another feminine sigh. She relented.

"Oh," Katy said when she opened the door, took the flowers and chocolates, and thanked him. Renaldo slipped past her, checked for other occupants. She informed him her parents were still in New Orleans then turned her head back outside and pointed to the curb, anticipated question descending from her lips.

Renaldo gave the planned response. She gave an "Oh," he aware she had more urgent troubles. She led him to the sofa. "Why do you want this?"

Renaldo laughed as if offended. "Because it's mine?"

"Didn't want it before."

"I told you, I—"

"Yes, I remember your..." Her voice took a mock Holy Roller tone. "Transformation." She apologized then said they were not psychologically ready, barely out of childhood themselves.

Renaldo squawked as if she'd said Bill Gates was bankrupt, bragged he was no child, had dealt with issues of applying for college, getting loans and grants, finding a work study program, and graduating from high school. And, yes, buying a car.

She repeated her fear about money. He promised in but a few years he would have a degree and be making decent money, she too. Katy asked what to do in the meantime, Renaldo mumbling something about making it work.

"There are obstacles," she said.

Renaldo demanded to know what they were.

She smiled as if he'd said he was the smartest man alive. "You're kidding. The obstacles? Yours? Ya know..." She put a circled hand to her mouth, moved her head back, mouth open.

The young man stiffened. "I can control that," he said as if accused of homicide.

"Like last night?" She touched his forehead. "Is this from then, you with the bottle?" She did the same motion of circled hand to mouth. "Who did you hurt?"

"No one." He moved as if poked. "I mean, I didn't hit anyone, they hit me. Almost. Forced me into a damn tree."

"I bet."

He protested but she talked over him, listed his past incidents, wanted to know how his child would feel about those. Would he introduce them to drink? At what age? She argued some believed alcoholism was hereditary.

Renaldo was on his feet. "So you have no faith in me?"

She joined him, voice calmer. "I know what I've seen." She rubbed a finger on his cheek, her eyes damp, throat hitching. "Do you really want an innocent child dealing with that?"

"I can handle it, damnit!" He slapped the girl's hand down, distanced himself from her. "But if that's how you feel, it's over!"

She grabbed his wrist. He loosened her grasp, asked her when the last time he drank was then wished he could take the question back, stomach now queasy.

"You forget? Last night? At the bar?"

"You don't know what I did after you left!"

"And your accident?" She made air quotes upon saying the last word. "How did it happen?"

His right thumb locked over knuckles. "I told you, bitch, it was an accident."

She wagged a finger. "Don't ever fucking call me that! I'm sure you were drunk, so smashed you couldn't fucking see stra—"

His palm cracked her cheek. Katy crumpled to the sofa. A red spot where he hit her stood out. Renaldo stared at the hand like it was a gun gone off accidentally. He broke from his trance, hurried to her, and offered a hand.

She brushed it back. "Go away, bastard! It's over, get the hell out! I'm doing this on my own. No way you can be a father. Never! Get the fuck out of here! Now!"

He straightened up, claimed he was the one who'd said they were finished.

"Who the hell cares? Just leave!"

"Katy, let's talk about this, I—"

She returned his favor, sound of her hand on skin not as harsh yet Renaldo toppled. She stood over him, swung her leg into his side. "Bastard! Get out. Fucking now!"

Renaldo clawed to his feet and stumbled to the door. Outside, his fingers sank into cold grass. He somersaulted and came back up as the front door slammed shut.

"And don't come back! Asshole!"

Birds chirped, a vulture squawked, squirrel's feet pitter-pattered on slanted slate. Kids' voices in the distance, a hum of a car a block away.

Renaldo gathered himself and slunk into his truck, searched for the keyhole, unsuccessful not only because of his mental state but also the vehicle was new to him. He found the ignition, slid the key in, started the truck, and left.

Back home, no convincing was required, his lips chapped. He bounded for the cabinet, opened the closest bottle—Everclear—and drank it straight.

"Smooth," he hissed then coughed, gagged. Another shot. He mixed a Tequila Sunrise then helped himself to cans of his parents' Christmas stash, uttered expletives at his former mate.

"We're fucking through when *I* say so!"

He mixed what he called *The X factor*, a concoction of a little of every drink on the shelves. It washed down his throat. His knees wavered, he fell on one side. Eyelids felt weighted. The last thought he had was how his parents would react should they see him. He forced himself up, plodded to the living room sofa, and collapsed.

The clank of the door roused him from the depths of dreaming.

"It's us," a female voice said.

The boy sat up, parents with half-grins, half-grimaces. Artificial light seared his eyes. He fell back, hand over his face. His mom queried as to his well-being.

"Fine," Renaldo said, droned he hadn't slept well, stayed up too late and had nodded off throughout the day.

"That's good," his mom said in sing-song drunkenness, asked how Katy was. Renaldo answered, "Good," came to his feet, and announced he was going to his room.

"Good luck," the mom said. Renaldo froze in mid-walk and turned, eyebrows now at a low angle.

His dad waved him off. "She's tipsy again."

Renaldo would have chided, "Whadya mean—again?" had he felt better, instead traipsed to his bed, teetered, fell on it, and took another trip beyond rapid eye movement.

* * * *

The gang commenced the week before spring semester, Wyatt there, Renaldo sans Katy. They questioned him about her as he sat down.

"Don't wanna talk about it." He rubbed his forehead. They pressed for details.

"Didn't you see—or hear—us at the bar last time?" Renaldo asked, but all denied they had. Renaldo looked at Wyatt, recalled the last thing he'd seen at the bar. "Did whatshername like it?"

Wyatt's face darkened. "Whatshername?"

"Yeah, the girl you talked to that night." Renaldo chuckled. "Morning, actually."

All heads moved like they'd heard some strange noise from Wyatt.

"Girl?" Wyatt's throat bobbed.

"Yeah. Whatshername." Renaldo snapped fingers, tittered. "Doesn't help it was New Year's Eve when I saw you two."

Everyone's face was stolid.

"Who?" Wyatt fanned himself with his shirt collar.

"The girl you dated."

"Dawn?" Sophia and Andrea said.

Renaldo hit his palms together. "Yeah. The girl you cheated on Conrad with."

"Thanks for reminding me," Wyatt groaned.

"Anytime, Benedict."

Wyatt straightened up.

"Hey, guys," Sophia intervened. "Let's get some pizza before it goes cold, shall we?"

All except Renaldo stood, he responding he had little appetite. Millicent kiddingly warned the pizza might be gone soon. Renaldo turned a lip up, assured her he wouldn't miss it, reminded her it was getting cold.

"I'm sure you two will work things out," Millicent said and moved to the buffet.

If only we could, Renaldo thought, glad to be alone, albeit for a minute.

When the group had eaten, Renaldo reminded Wyatt of what he'd seen. Wyatt said it was no big deal, he not having done anything that night. Renaldo teased he doubted that, wished he'd taken pictures, said if he was the paparazzi and Wyatt a celebrity, the caption would have read *Benedict turns coat again.*

Wyatt sat up and folded his arm. "Give it a rest."

Arturo smirked. "Sounds like you're still interested in her. Isn't betraying a friend once enough?" His grin widened. "Benedict."

"This is bullshit." Wyatt stood and gathered his jacket, reached to Arturo's plate then Renaldo's cup, swiped a pizza slice from Arturo, a shot of Coke from Renaldo then spit in the cup. Arturo clasped Wyatt's wrist. The other boy pulled free.

"Nothing happened." Wyatt put on his jacket. "We talked, she kissed me goodbye, end of story."

Renaldo smirked. "Looked like more than that. A sequel?"

"What would you know?" Wyatt's glare was as penetrable as a north wind on bare flesh. "Alkie."

Renaldo pushed off his seat.

"Later, dude," Wyatt sneered. "When you're sober. How about ten years?"

Renaldo was upright. Wyatt waved him down, turned, and marched out. The other boy glowered as if his stare could harm. When the door clanged, Renaldo slumped back into the booth and muttered, "Motherfucker" as the others changed the subject.

A tall, lanky waiter, with strong pectoral muscles seeming to break through a too-tight shirt, passed by the table, asked how everyone was, if he could be of assistance. Millicent's mouth moved.

"You can help me." Andrea sidled up to the guy, said he could satisfy her hunger. The guy laughed, Andrea talking him up. Little time had elapsed and they were arranging a date.

"Brad!" the manager called out.

The boy backpedaled toward the kitchen, lost his balance, caught himself with a chair, and gave a final flash of a hand to Andrea, and retreated into the kitchen, the girl radiant like the summer sun as she lifted a pizza slice to her lips. A gaping Millicent reached across, slapped at the piece. Andrea's face switched to an open mouth and wide eyes while Millicent took the slice, shoved it into her mouth, and grinned.

"What the hell was that for?"

Millicent's smile grew as she corrected Andrea not to end her sentences with a preposition.

"Whatever. What's your problem?" Andrea reached for her cup.

"Gee, nothing. You just swiped that guy from me."

Andrea's hand stopped halfway to the glass. "I what?"

"Like you didn't know, damnit!" Millicent thumped a plate-rattling fist on the table. The others jolted. "You stole him! I was talking to him and you cut me off!"

"Had no idea, didn't hear you." Andrea put a hand on Millicent's. "Gotta speak up, girl, or you'll lose every time."

"Shut up, bitch!" Millicent glanced over her shoulder, boy still in the kitchen. "He was mine."

"Possession's nine-tenths of the law." Andrea smiled, picked up another slice.

"Fine. You can have him." Millicent stood, stretched, and once more slapped pizza out of Andrea's hand, took it, and left, mumbled something as to why had she signed the lease then why others weren't conscious of their behavior, how kids were more mature than some adults.

* * * *

When Renaldo returned home and found the house vacant, his hands were soon around the Jack Daniels bourbon bottle then a Cutty Sark container, followed by Smirnoff vodka. His world spun. He retreated to his room, didn't even want his parents to see him like this.

The couple came home and went to their room.

The next time he came to, the sun was shining and his parents were gone. He left Katy a message and when she didn't return the call, left another, then another.

At nightfall, Renaldo gathered a few beers, took them to his room, and drank until he passed out, his mom coming in hours later to ask about him. He mumbled he was tired and had a headache so she left him alone.

Too depressed and drunk to visit Katy, let alone call her, Renaldo spent most of the week in his room sleeping, watching TV, or drinking, the latter two usually simultaneously. By Saturday he sobered, debated if he should make up with her, she his best defense versus the booze. But he had to ask quickly or the thing in her belly would be a memory of what could have been. Snapshots of future events scrolled across his mind. He dialed the number. Voice mail. He left a message about how they had to discuss things in a much more serious, mature conversation. He managed, "Love ya" at the end although his tone was like a local commercial actor.

By afternoon, with no reply from her and his head now clear, Renaldo went to her house, parents telling him she was back at her campus place. Once there, he exited the truck then froze. What to say if she'd done it? Was she there? He dialed her number. The jangle of Britney Spears' "Womanizer" was heard even from outside. He quickly turned his phone off, decided it'd be worse if she answered and knew he was right in front of her. He pattered to the door, knocked. No answer. He hit it faster, harder. As he was about to say he knew she was inside, the door opened.

"Oh my God." Renaldo viewed the girl's wrinkled shirt, the skin under her eyes red. He leaned on the doorframe. His eyes went hot. He bit his tongue, pushed air down his mouth. "Oh God." His voice trembled. "Please tell me you didn't. Please!"

The girl said nothing, her long face and unopened mouth creating dialogue for her.

Renaldo stepped back, his glance dropping straight to her abdomen. "Goddamn you! Bitch!" He shoved her. She stumbled back, hit the sofa and fell, head bumping the armrest. She rolled to the sofa, curled into fetal pose, and hid her face with her arms.

"Had to do it," was all she managed, words barely heard above sobs. She pleaded for understanding, said she wasn't ready, couldn't handle it, then begged to be alone.

"You will be. Forever." Renaldo slammed the door and trounced to his truck, his goodbye the sound of rubber moving in fast, circular motions on blacktop.

"Goddamn bitch." His eye ducts dripped, blurred his vision, he almost hitting two cars along the way. Fortunately, his parents weren't home, his mom's note only revealing they'd left and would be back later.

The cabinet welcomed him. He sucked up contents of the first bottle so fast he hadn't seen the label, didn't care. He downed several more, didn't stop until his eyesight became like night. He felt no pain upon crashing to the floor.

He awoke, groggy, stomach as if fighting a civil war, head like it'd been under a laundry-pressing machine. He tried to stand, slipped, and hit his head on the cabinet. More blackness.

Once back in the conscious world, he gathered himself and made it to his room. His mom's knocking on the door brought him out of his stupor enough to realize darkness had taken over the outdoors and to tell her he was tired, would talk later. She obeyed, asked if he was going to his apartment, classes to start the day after next. He said he would upon feeling up to it.

When it became bright enough to see things without turning on lights, Renaldo gained enough energy to rise and reach the cabinet. He opened it, groped, and pawed. A *clink*. Liquid dribbled off a shelf. Renaldo opened his mouth, caught some, swallowed it then touched a heavy container and swung it to him, grabbed another, then another until six were in his arms.

He squirmed to a halfway comfortable position, body sprawled on the floor, head leaning against the cabinet. He twisted the cap off a gin bottle and gulped its contents.

"Damn that bitch! Ruined my whole fucking future. Hell with her! Hope she's happy now. Two less people she'll have to worry about. Go to hell, fucking dipshit cunt of a whore!"

He finished this bottle then another. A few swallows into the third, he passed out. When he came to, he polished off what he'd left. A fourth container soon went dry. Renaldo felt as if in a spinning gyroscope, walls like a working trash compactor. The area of black around what little remained of his vision took over, the way a cartoon does when finished.

* * * *

Arturo called Renaldo Sunday, left a message as to when Renaldo was to return to the apartment. With no return call, he did the same on Monday. Tuesday, his phone rang. Checking ID and seeing the number, he picked up, asked his friend where he was. A much older, upset voice replied it wasn't Renaldo, told Arturo through broken sobs what had happened to his friend, thought Arturo should be the first of the friends to know. Hearing the cries, Arturo offered to call his friends and tell them himself. The other person thanked him, Arturo ordering the caller to notify him once they had a date set and he'd make sure all the friends would attend. He hoped.

* * * *

Wyatt's phone vibrated during biology. He pulled it from his pocket, checked the number, and shoved the phone back. Though they were roommates, he didn't have to talk to them, would avoid them as much as possible. Come summer, he'd look on his own for a fall location. Being with them was like having eaten the same food every day for a year.

Five minutes later, same caller. Wyatt uttered profanity, student next to him turning. Wyatt mumbled "Sorry," phone going back to its original place.

Ten minutes after this, Wyatt sounded more harsh words, exited the room, and flipped the phone open, sailor-esque dialogue coming out so fast he didn't hear Arturo's harried voice.

"Did you hear me?" Wyatt awaited a reply.

"Did you hear *me*?" Arturo's voice broke. "I can't believe it's true! I can't believe it!"

"What, damnit?"

Arturo wanted Wyatt's location. Wyatt demanded as to why. Arturo asked if the friend was in class.

"Fuck yes. Now let me get back, you've wasted enough time."

Arturo lectured him to get his books. Wyatt wanted to know why.

"An emergency," Arturo cried. "Do it! Now!"

Confused by the anger in his friend's voice, Wyatt did as told. "Okay, I got 'em. Now what the hell is going on?"

"It's…"

"Sophia?"

"No. It's…"

"What?"

"Renaldo." Arturo sobbed. "He…" He gagged. "Renaldo's gone."

"Gone?" Wyatt spun around, as if to see Renaldo behind him. "This a joke?"

"If only it was." Arturo's voice trembled. "Renaldo was found…dead. At his house."

Wyatt's phone clanked on white tile. He almost lost his footing reaching for the object then nearly dropped the phone a second time. "What are you talking about?"

"It's so early I don't have all the details. His parents found him on the floor, passed out. Or so they thought. When they failed to arouse him, paramedics came. Too late. I'm guessing it's alcohol poisoning." Sobs again. "He's fucking dead! What the hell happened?!"

Wyatt ordered Arturo to calm, asked where he was. When told, Wyatt said he'd be right over, ran so fast to the apartment he believed he would've qualified for the track team. Out of breath, he opened the door, saw Arturo with red eyes and wet cheeks. They hugged like soldier buddies sent out to fight, Wyatt in denial as he sank to the sofa, Arturo joining him.

Arturo blew his nose. "It's true. But he was just with us at the pizzeria. No mention of him and Katy having problems, they…"

"Hold on." Wyatt displayed a finger, his eyes glancing upward. "He said he didn't want to talk about it." He snarled.

"Then asked me about Dawn." As he reminded himself of his friend's fate, his mouth flattened. "Something was wrong. What?"

"Who knows? I don't have Katy's number nor does Sophia. Don't know where she lives. We have to find her, find out what happened. Maybe she doesn't know he's…" Arturo lipped the word *gone*, cleared his throat, and held out his hand. "Promise to call if you have problems. I know it's not manly to say but it's crucial. Promise me."

"Will do," Wyatt said, unblinking.

The two clasped hands then put an arm around each other, Wyatt holding Arturo to the same oath.

"Gotta find out what happened." Arturo shook his head. "Why the hell did he do this?" He stood. "We must find out. C'mon."

"What're we going to do?"

"Find Katy."

"How?"

"One of us had to remember. Renaldo or she must have said something about it. C'mon."

Though he frowned at Arturo's hope, Wyatt stood and joined his friend, classes forgotten.

* * * *

At the girls' apartment, Arturo asked if anyone knew Katy's number or address then searched his phone, sighed when he saw Conrad's name still listed, called, and got voice mail, left a message but doubted the boy would call back.

Sophia hugged Arturo. Tears stained his shirt. "Still can't believe it," she cried. "How did he do it? Why? What happened?"

"Who knows?" Millicent wiped her eyes, started to speak but choked up. Andrea remained quiet.

Arturo answered he didn't know but would find out, asked Sophia if she recalled Katy or Renaldo saying where Katy lived, what her place looked like, the neighborhood, at least in what part of town she lived. Sophia tapped a finger over her lips, mentioned Katy described a red brick house, deduced it had to be on campus. She snapped fingers, believed the girl had said it was at the corner of Monroe and something. Arturo asked if Sophia had seen a photo of the place. The girl's head shifted from shoulder to shoulder.

"C'mon." Arturo led all four to his car and when Sophia inquired what he was doing, he said they'd go past every corner on Monroe near campus and look for a red brick house.

Sophia folded her arms. "Do you realize how many of those there are?"

He stated in light yet firm tone they'd find it, said they had to try.

Of the first three red brick corner houses on Monroe none was the one. A fourth was vacant, fifth occupied though the car outside was not hers. They knocked and a scraggly, red-headed student said he'd never heard of the girl.

The next three corners had no red brick homes. A fourth block. Wyatt pointed. "There! Look."

As Arturo passed the place, Wyatt put his finger on the vehicle's window. "The car. Hers."

Arturo backed up and pulled to the curb.

At the door, Sophia's rapping garnered no answer. A second try. The door did not open. She tried a third, fourth time.

Wyatt made circles with his arm. "C'mon. She's not here."

Arturo again asked if anyone knew her cell number. No response. "I know I've checked but lemme see." He searched once more. "Knew I didn't have it. But that reminds me. Conrad. Let me try." A pause. "Shit" He left another message then stuffed the phone into a pocket and did as Wyatt had told Sophia.

"Hold on." Sophia gave several fist pumps on the door, peeked in a window. "Looks occupied. Think I saw movement." She hit the door harder. Wood creaked, a space between frame and door. It grew.

"Yes?" a familiar voice said though muted by hair dangling in front of the person's face.

The group didn't recognize her, eyes glazed and face pallid, her shirt unkempt, a few wet stains as well as many dried ones on it. Her feet were not covered.

"Katy? You okay?"

Katy tipped her head an inch forward, her *Uh-huh* more like *Uh-uh*. She sniffed, said she'd felt ill, rubbed her front, and cupped a hand on the doorframe as if it was the Rock of Gibraltar.

Sophia put an arm around the girl, requested to speak with her. Katy gave an *Mmm-mmm*. Sophia swept her arm, said all of them were there for support. The other girl mumbled she didn't feel like talking. Sophia cautioned she should as Arturo tapped his girlfriend, spoke into her ear.

Sophia moved away from the girl. "Katy, do you know where Renaldo is?"

The girl told them of when he left, said they hadn't talked since. Water in her eyes. She checked her front, sobbed, and wrapped herself around Sophia.

"Maybe she does know," Sophia whispered to the others as she patted the girl. "Katy? Honey? Do you know where he is, what happened?"

"Happened?"

Sophia gave the group an expanded-eye look, visually asked how to proceed. None had a response. "Katy." Sophia took the girl's face in her hands. "We have something to tell you. About Renaldo."

Katy hissed she never wanted to see him, he'd agreed on the abortion then changed his mind, demanded she do as he wished.

Sophia gasped. "Abortion?" Her voice sounded as if off in the distance.

"He got me pregnant," Katy said, tearful.

The group collectively blanched. Andrea blinked rapidly. Millicent's jaw opened. Wyatt was a stone carving. Arturo and Sophia gazed.

"Pregnant?" Sophia broke the cold silence. "You were pregnant?"

Katy nodded, informed them of the circumstances and the outcome then fell into Sophia's arms, Arturo assisting, the two leading the girl inside, she, Arturo, and Sophia on the sofa, the rest huddled around them.

"He was a nice guy," Katy said. "Loving, caring. He just had..." She gave a long, red-eyed face. "Other problems."

"We know," Sophia said, others nodding.

"One of these days he'll drink himself to death," Katy said. "But I don't care, we're through. He didn't try to understand me." She gagged. "I don't ever want to see him."

Sophia sighed, clasped an arm around Katy. "You won't. Ever."

Katy backed away, eyes growing as she asked what that meant. Her crooked brow smoothed, her face the color of paper. "You mean he..." She pointed a finger at her temple, thumb at a ninety degree angle. She lowered the thumb.

"Yes. And no." Sophia told her about Renaldo, described what few details they knew.

"Oh, God. No. No!" Katy fell into Sophia, who stroked the girl's hair while the others kept their silence.

"It's okay, let it out," Sophia said.

"It's not okay." Katy looked at the group. "Are you sure he's...no longer here?"

All showed agreement, Arturo somberly wondering if they could have done anything.

Sophia, Andrea, and Wyatt answered in the negative, it had been Renaldo's problem and he'd dealt with it best he knew how. Millicent only nodded.

They sat reticent for a long stretch before Katy sat up, resolved she'd overcome this, no one was going to destroy her. Sophia soothed her, Andrea said, "Attagirl," and the rest muttered encouragement. Katy stood, repeated her words, stated she would clean up, apologized then asked them to excuse her. The group did, said they'd be in contact regarding funeral arrangements. Katy vowed she'd be there to support the others, said she needed them to return the favor. Sophia hugged her, told Katy to call when she wished. Each gave the girl their number and she did the same for them.

"That's why Renaldo didn't want to talk at the pizzeria," Arturo said as they entered his car. "Maybe if we'd dragged it out of him, he might—"

"Don't torture yourself." Sophia placed an arm on him, rubbed his back, replied their friend had gone too far, reached the point of no return, his way the only way he knew how to deal with it. She let out a long breath. "Katy now knows. Thank God that part's over."

"Why are you thanking God?" Wyatt said bitterly then gave a twisted grin. "Or is this all His grand scheme?"

Sophia turned, eyes shriveled as she warned him about his poor timing. Wyatt flipped his palms up, said he was only asking. None of them spoke the rest of the way, all skipping their classes. They stayed up into the early morning hours, each sipping their drink, toasted the memory of their friend, and regaled each other with their favorite Renaldo moment. The question of why it happened didn't come up, all knowing the consequences if it did.

* * * *

That weekend, on a cloudless, calm day, the kind one imagined Thomas Kinkade had gotten up early for, canvas, paints, and easel in hand, the hearse weaved its way to the cemetery. At the gravesite, Arturo thought of his call and message. It had never been returned. He exhaled, shut his eyes. Too late now. Then a voice had him lift his head.

Chapter 20

"Conrad!" Arturo shook his friend's hand, clapped his back, and gave a brief hug. When the others saw their old friend, they did the same, asked how he was, where he'd been. He summarized his activities, funeral procession cutting him short.

The casket was lowered into the ground, Renaldo's parents crying, clinging to each other, the first time any of the group saw them cold sober.

Everyone gathered at the parents' house, hushed conversations abounded, words alcohol and poisoning often used together though never around the parents.

As the crowd abated, Arturo glanced to the kitchen. Renaldo's dad stood at the refrigerator, aluminum container in hand, lips pressed to its opening. Done with that one, the man started a second. Arturo shuddered, hurried away before being noticed, and met up with Sophia, swore he'd never do such a thing. He choked up, eh-hemmed, and spoke with Conrad.

"How are you? Glad you got my message. How'd you find out about the funeral?"

Conrad mentioned the college newspaper article, said he was sorry for not returning the call. "Why didn't you tell me what happened?"

Arturo said it was something he wanted to tell him live. Sophia joined them, told Conrad to stop by the apartments in the near future. Arturo offered going to the pizza place.

"Now?" Furrows above Sophia's eyebrows, Andrea and Millicent with like expressions.

Arturo said they'd just gather there to talk. He scanned the room, saw Renaldo's parents, each with drink in hand, motioned his head toward them, and whispered, "Anything to get away from them. Can't deal with it."

"You're right," Sophia said. "C'mon."

After changing, they met, the get-together sepulchral. At intervals, Arturo craned his neck, watched whenever the door jingled. Each time he slouched further in the booth.

"Who cares if he doesn't show?" Wyatt said. "He chose to leave."

"And how did that come about?" Arturo shot back. Wyatt wanted to know why he cared, it had happened months ago. Arturo said he simply wanted the truth to be told, known by all.

Wyatt grumbled Jack Nicholson's line from *A Few Good Men*. "Anyways, I was only doing God's plan." He turned to the girls, they in a quiet discussion. "Right, Sophia?"

"Huh?"

Wyatt told her. She frowned, asked why he was going there. The boy shrugged, said he merely wanted the truth, didn't it set one free? She scolded he didn't know the truth and never would.

"And you always will?"

"I'm just saying God wants us to do His will. Remember Thy Kingdom come?"

"A poem somebody made up. I have a will. It's my right to exercise it."

Sophia told him to do what he wished, he wasn't going to succeed if his will wasn't in concurrence with the Almighty's.

"So Renaldo's suicide was His plan?"

"Wyatt, shut up, I don't want to talk about it." Sophia faced the girls, involved herself with them.

"So you admit you were wrong?" Wyatt pushed.

"Whatever." Sophia waved a hand at him like he was a fly.

"It was Conrad's doing," Wyatt said to Arturo. "He could have worked things out with Dawn."

"You mean like you did on New Year's Eve?"

"Yeah. I, I mean... I mean no."

Arturo grinned, wanted to know which it was, leaned back as if he was a poker player possessing a royal flush. The other boy pounded the table, stated nothing had happened.

"Nothing?" Arturo arched his eyebrows.

"I mean after that night. Sure, we kissed on New Year's."

"So Renaldo was right?"

Wyatt sank. "Okay, we kissed. But nothing else. We did not have sex, we..."

The girls' heads turned synchronously, they looking at the boys as if both had raised sharpened knives to the females. Wyatt requested forgiveness and continued with Arturo. The girls listened as Wyatt said he and Dawn talked, made jokes, had drinks, and soon he found himself dancing to some ballad, she breathing down his chest. He closed his eyes.

The door jangled.

"God, her perfume was great," Wyatt went on, said the subject of the tryst came up, she saying Conrad bored her, too afraid, unexciting. "Like he didn't want to do it with her," Wyatt said with disgust, his voice rising.

"Wyatt," Arturo said in a low voice.

"Just a minute." Wyatt's eyes stayed shut. He laughed. "We joked maybe he'd been born a girl and changed things, if ya know what I mean."

"Wyatt," Arturo pronounced in song-like voice. "Look."

The boy opened his eyes. His face went from one dreaming of sex with the most gorgeous girl to one who'd been caught with his pants around his ankles. "Oh. Sorry." He frowned and sank in his seat.

"Yeah, sure." Conrad started to turn. The girls and Arturo begged him back. He motioned his head at Wyatt. "Why? So I can have my heart ripped out a second time? Now I find out he was with her *after* breaking up?" He leaned to Wyatt. "When? And what do you mean I was afraid to have sex?"

Wyatt pressed his back on the booth, chuckled rasply. "Her words, not mine."

"Whatever." Conrad spun. "I'm outta here. Pricks."

Sophia rushed to him, snuck her arm between his and his body, pleaded he stay. He swung the arm free, said he was never coming back, knew he shouldn't have, had only come to help everyone cope with their loss.

"But you all don't deserve that." Conrad kicked the door open and left.

"Way to go, Benedict," Arturo said.

Wyatt spread his arms. "*She* hit on *me*, not the other way around. I tried to leave. She kept me in her clutches."

Laughter from everyone else.

Wyatt seized the napkin, salt, and pepper holder then slammed it, others as if thunder clapped. Wyatt stood, said he was through, straggled out of the booth, and stomped away, did the same thing Conrad had done to the door, and left.

Arturo remarked how long the day had been, the year, how different things were two years ago, all of them together, a group. He scanned the restaurant, said it felt empty, unfamiliar. "C'mon." He took Sophia's hand. "Let's go."

The remaining members straggled out, Arturo aware Wyatt might be at the apartment. Now it'd be just the two of them.

What happened? How did it happen? Who's next?

They returned to the girls' place, talked into the early moments of a fresh day, Sophia wondering why Renaldo drank himself into oblivion, could have accomplished so much, had many years to live.

Millicent spoke of down times, how in low moments it felt life had ended. You'd found something, someone you really wanted, looked like you had it or them then it was taken away.

"Like traveling thousands of miles to visit the dream vacation spot only to find it's closed."

"Like Wallyworld." Andrea chuckled, *Vacation* one of her favorite films.

"I'm serious." Millicent looked at Andrea and listed incidents where her friend butted in on a guy she'd wanted.

Andrea jerked her head back. "I did?"

"Sure. So wrapped up in yourself you didn't notice."

Andrea gasped. "You have some nerve."

Millicent shrugged. "You were the one who told us after that male bimbo dumped you to let you know when you got full of yourself."

"Male bimbo?" Andrea was like she'd been accused of rape.

"C'mon," Millicent chided. "You know how slow he was." She smirked. "Guess that's why you liked him, had control. Isn't that what you want? Ya know, be a master to your slave?"

Andrea jumped up. "If I hadn't been taught not to fight, I'd kick your ass right now."

Millicent joined her. "Bring it on."

Andrea leapt at Millicent. Sophia bounded between them, one hand on each girl, rebuked them to relax, gently pushed Andrea to the sofa then Millicent, sat next to Arturo, they crammed between the two feuders. Sophia granted they'd had a very rough day, said they should gather themselves. For half a minute no one said anything, only exchanged glances.

"Doesn't that feel better?" Sophia ended the silence.

Andrea nodded. Millicent displayed upturned lips, said this was what she needed to regain her strength. Sophia sighed, about to put her arm around Arturo.

"Had to get my strength so I could kick her ass!" Millicent shot up. Sophia did too, pushed the friend back down, stood in front of her, and stated how Millicent had been so quiet, why the outburst.

Millicent pointed to the other end of the sofa. "Her."

Andrea leaned forward. Sophia extended a hand, nudged her roommate back, suggested they talk. Neither girl said anything.

"Millicent?" Sophia sat. "You have something to say?"

"Uh-uh. Unless you can have her vow never to steal another guy."

Andrea wanted proof. Millicent reeled off details like an actress who'd recited her monologue for weeks. "That enough?" she finished.

The other girl confessed she was unaware. Millicent gave a "Ha!" Andrea reiterated she hadn't been aware.

"Whatever happened, it's over." Sophia looked to Millicent. "Why do you bring this up now?"

"It hurts."

"That male bimbo, as you call him, was months ago." Andrea scrunched her nose. "Get over it."

"Then you took that other guy." Millicent described her latest disappointment, eyes clouding. "And then…" Her shoulders twitched, her eyes a water fountain. "Then..." She inhaled deeply.

"What?" Sophia stretched, put a hand on the friend's leg.

"Then... One of my friends dies." Millicent cried. "Barely into adulthood. Didn't he realize if he went too far, he couldn't come back?"

Sophia hugged her friend. "Guess not. But there are no mulligans in life, this isn't a dress rehearsal."

"Still can't convince myself it happened," Millicent said. "He was one of us. A good friend."

"Good friend?" Andrea asked. "Were you two—"

"Oh, God, no, girl." Millicent gave a half-chuckle through tears. "No way I'd be involved with someone who had those problems. It's hard not to succumb to those temptations when you confront them everyday." She wiped her eyes, tried to smile. "We become our parents."

The others gave quick *huhs*.

"You said God has a plan," Millicent spoke to Sophia. "You really believe this was part of it, Renaldo doing what he did?"

"Don't know what to think." Sophia turned to Arturo. "You're awful quiet."

Her boyfriend looked at each of them, said he had the same thought, now tired from asking. He stood, opted for nocturnal peace, and hoped Wyatt was asleep or perhaps had calmed.

Sophia rubbed a hand on her chin. "This whole thing's got everyone on edge. Let's call it a night."

Everyone nodded, girls doing as Arturo said he would. Sophia extended a finger, said she had an idea: a night of partying on Friday, carefree, no worries or concerns, just a time to be free.

The other two girls, though with eyes looking skyward, gave *Mmm-hmms*. Sophia asked Arturo, who concurred. She kissed him and he bade them good night, guaranteed a good time Friday, said he'd try to convince Wyatt into going, and left.

At his apartment, Arturo saw the living area unoccupied, Wyatt's door shut. He exhaled, repaired to his room, and fell asleep in his clothes.

Friendship

* * * *

Friday had things semi-normal. By nine o'clock the quintet was at the bar, Arturo with cup in hand, Sophia having knocked back a few, Millicent and Andrea with their share, Wyatt even joining the partying mood. Soon Andrea was with another guy, similar to the one Millicent had called a male bimbo though this one claimed to be a Finance major.

Millicent sat at the table with a Harvey Wallbanger, discovered how the drink got its name. After a few times on the dance floor with Sophia and speaking with Wyatt, she sobered though the buzz hadn't worn off, she almost toppling another bar goer as she headed to the ladies' room. The two caught themselves.

"Excuse me," a voice said.

"It's okay, I..." Millicent's glance met his. Her chest muscle thumped. Her mouth seemed super-glued shut. She righted herself, other person helping.

"You all right?"

Just the voice made Millicent go numb. "I...I'm fine," she said, now upright, could not resist staring at this person, his hazel eyes sedative, thick brown hair like it belonged in Hollywood, Polo cologne making her feel high.

"Good." His voice had the same effect on her as being at her favorite beach with the sun on her. He offered a hand as a song started. Millicent didn't think she could get on the dance floor fast enough.

They swayed to this song and several others, girl so into her scene, she hadn't noticed Wyatt on the floor, let alone whom he was with.

* * * *

When Wyatt'd heard the voice—he'd been tying his shoe then cleaning some stains off a pant leg—it was as if he was a glass of water placed in a room at fifty degrees below zero.

"How 'bout it?" the female voice said, voluptuous. "One time?"

Her perfume floated down to Wyatt's olfactory organs. He had trouble seeing, things seeming to shift as if on axis. It wasn't the beer, his last drink over fifteen minutes ago. He inhaled deeper, smiled. "Think we should?"

"Just once. C'mon." Dawn reached a hand, Wyatt finding himself half wanting to take it, half wanting to withdraw. Before he could decline, she had him on the floor. They brought each other up to date on happenings, she commenting sadly about Renaldo, Wyatt agreeing how tough it was, how they'd come here to forget and relax, if only temporarily. His throat tightened. A pause in the music gave the perfect chance. Then the thought of being alone and the temptation of her flesh and scent, combined with the next song being a slow one caused him to cup his hand around her. His mouth pressed against her cheek. She moaned pleasantly, to him the most beautiful sound. He lost track of time.

* * * *

Millicent continued with this boy while Whitney Houston's "Saving All My Love" played, a song before her time but one she liked despite its singer desiring a married man. Her eyes teared but she stuck her tongue between teeth and bit down. He felt as warm as tropical sun.

Whitney's voice faded. A hand on Millicent's back. She grunted. What about their conversation? Who did this girl think she was? Millicent did a one eighty.

"Andrea, don't you remember our talk about..." She viewed this person and forgot her words, asked the girl to forgive her.

"Just step aside," the tall, curvy, brown-haired girl said and shoved Millicent, pressed herself to this boy, and forced him to dance.

Millicent regained her balance and watched the two, his facial tone the color of a fire engine. Halfway through this song, their lips were interlocked. Millicent started toward them. The girl, noticing this, put a hand up.

"He's mine," she warned. "Come any closer and I'll take care of you. You had your fun—now get lost. He's been mine since last year, was trying to make me jealous. Right, Todd?"

"Yes, Gloria, dear." Todd looked to Millicent, mumbled something about being drunk as his girlfriend danced away from Millicent, Todd in her possession.

"Anyways," Gloria sniffed. "The only time you should have chosen that girl was if you were at the SPCA."

Millicent staggered, about to sit down. A yelp. She jumped.

"Sorry," Millicent said to the blonde female with pimples on her face like a pepperoni pizza.

"No big deal," the blonde said.

Millicent gathered herself, moved to the correct table, and slid into a chair, finished her drink. Tears welled. She wiped them away, had Arturo refill her cup, drank it faster than the others. As she finished it off, consciousness hit her. It had been but a few days since he'd died, how could she have forgotten? She'd asked why Renaldo had done it and now understood. She shook her head as if that would sober her up yet knew time was the only healer. She rose, gave farewell to Arturo and Sophia then, not seeing Wyatt or Andrea, left. At the apartment, she put on nightclothes and slid into bed, fell asleep though a few tears moistened the pillow beforehand as she asked when things would get better. High school and college were to be the best years of her life. Or so poetry, movies, music, and a few adults had told her. She was still waiting for the fun to begin.

* * * *

Wyatt spun Dawn, pulled her in, dipped her. They laughed, he bringing her back up, they doing a few moves separately. The song ended and they hugged, her lips on his face.

"Ya know," she said into his ear. "The moment I saw you, I knew you were for me. Conrad was nice but timid, afraid. I like—no, *need*—one who believes in what he's doing."

"That's me." Wyatt made his chest look larger. "Always believe in what I'm doing. Equivocal I'm not."

"Eee-quiv-a-what?"

"New word I learned." Wyatt bragged about his hard work and studying, how he always did what had to be done rather than what he wanted to do, how he did right, even when it didn't benefit him.

"Man of principles I like," Dawn said. "But the business before pleasure, I don't know." She chuckled. "You certainly have your principles. Conrad had no idea what he should or shouldn't do. He was... what was that word?"

"Equivocal," Wyatt said, thought of how she used Conrad in the past tense and couldn't rid himself of Conrad's reaction at the restaurant. His breathing became shallow.

"Yeah, that." Dawn tittered, said Conrad would never use such a word.

"Maybe not." Wyatt decided to sit, stated flatly he needed a break. And a drink. He had Arturo get him a beer, sat at their table, and drank the alcohol as if it was water, his tipsiness allowing the uneasy feeling to abate.

Following his third beer, the sensation in his gut forgotten, he led Dawn out. Uninhibited action followed, he twirling her, twisting and gyrating as if trying to win a dance contest.

"That was great," Dawn said during an interval. "Finally cut loose." With a laugh, she made an additional reference to her previous boyfriend, Wyatt too intoxicated to comprehend. She rested her head on him, her hair and perfume making him feel like Mr. Hyde.

"C'mon." Wyatt moved to the door.

"Where?"

He held her. "Someplace private, intimate, if only for a short time."

Dawn laughed. "You do believe strongly in what you're doing, don't sugar coat it."

"You bet." He led her to his car, glad they were but blocks from the apartment, and made it to the place without incident.

In less than sixty seconds they were as one in darkness, door shut. After climax, she rested on his shoulder, he fondling her back and hair, her perfume and hairspray a lingering aroma.

* * * *

Arturo held Sophia as they moved across the floor, he with a cheesy, wide smile. She quizzed him about it, he saying he was just thinking how long the two had dated. She hinted it might lead to bigger things. He said nothing, continued to dance. She sighed, resigned herself to the fact guys took longer. Who knew when "bigger things" would arrive?

As she was about to shut her eyes and lean on him, a body rubbed past Sophia. Her eyelids flipped open. When her brain interpreted what she saw, her pulse increased. She led Arturo away from this person, he resisting. She tightened her grip. He asked if she was all right. She responded, "Fine" but pulled him further from this other body.

The head turned. Sophia felt her latest meal rush up her esophagus. The person's eyes and nose were revealed. Sophia's innards relaxed, body temperature no longer at meltdown point. It was a stranger, only looked like someone she—they—knew. About to smile, the pulsating image from Sophia's memory promptly suspended the lips halfway up her face. Why couldn't she rid her mind of that picture? It'd happened practically two years ago. They'd stayed together. Her happy face re-formed. He intoned how beautiful she looked, how well she danced. She smiled. They had survived. Stronger, better, closer.

With the next song, Arturo lowered his hands and requested a break. Pictures reappeared to the girl like blinking neon. She held him in place, begged one more dance. He freed himself, went to the bar, Sophia watching. That same figure moved in his direction.

"Excuse me," he said, took a step away. The girl turned to the bar, ordered her drinks, and vanished into the bar's semi-darkness. Sophia confirmed it was not whom she thought—this person was shorter, face fuller, her waist bigger. Sophia sank to a chair at their table, rubbed her face as if to wash away the guilt. When Arturo handed her a cup, she drank half in one gulp, he cautioning her. The images floated away. She grinned, the rest of the night a routine of dancing and resting, drinking, and having fun.

* * * *

With sunrise, Wyatt rubbed his eyes, rolled to a side, and hit something, wondered what it was, his pounding head having trouble deducing the answer, as if a vacuum had sucked out his brain. He groaned, tried to move further in this direction, hit the object again.

"What the hell?" He pushed himself up with an elbow, opened his eyes despite brightness searing them. His mind registered what he'd touched: soft, creamy skin. Similar to the swells crashing a jetty, last night came to him. Then a second memory: Conrad's reaction at the pizza parlor. Wyatt sank on the mattress, his back to her. He wished for memory loss regarding the last twenty-four hours. His mind ignored the request.

How to tell her? His stomach had him thinking he'd never eat another meal. He slid a leg off the bed, his foot thudding on the floor, body listing in that direction. He twisted to the bed's edge, rolled away, and lifted himself up.

The girl stirred. Wyatt became like a character in a video whose viewer had hit the pause button. His ears were sonar.

Quiet beside him. Then breathing. Wyatt did the same in one big take, held it, and crept to the foot of the bed, leaned to the doorknob. His fingers touched metal. He drew himself to it, turned the knob. A *click*. He pulled the door to him, loosened his grasp. A loud *clack*. The figure under covers rustled.

"Wyatt?" Dawn propped herself up, a hand over slitted eyes. "Where're ya going?"

Wyatt released his hold, moved a half step to her. "Nowhere." His other foot followed the first. "Umm... nature calls." He shuffled feet, said he'd be right back, and took a wide step to the entryway.

"Wait."

Wyatt did as told, her voice some kind of automatic switch to his body. He leaned toward her. "Yes?"

She hit the bed. "Need to talk."

"I...uh." He pointed to the hallway room. "Can you hold that thought?"

"No." She repeated her action, harder. "C'mere." She stretched, took his arm, led him to her, and stroked his hair. "Had a great time last night. You really let loose, never saw you like that." She put lips on him. "Let's do it again soon."

"But I..." Wyatt poked frantically toward the other room. "Can I just..."

"Oh, go ahead." She freed him. "Hurry back."

"Will do." Two and half steps and Wyatt was in the bathroom, shut the door, used the sink for support, and looked in the mirror. Now what? A shower to kill time? It would only delay the problem. *Business first*, he told himself and opened the door. A figure made him jump back.

"Hey." Arturo smiled, motioned with his head to Wyatt's bedroom, and jabbed a finger at his friend's side. "Sneaky dog, you. Thought I saw someone with you when you left but was too drunk to know if I imagined it." He craned. "Who is she? Girl you met in class? At the bar?"

"Actually..."

"It's probably better you found someone else right away, after what happened with Conrad, ya know?" Arturo chuckled. "Hate to see that happen again."

"Arturo, I..."

"Wyatt?" Dawn came out. "Who's there? That Arturo?"

Arturo's face paled. "You?" His hands alternated, fingers pointing to the room. "In there?" He cringed. "With her? Really? After what happened at the pizza place?" His lips went up then down. "Don't know whether to pat your back or kick your ass."

"Would you excuse us?" Wyatt motioned his friend to his own room. Arturo did as told, finger over his lips as he shut his door.

Wyatt closed his door, back against it.

"Over here." Dawn hit the mattress.

The boy saw no other solutions, took a step forward but avoided the bed. "Dawn," he began.

"C'mon." She waggled a finger.

He stayed in place. His shoulders sagged and he sat on the bed's corner, rubbed his hair as if washing it. "Don't know how to say this."

"Oh God." The girl's body seemed to liquefy. It then returned to solid form. She jumped up. "I know that tone, those words." Dawn gathered her shirt, put it on as she spoke. "Know where this is headed." She slid arms through sleeves, straightened out the shirt, looked at him, and stepped to him, eyes like a bee had punctured her skin. "Why? What's wrong? Something I did?"

"Not at all. It's just... it's not you, it's me."

"Oh God," she repeated, headed to the door, put her pants on. "A fucking lie if ever I heard one. Hell with you. I'm outta here." Her hand twisted the knob.

Wyatt held her wrist and turned her around. "I'm sorry. Last night I got crazy, a little drunk."

"A little?"

"Okay, I was plastered. But I realize now we don't work. It's just all the..."

"Problems?"

"Yeah. It just doesn't work for me. I betrayed a friend."

"Ex-friend. Or so you say."

"But that's just it, we were friends. Until..."

"I ruined it?" She opened the door, attempted to exit. He blocked her, shut the door.

"No. That's what I meant by it's me. I ruined a good friendship. Not that I regret you, you're an attractive girl, nice. You're just not my type."

"Type?"

"You're too... shall I say, free? I have rules. And when I break them, it's like..." His hands moved in circles, one around the other.

"What?"

His hands continued. "Like I did something terribly wrong. Which I did, can't forget it. It's like someone who eats something spicy for the first time then gets sick. Every time they think of that food, it makes them ill." He gazed at her. "You understand?"

"Mmm-hmm." She cast her glance at the floor. "You don't like me, my lifestyle."

"That's not true, I..."

"Heard you loud and clear." Her eyes watered. She put both her hands on his side, thrust him away, stepped out, and turned, lectured he wasn't better than her, only pretended to have deeper values and stronger convictions. And if he did have them, he'd broken them so he was just as bad. She concluded he never forget that, yelled, "Good bye!" and pushed the door closed behind her.

"But, Dawn, wait, I ..."

The door hit his nose. He shut his eyes, about to follow her then sank on the bed, thought nothing, did nothing until a gentle knock broke his trance.

Arturo poked his head in. "You okay?"

Wyatt nodded, looked at the floor, and kicked a bed leg with his heel.

"You sure you're all right?" Arturo entered.

Wyatt stood, arms over his chest, mouth a wrinkled line. "I'm fine!" He shoved his friend aside, marched to the kitchen, poured a glass of water, gulped it, and moved to the sofa.

"You're sure?"

"Yes!"

Arturo tried to smile. "Did you get her?"

Wyatt stopped in mid-swallow then finished it off. "What?" He coughed a few times, set the cup down.

"Ya know..."

"Yes, I did."

"Good."

Wyatt scowled. "What does it matter?"

Arturo again attempted to curve his lips up. "You went out on a high note."

Wyatt acted as though a skunk had sprayed them. "What are you talking about? I fucked up."

"And in." Arturo laughed.

"Shut up." Wyatt got right in front of Arturo. "What the hell is so funny?"

Arturo spread his arms. "Was trying to lighten the mood, get you to look at the positives."

"How the hell can you be so insensitive? I betrayed a friend, remember? You're always reminding me. Benedict, right?"

Arturo's face blanched. "Sorry," he whispered. "Wasn't thinking."

"Damn right." Wyatt kicked the couch. "And you should be sorry. Excuse me." He thudded to his room, flung the door shut, and came out minutes later, fully dressed. "Going for a walk. A long, long walk." He slammed the exterior door so hard the glass he'd set on the counter fell and cracked.

Arturo kicked it across the floor. It shattered against a wall. He slouched on the sofa, shut his eyes.

* * * *

Wyatt walked around campus, cursed what he'd done as well as Arturo's nonchalance. Were all guys this immature? Was he the only one who saw what a real, mature relationship was about?

Who cares? His mind answered as he passed a small, two-bedroom brick house with shutters. A white sign out front had the words *For Rent* scrawled in black, a number below that. He thought ahead to fall, their lease up come spring. This area seemed nice and quiet. He made note of the house and a few others that appeared to be rentals though none had signs saying such. He'd worry about that in a few months.

Back at the apartment, he and Arturo made amends, felt no need to talk further.

* * * *

Things were calm the next couple of months, the gang—down to Arturo, Sophia, Andrea, Millicent, and Wyatt—planning spring break. They stayed at the same hotel in South Padre, Arturo doing a dry run, he and Sophia dining one morning on the balconied terrace of a beachfront restaurant. Waves crashed the sand every few seconds, gulls crying their sounds.

Arturo believed this would be the place. At sunset, she eating a favorite meal. Or perhaps at sunrise, no one else around. But that was a year away. She smiled as she ate eggs and hash browns, said how delicious it was.

"Indeed," he replied, was taken out of his daydream when she asked how he knew, he with a plate of pancakes. He only smiled. Three hundred and sixty five more days.

* * * *

The semester ended, each going separate ways though all promised to get together during summer despite no specific date set. When Arturo asked Wyatt about where to live next fall, Wyatt gave a non-committal response about talking later.

* * * *

Millicent worked full time at the daycare, kids seeming to keep her alive, her worries non-existent when with them as they discovered things for the first time, shared the moments with her. The experience strengthened her belief she could raise a family, small crises giving her a chance to learn how to handle kids. An instructor even told her she'd make a good parent.

If only I can find Mr. Right, she thought. *Though I have. It's just he's always with another girl.* Andrea came to mind. *Usually Ms. Wrong.*

When she saw Sophia in June at a store, Sophia made mention of going out for pizza and discussing fall plans, the apartment in particular. Millicent reacted as Wyatt had, the desire to be alone stronger. Like she'd outgrown everyone, they a collective Peter Pan. Time by herself sounded good.

* * * *

Andrea dated two guys that summer, neither lasting but a month. She took summer courses, made the grade in each.

* * * *

Arturo and Sophia spent much of the summer together since no one else was around. They ate pizza a few times, he commenting once how quiet it was.

Sophia squirmed next to him. "Allows us more time. Just the two of us." She sang the old Bill Withers song and when Arturo asked who sang it and she stated the name, he smiled, requested she keep it that way. She playfully slapped him and he laughed though his face quickly went long and stayed that way until Sophia asked if all was okay. He replied it was but with a long, deep exhale and swiveled to her. "Don't ya miss the good times?"

"Good times?"

"All of us here. Together. Talking about what we were going to do, how we would conquer the world."

Sophia's left lip ticked up. "I didn't say that."

"I mean in our own way."

Sophia leaned in. "I know."

"Don't ya miss it?"

"A little, sure. But it's not like we haven't seen the others in years, like we're over the hill." She sat up, said they hadn't even reached drinking age.

Arturo thrust his chest out. "*I* have."

"The rest of us. Anyways, we'll get together this summer. Bunch of times."

He mentioned they'd all be of drinking age, official adults in a few months.

She sighed, thanked him sarcastically for reminding her of her birthday.

"You just said how young we are."

"But I'm a woman." She sighed. "You guys have it so easy. Don't have to obsess about age, beauty, raising a family, being a good mother."

Arturo smiled at her last comment, pictured her playing with their kids. Only eight more months till spring break. And that first step.

"What're you grinning about? That you don't have to worry about that stuff?"

"Naw, just thinking ahead. Besides, guys have pressures. Have to make the first move for a date, no girl comes and asks me."

Sophia smiled. "Who'd want an ugly duck like you?"

Arturo poked her then lost his grin, said she knew what he meant: the paying for dates, having to pick up and drop off the girl, and how, after marriage, the guy had to be the breadwinner, the disciplinarian, the protector of wife and kids, repair broken things, and such.

Sophia put her chin in her hands, elbows on the table. "Guess it cuts both ways. Just seems easier for guys."

Arturo snickered. "I thought the same about women. Grass is greener, huh?"

Sophia held his hand. "We'll share chores and responsibilities when we get married."

The boy stiffened. "Who said anything about marriage?" He felt her hands fall away, watched her mouth curve down, jaw about to open. He moved his lips higher on his face, nuzzled next to her. "Gotcha."

She froze a second then laughed, kissed him. He wrapped his arms around her.

"Hey, hey, none of that around here," a familiar voice said, clapped hands.

The couple looked up.

"How's it going?" Andrea said, Millicent at her side.

"Great." Sophia slid over, invited the two into the booth. "How'd you meet up?"

Andrea said they bumped into each other at the dollar store, decided to grab a bite. "And this is like a second home to us."

"Second kitchen," Millicent joked. "Even better. Don't have to cook or clean up."

The four caught up on each other's activities, Andrea describing her latest relationship and how it'd ended, the others giving appropriate eye rolls.

"One of these centuries you'll find the right guy," Sophia teased then mentioned it was a month to fall semester, they with no plans about where to live, warned it had to be done soon. She squeezed past the others, went to the front, grabbed the apartment guidebook and the local paper next to it, returned, and flipped through ads.

"What about me and Wyatt?" Arturo said.

"Wyatt and I," Sophia corrected. "Don't sound so juvenile. You're an adult now."

Arturo stated her words about being nowhere near retirement. She sassed back in baby talk, her tongue out. He asked who was being juvenile now.

"Children, behave," Andrea said but with a grin.

Sophia found a few places, they either not as nice or more expensive than what they'd rented. "So." She folded the newspaper, stuffed the apartment guide in her purse, and smiled at the girls. "Looks like we're stuck for another year, same place, same roomies."

Andrea shrugged. "Okay by me."

Millicent shifted, scratched her chin. "I guess."

Andrea frowned. "Don't sound so enthusiastic."

Millicent protested she was, claimed she felt tired from shopping but looked forward to reuniting in the fall then sighed.

"Again," Andrea said. "Don't sound so excited."

Millicent repeated she was.

"Good." Sophia started to plan another meeting here to sign the lease and agree on a moving date. They chose the following weekend to sign, would move in right before the semester started.

"See ya then," Sophia said as everyone entered their cars.

"What about me?" Arturo asked, the two in her car.

"What about you?"

"I was thinking..." Arturo looked out the window, searched for the right words. He turned to her. "We've been together how long?"

Sophia tapped a finger on the wheel. "Three years."

"Going on four. I was thinking it was time we...took it a step further." He held his breath.

"A step further?" Her eyebrows sank.

"Yes. Three years is a long time."

"Seems a lot longer, actually," Sophia said then glanced at him. "Only kidding." She rubbed a hand on his thigh.

Arturo did not reciprocate, said he was serious, they'd gotten serious. He looked at her. "Don't ya think we should...live together?"

Sophia continued driving, non-responsive.

He tapped her. "You hear me?"

At a red light, the girl faced him. "Huh?"

"I said we should..."

"Oops." Sophia fingered the windshield. "Green." She hit the gas pedal. "You were saying?"

Arturo stared ahead. She encouraged him with a wave. Present time became the past.

"Well?" Sophia twisted her hand in a welcoming gesture. "I'm waiting."

Arturo looked out his window again, opened his mouth, words toppling out like dominoes knocked over. "I just thought we should be looking for an apartment. You and I."

Tires squealed. The two pitched forward, Arturo's head going forward then back.

"You think what?" Sophia gazed at him like he requested they get on the car's roof and perform a striptease.

Arturo withdrew, took in the passenger window view. "Only suggesting."

A horn from the car behind.

"Did you say what I thought? You and I? Should..." Her eyebrows were so low on her face they appeared to meet her nose.

"Live together. Co-habitate."

A second honk from the rear. Sophia looked up, moved forward at a slow pace. "Co-habitate?" She chuckled sarcastically. "What is that, a politically correct term?" She pulled the car to a side street and parked. Dogs barked. A lawn mower hummed in the distance. "I'm talking about us."

"So am I. Living together."

"You think we're ready for that?"

Arturo swallowed. "I do. Just for a year. You can move out if you want in six months."

"I don't know." Sophia glanced at her side mirror. "That's a big step. Read where people who live together first have a higher divorce rate than those who don't."

"Okay," Arturo said meekly. "Just an idea. If you're not ready for it..."

Sophia lectured him not to guilt her or make her feel inferior, believed two people should marry before living together. Plus, she already had an agreement with her friends.

"It's okay. If you can't handle—"

"Do you want to walk home?"

"No. It's okay, I'm fine. We'll do it your way."

"Good."

"So what about me? Where will I live?"

"What about Wyatt?"

"Hasn't returned my calls."

Sophia pulled the car back into traffic, tapped his knee. "Don't worry, there are one bedroom apartments. We'll find you one." She smiled. "That way when I'm not there, you can beat off and no one'll know."

"Very funny," Arturo said, not even hinting a grin.

"Just trying to get you to look at the bright side." She leaned over, pecked his face with her lips. "Don't worry, you'll be fine. Mama here will take care of ya."

The boy finally smiled, wondered aloud where Wyatt was, called him. No answer. He left a message.

* * * *

Not until the next day did Wyatt call back.

"Hey, pal, what's new?"

"Nothing," Wyatt mumbled. Arturo asked about the upcoming semester, his classes, plans for living arrangements. "Oh." Wyatt's voice dropped a level. "Didn't tell you. Already have a place."

"What?"

"Signed the lease last week." He described the two bedroom house. "And it's cheaper."

"I see. Well, that's nice. Hope you like it there."

"I think I will." Wyatt forced a laugh. "No one to call me Benedict, huh?"

Arturo tried to chuckle, told Wyatt to make sure he stopped by the old place, said the girls had the same apartment, he still looking. "And don't forget pizza. Haven't seen ya all summer, where ya been?"

"Here and there," Wyatt said vaguely, described a couple of classes.

"Well don't forget us." Arturo said he'd call an invite for pizza, Wyatt saying he wouldn't mind doing so.

"See ya around," Arturo said.

"Later," Wyatt said.

* * * *

The semester transpired with no significant events, Arturo and the girls out on the town though with the dwindling crowd, this occurred less frequently. For Arturo it mattered little, he focused on spring break. The big event. He'd saved some money, visited several jewelers to find the right one. The ones he thought she'd like were out of his range.

* * * *

Christmas break saw the gang get together at the restaurant, talk of plans for next year, spring break.

"I'm tired of Padre," Sophia said. "Let's hang out here."

Arturo became glassy-eyed and his heart seemed to have leapt into his throat, blocked his breathing. "What?"

Sophia said she wanted to use the break to catch up on sleep and relax. Arturo promised a great time, looked to Andrea, and said "Right?" in a firm tone. The girl nodded, called Sophia a spoilsport, wanted to know when the girl had become an AARP member.

Sophia grinned, said she wanted a slow spring break. Andrea moaned nothing was more relaxing than lounging on the beach and viewing all the guys. She then faced Arturo and apologized, said she meant her and Millicent would do that, asked Millicent if that would be fun.

The other girl nodded.

"See?" Arturo said to Sophia, hands clasped. "Whadya say? Please?"

Sophia's smile enlarged. She sighed. "If you guys are that adamant, okay."

"Great." Arturo wiped his forehead, licked his lips, mentally began a speech, where he'd do it and when. Now he needed the jewelry.

He found it at the end of January, made a down payment and monthly installments. Only remaining obstacle was her response.

To Arturo, the days leading up to the break appeared to last as long as the months before Christmas. The Friday before break had the gang on a torturous drive, four people in one car for twelve hours.

By the time the old day passed into the new, they were in their hotel, girls ready to crash. Arturo peeked through blinds, saw a bar in the distance, and asked if they wanted a drink, all now of legal age.

Sophia yawned. "After what we've been through? Need some shut eye." She smiled. "Anyway, you're sleeping with me, a room with two double beds all we could afford."

Andrea teased he could sleep on the floor then pointed past the window. "Better yet, outside."

"Aw, couldn't do that." Sophia planted kisses on Arturo. "Then my wittle cutesy pie baby'd weave. Wouldn't you?"

Arturo returned the kiss, said he wouldn't.

"Even if Selena Gomez invited you to her room?" Andrea said.

"Hmmm." Arturo rubbed his chin. Sophia punched him. He massaged the spot and observed the bed. Trying to enter la-la land tonight would be as easy as falling asleep on an interstate. He kept repeating the words, wanted to ask that morning and get it over with, fondled the object in his pocket then suggested they get up early.

"After this? And you? Up early, on a day off? You all right?"

Arturo proclaimed good health but couldn't prevent his face from flushing, said they needed to watch a sunrise together.

Sophia smiled, placed a hand on her heart. "Awww, how romantic. Didn't know you had it in you." She kissed him, agreed to his offer, and set the clock alarm for six, explained that'd give them time to snooze before the sun came up.

"Good idea," Arturo said though he knew he'd need no alarm, wondered if he'd even close his eyes. He crawled into bed, kissed Sophia, and as expected, did not sleep.

* * * *

Early that morning, with Millicent and Andrea in dreamland, he and Sophia did make out though it was nothing like the first time.

A pang of conscience stopped him in mid-motion. Sophia asked if something was wrong. Arturo continued. Had she guessed, even knew? If so, wouldn't she have mentioned it?

He told himself he didn't like that girl, it was he and Sophia until the end of time. And beyond. He smiled, laughed at the pet names she whispered, returned the favor. After she fell asleep, he went over what he'd say, how to say it, and when. And what to do if she gave the wrong reply. It had to be done early, Arturo positive if he waited he'd be like a soggy paper towel, his limbs all gelatin.

From five a.m. until the alarm beeped, he watched the clock then slapped the snooze button. After the third time it went off, he touched Sophia. She pulled covers up, rolled away. Arturo permitted her sleep as it wasn't light out yet and he had to edit his speech.

The next time the alarm sounded, he turned it off, put on clean clothes, and gently rubbed Sophia, tapped her shoulder, and whispered, "Time to get up."

"In a minute," the girl mumbled.

He took her. She swung her arm, told him to go away. He paused then shook her again, warned the sun was about to come up.

" 'morrow," she said, head half-raised off the pillow. "Do it 'morrow."

"Have to do it today."

She groaned she needed rest.

"C'mon." Arturo pinched her. No reply. He poked her ribs. She rose then fell back on the bed. He caught her, lifted her up, and said it was today or never.

She tried to free herself from his grasp. He did not let go, said it had to be done today.

"Why?"

Arturo's mind was blank so he repeated the words in beggar's tone.

She snapped covers off. "If it'll shut you up."

He thanked her over and over. She asked if he was okay and he professed he couldn't be better, added to himself *Except if you say yes,* and helped her out of bed.

"Never saw you in such a hurry."

"Need to watch a sunrise, remember?" He peeked out the window. Yellow had just taken over a thin strip of sky above the horizon, waves splashing in an eerie, yellowish hue, winds calm.

When ready, he waved her out of the room, dug a hand in his pocket. Empty. He checked the other. Same result. He opened the door.

"Whatsa matter? Thought we had to get out there."

"Forgot something. Be right out." He slid in, shut the door behind him. She asked what he was doing, other girls whining for quiet. Arturo searched the drawers, his shirt from yesterday, under the bed, by the nightstand. Where were his previous day's pants? He saw Sophia's clothes in a corner.

"What's going on, Arturo?"

"Be right out." He jumped over the bed to the pile, checked her clothes. Nothing fell out. Then, underneath them, he saw blue denim. His. He stuck a hand in a pocket. Nothing. The second pocket. His finger tapped a round, metal object. He gathered it, shoved the ring into his current pocket, and slipped out.

"What the hell was that all about?" she said. "You were the one in a hurry."

Arturo smiled, said the only thing he could think: he'd forgotten to put on deodorant then was unable to find the container. He tried to shut the door but lost his grip, clutched it a second time, and glanced to the window at the end of the hall. It remained dark blue except for a yellow tint at the bottom. He got ahold of the door handle, closed the door, and hurried to the front exit, she in tow.

"See?" she said when outside. "Sun's just coming up."

"Let's go."

A gentle wind blew through their hair. One fourth of the sun peeked over the horizon. He hurried her along, looked for a spot to sit.

"Why are you acting so weird?" She smiled. "Or are you acting?"

"Just follow me."

They walked for a minute, Arturo's chest pounding like thunder. She showed no hint of recognition then stopped.

"C'mon," he said.

"I'm tired. Let's do this tomorrow."

"You'll be too tired then."

"Am too tired now."

Arturo scanned the beach and saw a pile of rocks they could rest against. "C'mon." He ran to them.

"Slow down."

"Just follow me."

She jogged behind, he pulling at her. The sun neared one third exposure. He sat, let her sit on his legs, and pointed at the yellow orb.

"Isn't it beautiful? A great start to a new day."

Watching the sun as foamed water cascaded to shore, had her taking in a breath. "It is gorgeous."

"Almost as beautiful as you." He looked at her, took her hand. "Sophia?"

"Yes?"

"We've been together for quite some time."

She giggled. "Seems too damn long sometimes."

"I'm serious." He squeezed her hand. "You've been great for me, bring joy to me every day, mean so much, give me life." He waved a hand to the east. "Like the sun does to each day."

Sophia looked at him. He couldn't hide his smile. She squinted, studied him. Her lips began an upward curve. Moisture formed around the eyes. She sniffled.

"Sophia?"

"Yes?" Her smiled expanded.

Arturo stuck a hand in his pocket, clasped the object as if it was the edge of a cliff he was falling off. He slid his hand out, used his other to move her hand toward the one with the object.

He opened his fingers, slid the gold metal circle over her second largest digit, and looked at her.

"Sophia? Will you marry me?"

Tears flooded her eyes. She laughed and cried, drew a hand to her face, sniffed, and rubbed the eyes.

"Well? I'm waiting." Arturo sang out with a half smile.

She gazed at him.

Chapter 21

"Yes," Sophia cried then hugged him. "Yes, I will. Yes!"

He laughed as he wiped her tears away. They continued to hug.

"What a lovely day," Sophia said of the now completely-risen sun.

"And to think you wanted to sleep in." Arturo chortled. "I just hope it'll soon become the second best day."

"Second best? Wha..." She smiled and laid her head on him, he running fingers through her hair. They listened as the ocean washed up and birds squawked.

"Let's tell the others," Sophia said and the two walked hand in hand to the hotel, received hugs and congratulations from the other two, all celebrating with a big breakfast.

The afternoon was also better than any other for the two, light clouds scudding across the sky, gentle winds cooling a warm afternoon.

"So when's your Mr. Right coming?" Sophia, her face as bright as the day, asked Millicent.

The friend said she'd probably met him when he was with someone else, chuckled there were lots of other Mr. Rights.

Sophia placed a hand over her eyes and scanned. "Don't see any."

Everyone groaned. Sophia then asked if Millicent had seen any guys she liked.

"Plenty," the girl said as three young, well-built men strode past. "Just have to get them interested in me." Her head moved in the direction the boys went.

Andrea tugged Millicent's arm, pointed to the guys.

"Are you kidding?" Millicent loosened her arm. "I'm not desperate."

"Don't be ashamed, girls do it all the time now." Andrea elbowed her friend. "Guys like desperate girls."

Millicent giggled, cracked knuckles then rubbed one hand over the other. "I can't. It's not a womanly thing."

"You'll regret it."

"Besides, who are they, where are they from, what are they like?"

"Who cares?" Andrea said. "As long as they got great hair, great bod, and a cute butt. And plenty of this." She rubbed thumb and fingers. "At least, look like they're gonna make a lot of it."

Sophia scolded Andrea who countered it wasn't being greedy, it was practical, money the number one cause of divorce.

"Whatever." Sophia kissed Arturo a quick jab. He did the same. She volleyed another. Soon they had arms around each other.

"Hope I can get my guy," Millicent said. "College is almost done, soon out in the real world with no time to party, meet a guy, and grow with him. Is it too late already?"

The rest of the day she questioned out loud every time a guy passed yet never carried out Andrea's edict, said the right guy would come along and both she and he would know it.

The group enjoyed the rest of the break, Arturo and Sophia skinny-dipping a few times after dark, intimate both in the water and out.

"What a trip," Sophia said and sighed upon collapsing on the apartment sofa.

Arturo unpacked, discussed upcoming finals and next semester. "What about us? For our senior year?"

"Hmm?"

"It's early but I'm referring to living arrangements. We're engaged, ya know?" He smiled.

She spun the ring with her thumb. "So I've been told."

The two tittered. He moved to her, set her hand in his, said since they were together, they should act and live like it. Sophia pointed out they were not yet married and pulled her hand free. He said that was but a short passage of time.

She turned away. "But it hasn't happened yet." She faced him and fingered the ring. "Is that why you did this? To shack up with me?"

He kissed her hand. "Of course not. I just... I think we should do it, take that final step. We're getting married anyway, what's the big deal?"

"The big deal is about couples who live together." Sophia separated from him, went to her room, stopped at the dresser drawer, picked up a magazine, and quoted statistics from an article on living together before marriage and the divorce rates.

He entered the room. "Bullshit. Any research can be manipulated to fit an agenda. One group said breast feeding up to a certain age was bad, another said it wasn't. One study said kids sleeping with parents until ten was bad, another said it was good, a third claimed it had no effect."

"Let's not take chances." She glared. "You're sure you didn't propose just to live together?"

"I've already bopped you," he jeered.

Andrea and Millicent, in Millicent's room, reacted like photographers spotting a celebrity making out with someone other than their spouse.

Sophia pounded to her doorway. "Excuse us," she said and slammed her door then faced Arturo, arms in criss cross fashion. "I'm waiting."

The words made Arturo recall he'd said the same thing after asking the big question. He grinned.

"What's so damn funny?"

He told her, asked if she remembered.

She stayed silent. He re-told the moment: Sunrise, the view, his words, hers.

She smiled then laughed. "Funny how when we both needed an answer, we used the same words."

He took her in, pressed his face against hers. "Like attracts like."

She chortled. "Thought it was opposites attract."

"Who knows?" He kissed her. "I do know there's no one else I want to be with more than you." He pulled away to arms length, looked at her, and sighed. "If you think it's best we live separately until marriage, I'll go for that." He kissed her again. "You're the only one for me."

"You'd do that? For me?"

Another kiss. "For us."

They embraced. Only the knocking on the door minutes later caused them to separate, Andrea asking if they were okay. Sophia opened the door, told them they were fine, and they ate dinner. When Arturo stated he was headed to his place, his fiancé hugged him and thanked him for being so compromising.

"No problem," he said, kissed her, stepped away, and waved, Sophia blowing kisses as he shut the door.

* * * *

As she was about to fall asleep, an image streaked across Sophia's memory like an unexpected lightning strike. The photo. Where did she have it? Did she still have it? If so, she promised to burn it. It was their past, they to be together until death. After death. The memory would be like an old newscast about the coldest day ever. *Love overcomes everything*, she thought, drifted into the make-believe scenes the mind presents late at night.

* * * *

To Arturo, the semester lasted a day, he and Sophia spending warm spring nights together.

* * * *

"Perhaps with the wedding, I can woo your father back," Sophia's mother said.

With her head turned away from her mom, Sophia rolled her eyes. If she, Sophia, knew that would never happen, why didn't her mother? There was a plan for everyone and he wasn't in hers, no matter how much her mother wanted him to be.

* * * *

Andrea and Millicent were last to leave the apartment, Millicent observing Arturo and Sophia outside loading stuff. "Maybe someday soon we'll have our weddings," she said to Andrea then moaned. "If we're lucky."

"Not me, sister. Ain't ready for that. Am gonna have some fun."

"Don't ya think about finding the right guy, having a family?"

"Sure. For five minutes." Andrea picked up a small box, patted her roommate. "If it's meant to be, it's meant to be."

"Guess so." Millicent picked up a box. The two headed to their vehicles. Andrea passed a glance over her shoulder. "What about next semester?"

"Huh?"

"Three of us. Together again. Sounds good?"

Millicent halted. Visions of when she'd seen the right guy and her friend—*So-called friend,* she thought—had snatched him for herself, only to discard him like recyclable material, played in Millicent's mind. She shifted a leg under her box and pushed it up in her hands to re-secure her grasp. "We'll see. Have to talk with my parents."

"Your mom's right here."

"I mean at the right time."

"Gotcha." Andrea winked and loaded her box. As Millicent watched the girl, she already had her answer, an excuse all that was needed. To distract herself, she sized up a guy at the complex who loaded things into his car. He seemed geeky, wore horn-rimmed glasses, and seemed to weigh less than she did. "If it's meant to be, I suppose it's meant to be," she undertoned and loaded her box.

* * * *

Andrea dated a guy that summer for a few weeks though it was never serious, they kissing but a few times.

Millicent worked full time at the daycare, was told as soon as she graduated and got her teacher's certificate, she'd supervise a kindergarten class.

In mid-June the daycare doorbell jangled. Millicent opened the door. "How may I help..."

She absorbed the sight: crew-cut black hair, dark eyes, the box the young man held blocking the most important area to Millicent, after the eyes.

"How can I help me?" the girl said, then tried to laugh. "I mean you."

The guy smiled, said he was to deliver a copier, scanner, and fax machine.

"Oh, yeah," Millicent said in the tone a stereotypical airhead used. "One of those things you dial a number to send a sheet of paper."

"And make copies and scan documents to e-mail as attachments. May I, uh, come in?"

"Huh?" Millicent blinked. "Oh, yeah, sure." She backpedaled, nearly stumbled then, with an awkward laugh, asked for forgiveness. "What can I do for you?"

"I'm here to deliver this, remember?"

"Oh, right." Millicent hid her face with a hand. "Let me check."

"Can I set this down? It's pretty heavy."

"Someone like you, so strong?" Millicent gave an impish grin.

"If ya don't mind." The guy set the large box down, picked up the clipboard, dug in his back pocket, and retrieved a pen, his wallet falling out. Millicent bent and picked up the tri-folded object. One end opened and displayed photos, girl wishing it'd been his ID.

"Thanks." The guy took the wallet, checked a picture, and grinned, showed Millicent. "My girlfriend. Already serious, talking about moving in together. We get along great, haven't had an argument." He rapped his hand on the wood door then grinned wider.

"Yeah." Millicent's voice drained of enthusiasm. "That's great." Her throat restricted. She straightened up, forced her chest out. "My boyfriend and I are taking it slow, letting things evolve as they come."

"Great. Good luck."

Millicent signed for the package, muttered "Dickhead" then fled to the ladies' room where she stared in the mirror, asked "*Why?*" several times but, with no answer, went back to her job, a five-year-old boy requesting she read to him.

When the doorbell rang again near the end of the day, Millicent ignored it until an instructor requested the girl see who was there. Millicent whispered profanity, previous memory fresh in her mind as she trudged to the front. "How may I help you?" she said without looking up.

"I'm here to install a copier, scanner, and fax machine."

Millicent called out for her boss, about to check the order when she saw the guy's watch with Pistol Pete logo, the official Oklahoma State mascot, old west cowboy with chaps, ten gallon hat, and pistols, fingers at the trigger of each. She asked if he was a fan as she scanned the order.

"Am enrolled there," he said. "Education major."

"Really? So am I. Also at OS—" She met his glance, his soft brown eyes and small grin as inviting as a hot tub on winter solstice. He smiled big teeth.

Millicent also smiled, words flashing across her brain. Her mouth, however, remained closed.

"May I come in?"

"Huh?" Millicent broke from her trance. "Oh, sure." She sounded dry laughter, back of her hand high on her head. "My mind was elsewhere, I…"

Her boss interrupted, guy at the door stating who he was, Millicent taking in all details: Name was Adam, his pants clean and ironed. She did not move.

"Millicent? Shouldn't you be looking after the kids?" her boss asked.

The girl did not respond. The boss nudged her, said her name a second time.

"What? I'm sorry." Millicent could not keep her mouth down.

Her boss told her to watch the children.

"Yes, sure. Right." With her stomach seeming to cave, Millicent trudged to the kids, checked over her shoulder so long a boy asked what she was doing. Millicent mumbled, "Nothing," watched the guy move to the back, and followed him, he setting up the machine, showed employees how it worked. Millicent had trouble preventing her legs from twitching.

"There you are," the guy said as he headed to the front.

The young girl's head ached, thumped. She opened her mouth, feebly said, "Excuse me." The guy continued to the door. As if starving and seeing the last morsel of food on the table, Millicent reached out. Her arm was too short. She lowered it, about to sigh.

"Hmm?" The guy did a half turn.

"What?" Millicent found herself saying.

"You need something?"

The girl blushed. "No. Uh-uh." She immediately took the Lord's name in vain under her breath.

"Okay." The guy lifted an arm, fingers on the doorknob. He opened the door.

Words in Millicent's mouth. Her lips, however, would not move. The boy waved, thanked the girl, and started to leave.

"Wait." Millicent stuck out her arm. It hit the door. She shivered, wrung the hand, still looking at the entrance. It closed. "Damnit. Golden opportun—"

The entryway opened. "You say something?"

"Hmmm?"

"Thought you said something." The guy's creased eyes relaxed. "Guess I'm hearing things. Bye."

The words crashed, a hurricane wave on the beach of Millicent's mind. "Hold on."

The boy chuckled, his face like she'd turned into a frog. "Yes?"

"I was wondering..." Millicent scratched her arm, pulled at her shirt.

"Yes?"

"What?" Millicent blinked, her heart feeling too big in her chest. "Oh." Uneasy laughter. She pointed to the guys' hand. "Your watch. Where'd you get it?"

He extended his wrist, flipped the watch over, read the name of the business, said it was a good place for OSU apparel.

She grinned. "You said you're at OSU? Education major?"

He showed agreement. She asked what year, he saying sophomore.

Younger man, she thought, pinched back her grin, repeated she had the same major, and waved a hand at the room like a game show hostess in front of a prize. "Work here part time during the semester, full time in the summer."

"Like it?"

Millicent moved her head up and down. "Not bad. Kids are fun." One tapped her leg, requested she finish reading. She promised she would, told him to wait then looked at the guy. "When they're behaving."

"Which is about zero percent of the time." The guy flashed his big teeth as he laughed.

Millicent felt she'd never need a jacket again, no matter the temperature, and giggled. "They're fun most of the time."

"They are."

The little boy continued tapping the leg. Millicent told him to wait then spoke to the guy. "I'm Millicent. I assume your current job is to pay tuition."

He admitted such then beamed, bragged next week he was to start as a teacher's assistant for summer school. Millicent congratulated him, talked about the OSU campus, her experiences and friends, how they'd gone to high school here, remained pals in college, told of how they met for pizza. Her eyes brightened and she snapped thumb and finger. "Wanna join us? You'd like it. We just eat, talk about classes, upcoming stuff, philosophy."

"I don't know. Sounds pretty deep, philosophy."

"It's not much. College stuff, guys discussing sports and other interests, girls their interests."

"You mean guys?"

"Huh?" Millicent's smile vanished.

"That's what women are interested in. Guys like simple things. Sports, cars, umm…"

"Who can burp the loudest?" Millicent smiled coyly.

The guy didn't miss a beat. "Exactly."

The two chuckled. He said he might like it, extended a hand, and introduced himself as Adam Timson. She stated her name, shook his hand.

"Why don't we get together first?" he said. "Then I'll join your friends."

"Fine by me." Millicent lost her grin, said the gang hadn't gotten together as much. "But we can go out first."

"Student Union? Dinner?" He checked his watch. "Get off at five."

"I'll be done at six, parents of these kids off at five and pick them up after that."

"See you then."

"You bet." She winked. "Bye." She shut the door, boy at her leg bringing her back to reality. She scooped him up and kissed him.

"Yuck!" the boy wiped his mouth.

Millicent giggled, twirled him around, rest of her day as clear as watching a video at fast forward speed.

Six o'clock had her out the door and in her car, she driving faster than she ever had. At the Union cafeteria, she did a visual, did not see him nor any young males with brown hair. She found a spot seeming to cover all entrances.

"Why not sit over here?"

Millicent turned to the sound. In a corner, a hand motioned and a smile flashed. She respired, sat where she'd been invited. "Didn't see ya there."

"Guess I shoulda sat at the front. This is my favorite spot, away from the crowd, able to observe all. See those two?" Adam fingered the two red-head girls, said they came on Mondays, Wednesdays, and Fridays, mentioned an elderly couple whom he saw at this time most days.

Millicent complimented his observation skills, he saying he'd taken psychology classes, it his minor.

"May go into child psychology, though for now, I'll stick with teaching. Being a shrink seems too hard." He circled his ear with a finger.

Millicent chuckled and they talked, he saying he'd meet with the group next time they met. They exchanged numbers as they left.

"I'll let you know," she said. He gave a gentle kiss on her cheek. She blushed so deep she worried he'd think she was bleeding. Instead, he smiled and waved goodbye. Driving home, Millicent had trouble focusing on the road, her emotional state going at supersonic speed.

Her mother asked where she'd been. Millicent gave no expression. The clock made her aware of the time. "Forgot. Sorry."

"Don't sorry me, you should be here when you're supposed to. As long as you're living here—"

"Mom, I'm an adult, you shouldn't—"

"Don't tell me how to parent. Wait till you raise kids, you'll see. You're supposed to be here for dinner no later than six thirty. It's almost an hour later."

"But, Mom, I—"

"I don't want to hear it." The mother retreated to her room, door closing loud enough to make Millicent flinch.

Who cares? the girl said to herself, thoughts returning to Adam.

She had to tell someone. Her brother breezed past, sneered at her, tongue out, teased in musical tone how she'd gotten in trouble. Millicent flipped the bird.

"I'm telling!"

Millicent called his bluff. The boy frowned, then returned to the family room to watch TV, girl telephoning Sophia, talked so fast she had to tell the story twice. Sophia congratulated her, Millicent saying he'd be there the next time the group met.

"Yeah." Sophia's voice dropped. "Haven't done that this summer, been so long since we met, I forget when it was. I hope we're not..." She paused so long Millicent spoke.

"We're not what?"

Sophia let out a breath. "Drifting apart."

"We're just busy. When fall semester starts, we'll be together again, like magnets."

"Hope you're right. Next year I won't have so much time, will be looking for a job. And the wedding. Oh my gosh, the wedding. Invitations. The church. The reception. All that stuff."

"Hey, I'll trade places with you and get married."

Sophia laughed. "I'm not complaining. It's just different."

"It's called growing up."

"Guess so."

The two vowed to meet up soon. Millicent had trouble sleeping although for once she was glad, savored each moment.

* * * *

A fortnight passed before the group was able to descend on the restaurant in unison, Andrea by herself, Millicent next to Arturo and Sophia. Andrea spoke to the person beside Millicent. "And you are?"

Millicent introduced him, all trading pleasantries, then ate.

"What about apartment plans?" Andrea asked. "The three of us sharing the place?"

Millicent considered the possibility: Andrea and her together nine more months? How many chances would that give her friend to steal Adam? She didn't want to find out.

"I'm not sure," Millicent said.

"Why not?" Andrea asked.

Millicent gave a few *Umms* and *Wells*.

Adam brought her to him, arm around her neck. "We could live together."

Millicent reacted as if white light from a thundercloud had struck the table. "What?"

He said it a second time, cuddled with her, his lips on hers. "It'd be good." He snickered. "And cheaper."

Millicent lifted his arm. "I don't think so."

He distanced himself from her. "Why not?"

She chuckled. "Duh? We've been together but three weeks. No way I'm ready for that."

"Don't be a prude." He put his arm back around her.

"I'm not." She escaped his grasp, patted him. "Maybe next semester. We'll see."

Adam portrayed a broken smile, his voice in surrender mode. "Okay."

The group switched to other things, Sophia saying they had to sign the lease before fall classes, teased she'd have to find Arturo a place, he all by his lonesome.

"At least you can masturbate in private now," Andrea said.

Sophia burst into laughter. "I said the same thing. See? There's an advantage to us not living together."

Arturo ha-ha'ed though his face showed no upturned mouth. Sophia squeezed his cheek, said she was kidding.

Millicent said quietly she wasn't sure about arrangements. Thinking she might find Andrea in bed with her boyfriend—She couldn't believe she thought that last word in reference to herself—had her lunch rising in her stomach. She awaited her girlfriends' reactions. They went on as though Millicent had announced she was going to try a new pizza. Had they heard?

Adam rose, said he had to leave. Millicent followed him out. The more she considered living with her friends, the more her insides felt like a roller coaster doing a loop the loop. She pushed the sensation away.

He smiled, asked if she was all right, opened her car door. This allowed her muscles to ease. Maybe he'd meant living together as a joke. Had to.

She perused ads for a one bedroom place over the next two weeks, wanted a house yet didn't feel comfortable living alone or having Adam over, they by themselves, she aware of what every young male wanted.

A week later she saw a likeable place and her parents approved of it. She signed the contract, gulped at how to explain her decision to the others. When Sophia offered to meet that weekend, the scene in Millicent's mind was like a DeNiro movie for women, she the good girl protagonist, Andrea the female DeNiro. She declined, Sophia joking Millicent and Adam must be getting serious. Millicent played along.

Shortly prior to fall semester, the phone rang. Millicent saw the number, aware it was that time. "Hello?"

Sophia gave greetings, offered pizza after they scrawled their signatures for the landlord.

"Ummm…I don't know," Millicent replied.

"What does that mean?"

"I just…" Millicent clutched her free ear with a hand. How to say it? She knew only one way. "I've already signed a lease."

Silence.

"Sophia?"

"You what?"

Millicent shut her eyes, took in air, and said it again.

"When? Why? What about us?" Sophia gave awkward laughter. *"Is there something about me you don't like?"*

Millicent sounded a similar reaction. "It's not you, it's me."

The two chuckled uneasily.

"When did this come about?" Sophia asked.

"Been thinking a while. Wanted some space, never been by myself." She breathed, added, "Nothing personal."

"Sure. If you say so."

"I do. And I'm sorry." Millicent tried to perk up her voice. "But let's still meet whenever for pizza."

"Okay," Sophia said although her voice trailed off as they hung up.

* * * *

"Better for us," Andrea said when Sophia told her the news. "We can have a good time together."

"Glad you're not letting it affect you." Sophia mentally noted they were down to three of them and bit her lip. Were these events a form of friendship apocalypse? How could they avoid this? Could they?

Arturo's call to discuss wedding plans improved Sophia's mood though questions about the group's demise never completely left her mind.

* * * *

Things settled down for a week, Arturo and Sophia going out, their last fling as college students. With the start of classes, thoughts of the gang dispersing melted from Sophia's conscience.

August passed into September, September receding into fall break, then Thanksgiving. The week before finals, Sophia and Arturo looked over wedding invitations at her apartment, Andrea on a date, the couple agreeing to study the next morning.

"These are nice," Arturo said of an ivory-colored card, announcement in raised calligraphy script.

Sophia shook her head. "Too creamy."

"What the hell does that mean?"

"Girl thing, you wouldn't understand." She showed him white ones. His face was like he'd drank rancid milk.

"These?" she said of bright yellow ones.

He laughed. "You're kidding."

They looked at a few others, never finding one they both liked. Sophia rubbed her forehead, decided to try other things. "Honeymoon?"

"Paris?"

"Be reasonable."

"It's the romantic capital of the world. Girls love it."

"*Now* you decide to be romantic. How come you were so afraid to open your wallet before?"

Arturo's voice rose. "When was I not generous?"

Sophia cackled. "Like always."

He demanded an example. She stated dinner last Valentine's Day.

"We went somewhere nice. And I bought flowers."

"Yeah, but..."

"But what?" He started to rise off the sofa. She gently pushed him down. He wanted an explanation.

She grunted, eyes heavenward. "Can we drop it? We're discussing the wedding."

"No." Arturo jumped up. "I want to know. How am I cheap? What was wrong with my Valentine's Day gift? Or any gift?"

"Arturo, I didn't mean it like—"

"Tell me, damnit."

Sophia grimaced and stood. "Since you want to know so damn bad, those pink carnations were cheap, wilted before our date ended."

"So?" He spread his arms. "They were going to die anyway."

"Coulda gotten some that lasted."

"Forgive me, next time, I'll ask how long you want them to last. What else are you pissed about?"

Sophia touched him. "Don't get carried away, it's only—"

"Our lives. Maybe we should think about this. Maybe we should consider—"

"No! We've come this far, I've put up with so much!" The photos emerged in her mind, blinded her sight like a migraine aura.

"Like what?" Arturo heckled.

Sophia thought about that night. Why had she brought it up? Couldn't she let it go? Was something telling her not to? A warning sign?

"I'm waiting."

Those words made her revisit spring break. The proposal. How they'd wound up laughing because of those two words during their last serious argument. This time, water toppled out of the girl's eyes. "Don't do this to me," she cried.

"What?"

"Don't." She opened the door. "I think you should leave."

"Fine." He took her advice. She slammed the door on him, pressed fists to her eyes, and fell on the sofa, lay there, then on her bed, face in a pillow. What was happening? First Conrad. Then Renaldo. Wyatt. Now Millicent. Was it a curse, she and Arturo next? What was going on?

She cried herself to sleep.

* * * *

Upon stomping to his apartment, Arturo frowned at the discovery he'd have no one to talk to, needed an escape, decided to take a walk. And found himself on Washington Avenue. Though the bar was open, the crowd was sparse. There was a reason the time preceding finals was called Dead Week.

He entered, pushed through the crowd to the bar, set his elbows on it, and asked for a beer. A voice next to him said the same. A familiar voice though he couldn't place it, like a song from years ago, its title forgotten. He turned. And smiled.

"Hey, my handsome, gorgeous stud," the voice said. "How's it going?"

Chapter 22

"Great," Arturo said. "How are ya?" He swallowed. "Phoebe?"

The girl's face radiated. "You remembered. I'm great, getting smashed after hours of studying, now looking for fresh meat." She sidled up to him, snapped a hand around his waist. "Looks like I found some."

He took a drink of his beer. "Thought you graduated."

"Did. Working on a masters." She squeezed him tighter.

Arturo wiggled his fingers. "I'm taken."

Phoebe studied his hands. "Don't see a ring."

"Engaged." He updated her.

She congratulated him. "Wish I'd have taken advantage of you when I had the chance. When's the date?"

He told her.

"Am I invited?"

Arturo hesitated.

Phoebe held up her hand. "Say no more." Yet she continued to hold him. The bartender gave her a drink.

Arturo finished his, bought another.

"My kind of guy." She invited him to dance. He resisted. "Just one?"

Arturo took a long gulp. Phoebe pulled his arm down, set his cup on the bar.

"One time?"

He followed her out. They did a fast dance. When the next song, Eric Clapton's "Wonderful Tonight" played, she didn't let him go. He gave light protest though they remained close even after the song was done, danced a few more numbers. She said breathily how she'd wished he'd be back. Now he was—it their destiny.

"Maybe," he mumbled, had a third beer, now felt light-headed.

She kissed him, first on the lips then French-kissed him. "C'mon. Let's go." She combed fingers through his hair.

"Where?"

"Someplace private. We..." She stomped a foot, cursed.

"Something wrong?"

"Forgot my roommate's home studying."

"Thought you lived alone."

"Too expensive. And the only time she stays home to study, I want the place to myself." She held his hand. "Ourselves."

In spite of his inebriation, the idea crystallized in his mind. Arturo brushed it aside. It came back as he looked at her then thought of how he disliked their initial tryst. He reminded himself that was four years ago. She'd probably gained lots of experience.

"Ya know," he said, unable to stop himself, "I live alone now, all my buddies have their own places." He chuckled, then frowned at the memory of Renaldo but quickly rid his mind of that portrait. "Guess I drove 'em crazy."

She moved to him. "Just like you're doing to me. C'mon." She headed for the exit.

"What?"

"Duh? Let me take you to your humble abode." Phoebe smiled. "College learnt me a fancy word. Now come on."

He tittered, her eye-candy look and now well-developed figure not helping.

As she pulled in front of his place, he thought of Sophia. How does someone call a boyfriend who considers Paris for a honeymoon cheap? Or unromantic? Maybe it was all leading to this moment. An epiphany. Fated change. Corrected fate, a chance to put him on the right path.

"C'mon." He opened the apartment door.

"Glad you're as excited as I am."

He led her in. They hopped in bed, clothes lost to the floor.

"That was great," she breathed when done. "How about you?"

"Much better than the first time." With his thoughts clearer, he recalled that night, compared it to this one. It was like hearing Bruce Hornsby on piano after listening to someone practice scales.

They fell asleep together.

When Arturo tried to get up that morning—not easy to do, considering his pounding headache—he couldn't figure out what was so heavy next to him. He looked. And felt the way a man strapped into the chair at a maximum security prison felt.

Friendship

* * * *

Millicent and Adam remained steadies, she guiding him in classes she'd taken, they studying for upcoming finals.

"This is great," Adam said during a break, she preparing a chicken and rice dish. "Studying together, taking a break. Maybe a little more."

The girl gave a fractured smile at the last two words, viewed her bedroom furtively. Not the first time he'd hinted about sharing supine positions, she rebuffing him with "In due time" and now encouraged him to eat up.

Upon seeing his dreamy-smile side glances, she had him work a problem while she oscillated mentally: *Hold him off. Submit to his desires. Continue to offer future opportunities.* Did he have much more patience?

"Okay." He finished his work.

"Let's see." She checked what he'd done.

"Ya know…" He moved his chair closer, hand on her leg then her side. For Millicent it was a massage, she straining to prevent a smile.

He kissed a side of her face. "Was thinking…"

"You were?" Millicent felt cartilage in her throat move.

"Yes. Been together how long?"

"Six months."

"Right." His mouth glided up her cheek. "And we still haven't…" His lips suctioned her skin.

"Haven't what?" she said, shut her eyes, and inhaled as if breathing mountain air.

"You know." He stroked her locks, hands finding the back of her neck then the front of her shirt. He undid a button. "It."

"It?" she asked, her foot moving toward the correct room despite part of her wanting any excuse to avoid it.

"We can do it here." He motioned to the sofa. "If you like."

"Do what?"

"You know."

She feigned a giggle. "No, I don't."

He pulled away, his look of having eaten his favorite meal now morphing into one of a hungry man seeing someone with a cart full of groceries. "Do I have to spell it out for you?"

"Yes." She kept her mouth in a straight line.

"Ess-eee-exx." He nodded to the bedroom. "Are you that obtuse?"

"Oooh, obtuse. How did we get so smart?"

"From you." He aimed for her lips.

She dodged him, snickered. "Nice try."

He contrived a gasp. "What are you saying?"

"Some other time. Doesn't feel right today."

"When will it? Don't you know how long I've waited?"

"Six months." She pushed herself away. "And you're going to wait a little longer."

Adam stood, chair falling over. "How much longer? You should be thankful I'm not most guys."

"How is that?" She joined him in like pose.

"Most would've demanded sex or left. I'm patient." His face relaxed. The boy smiled, encircled his hand around hers. "And I like you. I mean it."

"Then you can wait."

"How much longer?"

"I don't know." She turned away, about to say there was more to a relationship when he seized her, spun her around, and tried to lead her to the bedroom.

"Let me go!" Millicent twisted free.

"Come on!" He grabbed at her. She slapped the arm away.

"I'm not trying to force you, just saying try it. If ya don't like it, we'll stop and I won't ask again."

She paused. He placed a hand on her back and nudged her to the room. Halfway there, she interpreted his words. And escaped his hold.

"Honey." The boy touched her shoulder lightly. "C'mon." He escorted her to the room.

Millicent thought how no other male had taken an interest in her. He'd been nice, bought flowers, recited poetry, and celebrated anniversaries: one month, two months, half a year.

"It'll be great." His voice was sunshine on a cold day. Then his grip tightened.

Her eyes grew. She sucked in a quick breath. And snapped herself free. "No. Maybe later."

"Damnit, Millicent, what the hell is your problem? I take you out, buy you stuff, read poetry, and you won't let up and get intimate, even once. Won't take ten minutes." His eyes seemed to blaze, his mouth ugly, twisted so tight it seemed to disappear.

The girl watched then shivered. "No."

He rushed her. "Damnit, I'm gonna show you a good time if I must drag you there. Now let's do it!"

She resisted.

He looked to the ceiling. "What a bitch. Most girls give in by now."

Her heart ached, she viewing him like he was one of the daycare kids who'd skinned his knee, yet her tone remained firm. "I'm not most girls."

He approached her again.

She raised a leg. It landed between both of his. He *oomphed*, bent, and fell. She kicked him, surprised by her determination, did not let up, drug him to the door.

"Now get out! No one takes advantage of me!" It seemed as if another girl was saying this, Millicent watching. She opened the door, flung him out, gathered his books, and tossed them at his side.

"And don't come back!" She slammed the door. It rattled in its frame. "Bastard!" She pressed her back to the entry, shut her eyes. Her chin quivered. She cried, hands over her face as she wandered to her room, shoulder hitting the door frame. She collapsed onto the bed.

Why she wondered between sniffles. *Finally get a guy attracted to me and he treats me like this. Now what?*

She cried herself to sleep, dozed off and on, thought of calling one of the old friends but declined. If only she hadn't moved out. Her eyes were puffy by morning.

* * * *

"Oh, God," Arturo whispered, Sophia instantly coming to mind, his head clearing. Their plans. He pressed steepled fingers on his nose. "What have I done? Why did I do this?" He checked the clock. Past ten. They were to study at ten thirty. Here. He awaited her hand rapping the door. *Then again*, he thought, *considering what happened last night, maybe she won't show*. He slithered out of bed, rattled drawers. His guest stirred, watched as he stepped into jeans.

She motioned a finger. "Take those off."

"No can do."

"Why not?"

He sat on the bed's edge. "Phoebe, you're a nice girl, attractive—"

"Oh no." She sat up. "Stop. You'll regret it." She put her arm around him. "Wasn't last night great?"

"It was. At—"

She forced her lips on his. "This will be better."

"You didn't let me finish," he said although her mouth was over his. "I was going..." He pushed her off. "Was saying it was good. At that moment. Now..." Arturo grasped the sheet. "I feel different."

"Ha! A guy? Talking feelings? What's wrong with you?" She coddled him. "Just try."

"No."

"What's wrong?"

He explained his and Sophia's argument. "She's going to kill me. How can I make it up to her?" He went for his phone but put it back down, said he had to do it in person yet knew Sophia wasn't going to listen to him when she arrived.

"You've got to leave. Now. I'm sorry, this was stupid, I totally fucked up. Sophia will kill me. I'm sorry, we just can't—"

The sound of knocking on the front door was a sharp needle injected in Arturo's side.

"Oh fuck!" He choked back the chunky liquids that rose from his stomach.

"What?" Phoebe asked.

"Arturo?" Sophia called out. "Arturo?" More knocking. "You there? We're supposed to study."

"Be there in a sec. Hold on."

Sophia's hand persisted. "I know we fought and I'm sorry. I hope you are too. But let's move on, go to the library, study, and talk about invitations."

"It's okay," he yelled. "I'm coming."

Phoebe chuckled. "Do you mean that literally?"

Arturo gagged and shoved a hand over her lips, she wide-eyed. He ordered her out of bed, shoved her clothes in her hands. She dressed quickly. He pointed to the window and opened it. She looked at him like they were on the top floor of a high rise.

"Just go," he said in a whispered yell. "Now!"

She did not move.

"You heard me! Go!" He waved hands at her.

"My purse!" she said in a whispered plea.

Arturo eyed the room and found it, shoved it at her. She juggled it, contents spilling.

"Damnit!" he said.

"Arturo?" Sophia called out. "You hear me?"

"Be right there. Was cleaning up this mess. On my way." He and Phoebe collected her things, she again juggling the purse as he lifted her over the window sill, pushed her out. She grunted while he apologized and shut the window, leapt toward the door then buttoned his jeans, still bare-chested. He turned the knob. The door remained shut.

"Uh, ya gotta unlock it," Sophia said.

"Sorry." He undid the lock, opened the door, and let her in, she wanting to know why delay.

"Uh…" His mind processed at warp speed. "Was studying last night and made a huge mess, books and papers and all, then overslept." He forced a smile.

She took him in her possession, said she was sorry for the previous night's dispute. He did the same, chuckled at the question of what they were arguing about. Sophia offered news headlines: Fiancés cancel wedding over invitations dispute. Laughter escaped her lips.

"We'd get paid a lot by the tabloids," Arturo snickered then did a quick scan at the bedroom. All clear. He viewed the window, didn't see a figure beyond it. Sophia asked what he was doing.

"Need to clean in there."

He watched her visual inspection, bit the corners of his mouth.

She looked at him. "Not too bad. For a college guy's room. Anyway, what twenty year old male cares about a clean apartment?"

"Twenty-one," he corrected, knew switching subjects was paramount. "Maybe we should do that."

"Do what?"

He felt sweat on him as she made a second reconnaissance of the room. "Say we broke up over invitations, sell our story."

She chortled. "You are one weird dude."

"But I'm funny. Girls say they want a guy who'll make 'em laugh. Now excuse me." His chest pounded and he did his best to keep his face from going red, said he had to finish dressing. He put on shirt and socks and stepped into the bathroom. "Let me comb my hair, do my thing, and we'll go." He shut the door…

"Okay," he said a few minutes later, stepped out. "I'm ready."

"Are you?" Sophia's tone had changed. Lower.

Arturo bowed his head, inspected his clothes then went back to the bathroom mirror. "Whadya mean?"

"Seems like you've already gone out."

"Huh?"

"How was last night?"

"Last night?" he asked, words coming out in a high tone.

"Mmm-hmm."

"Terrible. We fought, remember?"

"Yes. And then…"

"I came here."

"And..."

"Tried studying. Finals, ya know. However, I was too upset, went to bed. But you're right, we blew it out of proportion. Glad you're so understanding." He placed hands on her arms, kissed her forehead. "Let's go." He started for the front door.

"You were upset, huh?"

"Definitely." He waved her over.

"So upset you probably felt like talking to someone. And more."

He ingested oxygen. "What does that mean?"

"You were upset?" With heavy steps, she neared him.

"I was, didn't sleep well."

"I'll bet."

"What?" His voice cracked.

"Kinda tough sleeping in a twin bed with two people." Her eyes were like a tiger's when attacking a small prey.

"What are you talking about?" His side hit the door.

"This!" She raised the pink watch with wide pink band, shoved it in his face. "How was she? Good? Better than me?"

Arturo felt his eyes enlarge. "Where did you get that?"

"Where do you think?" She motioned her head to his bedroom.

Arturo blurted his first thought: The watch was his.

"Pink? Not a manly color."

He tried to laugh. "I'm man enough I don't see pink as feminine."

"Funny," Sophia said but kept a straight face. "You may have a future in comedy. But truth telling?" She shook her head. "Uh-uh. I know this is not yours. See?" She flipped the watch over, showed him the inscription.

Phoebe. Congratulations. 5-25. PBM

"Obviously her initials," Sophia said, assumed the date was her birthday, perhaps high school graduation.

"Sophia..." Arturo extended his hands. "Let me explain, it's not what you think."

"Really?" She crossed arms over her chest. "What am I thinking?"

"You're thinking..." He swallowed. "I was with someone else last night. In there." He did the same with his head as she'd done.

"And were you?"

Arturo slid away from her, scrambled past the table, and hit a chair. "Yes. I mean no."

"Either you did or you didn't. Tell the truth."

He felt his face lose color.

"Arturo? The truth."

No words came to him.

Sophia cried. "Your response is deafening. Who was it with? That girl from high school? Phyllis?"

"Phoebe," he said, unthinking, immediately wished he'd thought first.

She threw the watch at him. "Why did I trust you! I had evidence to show you couldn't be! But I had faith, believed it was a fluke, you were young, wanted to tell your buddies you'd done it before them, didn't care who it was with, whose heart you shattered."

"What are you talking about?" He eyed her as if she'd sprouted wings.

"I know all about that night." She inhaled, wiped her eyes and nose, more water rolling down her face. "You and her. The night *we* were to be together. How could you? Couldn't you wait? Why did you have to do it with her? Goddamn Phyllis."

Arturo corrected her a second time.

She slapped him, punched him in the gut. "I don't give a fuck what her name is, bastard! The hell with you! It's over! Everything! The wedding! Our relationship! Go burn in hell!"

"Sophia, let me explain."

"Explain what?"

"That night. Last night. And what evidence are you talking about?"

She held up a finger. "Hold on."

"But Sophia, I—"

"Fuck you!" She opened the door, swung it shut.

Arturo opened it, followed her. At her place, she once more slammed a door at him.

"Sophia!" He hit the door. "Let me in, I can explain!"

"The hell you can! But I'll show you evidence!"

Arturo pounded fists on the entrance. It swung wide.

"Here!" She flung the photo at his face.

His hand, in mid motion for another knock, halted. He watched the object flutter to the ground, lowered his arm, took possession of the snapshot like it was a relic, and examined it. Slowly, he lifted his glance. "How did you find this?"

"Who gives a fuck? I found it and that's all that matters. Care to explain now?"

Arturo heaved a breath. "Honey, that was years ago."

"Don't honey me. Three and a half years wasn't that goddamn long ago. Besides, what about that pink thing in your bedroom? That wasn't from three and a half years ago. More like three and a half minutes ago."

Arturo entered the place, shut the door, swayed to the sofa, concentrated on the photo, and squeezed his eyes shut.

"Aren't you going to explain yourself?"

"I can't." Arturo choked up. "I can't. I just... Got caught up in the moment."

"I know, a man's sex drive. Well, fine, you can have that. It's over for us!" She snatched the picture. "Over! Now get out!" She gathered part of his shirt in her fist then threw him toward the front.

Arturo pleaded to speak. She shoved him further to the door, said he'd had his chance and blew it.

"Now get the hell outta here! And get the hell out of my goddamned life!" She swung a forearm at his face. He toppled, head hitting the door, eyes moving in parallel ellipses. She grabbed him then opened the entrance and pushed him out, kicked his stomach, and returned the door to its frame with a room shaking rattle. "And don't ever fucking come back!"

After a few seconds' blackness, Arturo blinked. His surroundings were blurry. He rubbed eyes. Everything cleared including his memory. He pushed tears back, attempted an upright position.

"Ahh!" The boy rubbed his joints and muscles. His head felt it was being drilled into, back of it damp. He touched it, checked his hand. Red splotches. He wiped the hand, placed it on the ground, pushed, and collapsed. Two more times before he could manage so much as an infant's position, knees like someone was hammering nails into them. When the sensation eased, he attempted a standing pose. The knees gave out, he slapping palms on the wall, used them as quasi-suction cups, able to stand. He lifted a foot, built momentum with each step, body moving quicker, to his place, where he tottered to the couch and fell. Blackness spread over his sight.

When he came to, he felt better, stood with minimal effort, treated the wound on the back of his head and the cuts on his fingers, considered visiting the emergency room, even pressing charges. He quickly ran these thoughts out of his mind, ridicule for the latter more painful than his current condition. He imagined the taunt:

"You're the guy who got whipped by his ex. What a wuss!"

He thought about Sophia. His body ached even more. How to convince her he loved her? The stabbing at his heart hurt worse than his physical pain. Were they through? If so, would he find another as good as her? Why go on?

With these thoughts, he trudged to his room and drifted off, woke briefly at intervals, each time she being the answer to why he should go on.

* * * *

Though awake, Millicent acted as if paralyzed, tears flowing then ebbing as she kept asking why, despite knowing she'd never get an answer. With sleep came dreams, bad dreams, Adam threatening to kill her, Millicent awakening with a "No!" then lying silent, to fall asleep again. She went to but one of her three classes then retreated to her mattress.

* * * *

Sophia kept her door shut for two days, Andrea finally asking if she was okay. Sophia ordered her away, claimed she'd gotten a nasty flu bug, stated the word contagious emphatically. The roommate asked no further questions. When the third day arrived, Sophia arose though her puffy eyes and lackluster movement had her looking like the undead.

"You okay?" Andrea asked when Sophia stepped out of her room. "What's wrong?"

"Nothing."

"Nothing? Sure don't look like nothing's wrong. School? Arturo? He getting cold feet?"

Water cascaded from Sophia's visual ducts. Andrea held her, wanted the whole story, Sophia speaking though half of her words came out in unintelligible sobs and hitches of the throat.

"At least you made him feel significant pain," Andrea said.

Sophia gave an emotionless, "Yeah. Huh."

* * * *

For three nights, Arturo got no sleep though the first was due to his injuries. He went to classes in a catatonic state, couldn't slack off on grades during the semesters before the realtor's exam. Notes he'd taken looked to be in Chinese, hand barely able to grip his pencil. It felt like a bowling ball was stuck in his throat. Thoughts of how to gain redemption went across his mind, none a plausible solution.

Each day seemed longer than a year. The fact it was the time when colored lights decorated houses and people opened their blinds at night to show off multi-hued trees stabbed at Arturo deeper than any natural wound could. It was like someone ordered him to take over Atlas' duties with a one hundred-ton weight added. Only after a few more todays became yesterdays did Arturo take out his phone and call, prepared the message he'd leave, knew she wouldn't answer. He hung up a series of times before leaving a message. After doing so, he called back to correct what he'd said, added again how sorry he was and begged for mercy.

Her response was as expected.

During finals week, he left more messages, tried a few jokes. No returns. An idea during Christmas break.

Christmas day he had a rose delivered to her house. The second day, he had two diamond bracelets brought to Sophia. Third day it was three sets of earrings she liked. He sent something each day for twelve days, last day sending a dozen roses and a gold necklace, had to hock prized possessions for it. He also left several poems, told her she needn't return the engagement ring.

The thirteenth day seemed to not want to pass. Arturo's phone remained quiet and no one rang the doorbell. He went to bed earlier than any time in the past six years. When his parents asked why, he mumbled, "Tired," hadn't told them what had happened though they noticed she hadn't been around nor had he gone out for New Year's. He fell asleep with a heaviness in his chest.

* * * *

Sophia was a living cadaver during the break. Her mom questioned the boyfriend's absence, daughter saying they'd had a spat and she wished not to elaborate. When the gifts came, the girl told her mom to enjoy them. With the twelfth present, her mom advised to call him.

"Hell no! *He* betrayed *me*. Not once but twice. No way I'm letting it happen any more."

"Just call and acknowledge the gifts. You don't even need to say thank you."

Sophia did not. Her mother kept after her. The day before spring semester began, the elder female repeated the request. Sophia grabbed her mom's shirt collar, the two bumping noses.

"When are you going to get it? It's over, he's never coming back into my life. Ever!" She pushed her mom away, reacted as if the woman hadn't used deodorant. "Why are you nagging me?" She hit a hand on her forehead. "Forgive me, I forgot you've spent your whole goddamn, pathetic life chasing a guy you'll never get back. Let it go, Mom." She closed then opened a hand. "Let it go. He doesn't want you, it's too late. Like Arturo and I."

The mother teared up. "I'd slap you for what you said except you're right. I don't want to believe it, love him too much." She blinked steadily as she stared at her offspring. "You're right." She held Sophia. "Thank you. It's over. I must move on."

The girl smiled. "Glad you finally see it. Just wasn't meant to be. Isn't that what you always said when things went against my wishes? It's the same with Arturo and I, wasn't meant to be." Sophia fought the tears. "He cheated on me with another girl. And I ignored the signals." She lifted her lips up. "Like someone else I know." She shuddered. "Oh my God," she said, hushed. "Oh my God."

"What?"

Sophia gazed at her mom. "I've become you."

The mother smiled gently. "One event doesn't define who you are. You're a beautiful young woman with the whole world waiting for you. Do you want to lose that?"

"Mom, it's over."

"Fine. Maybe." Mother put arm around daughter. "Or maybe this is a test to see if you two can handle each other. If you can get through this, you'll survive anything."

"But, Mom, it's not..."

The lady held up a digit. "I'm just saying think about it."

Sophia's phone rang. She observed the number. And buried the phone in her purse then glared at her mom. "You planned this."

A chuckle. "Planned what?"

"That whole damn speech, his call now."

The mother laughed. "You really think I did that?"

"I know you did. Tried to convince me he's the right one after I said we're through then, *voila*, he calls."

"Sophia, I had no clue." The woman continued laughing. "It was a coincidence." She looked upwards. "Or maybe not. Maybe—"

"Don't give me that. If we were meant to be, all this crap never would've happened. Failure doesn't teach you how to succeed, success does." She recalled who'd said that. Her eyes teared from the memory of her deceased friend. She thought how many of her previous perceptions were now in question, some having already changed. She had changed. For the better? Her current situation certainly wasn't. She looked at her mom, debated which choice to make. She inhaled then exhaled. "Forget it, it's over. Like you and Dad."

"If you say so."

"I do." Sophia picked up her purse, announced she was going shopping.

"Have fun. See ya later."

Sophia trounced out and did several errands, asked herself if what her mother said was true, and decided it wasn't. She visited campus, went to Theta Pond and fed the ducks, it a mild January day, then got a salad at the Student Union cafeteria, sat down, and watched students pass. A familiar person.

"Hey." She waved. "C'mere!" She ran to the person, put an arm around their shoulder. "Girl, how're ya doing? Sit down with me."

"Hi." Millicent hugged Sophia.

"Over here." Sophia led the girl by the arm. Millicent protested she had things to do. Sophia asked to borrow just one minute. Millicent sighed, followed Sophia who questioned her about her circumstances, Millicent telling about school and work.

"How are you and Adam?"

Millicent lowered her head. "We…" Her face twisted.

Sophia set her hand on Millicent's, told her she didn't have to go any further. Millicent said she did, gave details, and choked up when describing that night. Sophia rubbed her friend's back, hugged her when done then gave a peck on the cheek.

"How about you?" Millicent asked. "When's the big day?"

Sophia's body went numb. She checked her shoes, ran upper teeth across lower lip.

Millicent questioned if something was wrong.

Sophia hesitated then spoke though the words were hardly audible. She finished and put her head on the table.

Millicent held Sophia, assured her it would be all right, told her not to fret. With head still down, Sophia described her mother's comment and the group's discussions. She raised her head. "Is there a greater plan?"

"Who knows? Went through the same thing, got no answer. Guess we have to keep on keeping on."

"Guess so."

Millicent requested further details, Sophia casually mentioned he'd called.

"He called?"

"Bunch of times. Even tried to bribe me with gifts."

"Such as?"

Sophia described them.

Millicent whistled. "Not bad."

"What?"

"He's trying."

"Yeah, well, he'll never have me again."

"You sure?"

Sophia sat up. "Yes."

"I mean, you're sure it's meant to be, you two apart?"

"I don't know. I just—"

The phone rang. Sophia emitted a deep breath. "It's not going to work. Watch."

She answered the phone saying, "Nice try. Bye." and hung up, glowered at Millicent, said her plan wouldn't work. Millicent denied the accusation then asked what Sophia was accusing her of. Sophia laughed, said no matter how much anyone tried to reunite them, it wasn't going to happen. Millicent protested she hadn't tried, didn't know Arturo's number, had deleted it from her phone.

"Hell," she finished. "Didn't know you two'd broken up."

Sophia recalled her friend's inquiry and the girl's reaction when told the couple were done. "Oh." She studied her friend. "Hmmm." She stuffed her phone into her purse. "Well, anyway…"

The two talked, attempted to meet again but found no agreeable date and time. They said goodbye, about to separate.

"Don't forget," Millicent said. "Think about it. If he'd sent me those things and called that many times, I'd listen. Maybe it *is* meant to be." She waved. "See ya later."

Sophia did think about it. Twice when talking about him, he'd called, both mother and friend adamant in denying collusion. The presents were nice. Romantic. But she wasn't going to succumb, he wasn't getting off easy. She headed to the apartment, Andrea back. Sophia told her what happened.

"Hell with him," Andrea said. "He's gone, old news. Adios, caballero. Sayonara."

Sophia mentioned her roommate was outvoted two to one. Andrea replied they were wrong, boasted she knew when a guy was genuine, had lots of experience with them. Sophia chuckled as to how long those experiences lasted, Andrea arguing that was beside the point. Sophia then said someone with so many relationships that ended unfulfilled wasn't one to take up the relationship mantle.

"Whatever," Andrea replied. "I'm sure I'm right." She reached into a counter drawer, held up a pack of cards. "Poker?"

They played a few hands, Sophia losing them all, constantly asked herself who was right.

* * * *

More calls that first week of spring semester. She responded to none.

That weekend, a knock on the door.

"Sophia?" Andrea called out. "For you."

Before Sophia could order Andrea to say she wasn't there, a figure moved across her bedroom entryway.

"Hello," she said as if speaking to a stranger.

Andrea stepped behind Arturo. "Guess I'll leave you two kids alone." She exited the place.

He took a step. Sophia warned him to stop. He smirked. "Mother may I take one giant step forward?"

Sophia remained straight-faced. "Ha-ha. Very funny. Too late."

"Sophia, let's cut the bullcrap. You know why I'm here." He sat on her bed.

She moved away. "Yes. Sex."

"If I wanted that, I'd call Phoebe."

"Why don't you?"

Arturo sighed. "I don't want sex. I mean, I do, if it's offered."

"Well, you are a male." Sophia went to the sofa, told him to sit in the chair. He did.

"But I want more."

She frowned. "More sex?"

"Damnit, Sophia, I'm trying to beg your forgiveness."

"And you aren't getting it."

"Listen to me, please." He moved toward her. She pushed him away. "Hear me out. I love you, more than ever, made a huge mistake. I was angry, upset, hurt that day. Doesn't make what I did right. Understand, the next morning I hated myself, what I'd done. Ask Phoebe."

"Probably told her what to say."

Arturo stood. "Damnit, I'm trying to make this work! A relationship requires compromise. But I'm the only one compromising. Can you meet me halfway?"

"Okay. I'll listen though I can't say I'll agree."

He sat, held her hands. "Sophia, I mean it when I say I love you. We're meant to be. We all screw up, some worse than others, true. But not forgiving someone who's truly sorry is almost as bad."

She sneered.

"It is. To not let someone prove they're sorry is selfish. Let me show you I'm sorry. Please?"

Sophia said nothing.

"How about it? A date? Just out to eat?"

"Let me think about it."

"Great." Arturo stood.

"Nope."

"What?"

"I thought about it. No."

He sat down. "You mean you won't even consider it?"

"Did."

"Give it some time."

"Already have. The answer is no." She headed to the door, opened it. "Bye."

Arturo walked up to her. "Sophia, just listen to—"

"Bye." She led him out then shut the door right behind him.

He knocked.

"Bye, Arturo. You had your chance."

Several more knocks. Then silence.

* * * *

"Way to go," Andrea said when told. "Put him in his place. Awesome." She and Sophia exchanged a high five though Sophia put little *oomph* behind hers then sat down, hand on her chin, and went quiet.

"Something wrong?"

"I don't know. Am all mixed up."

Andrea groaned. "Not second thoughts?"

"Do you believe if something's meant to be, you shouldn't fight it?"

"I don't know if anything's meant to be. I just don't think he deserves any more chances."

"I'm confused." Sophia changed the subject though her insides gnawed at her, a tapeworm, her mother's and Millicent's question not leaving the forefront of her mind.

* * * *

Valentine's Day had Sophia with a long face, she blowing off classes, called Millicent, promised again to get together yet still set no specific date. Darkness had her face growing longer though she rationalized the day was nearly over.

A knock on the door. She answered it, observed the guest, and frowned. "What the hell're you doing here?"

Arturo put a finger on his lips. "Wait." He fell to a knee, reached beside the door, grabbed something, and extended it to her. A rose bouquet.

She sniffed them, couldn't deny they were nice. Her voice firmed up. "If you think—"

He quieted her again, read a poem he'd written of how a town had a disease until a mysterious, beautiful woman came through, all smiles and positive thoughts, and rid the place of its illness.

"Like you," he said. "Rid me of my ills, made me better. I screwed up but you stuck with me. Please stand by me this time. I am sorry." He stood, hands clasped before her. "What must I do to prove I still love you? Let me take you out. Can't stand being alone on Valentine's Day. Are you aware the last time I was by myself on February fourteenth was…" He touched a finger of one hand on the others.

"Can't you subtract?"

"Hold on." He continued then lowered the hand. "Five years ago, before I met you. That was tough. Didn't know how to masturbate then."

Both chuckled.

"Made you laugh." Arturo looked like he'd burst. "You don't know how long I've wanted to see that cute, child-like grin." He went to a knee once more. "Please, go out with me. One night. After that, fine, we'll forget it. Please?"

The corners of her lips went up. "Okay. But only because it's Valentine's and I hate being alone too."

"Great. Let's go."

"Where?"

"Sleepy Hollow."

Sophia's mouth watered, the expensive restaurant a place she'd never been, it in a secluded, wooded area north of town. "Let's go." She went for her things then paused. "Don't we need a reservation?"

He said he'd made one.

"Don't they charge quite a bit if you cancel?"

"Mmm-hmm."

"But you didn't know I'd say yes."

He shrugged. "Took a chance." He took her hand. "Worth the risk. Like the other things I did for you."

She thought of the Christmas gifts. The calls. His poetry. She sighed. "This latest poem was a nice attempt though Emerson or Frost, you aren't."

"I tried. Anyway, poet isn't my goal."

"Thank God. You'd die broke if it was."

Arturo laughed. "C'mon."

They dined under moonlight, temperature chilly though warm enough for outside eating. They reconciled the past, talked of future plans like the one to occur in four months though Sophia cautioned him not to move too fast. Yet before the hands of clocks merged at the top that evening, they were making out in the car, arms around each other.

* * * *

The following month had them making up and talking wedding. They found the right announcements and mailed them, the big day moved back to late September, honeymoon in South Padre.

"Damn you," Andrea teased when hearing the news. "Told you to ditch him."

Sophia smiled at Arturo, held his hand. "I'm a sucker for a happy ending, believe in fairy tales."

"And miracles," Arturo added.

* * * *

Two months later the remaining four friends were at each other's graduation ceremony. After hugs, praises, and spending time with parents and relatives, the quartet congregated for pizza, toasted themselves with soft drinks, had bigger plans for partying that night at the bar.

Sophia sighed, wished they were all together. Arturo pointed out the only way that'd happen was if the six living friends died. She did not laugh, told him he knew what she meant, said they should've gone to other ceremonies, might have found Conrad or Wyatt. Arturo mentioned they probably had theirs at the same time as his or hers.

"True." She slid lower in the booth, commented it was the real world now.

"I'm looking forward to it," Millicent said of her teaching kindergarten.

"I am too, the Bursar's office job sounds interesting. However, going from fifteen hours a week to forty, maybe more, will be hard." Sophia held Arturo's hand. "Glad we had our time. Gonna get busy. Wedding, work, buying a home."

"House'll be easy." Arturo stuck out his chest. "I'll be real estate king and will have no trouble getting a deal on a dream house."

Sophia said there were other things. Arturo sat up, inquired what. She stared at him. "Don't you want a family?"

"In due time." He held her. "Right now, let's enjoy this time. Then we'll talk babies."

"You're right." Sophia smiled. "Let's appreciate us while it's only us two."

"Gotta have some fun," Andrea said. "Before ya know it, you'll be thirty."

Sophia put the back of her hand to her head. "Oh, God, I'll be an old maid, will have to go to a nursing home and live out my final days."

The others chuckled, Andrea warning life didn't slow down, they had to savor it while they could.

"That's what we've done." Sophia leaned on her boyfriend. "And will continue to do. Right, honey?"

Arturo brought her close. "You bet."

She raised her glass and gave a second toast. They clinked cups, smiled at each other, and drank up.

Things did get busy shortly after graduation, Sophia and Millicent beginning their jobs the following week, Andrea hired by the public relations section of the water department. Arturo passed the realtor's exam and was picked up by a local realty firm, made his first sale shortly thereafter.

* * * *

Wedding day was muggy and overcast. They'd tracked down Conrad and Wyatt, invited them, Sophia with tears as she said her *I do's*, Arturo rubbing a corner of his eye, everyone applauding as they kissed.

The reception was a grand affair at the Student Union Ballroom, the couple dancing to every number, they alone on the floor with the last song, Bryan Adams' "Heaven," Sophia crying and laughing simultaneously, reminded Arturo it was the first song they'd slow danced to. He merely nodded and smiled, cleared his throat several times. At the end, they exchanged a long kiss to more applause.

Honeymoon had them up before sunrise on that first day as they'd done when he'd proposed.

"Well, we didn't exactly have the yellow brick road to our land of Oz," she said as the sun lit their faces and surf lapped their feet.

"I don't care as long as we made it. And on time." Arturo kissed her. "Didn't want to be late to this moment."

"Me neither. And we weren't."

They hugged and kissed then skinny-dipped, back in their clothes and on the sand prior to anyone's arrival.

"Refreshing," he said.

"Scintillating," she replied.

He pointed to the sky and ocean. "Breathtaking."

"Life invigorating."

"Just like you," he said.

More hugs and kisses, Sophia feeling like she was in a movie. One that wouldn't be nominated. She couldn't prevent her lips from grinning even though they were on his.

Chapter 23

"Way to go." Sophia smiled after eating a pizza slice, Arturo showing sales for his first four months, he top seller. Her smile weakened as she surveyed the empty booth. "Not so fun when no one's here to share the joy, eh?"

"Misery loves company but so does success.'"

Sophia asked when he'd become the deep thinker. He argued he'd been this way for a couple of years. She wished they'd done something to maintain the friendships.

"We've got each other. Means everything to me." His eyes glistened. "What good is the other stuff, including friends, if I don't have you?"

"Amen to that."

They clinked glasses and ate, though it was a subdued meal.

* * * *

Arturo's talent for selling homes continued, he quickly promoted, traveled to a Las Vegas conference then sold a four thousand square foot house in the most exclusive section of town right before Christmas, his commission more than they'd ever seen on a check with his name. They celebrated at Sleepy Hollow restaurant, ordered the most expensive wine, chose the costliest meals.

"Awesome." Sophia toasted Arturo's success, tee-hee'd she hoped this Midas touch wouldn't go away, they'd buy their dream house, set up retirement funds. "And then..." She sighed. "Start a family."

Arturo shifted his head back and forth, promised the best education for their offspring, vowed to take care of Sophia when they got old.

"Sounds great." Sophia hit her glass on his.

They drank up, spoke of possible home buying situations.

* * * *

The couple soon had new cars, big screen televisions, plans for their own home at the front of their minds. They rented a beachfront cottage in South Padre to celebrate their first anniversary, sat in wooden lounge chairs as water rushed over their toes then retreated in a constant rhythm. Sophia took in a deep breath, let it out slowly. "Oh, the good old spring break days, everyone here. We must get together, catch up on old times."

"Or are you trying to bring them back?"

"I don't know." Sophia sipped champagne they'd bought. "Money and success, we all want it. But your statement about sharing it is right."

"Need money. A family. A home. Dream job. Gotta have everything."

"Not everything. Just what we deem important."

He hit his glass on hers. "May we have a little of everything."

The two finished their drinks then chased one another to the water, dived in, and swam for a long stretch.

Watching the yellow orb call it a day on their last evening there had both of them quiet, sky passing from blue to black. They held each other, kissed one last time before returning to the hotel then home the next day.

* * * *

While snacking at the Student Union cafeteria a few weeks later, a figure passed Sophia, who gave a double glance and shot up from her chair, rushed to the person, and hugged them.

"How ya doing?"

"Hey, girl," Andrea said. "What's happening? Been a while."

"Too damn long. C'mere."

They sat down, chatted up what they'd been doing, Sophia telling of Arturo's success.

"Sweet," Andrea said. "Can't complain about my financial situation either. But my romantic one..." She laughed. "You know the story." She touched Sophia. "Lucky you, found yours quickly. Millicent envied you guys, how you found each other early, had few problems."

The difficult times came to Sophia like an old wound reopened. She smiled sadly. "You seem to have forgotten the one before our wedding."

Andrea responded they'd made up. Sophia commented they had other problems, as did everyone, from Renaldo's alcoholism to the other two boys' affairs and failed friendship. Air escaped her lungs in a long exhalation. "That's life."

"Don't I know it," Andrea concluded.

Sophia found her cell phone, wondered if the numbers were still good.

Millicent's number gave the *We're sorry, this number is no longer in service*...recording. She dialed Conrad, line ringing and ringing. Wyatt's had a recording and she left a message.

"Doubt he'll call." She picked at her salad. "Times change. People change."

"C'est la vie." Andrea checked her watch. "Back to work, boss is anal about being late. What fun."

"Yeah, fun." Sophia viewed the time, she just starting her lunch. Andrea went to leave. Sophia seized her elbow. "Promise you'll call. And if you see any of the old crowd, give them my number. Yours still the same?"

Andrea nodded, Sophia reminding the friend of her own cell number. However not once, she thought, had Andrea called.

Then again she thought. *Who had the time?*

* * * *

Sophia received no calls from Andrea nor did Sophia call her friend. After a busy week, she and Arturo were on their way to a downtown Italian eatery in an historic, two story brownstone when they passed the old place. She clutched Arturo's forearm, he nearly losing control of the wheel. She suggested eating there for old time's sake.

They drove up. And frowned, place with no cars. After getting out and checking the door, they discovered why.

"Oh, no." To Sophia, her heart seemed to increase in weight. "Out of business? When?" She kicked the door. "Why did this happen? How? What's going on around here?" She pressed fists to her eyes. "Damnit!"

"Calm down." Arturo held her. "They're closed, this isn't Last Judgment."

"I know," she whispered. "It's just hard. What happened? Why? How did we miss it, allow it to happen?"

"Some things just happen. Changes aren't permanent but change is."

"My husband, the great thinker." Sophia smiled and they slowly returned to the car, Arturo driving to their original destination. A muted dinner of small talk.

At home they watched television, listless, retired early, shared nothing in bed that evening but a good night kiss.

Arturo's commissions improved, he promoted again although routine remained their constant, no special get togethers occurring.

* * * *

Right before Christmas, they attained the one thing they really desired: A new home. Thirty-five hundred square feet with game room, pool, and indoor sauna, place in a gated community, old fashioned street lamps along the sidewalks.

With Arturo's current position came more travel, he gone nine out of the first twelve weeks of the new year, Sophia wandering the house feeling she was in a gothic movie. She called him every night. A few times when they conversed, she heard background voices, at least one of which had a high lilt. He'd said they were other realtors, always concluded with "You're the greatest" although once she thought she heard him laugh and say "Calm down," comment not directed at her. She did not fall asleep right away that night then told herself she was closer to Pollyana than Chicken Little, wasn't going to lose that perspective. They were different now. Adults. More mature. Loyal. And trusting.

* * * *

By the time of year when the afternoon sun scorches pavement, Sophia believed her suspicions had grown to possible truths. Arturo was gone for another week in Vegas. When she offered to join him, he told her he had nothing but long, boring meetings all day, into the night.

She thought of the photo. He'd changed. And so had she—was less trusting. She reprimanded herself, thought of their future, their children swimming in the pool, splashing and carrying on, kids' laughter creating its own kind of music. She managed a smile, made a mental note to broach this subject with him.

When he called on the last day of the conference, Sophia's words came out so fast she didn't stop until he'd yelled her name.

"What?" she said.

"Bad news. Gonna be here a few more days."

"What?" She believed she heard laughter, voices, their pitch similar to hers, and told herself he only dealt with them on a business level.

"No big thing, only three days," he said.

"What's going on?" Those times of him with whatshername flowed into her mind. Did she hear a giggle?

"A last minute conference nearby. Be home in no time."

"Arturo?" Her eyes stung, blinked faster than normal. "We need to talk."

"When I get home, will be there soon. Faster than a roadrunner crosses the street."

Sophia mustered a chuckle.

"Miss you. Love ya. You're the greatest."

"Bye." She hung up, her lips low on her face.

* * * *

When she picked him up at the airport, he gave but a light touch on her cheek, brushed past her to the exit. She asked if he was okay. He said he was. Were her fears correct?

They were forgotten by the next day though he didn't return until after eight that evening, had to show a series of places after hours then did paperwork in the room they'd made their office, books dotting half-empty shelves. She ate alone while he consumed a snack at his desk.

Sophia went to bed by herself. When the alarm went off the next morning, they arose together.

"Need to tell you," he said. "Have another meeting, this one in Los Angeles."

She halted. "When?"

Arturo's glance fell. "Leave this morning."

"Why didn't you tell me?"

"Knew you'd be mad."

She stood in front of him. "Why the hell would I be mad? Only because you're going away on another trip?"

"But look at the money I make, this house, our success. I am extremely passionate about it."

"What good is this stuff if we can't enjoy it?" Snapshots formed in her mind: He and the girl fleeing the house, he with the girl in his apartment. She pushed these aside, uttered profanities at herself for being too critical. The last time was over two damn years ago. What had he done since? Loved her despite not being with her as much as she'd wanted. He was being successful, what she expected in her man.

She allowed air to exit her mouth. "I'm sorry. You are doing great, just need to slow down. A little, okay?"

"I'll think about it." Arturo looked at her. "After I get back. Does that work?"

Sophia nodded. "We'll talk then."

"Great." He kissed her, said he was late for his flight.

She waved to him as he drove away then went inside and checked the time, her day still ninety minutes from starting. She showered, readied herself, ate a light breakfast, and glanced at the TV. Another report of how failed marriages were increasing every year. She glanced skyward, offered a prayer, and changed the channel, watched morning shows until it was almost time for her to leave.

Passing his office, she observed the mound of papers, wondered how he kept track of them, she preferring to keep things organized. Unable to help herself, she entered the room, sifted through pages, and tried to organize them, read a few. Realtor documents and forms, photos and listings of homes, one place twice as big as theirs with an indoor and outdoor pool. She whistled, thought maybe someday they'd have that place then caught herself in the contradiction of wanting the best but scolding Arturo for working so much. What they had was fine.

She straightened more pages, memories of their past flashing in her mind like photo album mementos: The times at the pizzeria. South Padre. His proposal. And determination to win her back. Their honeymoon.

We'll make it work, she thought. *Our struggles, failures teach us...*

She recalled the gang's discussion and whether the statement was accurate.

In our case, she told herself, *it will be. We have always conquered and succ...*

A page with handwriting buried in the midst of the stack caught her eye. She pulled it out, handwriting a lovely script, she envious of the penmanship. Until she read the contents. Her eyes narrowed, her body temperature like a freezer's. She ceased blinking. Tears formed. She trembled, searched for a chair, almost missed it.

"No!" she cried. "No, it can't be! Bastard! Hell no!"

She re-read the note. Three times. Five. Ten. It stayed the same.

Dear Arturo,

Had a great time with you here in Vegas. Imagine you being here on conference at the same time my girlfriends and I are on vacation. A sign? Some believe coincidences are messages from God. Like when Denzel Washington first met his wife he didn't have the courage to speak to her. Later, he

*spoke with her but was too afraid to ask for her
number. He was then offered a ticket to an off-
Broadway play. And the person who sat next to
him? The same woman he'd been too afraid to ask!
Don't you think that could be true for us? We keep
meeting without planning it. Wish we could have
gotten more intimate this time but I guess a hug and
kiss is all we could manage. We'd be great together,
as you know from past encounters. Please think
about this. Us. E-mail or call anytime.*

Love,
Phoebe

"Damnit, no! No!" Sophia grabbed the phone, found his
cell number, dialed.

"Yes, honey?" Arturo said.

Sophia gritted her teeth. "Don't honey me. What the fuck
have you been doing on these trips?"

"Business."

"Mixed with a little pleasure, hmm?"

Arturo asked what she meant.

"With others."

A *yuk* of laughter from the man, he giving an "Of
course," said that was his job, what was he going to do, stand
around and say nothing?

"I'm talking about getting intimate. *Real* intimate, if ya
know what I mean."

"Honey, you're sounding very strange. Can we talk
later?"

"No, damnit! We're going to talk now!"

Arturo's voice cracked. "Sophia, what is wrong?"

She insisted he knew. He replied he was clueless, needed help.

"Fine. Listen and see if this sounds familiar." She read the note, stated the words emphatically. He tried to stop her.

"Don't fucking interrupt me! You're just trying to cover your ass!"

"Sophia—"

"Shut up!" She finished reading. "Care to explain?"

A light chuckle. She demanded to know what was so funny.

"Nothing happened with us," he said, his tone serious. "I'm telling the truth."

"Like other times with Phyllis?"

"Phoebe," he corrected.

"So you remember her name?"

"Sophia, that letter was written a week and a half ago. Of course I'd remember."

"Bet you always have."

"Honey, let me explain."

"I don't want to hear your excuses."

"They're not excuses."

"Yeah, right."

"Just let me explain. I have a very good excuse. I mean, reason."

"Really? I'd like to hear it."

Arturo told her she could see it, read it. She wanted to know how. He instructed her to turn on the computer, gave her a website he used to access work e-mail remotely, told her his password. She entered the information. The e-mail box came up.

"So?" Sophia said.

He said to click the *Sent* option. She did. "And?"

"Scroll down to the e-mail that starts with her name."

Sophia found it, it having been sent late in the evening, two days previous. Her heart throbbed and she felt dizzy. She clicked on the message, said she'd opened it. He had her read it. Out loud:

> *Phoebe,*
> *Read the note u left at my room in Vegas. Thought about it. And am glad we did nothing more than a kiss and hug, because I know—this last time we met confirmed it—there is only 1 woman for me. And u know who that is. I love my wife intensely, made mistakes against her with u and deeply regret them. I'm sorry but there just isn't the spark with u I feel when I'm with Sophia. She is the 1 I'm meant to be with. Good luck on any future endeavors—work or otherwise.*

Sophia noticed he hadn't typed the word dear or a closing remark or his name. Her stomach ached. She apologized, tried to tell him why she felt the way she had.

"I understand," he replied. "Don't blame you, considering the past. Of course, I'm hurt by your accusation. But I can see how you reached such a conclusion. Trust me, I'm not interested in her. Do you believe me?"

"Mmm-hmm." Sophia sniffed, dried her eyes.

"I swear, nothing happened. Never will." He sniffled, cleared his throat. "I love you, Sophia. More than anyone else." He gave a chuckle. "Even myself."

Sophia managed light laughter, read the note again, and once more expressed regret. "When I saw the note, I just—"

"It's okay." His voice broke. "I really messed up. Twice. Shouldn't have. I am upset but I'd have felt the same as you if the roles were reversed."

"Thanks." She inhaled deeply through her nose then wiped her eyes. "Just don't think I approve of what you did."

"I don't. It was stupid."

"Damn right."

"But I really love you, hope I proved it after all I went through trying to win you back." An empty chuckle. "Took three damn months just to have you going out with me again on a steady basis."

"Well, considering..."

Arturo said he wasn't disagreeing, knew he had to prove himself, said it was like maintaining clients, how it took a lot more to find a new one than to keep a current one. "Should have thought before I did what I did to you."

"Thanks. Again." Sophia collected herself.

His voice cracked again. "I don't want to lose the most important person in my world. I promise I'll slow down. We're doing well financially, will take a vacation, relax, appreciate each other, and talk about future plans. Like what you want."

"You mean..." She touched her flat belly, heard light patter of feet in her mind.

"Yes. I think it's time."

"Really?" She sat back.

"Yes. Haven't had a good night in bed in months."

They laughed.

"Seriously, we will talk. I'm back in two days, won't have to go out of town for three months. Maybe have someone else go then." He exhaled. "We need to work on this, are meant to be together. Some just are."

Sophia tittered. "My little philosopher."

"That's me. Aristotle the second."

"I won't go that far. Money is great but time, once it's gone, is not coming back. A vacation sounds lovely. You're right, we're meant to be together."

"Definitely."

They talked about several restaurants and movies, a vacation spot. An intercom voice behind Arturo.

"That's my flight. Gotta go." He waited a few seconds. "Love you. You're the greatest."

"Love you, too. Bye."

They hung up. Sophia sighed, wiped her eyes, and went to work.

During lunch at the Student Union, she watched the twenty-four-hour news station absentmindedly. A change in the TV background had her pay attention to what was showing. The female announcer's voice was choppy, gaps between each shrinking as she attained new information.

Sophia watched the pictures. Flames and smoke wafted from concrete. A tarmac, she noticed, announcer saying it'd happened minutes ago, cause unclear. Sophia read the caption. And goosefleshed, checked her watch. About the right time. *Or wrong time,* she thought, dug her cell phone out, and pressed the numbers. Voice mail. She left a message, wishing he got there with no delays and was at his hotel.

"Alone," she said then chuckled. "Only joking. Call me when you get this. Love you. Bye."

He did not return the call immediately. Nor when she was done eating. And not when she called him at the office. Her stomach was like she'd eaten spoiled food. She wanted to check internet news or the break room TV but just as much, *didn't* want to.

"Hey," Sophia heard someone say. "Didja hear about the Oklahoma City to Los Angeles flight this morning? Crashed at L.A.X. earlier this afternoon."

Another inquired as to the damage. Sophia rose in her chair.

"News said it was too early to speculate but added it didn't look good."

Sophia ran out, rushed to her car, and sped off. To where, she had no idea, chose to go home. At the first red traffic light, she dialed his number. No answer. She flung the phone to the floor and drove twice the speed limit.

At home, she turned on the television, sucked in air as she watched, and read the captioning. She sank on the sofa.

"Oh, God, no! Why? It can't be! No!" She dialed him again, hung up without hearing his recording, and thrashed on the couch, fists over her eyes. She had to call someone, searched her phone, chose the call option for the first name she saw.

A ringing.

"C'mon, answer," she breathed. "Please, please answer. C'mon. Gotta talk to someone. Please."

No response.

"Damnit, damnit, damnit!" She shut her eyes to repress what came out of them.

More ringing. Then the message.

"Goddamnit!" Her thumb shifted to the red button.

"Hello?" A voice.

Sophia pressed the phone to her ear. "Andrea, thank God you're there!" She sobbed.

"Sophia, what's wrong. You okay?"

Caterwauling. "I can't believe it's happened."

"What? What?"

"Arturo. He's dead."

"What? What are you talking about?"

"Didn't you hear? The plane crash in Los Angeles. He was on it. Oh God, why me? Why us?" The phone slid from her clutches. Crying and wailing reverberated through the empty house.

Chapter 24

Andrea shouted her friend's name. Sophia retrieved the phone.

"Andrea, what am I going to do?"

"First, calm down. Are you sure he was on that plane?"

"Positive. And I called his cell hours ago, no answer. What do I do?"

"I'll be there shortly. Don't do anything rash, please. And Sophia?"

The other girl was quiet.

"Sophia? I love you. I'm on my way."

"Please hurry! Don't think I can be alone like this for long. Please!"

Things were quiet for what seemed an entire day before Andrea called, Sophia allowing her into the gated community. A rap at Sophia's door. She opened it.

Andrea's mien went from normal to a sickly pale. The friend questioned Sophia's mental state, the latter saying she was okay but added, "For someone who's lost their spouse," and burst into tears. Andrea embraced her like they weren't to see each other for years. Sophia apologized for her appearance. Andrea dismissed that and tightened her grasp. Sophia allowed her inside, Andrea craning her neck in all directions, tried to joke why she hadn't been asked to live here or at least visit.

Sophia found herself chuckling, wiped her nose. "Shoulda figured you couldn't resist a wisecrack. Would probably spew jokes as an asteroid destroyed earth."

"Sorry, it's my most salient way of coping."

Sophia managed another small chuckle. "Salient? Where did you hear that?"

"Some place called college."

"Didn't think you learned anything there." Sophia tried to smile.

"Well, I did." She flicked out her left hand, no jewelry on it. "Learned every Mr. Right will only be Mr. Wrong."

Tears poured out Sophia's eyes. "My Mr. Right's gone. Forever." She sobbed.

"Sorry," Andrea said, led Sophia to the living room sofa, commented on the luxurious accommodations. The friend continued to cry, conversation finally switching to years past, the get togethers.

"God, how I need you guys more than ever." Sophia spoke of the last time she and Arturo passed the pizzeria.

"Closed? After all these years?"

"Like we said, times change, people change."

"Wow." Andrea breathed. "That was *our* place. Gone." Her eyes went from damp to wet and she forced air down her lungs. "Where do we go now?"

"Who knows? But I need you guys, all of you. Have to find out who's still here, where they live, their number." Playing back the times in her mind made Sophia's cheeks wetter. "God how I need you."

Andrea hugged her tight, the two like this a long time. They turned on the television, twenty-four-hour news having switched to other events and updated the story at intervals. No survivors, cause yet unknown. Local ten o'clock news ran it as their top story. Soon after, names were released, Arturo's one of them. Calls came, Andrea answering the phone. More tears for Sophia. The two talked early into the next morning.

* * * *

Sophia spoke with a few media the following day, local paper with a brief article on Arturo and his success as a real estate agent, mentioned Sophia survived him. Thinking how they'd had no family of their own caused Sophia some tears and had her stomach tightening.

She stayed home the rest of the week, Andrea there the first twenty-four hours, then visited at lunch and after work, stayed over on nights and into the weekend. The funeral was held at the end of the following week.

"Thank God I found Wyatt's and Millicent's numbers," Andrea said then grunted. "Couldn't get Conrad's though."

Sophia nodded and her vision blurred, her stomach hollow, body as if it had fallen asleep.

The day had light cloud cover with gusty winds. As the hearse chugged to the cemetery, Sophia awaited for him to jump out, everyone chortling at the prank. Only when the last shovelful of dirt covered the coffin did she accept his fate.

About to enter her car, Sophia felt a touch on her shoulder. She half turned. An older yet familiar person. The urge to retch overcame her. She forced it back down and clenched her teeth.

"Hello, Phyllis," she said, her tone like the clichéd husband seeing his mother in law.

"Phoebe," the girl corrected although her voice stayed level, her eyes not dry. She lifted a hand to Sophia, who swatted it away.

"What the hell are you doing here?"

"Being respectful."

"Only if you get the hell out of here." Sophia went to push the woman. "I read your fucking letter. Why the hell didn't you find your own man!? I'm going to kill you, you—"

Someone intervened.

Sophia turned, her iciness thawing though it was replaced by overlapping desires. To strangle the guy. Or hug him.

"Conrad," she said, unsure if she should raise her voice or speak softly. "How did you find out?"

"Television regarding the accident, newspaper this event." He mentioned the article, said Phoebe introduced herself to him before the service, he with Wyatt.

"Okay. So why the hell are *you* here?" Sophia said to the girl.

Phoebe blinked rapidly. "Had to tell you."

Sophia folded her arms. "What?"

Phoebe slid her tongue over her teeth, inched closer. "He loved you," she rasped. "*Really* loved you. I'm not saying that just because he's gone. He told me when we were together at his apartment."

"You mean when you were in bed together," Sophia snapped.

Phoebe held up both hands. "I admit it. But he despised himself afterwards, told me you were the one for him, you guys had some kind of fight, he went to the bar, and, only by fluke, bumped into me, and had a few."

"A few?"

"Okay, more than he should have. And when we met in Vegas, he showed no attraction to me, I swear. Before you came that morning to his apartment, he told me he was sorry, said he'd slept with me out of spite. He was young, please forgive him. And me." She bowed her head, tears splattering the ground. "I'm sorry for what I did. And what happened to him. He was a great guy."

She hurried away, head down. Conrad started to follow but stopped, faced Sophia, and promised if she needed to talk or meet to let him know, said he'd do whatever he could. He handed her a business card.

She read it and smiled. "Professor of computer science? Impressive. Bet you make good money."

Conrad displayed a small smile, corrected he was an associate professor, hoped soon to have the first word in the title removed.

Sophia thought about her comment and felt her face redden, able to grin albeit briefly. "I'm sorry, shouldn't have made that last comment. Arturo was right, women do judge men by their jobs. Or their money."

"That wasn't what attracted you to Arturo."

She laughed, repeated what Arturo had said about meeting him before money mattered to a girl then asked for forgiveness. Her eyes filled up. Conrad held her, said he didn't care, and reminded her to call. She looked at him, saw him from memories in high school. In college. At the pizzeria. Her waterworks worsened. "I will," she said, and updated him regarding the pizza place.

"You're kidding? Where will we meet?"

Sophia sniffed. "Had the same reaction." She gave a quick, dry, *ha-ha*. "Of course, we had to find everybody before worrying about where to go."

Conrad laughed uneasily. "Yeah." His face smoothed out. "Maybe we could get together."

"Thanks." She hugged him. He went to his car, repeated she could call if needing to talk. Sophia waved, promised she would. Seeing Millicent, having spoken with her prior to the service, had her smiling. She opened her arms. "Thanks for being here."

Millicent hugged her, wiped her eyes, and gave condolences again, inquired as to Sophia's emotional state, friend saying she was surviving. They held hands.

"Sure do need you guys. Just talked with Conrad. You know he's a professor?"

Millicent nodded, wondered aloud about his salary. Sophia quoted Arturo's words, her former roommate agreeing. Sophia mentioned their times at the restaurant, how the subject matter had changed as the years flowed past. She requested an update on Millicent's job then said to forget that, laughed at how quickly she'd forgotten her new lesson.

Millicent replied she wasn't offended, liked the position, and described how the kids were fun—most of the time. "They keep me busy. If only I could find a man so we could have our own."

The words made Sophia rub her eyes. Why hadn't he agreed earlier to her plan?

"You okay?"

"I think so." Sophia took a couple of uneven breaths.

"Sorry. If you need, call me. Anytime."

Sophia retrieved her cell phone, entered Millicent's number, and thanked her then put a hand on her. "How about you follow me to my house now? Need someone to talk to."

"I'm there. Lead the way."

"In a minute." Sophia saw the other person, had also spoken with him before services. He hurried to her, held her.

"How are you?" Wyatt said in a hush.

"Surviving." Sophia ran a finger over an eye as he patted her shoulder. They caught up on each other's lives, Wyatt still single, no one since his time with Dawn, he kicking the ground while saying this, ah-hemmed then looked up, face brighter. "Talked with Conrad."

Sophia smiled. "How'd it go?"

"Okay." He lifted his shoulders. "Even exchanged numbers."

"Good for you."

He volunteered his number and she gave him hers, he instructing her he was ready to talk if she needed to. Sophia mentioned her invitation to Millicent, asked him to join them then hit her head with a hand. "Totally forgot to ask Conrad for his number when he offered to talk. Damnit."

"No problem." Wyatt dialed the number and left a message. "There."

"That was sweet. Especially considering you two's previous circumstances."

He waved a hand, said it was over, they were meant to be friends.

Sophia smiled, asked if it was he or Renaldo who'd said they didn't believe in such.

With a half grin, Wyatt answered he had no idea then explained he'd been immature.

Sophia touched his hand, re-invited him to her house. His fingers squeezed into her palm. She then saw Andrea at her car, waved her over, the friend agreeing to go then laughed she thought she'd already moved in. Her smile waned while she swore eternal friendship should Sophia need it, instructed she talk until talked out. Sophia hugged her, gave thanks, and entered her car, guided them to her home where they discussed Arturo and he and Sophia's relationship.

Millicent stated her envy of the couple, how when she and Andrea spoke before the funeral, Andrea repeated Sophia's comment about others only seeing the good side.

Sophia exhibited a droopy smile. The group talked of other things.

Hours later, they started to wind things down.

"Oh no." Sophia looked to Wyatt. "Forgot about Conrad. He ever call back?"

"Damn." Wyatt pulled out his phone. "Sure didn't."

"If only he were here," Sophia lamented. "Like old times."

Andrea half smiled. "Except no pizzeria."

"Let's go someplace else," Wyatt said, offered a fish place that had been around almost as long.

Everyone bobbed heads then followed Wyatt. Though quiet, they dined on salmon, catfish, and tilapia, and shared platters of fries, Millicent and Sophia misty-eyed when the past was brought up, all staying until the place closed then hung out in the parking lot.

"We must get together again," Sophia said. "Soon. All of us, Conrad included."

The other three promised. Sophia tried to set a date but either someone was working or had other commitments.

"Let's just keep our options open," Andrea said.

Sophia frowned but seeing her friends move heads back and forth, did the same, kidded she was holding them to it.

The others laughed, promised they'd keep up their end, and said final goodbyes, save for Andrea. Only when she entered her bedroom did Sophia return to her demoralized state despite Andrea sleeping in a spare room. She contemplated talking to Andrea then, seeing how late it was, slipped into bed feeling a little better, told herself it was like the old days then touched the empty half of the bed, and whispered, "Almost."

She barely slept, face wet, dry, wet again.

Questions scrolled across her mind the next few weeks, she telling Andrea she needn't be at the house unless requested, Sophia having hoped to lose herself in her job. Yet the questions always returned: Why had it happened? Why him? Why now instead of fifty years later, when she'd had her share of him and vice versa? After they'd had others to carry on their name.

She spoke with Millicent, Andrea, and Wyatt, made small talk though none seemed eager to delve into philosophy. When Sophia spoke of getting together, the response was the same prattle about having plans, busy lives, jobs, and responsibilities, Andrea and Wyatt each looking to buy their own home, Millicent a new car. The calls diminished as summer reached its peak.

* * * *

Days felt like decades to Sophia as she trudged through her routine of work then home, vegging out with the TV. She visited Arturo's grave most days, always left in tears. She took off from work until her leave was used up.

* * * *

After work on a Friday in early December, Sophia gave heavy sighs as she played with a salad at the Student Union. First Yuletide season without him. Her eyes teared. Spotting someone shifted her glance. "How are ya?" She managed a smile and stood, put arms around the other girl, and gave usual pleasantries. Her friend's grin sank.

"What's wrong?"

Millicent slumped in a chair, hand on her chin. "Lost my job."

"Oh no. When?" Sophia sat next to her.

"Over three months ago."

"What happened?"

"Said they were losing money. Guess some other places opened and are taking their business."

"You apply at those places?"

"Mmm-hmm. Applied for any job I could find. Office work, secretarial." She forced a chuckle. "Though I haven't looked at burger flipper. Yet."

Sophia gave a quick smirk.

Millicent sighed she couldn't so much as find part time work, was nearly broke, about to lose her car, still hadn't found the right guy, rubbed her eyes, and looked at Sophia. "You ever think about that?"

"Duh. All the time."

Millicent touched her friend. "Sorry. Not thinking, just—"

"Hey, you two, what's going on?" someone interrupted.

The two raised their glances. Conrad gave each a quick hug, occupied a chair. They updated him on things then proceeded with their discussion.

"I first asked why this happened," Sophia said. "Then what I could have done different. Wanted him to cut back on his trips, needed time with him. If only I'd done so earlier. Thought I was being selfish since he enjoyed his work so much."

"And the money was great," Conrad said.

Sophia shook her head. "That helped though only so much. I mean, I didn't want to be poor. However, his income wasn't a panacea."

"We need balance," Millicent said.

"Exactly. Now I..." Sophia looked at Millicent. "We have nothing."

"You've got a lot," Conrad said. Sophia demanded examples. He mentioned her money. She grimaced, asked if he'd gone deaf or senile.

"Okay." Conrad thought. "Your health."

Sophia cringed. "Only the biggest loser is thankful for that."

Millicent agreed. "What's the point of it all? Who knows if it's going to get better."

"Yeah." Sophia continued with her salad but ate none of it. "They say things work out."

"Has just gotten to be a drag, a burden," Millicent contributed.

"C'mon." Conrad tried to laugh. "Don't get down, it's not that bad."

Sophia's eyes expanded. Conrad lowered his head, mumbled, "Sorry," and asked Millicent about her job. She told him.

"Oh." He looked away.

"I'm just so drained." Sophia stirred her bowl.

"It will get better," Conrad said.

"When?" Both girls asked.

He shrank. "Don't worry, it will. Cheer up." He made his back straight. "Put on a smile, inhale, exhale. Ahh. Doesn't that feel better?"

"No," Millicent grumbled.

"Uh-uh," Sophia said in like tone.

Conrad put a hand to his face. "Sorry."

"It's okay." Sophia touched him. "You tried."

"Yeah, well..." Conrad looked at the clock, stood, and announced he had an evening class to teach. "Don't get so down, leads to crazy thoughts." He turned a lip up, told both to call if needed.

On his way out, Conrad passed the Oklahoma State Novelty store, noticed the one thing he'd been looking for: OSU stone coasters, had seen them months ago, decided against them, and when he next checked, they were gone. He now picked them up, saw the price, and fondled the products, flipped them over and over.

* * * *

"Just hurts so much," Sophia said to Millicent back in the cafeteria. "Each day seems longer, more torturous."

"You did have your man."

Sophia lowered the hand resting on her chin. "So? He's gone."

"Well, what about how it's better to have loved and lost than never to have loved at all?"

"Not true if it ends way earlier than you wished. And how is not having someone worse than losing your spouse?"

"It's like we were injured in a plane crash and..."

Sophia sniffed, whimpered.

"Bad example," Millicent said. "Let's just say you're having a heart attack, I have broken legs. The fact you have a more serious predicament doesn't make my pain go away or solve my problem. I'm still hurting, need attention too. Make sense?"

Sophia put her hand on Millicent's. "Think so. I just feel so tired, hurt so much, don't feel like going on."

Millicent released a long, slow breath. "I'm with you, sister. If it's too painful doing something, why keep doing it?"

"Agreed." Sophia felt her body tingle. She clutched her friend's hand. "I really don't want to go on."

Millicent mumbled, "Me neither," then thought about her friend's words, gazed at her. "You don't mean..."

Sophia's head went back and forth. Millicent asked how. Sophia froze, said she had no idea, suggested drugs, Millicent saying they didn't always work. Sophia said "Gun," then gave a humorless chuckle, aware neither owned, let alone knew how to use, one.

Millicent placed the palm of her hand under her chin. Suddenly, the hand went up, index finger raised. She described the legend she'd heard, how it'd happened years ahead of her time, had told it to Andrea. Teen boys doing it with one of the guy's car, they both having been jilted.

"Sangre Cliff," she said of the location on the south side. "Supposedly older locals familiar with the story give it another name."

"I don't care, just want to get it over with. Why not tonight?"

"Was going to suggest that, only need a little time to work out the plan. C'mon."

The two stood, meandered by the OSU Novelty Store, stopped in the hall due to the crowd, classes and work having ended, students hungry for dinner.

"Let's get this over with, end it for us as soon as we can," Sophia said.

"Finish the job right now," Millicent replied.

"No point in going on. Tonight. After dark. That way I won't see it, won't get scared."

"Right. No headlights on. You want to?"

The two slapped palms. And left.

* * * *

In the shop, Conrad recognized the voices, turned to see if it was them. They were gone. He re-heard the words in his mind to convince himself he hadn't misinterpreted them, believed he hadn't despite knowing he'd heard only part of the conversation. Something without headlights. After dark.

To end things. The two of them. His mind processed what that meant. When he reached a possible translation, he sucked in his breath, uttered the Deity's name. They wouldn't, were too sane. The exchange he'd had with them was fresh in his mind, like lines from a favorite movie. Were they that down? If so, he had part of the how, the when, and why but not the other vital clue: Where?

Another question: What to do? He did a quick turn. Plastic cups tumbled, rolled off shelves. A key chain stand toppled, the twenty something store employee giving a narrow stare, muttered something about Conrad experiencing a long time in the place Beelzebub existed.

Conrad said he was sorry, helped the employee re-stock items then sprinted out, dodged a woman, raced around a corner, and searched. The two were not there. He pressed his way through the hall, throngs of students, teachers, and workers, the mob of bodies almost as dense as a football Saturday. He made it to the front entrance doors, looked left then right. No Millicent or Sophia.

"Damnit!" He kicked one of the building's pillars. "Now what?" He fished out his cell phone but at that moment thought of some important facts: He didn't have their current numbers, realized he hadn't given his own new number nor asked for theirs when advising them to call if they wanted.

"Now what?" He scanned the phone to be sure. No number with Sophia's or Millicent's name. "Damn!" About to turn it off, he saw the last name and number. One he'd gotten after the funeral. He smiled. And frowned just as quickly. What good would his number do? Did he have theirs?

Conrad pressed *call*. A *doo-doo-doo* sounded, followed by the recording: *We're sorry, your number cannot be completed as dialed. Please hang up and...*

"Fuck!" He slowed down, read the name on the screen before pressing the dial option. He held the phone to his ear.

A ring. A second. Third. Fourth.

"Answer, damnit, answer! If only this one time. Come on!"

No response. Voice mail:

"This is Wyatt. Please leave a message. Thanks."

He's gonna think I'm crazy, probably won't even call back, Conrad thought but was aware of the result if he did nothing. His words spilled out:

"Wyatt, this is Conrad. Call as soon as you get this. Please! It's an emergency!" He hung up.

No return call immediately. Not five minutes later. Ten minutes. He went to his class but cut it short, unable to lecture, his thoughts scattershot. He called Wyatt twice more, same result.

"Damnit, Wyatt, where are you?" He left another message.

The sun neared the horizon. Hadn't they said after dark? And where?

He dialed yet again, left another fast-paced message:

"Wyatt, please call. It's an emergency. Regarding Sophia and Millicent. I think they're..." He contemplated what to say. "They seemed upset when I saw them today, really down. Overheard them talking about doing something drastic, something about ending things. Call as soon as you get this. Please! Hurry!"

Time seemed to have frozen. At home, he writhed on the sofa, considered calling police. What could he tell them?

A jangle had him off the sofa. A second ring. He checked the number. "Thank God." He pressed the talk button. "Hello?"

"Conrad? You okay? Left some confusing messages. Is everything—"

"No. Listen to me," Conrad cut him off, explained the circumstances.

"You sure?" Wyatt said.

"Positive. They were really down. We should at least check on them, call. You have their numbers?"

"Yeah, thanks to Arturo's funeral. Let me try and I'll call back."

They hung up. Conrad could not stay seated. Ten minutes expired. Fifteen.

"Damnit, Wyatt, what're ya doing, jerking off? Fucking Dawn again?"

Those memories made Conrad's heart thick. His lips curled down. "Bastard." He brought himself back to current times, more important matters, and went to dial. The ring nearly caused him to fall backward.

"Wyatt?"

"I called both, left messages, waited for call backs but no response. You try." He gave Conrad the numbers, the other friend dialing and also leaving messages, pleaded with them, said he'd heard them, implored them to call. Nothing after twenty minutes. Wyatt called Conrad who said he'd met with the same results.

"I'm gonna try Andrea, see what she might know." Wyatt found her number, told her what was happening, she in denial at first. He had her call Conrad.

Conrad saw the name and number, immediately pressed the green button, gave a quick "Hello" then told Andrea what he knew.

"Any ideas?" he asked. "No headlights, what does that mean? Something about a car?" He peeked through blinds. "Almost totally dark, we gotta do something."

"You're sure about what they said?"

"Definitely. Andrea, think. Where might Millicent go, what would she do? Sophia too."

"Sophia, I don't know. Has always been upbeat. Of course, friends can make other friends do things they normally wouldn't. And Sophia's still grieving. Millicent's had plenty of down moments. I remember in high school after she saw a guy she liked dating someone else, how depressed she was, talked about two teens who supposedly years ago..." She sucked in air. "Oh my God!"

"What?"

Andrea snapped fingers. "You said they sounded desperate? Mentioned the words *Ending things*?"

"Something like that."

"And they mentioned a car?"

"Headlights. I assumed they meant a car."

"We must get out there. Now!"

"Where?"

"Sangre Cliff, out by the golf course on the west side of town where Sangre Road and twenty fifth meet. There's a side road, all gravel. Goes up a steep incline, Sangre Hill.

This road dead ends to Sangre Cliff overlooking a huge field. Millicent said two boys drove over that cliff years ago, after their girlfriends broke up with them, police saying they did so after dark, headlights not on. A few older folks call the spot Suicide Cliff."

"We have to stop them. Where is it?"

Andrea gave directions while Conrad entered his car, ordered her to meet him out there. Conrad called Wyatt.

"Be there as soon as I can."

"And if a cop wants to pull you over, keep going."

"Good point," Wyatt said.

The three sped to the scene.

Chapter 25

"Maybe you'd better turn the lights on," Sophia said. "Just in case."

Millicent scoffed. "In case what?"

"I don't know. You won't see how far to the edge, might not go fast enough and we wind up alive, paralyzed for life."

"Whatever. Doesn't matter to me."

In the distance motors rumbled, rush of engines louder, the vibrations at the girls' feet. A barely audible squeak of what sounded like rubber in the distance.

Sophia lowered her brow. "What was that?"

The other girl pressed a shoulder to her ear. "Who knows? Or cares? C'mon." Millicent turned to Sophia with wide eyes. "Ready?"

"Let's do it."

Millicent gripped the key, Sophia thinking of financially trying times when Arturo tried to start his old car and it wouldn't turn over, needed another repair.

The good old days, she thought then sighed. They weren't so good anymore.

Engines hummed louder, sound of metal bouncing on gravel behind the two girls.

Sophia blinked faster, sniffled then faced Millicent, about to tell her to start the car when the drone of engines could be heard through Millicent's partially open window. Sophia looked behind her. "What's that?"

"Who cares? Let's go."

Millicent shifted the key. The engine roared. She smiled, the two shaking hands. Sophia sat up. Millicent slid her hand to the gearshift. "Ready?"

Headlights shone in the rear view mirror.

"You bet." Sophia pointed to the windshield. "Go!"

A horn honked. The females glanced over their shoulders.

"Who the hell is that?" Millicent watched her side mirror.

"Like you said, who cares? We're ready."

Brakes squealed, both girls hunching, shoulders up, each looking out her side mirror to the two, then four, then six headlights.

"What the hell?" Millicent checked behind them.

Doors slammed, engines still running, headlights blinding the darkness. Feet sha-shushed on dirt and grass. Figures came close. Two males, one female.

"No! No! Stop!" Conrad and Wyatt said, Conrad sprinting to Millicent's side, Wyatt at Sophia's. Conrad snaked an arm through the window, clutched Millicent's forearm.

"What the hell are you doing?" Millicent broke free.

Conrad grabbed again. "No!"

Millicent struggled.

Wyatt tried to open Sophia's door. Locked. He hit the window, glass not breaking.

"What are you doing?" Sophia shouted.

"What are *you* doing?"

"Nothing is going to stop us."

"We'll see," Conrad said, continued to hold on to Millicent.

Millicent gave a twisted grin. "Yes, you will." She reached her right hand under her left, touched the button. The window went up.

"Ah! Shit!" Conrad screamed.

Millicent's grin expanded. "Let go or I'll keep this pressed on your arm till the circulation is cut off."

Conrad did not obey. She pressed the button harder. He groaned, shut his eyes, clenched his teeth.

"You'll be sorry." Millicent kept a finger on the button. Conrad shouted, screamed, twisted his head skyward, downward, left then right. "C'mon!" he pleaded. "Stop!"

"Not until you let go."

Conrad's fingers lost their grasp. The girl freed her arm and lowered the window, thanked Conrad then pushed the window shut.

"Damnit!" Conrad stomped a foot. "Stop this! Now! This is crazy!"

"You're crazy!" Sophia said. "We want to do this, you're the one trying to stop us. Why?"

"C'mon, girls. Please?" Andrea cried, came up to Millicent's window. "You don't want to do this."

"Like hell!" Millicent looked to Sophia. "Ready?"

"Mmm-hmm."

Millicent backed up.

"Wait a minute," Andrea said to the two males. "Got an idea. C'mon." She ran ahead of the car, turned right, waved the two guys over.

"Are you nuts?" Conrad said.

"Let's see. We'll find out if our friendship is for real. Get over here. Wyatt, you too. Right here. All three of us. They think they have no reason to live? We'll show them otherwise."

The three stood, arms entwined.

Millicent watched, looked at Sophia, and revved the engine. Sophia was mute though her eyes, and Millicent's, were giant circles.

"Go ahead!" Andrea shouted. "Right at us!"

Millicent ran her tongue on the outside of her mouth. Sophia squirmed.

"Let's do it!" they both said. Tires squealed.

"Jesus Christ!" Conrad flashed a glance at Andrea, Wyatt doing the same.

"Don't worry," Andrea said. "It'll be okay. Trust me."

"This is fucking crazy!" Conrad said.

"Just do as I say, trust me. Can't bail on them now."

Conrad and Wyatt stared at her. She smiled.

The car lurched ahead. Its speed increased. Both boys closed their eyes, Andrea with lips pressed together.

Brakes seemed to pierce everyone's eardrums. The car did not decrease its speed quick enough.

Sophia yelled for Millicent to do something. The other girl lifted the emergency brake. They still went too fast.

Conrad opened his eyes. They seemed to grow as big as the sun. He shut them.

"Stop! Stop!" Sophia screamed.

"I'm trying!" Millicent yelled.

Sophia reached across to the wheel. Her hand touched it. She spun it, Millicent's hand doing the same. The car fishtailed. Dirt and dust wafted into the air so thick it blocked the view of the other three.

Metal approached the trio. Closer. Then stopped as did the squealing of pads on wheels. Only the sound of the four car engines.

The three friends opened their eyes. The vehicle was in front of them, parallel to their bodies, and just out of arm's length. They traded glances. All three smiled. And laughed, unloosened interlocked arms, fell into each other then rushed the car, guys opening doors, Andrea hugging Sophia then Millicent, all the girls getting each other's shirts wet, guys rubbing their own eyes.

"Why would you do this?" Andrea asked.

"We just didn't want to go on." Sophia wiped her eyes. "Was too painful; death felt more pleasurable than living."

"Why didn't you call?" Wyatt said to Sophia. "I told you."

"Right. And when I suggested we get together, what was your reaction?"

Wyatt pointed a finger. "But I..." He lowered the hand.

"Andrea?" Sophia said, other girl with chin on her chest, she mumbling weak denials.

"See? I felt alone, the worst I'd ever felt." She hugged Millicent. "She felt the same way."

The other three displayed nods. Andrea sighed, said it usually took something drastic to make an emotionally troubled person see what was good.

Sophia smiled. "At least you guys had the nerve and courage to show us."

Millicent shook her head. "And that was one crazy stand."

"Guess you gotta be crazy to fight crazy," Andrea said.

"Whatever it was, it worked." More tears from Sophia. She wrapped arms around the other girl. "Boy, did it work!"

Millicent joined them. "It sure did!"

The guys did the same.

"Friends," Andrea said. "For eternity."

"Always," Sophia replied.

"Past the end of time," Millicent said.

"For infinity," Wyatt responded.

"Never ending," Conrad answered.

The five hugged tight, as if afraid once they let go, they'd lose each other.

Chapter 26

The group retreated to Sophia's house, she giving them the grand tour this time, Millicent, Conrad, and Wyatt chuckling how sore their necks were when done.

"Awesome," Conrad said.

"Sweet," Wyatt added.

"It's lovely," Millicent said then noticed the place lacked seasonal decorations.

Sophia frowned. Millicent gave profuse regrets, hugged her friend who said it was okay.

"When can we move in?" Millicent said to light laughter, Sophia answering she'd considered selling the place, needed a new beginning. "Place is too damn big anyway. Too much to clean."

The other girl smiled sadly.

"Well," Wyatt looked to the grandfather clock in the living room, "it's late, think I'll turn in."

Sophia gave a melancholy smile, mentioned how just a few years ago this was the beginning of the evening to them, the night in its infancy.

"Guess we grew up." Wyatt stretched. "Became old."

Andrea vowed she'd never get old, pointed to her heart then head, said that was where she'd stay young. Wyatt countered how those two were the last to fail, it was the body that gave out, one needed to take care of that. "Early to bed, early to rise," he quoted.

"You're just an old fart," Andrea said. "Let's go out, a fling for old time's sake. Who's with me?" She went toward the front.

Everyone stayed their ground. Andrea halted, turned her arm in circular motion. "Come on."

The rest exchanged blank faces, shoulders raised.

"I have an idea," Sophia said, brought Andrea back to the group, they in a circle. "Why don't you all stay overnight?"

"Yeah." Conrad leaned around the rest of them to scan the backyard. "We can go swimming."

"Now?" Sophia laughed. "Pool's covered, it's winter."

"So? Let's jump in."

"Well, it has a heater." Sophia smiled, led them out, guys taking the tarp off, she turning on the heat pump.

Inside, they sat for a spell, waited for the pool to warm.

"What do we do for swim trunks?" Wyatt said.

"Why not Arturo's," Sophia said, pushed back tears, and put on a grin. "He had several, should fit you guys." Her eyes remained wet until she recalled a specific outfit. "I know you'd like one in particular, Wyatt." She went to the bedroom, searched a drawer, came back, and held it up.

"You'll never get me in that thing." Wyatt backed away, hands out. "Couldn't pay me enough."

"Why not? You'd looked cute." Sophia smiled. "Wouldn't he?" she asked the girls, who *Mmm-hmm*'ed. Sophia offered the outfit. "Arturo liked Speedos though thank God he only wore this once. Try it."

His face the color of an apple, Conrad said he no longer felt like swimming.

"Wyatt?" Sophia asked.

The friend hid his face with both arms. "Thanks, no."

"Chicken," Sophia taunted.

"You bet," Wyatt agreed.

"Whatsa matter, too old?" Andrea said. "Can't believe two young men are afraid of one tiny outfit."

"I'm old," Wyatt said.

"Over the hill," Conrad chimed in.

Sophia laughed. "I'll get you some stuff." She waved the girls to join her, said they could wear one of her outfits.

"Let's go out," Andrea said. "Have some fun first. Just for a while. Please?"

Again, none of the others responded.

"For an hour. C'mon."

Conrad looked at Wyatt who glanced at Millicent, she passing the expression on to Sophia.

"Isn't this what you wanted?" Andrea said. "Old times again?"

Sophia hesitated. And yawned.

Andrea's body sagged.

"Let's go!" Sophia winked at her friend, rushed to the garage, others in tow.

At the bar, they drank, danced, and celebrated, Andrea trying to pick up any guy she found attractive, wound up sticking with none of the four she met. Millicent elbowed Sophia, gave an okay sign as a square-jawed red-head with crew cut and clipped beard passed the table.

"So go after him," Sophia said.

"You like him?" Millicent said then held a hand over her mouth. "Sorry. Wasn't thinking."

Sophia forced air down her lungs. "It's okay." She nudged Millicent in the guy's direction. Millicent stayed put.

"What're ya waiting for?" Sophia pleaded. "Who knows when you'll get another chance?"

"Exactly," Andrea said. "You've said how guys don't come up to you. So do like me, make the first move, take a chance, be bold."

"Think so?"

Andrea put a hand on her. "Told ya a guy loves it when a woman comes up to him like she's desperate."

Millicent squinted. "I'm not desperate."

Andrea smiled. "Are you? Be honest."

"No, I just..." Millicent gnawed her lip.

"Just go on," Sophia said.

Millicent leaned forward, palms pressing the seat of her chair. She sank back down, put her hands under her legs.

"For Chrissakes, go on," Andrea said and, in half-singing tone, "You'll regret it."

Millicent sprang up, shot the two a look like they'd said they would bet a million dollars she couldn't do it. She tromped to the guy, about to extend her arm, finger out to touch his shoulder. In mid-motion, she froze.

"Oh, shit." Andrea's hand went to her forehead. "Don't quit now, girl." She and Sophia watched, mouths slightly ajar.

The guy saw the arm, turned, and flinched. "Whoa. Sorry."

Millicent withdrew a step.

"C'mon, girl," Andrea muttered.

The guy began to slide past Millicent, space between them increasing. She sagged.

"It's over." Andrea slid down in her chair.

"Don't be so negative," Sophia said. "She'll recover."

Millicent started for the table. Sophia pointed in the direction of the guy, Andrea with her hand like she had a sock puppet, her other hand pointed at the guy also.

"You'll regret it," Andrea sing-songed again.

The girl on the floor straightened up, moved to the stranger. The guy turned.

"Excuse me." Millicent held out her hand. "Wanna dance?" She gave a child-like smile, chin tucked to her shoulder.

The guy remained with arms at his sides.

"Oh, God, no." Andrea put her elbows on the table, bent her head into her hands. "Not after all that. It's over. Damnit. She gonna be so depress—"

"Wait. Look!" Sophia tapped her friend.

The young man lifted an arm, touched Millicent's shoulder. She took his free hand, put it in hers, and led him in a dance of Creed's "Higher."

"Oh, thank heavens." Andrea's upper half was sprawled across the table.

"Success." Sophia gave a muted clap.

The two danced several more numbers before Millicent led him back to the table, introduced him—Justin—to her friends. He gave a small grin, the two got drinks, sat, and talked, had a few more dances.

"Sophia?" Andrea said, motioned to the dance floor. The other girl's eyes became wet. Andrea apologized, Sophia saying it was okay. The former held the latter's hand.

The gang stayed out past two, returned to Sophia's— Millicent bringing her new friend—and swam in the now warm enough pool, Justin not afraid to wear the Speedo though it was snug, girls cat-calling him. He played along.

They all stayed the night, did not awaken until the noon hour, each clamoring for food.

Sophia hit the back of one hand in the palm of the other. "Why not go out for lunch? Someplace different, start a new trend, new place to meet." She smiled. "But like old times."

They agreed, crammed into Sophia's Escalade, drove by a few places, none very appealing. Soon they were in the old neighborhood and passed the familiar structure.

Andrea put a finger on the window. "Look! It's open!"

All craned their necks.

"The pizzeria?" Wyatt said.

"Uh-huh. Same name, too. See?"

Sophia did a one eighty with the vehicle, occupants slapping a hand on the dash or seat in front of them, Wyatt thanking Sophia for the amusement ride, said he hadn't been on the spinning teacups since he was a kid. Everyone chuckled.

"Here we are." Sophia pulled into the lot. Lights shone out through the buildings' windows. Bodies flashed past glass. Doors opened and shut.

"Oh my gosh, they *are* open." Sophia parked, hopped out, and waved the others inside.

The gang entered, held their breaths. And let them out as one. Very little had changed, chandeliers refurbished and polished, new pictures of land and seascapes decorated newly painted powder blue walls. Sophia led the gang to their old table.

"This is great," she said. "Brings back lots of memories."

"How about we create some new ones?" Andrea said, thumb in Justin's direction. "Starting with him."

Justin slunk down in the booth as if accused of wrongdoing. "Me?"

"Sure. Tell us about yourself," Andrea said.

Millicent covered her chest with overlapped arms. "Why? So you can hit on him?"

"Give me some credit, I've matured. Plus, I've gotten too old for that kind of thing."

"Too old?" Wyatt cracked. "Thought you said you were going to stay young."

"At heart, buddy boy, at heart. And in mind. We all must mature. And..." She sighed. "Last night had me wondering. I've spent so much time trying to find the perfect guy, I passed on many a good one. Who knows, one of them might have been *the* guy if only I'd given them a chance. None of us are getting younger and the older you get, the less chances you have of meeting Mr. Right."

"I'm th'till waiting for him," Wyatt said to a few giggles.

"Or Ms. Right," Andrea corrected. Her smile shrank, she with hand on chin. "I just wonder, *What if I'd stayed with one of them?* We could be happily married, I a mother." She blinked rapidly. "Never thought I'd see the day I'd be pining for that."

"So what happened?" Conrad said.

"Don't know. It just happened." Andrea stood. "Gotta move on, though." She rubbed her abdomen. "There are more immediate, pressing needs. Who'll join me?"

Everyone stood and headed for the buffet. A stocky, brown-haired guy by the counter leaned on the door to the back, he with a blue apron, restaurant logo and name on it in white cursive.

Andrea tapped Sophia and pointed. Sophia showed downturned lips, gave a visual denial with her head. She looked again but choked up and turned to Andrea. "Not yet."

"Just checking."

Sophia managed another glimpse. "Is handsome, though."

They returned to their table. Sophia peered over her shoulder then looked away, her mouth flat as the guy moved to the back. He didn't return.

Done with the meal, the six talked future plans. Millicent's phone rang.

"Hello? Oh yes." She listened. Her face brightened, she agreeing to meet that Tuesday, wrote down the date and time on a napkin. "Will be there. Thank you."

"Another date?" Andrea said, motioned to Justin. "You've got him."

"It's an interview for a job as kindergarten teacher at The Academy."

"Ooh, new private school on the north side," Sophia said. "Bet they pay well."

"They do," Millicent agreed. "But remember, money isn't..."

"I know, I know. Forgive me."

"Sounds like what I want." Millicent rubbed hands together. "I feel good about this."

"Don't get your hopes up," Justin warned.

Millicent elbowed him. "And don't be so negative."

"Sorry." He grinned. "Just when someone keeps me up past two the night before then drags me out to eat the next morning, I sometimes get cranky, pessimistic."

"Only it's not morning, just feels like it," Andrea said.

"True." Sophia rubbed her head. "Woke up at six with a nice hangover. Amazing how six more hours of sleep cured that."

They laughed while a shadow moved near them. Andrea glanced to the source. The figure stepped forward.

"Y'all enjoying this?" the man with blue apron asked in a baritone.

"You bet," Andrea crowed. "Used to come here for years in high school and college till the place went out of business."

The man smiled. "You guys that old?" He pointed at Sophia. "Assumed she was a sophomore."

Sophia blushed as Andrea slapped her gently, whispered, "You don't believe that?" then faced the guy. "She got her degree over two years ago."

The guy smiled wider. "I meant a sophomore in high school."

Andrea put the heels of both hands on her eyes, tilted her head side to side. "It's getting really deep in here."

"Let me get a shovel," the guy said as the others laughed. He introduced himself as Dale, owner of the place, said he'd eaten here a few times in college, he a restaurant management major, loved the food, and when he saw the building vacated and for sale, decided to buy it.

"Love to cook," he explained then placed a hand over his front. "Even more so, eating."

"What's your favorite?" Andrea said. "To cook, I mean."

"Filet Mignon." He pressed fingers on puckered lips, opened the hand. "Delicioso."

"Sounds tasty." Andrea tapped her friend's elbow. "Doesn't it, Sophia?"

The other girl glared.

"Would love to have you try it." The owner leaned toward Sophia. "Want to?"

"Here? You don't have the ingredients for it."

"I don't mean here." He grinned. "Have them on a shelf at home."

Andrea viewed Sophia who dabbed an eye with a knuckle. "Umm, I don't believe she's ready for that, been through a rough time."

Sophia now rubbed hands on both eyes.

"Maybe in the future," Andrea said.

Sophia gasped, leaned to Andrea, and whispered for the friend to stop, she not ready.

"I have an idea," Andrea said to the man. "Bring the ingredients here some time, say in the next week or two and we can try it." She motioned her hand at the others. "All of us." The corner of her mouth near Sophia moved. "How's that?" she mumbled. "Nice and slow. *Real* slow. Can you handle that?"

Sophia gave a half frown, half grin, feebly lifted a shoulder.

"Let's see what happens. If you're not ready, we'll stop then. Okay?" With no reply from her friend, Andrea asked Dale if he could agree to her offer, said the friends had unusual dating habits, tittered it was their religious beliefs.

When Dale half smiled and said he'd never heard of any religion requiring group approval for dates, Andrea responded it was a new offshoot. He inquired as to what branch.

"Umm, spawned from several different ones. Catholic, Protestant, Baptist, Seventh Day Adventist, Amish."

"Amish?" Dale lifted an eyebrow as well as his lips. "Didn't know they were prevalent out here."

"Ooh, big word, prevalent." Andrea tapped Sophia, gave an upturned-lip expression.

"Got that from college." Dale winked at Sophia, who stirred but kept a straight face.

Andrea snickered. "That's what we always say. Right, Sophia?" When her friend said nothing, Andrea touched a finger at Sophia's side. "Right?"

Sophia blinked. "Huh? Oh, yeah." A rough laugh. "Inside joke."

"Well, we are inside..." Dale said.

Sophia found herself chuckling. Andrea reminded the guy they'd all be here for Filet Mignon, offered two weeks from now.

"Okay. Looking forward to it."

A voice called the owner's name, employee asking for assistance.

"See ya in two weeks," Dale said and retreated.

Andrea nudged Sophia. "Do you want to do this? If not, say so and I'll cancel it." She glanced over her shoulder. "Though he is handsome. Wealthy, too."

Sophia frowned. "How do you know?"

"He owns this place. Had to have money to buy it."

"May have gotten a loan. Anyways, who cares? Right, Millicent?"

"Exactly."

Sophia commented how each table in the restaurant was occupied, a few waiting for an empty spot. She leaned to Andrea. "Place is doing well. How much do you think he has?"

Andrea mentioned she saw a Lexus in back. The two playfully slapped each other, Millicent scolding them.

"But money is nice, isn't it?" Sophia said.

Millicent smiled. "Yeah, guess so." She sighed. "Learned a lot with you guys." She slid closer to Justin. "What would I have done without y'all?"

Sophia raised her cup. "To us. Friends. Always."

"For eternity." Andrea held up her drink.

Wyatt did the same. "For infinity."

"Never ending," Conrad said.

"Till our last days. And beyond," Millicent replied.

All were quiet. The five looked at Justin who shrugged, looked at his new girlfriend.

"Say something," she said.

"Uh... to good times."

"Yeah," everyone said, about to hit glasses.

"Even if I don't have any with you guys, don't know what the hell you're talking about," Justin added.

Laughter, followed by the heavy *clunk* of plastic.

"So when will we get together again?" Sophia asked.

Andrea mentioned the group date with Dale.

"I mean us as a group," Sophia said. "Like we always did. Only now as adults. And on a consistent basis."

"I don't know." Wyatt let out a breath. "Work's getting busy and..."

"He's right," Conrad said. "And I'm taking classes for a masters."

Millicent pointed to Justin. Andrea shrugged, swallowed her drink.

"Come on," Sophia begged. "We can do it, need each other. Don't we?"

All nodded.

"Next Saturday," Sophia said. "Noon. All of us. We'll meet every week."

Andrea's eyebrows rose. "Every week?"

"Every other week?"

No one spoke.

"Once a month?" Sophia offered. "On a Saturday? For lunch, that's all."

Everyone's heads moved toward their chest then back up.

"Great." Sophia beamed. "Again to us." Her face went solemn as her glance rose. "And to Arturo. Renaldo. We're always thinking of you, you'll always be our friends. All of us. Long after the end of time."

They clinked cups again, drank up, and smiled at one another. Friends. Eternally.

ABOUT THE AUTHOR

David DeGeorge is the published author of numerous short stories in multiple genres, several of which were finalists in writing contests and his artwork has received a couple of awards at art shows. If he's not writing, reading, or drawing, he's spending time with his nieces and nephews.

For your reading pleasure, we invite you to visit our web bookstore

WHISKEY CREEK PRESS

www.whiskeycreekpress.com